The Old Trading Store

Mereo Books

2nd Floor, 6-8 Dyer Street, Cirencester, Gloucestershire, GL7 2PF
An imprint of Memoirs Books. www.mereobooks.com
and www.memoirsbooks.co.uk

The Old Trading Store

ISBN: 978-1-9191788-9-9

First published in Great Britain in 2025
by Mereo Books, an imprint of Memoirs Books.

The address for Memoirs Books can be
found at www.mereobooks.com

Mereo Books Ltd. Reg. No. 12157152

Typeset in 11/16pt Garamond
by Wiltshire Associates.
Printed and bound in Great Britain

THE OLD TRADING STORE

A LIFE STORY FROM THE TRUE HEART OF IRELAND

JOE O'FLAHERTY

To the memory of our dear daughter Marise

Romance blooms, 1965

This is a tale told through the eyes of Jonsie, the name I was known by as a child growing up long ago in the misty midlands of Ireland, a time and a place where the world was more innocent and more forgiving. There are harrowing stories of troubled times, but there's plenty of good humour along the way to keep the story going. We all have a story to tell, and this is mine; Jonsie's reflections, if you like.

Joe O'Flaherty
September 2025

CHAPTER 1

When a little boy fell on rough ground near the old building, the young woman picked him up in her arms. The whispered sound of maternal love was very consoling, so she took great care putting him down again. On some previous occasion, a stray dog had knocked his bottle to the ground. As he stood watching him lapping up the precious milk, he'd remember that annoyance. This time the mongrel was missing.

Holding the milk bottle to his chest, Jonsie waddled off on his way towards the front door. Hanna smiled after him, knowing how he liked making his own way about. Time with his father gave her peace to get the washing done. She could hear laughter from the trading store and knew what that was all about. Someone was getting a good roasting.

It was bound to be rough.

There were times when the compliments she received, in these male-dominated situations, fell short on respect. She'd endured the flush of embarrassment at their innuendo in the past. Their absurd banter wasn't appreciated, so she made them aware of it, using a sharp tone that didn't readily fit her pleasant demeanour.

'When boys get together they forget their manners,' she scolded. But it didn't appear to have any lasting effect. She couldn't be bothered listening to it anymore.

There were jobs to do.

Her primed disposition made them very wary. There was something of a rogue element there, inclined towards facing down certain issues. That made her unpredictable. So they remained silent whenever she put a damper on their improper behaviour.

She wasn't used to foul language growing up; her family, immersed in farm work every day, hadn't time to indulge the banter of crude behaviour. The land was in her blood and her marriage didn't take her far from home. Hanna would let them enjoy their own company. She'd never tolerated it on that busy day when it looked like everybody in the whole parish called into the store.

That social contact made it a pleasurable occasion; a time for neighbours to chat with people they didn't see often enough. They placed orders for Danny's run. He used horse-drawn transport to deliver supplies, and even when the big river burst its banks, flooding all the roads, the provisions always arrived. He drove a four-wheeled wagon, with a horseshoe canvas cover, along narrow winding roads, in all weather conditions.

War had just ended in Europe, and petrol was rationed in Ireland. So the horse provided a reliable mode of transport. This noble creature, ably assisted by the humble donkey, was essential to the rustic way of country living at that time.

The month of February lay ahead. Its dark moody mists hid

Hanna's picturesque countryside from view, but today had turned up sunny. She had learned from her mother how to predict conditions for a perfect drying day. She claimed that changing winds favoured different kinds of texture in the drying process. You would get softer bedclothes when they were hung out in a gentle river breeze. A starched linen sheet was a result of the east wind's harsh feel, she explained.

Hanna arrived home to make tea for the old woman who had caused her so much anxiety. She'd settle herself with a cup of her own in the process. Her pregnancy or awkward circumstances didn't matter.

She boiled water in a metal pot hooked over flames and half-filled a big washtub on the kitchen table. It was high enough to ease her troubled back while she was diligently scrubbing bed-linen.

Her strong, wiry hands made sounds on a tin-ribbed-washboard, to suit her own company. She positioned herself looking out of the window, averting her gaze from the silent woman behind her.

Hanging sheets out on the clothes line before airing them in front of the fire would give her plenty to do. Then there were vegetables to prepare and a chicken to stuff for the pot oven. Her husband Bill would be hungry when he got home from the store.

A quiet breeze from the River Shannon drifted over the still countryside. It barely ruffled the stout blackberry brambles sprawling lazily, their tentacles probing the hedgerows. Soon, tiny flowers would render these stems a gift of fruit. Homemade jam was favoured in every household.

As life moved casually along in this widespread rural community, there was a general air of contentment about the place. Except when inclement weather flooded the big river, winding its course to the sea. That annoyance made things inconvenient for a while. But people treated their neighbours like extended family members. Everybody knew help wasn't far away.

In the cramped confines of the trading store with everything scattered on the floor, Bill, the owner, sat on a high stool, his money box on the counter beside him. He was telling two eager listeners about certain things they'd like to know more about. Until he stopped abruptly; what couldn't be said in front of the child? With his attention on the boy coming in, he lowered his tone to a whispered drawl.

'Jonsie picks things up very quick, quiet now!'

A son with intelligence was a good thing to have.

Bill, a rugged young man with a dimpled chin, had a mop of black hair tousled over his forehead. A tweed cap kept it right and he always wore a waistcoat. There was a leather belt with a big brass buckle holding the brown corduroy trousers up, in a comical way. It was a source of fun for his humorous wife.

'All you need now is a parrot on your shoulder, like Long John Silver, ready to sail,' she laughed.

He joined in the banter, asking why she'd never noticed anything wrong with him before they were married. Hanna wasn't interested in answering that question. He might get bad ideas.

Jonsie ran into the kitchen; something was bothering his

head. The rocking horse felt hungry and he could see food on the table. His father was getting ready to enjoy the chicken, and there wouldn't be much left over. Giving some away was something he'd never consider. But the boy was demanding food for his horse. And he wasn't giving up.

So Bill took the easy way out.

The small portion he cut off the leg was thrown back at him. The boy scowled, pointing to the breast meat, whingeing at his father for giving 'bad stuff' to his horse.

Jonsie was sharp all right. That dark leg meat looked like it had gone off. But Bill enjoyed the boy's reaction. This single-mindedness was a well-noted family trait. That mind-set of never giving up when you wanted something was in them all. He cut a thin slice of chicken breast and sent him out the door with it.

'Pity he wasn't as particular rolling around in the long grass.' The annoyance of parting with the chicken breast triggered him.

Hanna heard what he said, and she couldn't let that comment go.

'There shouldn't be broken bottles left lying around. It could have been worse, Bill. He's doing little boy things, part of growing up.' Big boys head for the dark side deliberately; little fellows drift along with simple innocence in their heads. But it's the love of freedom that gets all of them in trouble, of course. They cannot adapt to being held down for long, with this careful eye directly at him. The company he revelled with in Freddy's bar she'd heard all about. And she'd let him know anytime he crossed the line.

'Stop drawing attention to my pregnancy with those leering imbeciles in the store,' she warned him, when she thought of it.

He was thoughtful before giving his answer.

Men who enjoy that sort of talk live alone. It was no harm reminding them what they were missing, as if anyone could miss the wonder of that. He was looking her over, visibly approving.

Hanna was well tuned into the changing mood. She knew his intention. That dimple on his chin was twitching with good humour, but she was having none of it under the present circumstances.

The old woman had surprised them once, arriving home from town in the middle of the action. Hanna vowed she'd never be 'seduced' in that situation again. Her early religious instruction wasn't favourably inclined to indulging spontaneous acts of sexual adventure. She found it difficult to relax in a creaky bed, with the insomniac old woman lying awake underneath. Her husband wasn't that easy to distract when the mood hit him. But there must be some kind of rules laid down in these overcrowded conditions.

How Hanna wished for more privacy.

WT Flanagan said it all in his long-winded wedding speech: his boy thought the sun, moon and stars shone from Hanna's eyes. And she would never want for anything, if he worked hard. He would be successful in business, like him.

The 'boss' took the wedding opportunity to put things in proper order. That was his stock in trade. His pressure game affected everyone around him, at some time or another. This constant barrage made Bill feel restless. He got an idea to open his own store. And he made a 'fair dealing' arrangement for ownership of the old stone building nobody wanted, paid off as small rent, to help with financial arrangements. And one day he'd have something to sell.

A legal route was never considered, to break a decent man's word. Things were agreed on the strength of a handshake. The eye-to-eye reassurance indicated it was proper, and the words 'My word is my bond' announced its real intention.

WT supplied Bill with enough stock to start off. He was genuinely interested in his son's future ambitions. And there were some items too long in his hardware store. A new location might speed up their disposal. The old man was inclined towards business first; sentiment might develop at some later date.

The front door of their dwelling house opened into the kitchen. Here, the hearth fire took central position, and a traditional pine dresser adorned with colourful plates from bygone times stood against the back wall. A big pine table scrubbed clean over decades was strategically placed underneath the front window to keep an eye on the boy outside while he rocked his horse on green grass, bordering the road.

He watched for his friend to pass by on her horse every day. She always greeted him cheerfully. If only for a short time they were heading in the same direction, together. The pleasure of being in her company stayed with him.

There was a big mirror hanging over the fireplace. And the comforting smells of burning turf filled the air.

Bill was a more serious man in the house. That store bravado was how businessmen talked. He was good at it. They discussed everything going on together, a close couple. Hanna was prepared to do anything to reach their goal.

The old woman who shared their home owned a drapery shop in town. Bill was inheriting this property, she'd promised him that when he agreed to mind her, so peace was essential at all times. She might change her mind about everything if things didn't go her way. Hanna had to dig deep. She tried pleasing the solitary old dear, but she was intent on keeping it miserable, just by saying nothing. 'When will it end?' Hanna asked herself, quietly.

Jonsie had a lot going on in his life.

At the back door a drainpipe filled a half-barrel with water. He had a little boat to sail on it. When he got tired of this, his mother brought him to visit his father in the store. There was a lot to wonder at in this place. Big wooden chests of tea were stacked on top of each other and large white sacks of flour were piled against a wall. There was a stack of wooden drawers filled with nails, and there were horseshoes, looped over a pole, cut specially from the hedge. Here old men watched quietly as his father cut squares of pipe tobacco with a guillotine blade on the counter. They took turns smelling it before making a purchase. There was ceremony attached to pipe smoking. Old men knew the smell of a real one.

When rain poured continuously, the big river swelled its banks. It had been going through the same routine for centuries. There were drowning accidents, over the years. Everyone was aware of it. The loss of two young children people found difficult to bear.

Bill wanted to teach his son about the dangers of the river. They arrived on the bridge for a realistic lesson. The old sack was a bad memory for the young boy; he recoiled when his father held it up in front of him.

The boy remembered when the dresser door was hanging open, and he had dragged that sack across the kitchen floor. The noise woke the old woman on the chair, and she told his father how he tried to blow up the house. It was the first time Bill had roared at his son, frightening him. When the story started doing the rounds after, it marked him out as a 'wild boy' in the making, from this early beginning. Didn't he try and blow up the whole house?

It doesn't take much to get misrepresented.

Bill was holding the sack out in front of him now, shoulder high.

'Look here Jonsie, look.'

When the boy saw it drop into the rushing water, a shiver came over him, and he got afraid looking down on the river.

'Gone,' said his father.

Jonsie looked up his eyes widening. 'Gone,' he said, backing away from him.

There were bullets and hand grenades belonging to his dead brother in that sack. Bill knew it was time to get rid of them.

It looked like this play acting made an impression. The sight of churning water would frighten the boy for a long time. And he told his mother he'd never go near the river again.

Bill could see that the friendship between Hanna and the old woman wasn't developing as he'd hoped. It was time for more talks about things going on in the house. He felt the bad atmosphere and understood how much it annoyed his wife. Everything must be kept in harmony; a lot depended on that.

He took the little boy's hand walking down the middle of the street. There wasn't another person to be seen around the town at midday. Cody's Cross was a quiet little place.

A fluffy grey cloud spread across the blue sky. Like steam rising from a cooking pot, it drifted. Rays of sunshine beamed through, warming the land with a hue of yellow. This growing mist was turning the whole countryside green. And nature called on all living things to welcome the arrival of spring.'

The wagon driver left the reins down very deliberately.

'You'd best go inside Danny; she's been waiting for you all morning. Make tea if you want.' He jumped down, grinning at her.

'I won't stay long Hanna, but she likes to know what's going on.'

'She never talks to me, I gave up trying.'

Hanna always thought the wagon looked like something from the wild west of America. The picture hall kept people informed on the world outside. What you saw on the big screen was true life somewhere else. She lifted the boy up on the wooden bench seat, over the horse's tail. 'Watch out for the Indians!' She laughed. The reassuring presence of the driver was consoling.

He'd been part of her husband's family for longer than she could remember. And she was pleased when he visited the old woman. It took her out of her sullen way, and that gave Hanna some peace of mind for a while.

Bill told her how the Kellys had tried getting rid of Danny once, when they thought a friendship had developed with their precious only child. But Mary threatened to leave home on account of it, and he was reinstated. So this bond had withstood the test of time.

Jonsie was taken on the wagon journey once a week; on the day his mother worked in the trading store. She enjoyed harmless gossip with the women, though some stories that came out so easily might be better off left unsaid. All this private chat was for Hanna's ears only. These were excitable country people, enjoying a carefree atmosphere in the scandal-loving store. Keeping her up to date about things happening in the place she grew up.

No wonder it felt like a family gathering.

Danny came out of the house shaking his head. 'Once upon a time she was full of the joys of spring,' he said.

Getting back up on the wagon again, Hanna gave the boy his milk bottle. He wouldn't go anywhere without it.

They rolled along a quiet road with birds warbling in the hedgerows around them. Danny shouted to the boy, explaining how these songs were for other birds, warning them to keep away from their nests. He was convinced Jonsie understood everything, it was just that he didn't know how to say it yet. But he knew.

The old covered wagon's seasoned timbers creaked. Iron-shod wheels rattled off a gravel road, jolting the axles with a sturdy sound. This long-time traveller knew there was nothing to worry about when it shook like that. It gladdened his heart. The boy took everything in.

When the wagon came to a flooded road, he saw the big river coming to take him. There were straps holding him back. He threw his bottle at the water in temper; it sailed on top like a boat. 'I'll get it!' The driver rushed to retrieve it.

Danny didn't disappear when he collected the bottle. The horse wasn't going down under the water like a sack. It made Jonsie think.

Everything felt good, same as on his rocking horse. When the horse was with him, he was safe. He figured it all out for himself that day, for sure.

They stopped at a small thatched house.

He could see the same little yellow birds playing games again, sailing on the water like boats with their mother. They were laughing, and she laughed loudest of all. He'd only seen them once before. And he shouted at them with pure delight.

Danny said their name. 'Ducks, Jonsie, they're little ducks.'

The driver picked the woman's groceries up off the floor. It was a heavy box, so he had to be careful. One slip in his rubber boots and he was down in the water. There was a red order book sticking out from the coat pocket and a pencil behind his ear.

Even though the road was flooded, the house was standing on high ground. And the wellingtons kept him dry, to walk to the door.

A smiling grey-haired woman stood waiting patiently for him, brushing her hands softly down her apron. She had a few dozen eggs in a basin and some small blocks of homemade butter, wrapped in greaseproof paper. They would be sold in the store. These items were bartered for groceries. This woman's produce was eagerly sought after; her reputation for cleanliness assured that. She washed the eggs before Danny collected them; that attention to detail made her produce popular.

A record of every transaction was entered in Hanna's book. Back at the store, she was deep in thought. The bad news she heard still bothered her. Her 'old cronies', as she fondly referred to them, placed orders. All accounts were paid for in one month, unless otherwise arranged. Fair day was best.

Sometimes she left her position at the counter. It was on such an occasion that she heard troubling news, coming straight from the lips of a well-known gossip.

'Hanna, that woman Miss Kelly you have given shelter to in your home is some imposter, I'll tell you.' She spoke with a nasty curl on her top lip intended to convey more than a thousand words. Hanna was going to hear it all, whether she liked it or not. She told in whispers how another of Miss Kelly's relations had persuaded her to sign the shop over to him. He was a big shot pub owner in London, with lots of money.

He'd leave her decent hard-working husband standing with one hand as long as the other. Everyone knew Bill was more entitled to inherit the place; she said that 'for Hanna's benefit'.

And there was badness to spread when she started giving out.

'It wasn't funny having a contrary old hag to look at every day, especially when there was nothing to be gained from it'. She looked closer at Hanna for some sign of resentment, but she maintained composure, listening to the woman's story. She knew well to say nothing, so as not to be quoted.

'The whole parish is talking about it,' she was informed. 'The honest truth wouldn't be her first thought, Hanna. It won't be in her last gasp either.

She won't change her will I assure you. But your husband will have to do everything she wants even if you don't agree with it. She owns him now. You see. You poor woman, God help you, I'll say a wee prayer for you.'

The gossip seemed pleased to make that final remark. In some way it vindicated everything she said. God was in on it too.

She was known for making religious promises to conceal her real intentions, and creating as much trouble as she could. It came easy to her when it was a holy sermon. In this way she was doing a good deed for all concerned.

Later in the day, when Danny arrived back from deliveries, Hanna headed home with her son in a hurry. She'd like to tackle the old one immediately, but knew she couldn't.

That was the hardest part. Knowing it and not saying it. Under any normal course of events she'd tell Bill everything. But this was no usual occurrence.

He had endured a tough struggle, setting the store up while trying to pay off money he owed. He'd got on top of it. Happy trading, doing what he was good at. How could she bring him down with all this crooked business talk?

She had a gut feeling it wouldn't be resolved easily.

After she'd left the store, Bill wondered why there weren't any cheerful goodbyes.

She always made a fuss over everybody when she was going home. He noticed she wasn't looking her usual bright self; with that deep furrow across her brow and her face the colour of death. She might be better off resting herself at home.

Her pregnancy was slowing her down. He blamed himself

for not taking proper care of her. She was very independent, and could take exception to some well-meaning consideration; a proud woman who wouldn't want to burden anyone with her problems.

Maybe sometimes, he took her great strength for granted.

The right thing to do was get help for her, with all the work she did. But she wouldn't want anyone else working in her kitchen.

He was expecting the two farmers to call; he'd been grooming them as potential buyers. They knew how the business operated now and why it was such a good retirement plan for them. They had approached Bill to sell the store in the first place. They'd sold their smallholdings for cash. He'd explained what running a country store entailed. And they would do a deal.

Bill put together a price for all stock that included a sum of money for the old building; a favourable settlement for the value of goodwill.

That transaction would finance their next move.

A bar in the town; three years was a long time to wait. He was hoping to tell Hanna the good news. It might give her a lift. Something she needed, by the looks of it.

When Hanna arrived home, Miss Kelly was on Bill's chair at the fire, seemingly without a care in the world. She would never occupy Hanna's identical chair, for some unknown reason. She didn't want her on her chair anyway, so she was grateful for little mercies, when that annoying thought struck her again.

That bad story she'd heard earlier never left her head.

Hanna considered how 'the old one was portrayed as a manipulative hag that knew exactly what she was doing'.

'Playing cat and mouse on a good man's decency,' was the way the 'old gossip' put it.

But Hanna was prepared to bluff it out, as usual.

'Good afternoon Miss Kelly, how are you today?'

The greeting wasn't acknowledged by the silent old woman in black sitting down at her fireside. She couldn't be bothered listening, except to 'the man of the house', as she kept referring to Bill. It seemed no one else existed in her solitary world.

Hanna was inclined to leave things just like that; this time, there wouldn't be any effort on her part, playing the game, 'helping her to hear'. Fussing over her with more tea or a biscuit, the days when that consideration existed, were resigned to the past.

Hanna would get dinner ready, and plot her strategy. There was more than one way to cook a goose, her mother always said. She was always willing to learn more about cooking.

And whatever else it took to sort it.

When she sat down to dinner that evening her stomach heaved looking at the plate in front of her. She had diced up a small amount for the old one to have on her knees, the way she liked it. She sat shaking her leg, tipping her heel on the floor, a sign she was relishing it. But she'd never admit to that.

Hanna placed her hands across her pregnant bump to ease herself. Bill noticed her discomfort; he'd been watching her anxiously since he came in the door.

'You looked tired today, Hanna,' he said, reaching his big hand across the table to give her arm a gentle stroke. 'Do you not think you're doing too much? We could get one of the country women in to give you a helping hand for a while. If you could tell me which one you really like, I'd ask her.'

It wasn't the pregnancy causing all her discomfort. The one responsible for that was sitting behind them; listening to everything, knowing it all and saying nothing.

'It's the baby, Bill, a little extra weight to carry around for a while longer. I'm fine, no pains yet, please God the doctor will call at the weekend, and I'll be okay till then.'

She thought for a little while before saying what was on her mind. 'If we had a business in town it might be easier if everything was nearer to hand. Jonsie would be beside the school.'

Bill picked up his ears when he heard that. It was the first time his wife had made public reference to their personal goal, a very private topic. His reaction was to change the subject, in case Miss Kelly thought he was moving on her property prematurely.

'What business in town, Hanna?'

He winked over the cup, to put her on guard; she was getting very close to the bone.

'My father will not be retiring for many years yet,' he went on. 'I may not inherit the place anyway; my brother must be taken care of in that arrangement also. You'd never know how it would go.'

She was determined to have her say.

'It's always been your dream Bill, having your own business in Cody's Cross to carry on the family tradition.' She continued talking, in a steady voice. 'I'm sure there must be some other property you could obtain to realise that dream. After I have this baby we'll discuss it more. We have to think of schools and medical treatment now. Moving to a business in town makes more sense.'

She could see the one at the fire was taking it all in. Hanna was watching her with the corner of her eye during the exchanges. It wouldn't be like her to show any emotion.

Bill wondered what had brought about this sudden change in his wife. He had a secret concerning the store that couldn't be revealed. That would come up for discussion now, the sale agreed.

It was well known that the bar business was the surest way of making your fortune. Freddy Brown was coming to the end of his days a wealthy man. He'd steadfastly refused all offers for his old pub. He was prejudiced against a Catholic family living in his home. They had threatened to burn his father out, in the troubled past. A quiet man on the surface, he could be bitter. It was difficult to distinguish bigots. The nature of that unpleasant condition remained hidden, until a perceived threat bothered someone enough to reveal their true intent.

That's when the real bastard turned up.

Bill was going to open his pub in the premises that had once been a lady's drapery store. All he had to do was apply for a licence to sell alcohol. So he was obliged to care for the old lady, no matter how contrary she turned out to be. There was nothing in writing that bound her to their verbal agreement. He understood how these two women couldn't hit it off. Both had that same independent streak. That didn't make room for compromise.

The story of deceit was still troubling Hanna's weary head. She was thinking of bringing the subject up for discussion when the old woman informed her in that distant tone of voice that there was something she needed to do in the town.

That was all she said, walking out the door.

Hanna figured she was consulting a solicitor, to change her will. Danny must have organised a lift for her.

Hanna had been dropping hints for her ears long enough. It finally clicked, it seemed, so she made a cup of tea for herself. It looked as if the issue was about to be resolved amicably, after all. She'd quiz her more thoroughly when she returned though.

And insist on seeing written proof.

Catching a glimpse of herself in the big mirror was a shock to behold. There was a lot of work to be done. She vowed that after the birth, getting her figure back would top the list. The 'pasty white face' would be next. Her mother was on to her about it already, saying she looked like she had TB.

That evening Jonsie was given strict orders to stay quiet in the chair, or his horse would be put out in the rain.

The old witch complained 'this horse shouldn't be in the kitchen'. 'Outside!' she shrieked, but nobody listened.

Jonsie wondered why she came back again when nobody wanted her. He'd picked up on his mother's negative reaction to the old woman for a long time. Now she was fussing about a box in her hands. It was full of holes with squeaks coming from it. Jonsie thought it could be biscuits.

He watched her placing it carefully on the table. She stooped down, pulling a long pin slowly from her black hat, with the great coat brushing the floor around her, like a witch his mother had showed him in a book. He stared at the box of holes.

'I have everything ready for them,' his father was saying. 'We'll put them to bed now, so they won't get cold.'

Out in the shed, he watched him lifting them gently, placing them on straw, under a red lamp hung from the ceiling.

'To keep them warm', his father said, 'we'll let them sleep for a while. They're only babies yet, Jonsie.'

He watched the little yellow birds huddling into a warm bundle. They looked so cosy together as everyone headed off for tea.

Hanna was thinking 'it was chickens'. She went into town for, nothing to do with her old shop. The panic returned. She couldn't mention a solicitor with her husband sitting there. She'd wait until they were alone.

As she prepared scones and jam, she asked Miss Kelly politely to fetch her son.

'He's enthralled with the chickens,' she said. She sighed dreamily to sound more cheerful.

It took a while for the scene to register with the old woman. She was horrified at what she saw. Like a total massacre. The chickens lay motionless on top of the water barrel, their legs sticking up, like yellow withered waterlilies.

The little brat responsible was on his toes holding on to the barrel with his fingers, laughing at them.

She closed her fist. 'The monster killed all my chickens!' She shrieked like a mad woman, grabbing his hair, smashing her bony fist on his nose, making him howl.

His mother, hearing all the shouting, came running from the kitchen to see her son with a bloody nose and the old one still laying into him like a woman possessed.

Hanna pushed her away from him roughly.

Bill became agitated when he saw what was going on. He picked the boy up and went back inside. When things settled and

Jonsie was in the chair again, his mother held a damp towel on his nose.

The old one sat still on her settle bed, glaring at the evil little brat that had drowned her chickens. The sole reason for her trip to town was getting a few chickens to rear for laying eggs, so she and Bill could have a boiled egg for breakfast. That young fellow had ruined everything and he was sitting there, defying her now and staring at her coldly. He'd get another clout if there was no one about.

There wasn't a minute of the day that he wasn't up to some kind of mischief. And she was sometimes left in charge, minding him.

She sat listening to what the man of the house was saying. He spoke at her from the table, his stern face displaying the roughness of him. Vexed at what he'd just witnessed, and making no bones about what could happen next.

'How can you beat our son like that?' he demanded quietly, a deadly feel to it.

She answered coldly. 'He murdered all my chickens.'

'We never hit children in this house; you've never seen it, so don't ever let it happen again. Or you'll finish up in the county home. I swear to God I mean that too.'

When he growled that out, it sounded frightening.

Hanna noticed the old one's wrinkled face twitching. Her mother's final years in the county home were badly remembered. The fear was that she would finish up in one too.

'Never mind talking about the county home for me, I have a drapery store you want in the town, if you sign with a solicitor to say that you'll look after me till the day I die. You can have the lot.

I will sign all over to you tomorrow, if you want.'

'Right, I'll put my suit on. Hanna will come with us, and we'll do it right this time. Those days for dealing on a handshake are gone. We won't wait another day to make it right.'

He turned to wink at his wife. Then he proceeded to tell them how the two farmers were going ahead with the store purchase. There would be enough money now to fund their pub venture. He promised to do up the parlour room downstairs especially for Miss Kelly, 'her private fireside in her own home', he explained, where she could relax from the stress of childminding to enjoy the quiet retirement she deserved.

'Hopefully there will be lots of distance between girls with different interests.'

Hanna spoke out hurriedly, to get her say in. She was still very cautious.

Bill knew Miss Kelly had the property left to someone else. His father had told him the story and he decided to bide his time. He couldn't test Hanna's resolve; she mightn't want to tolerate her anymore. That's why it remained such a secret.

When Danny told Hanna about her son's fascination with young ducks 'on the flooded road', she was delighted to hear the story. She'd agonised about how her little boy could carry out such an act of cruelty. Now she understood everything. He had thought the little yellow chickens were ducks, and he only wanted to look at them swimming.

She hoped he'd never remember how it had gone so badly wrong.

CHAPTER 2

It didn't take long to convert the drapery store to a pub. For the part-timers involved, it was a labour of love; loaded with self-interest too, of course. You don't often get a chance to build the perfect place to booze in. Bill's pals pitched in to help out with the renovations. They did it after work, excited at having a new hangout where they could raise hell without getting barred.

So he knew he'd pay dearly for their kindness; they'd live off it forever. But there was a big saving on much-needed cash.

His pub was everybody's pub, he shouted, when excitement hit him. When they asked if the town undesirable, Ned Goat, was welcome, Bill was not amused. 'That man won't be tolerated. I'd have to get the place fumigated after him', he swore.

He didn't see the winking going on behind his back. This opportunity might make room for a bit of 'craic'. Everyone knew about this Irish expression for all kinds of fun and banter. Its subtle magic wasn't easily understood by strangers, but the Irish knew it made good sense to them.

If you didn't have any craic in you; you were disadvantaged. And you wouldn't find anyone to spend time with, especially in a small town like Cody's Cross, where everyone was full of craic.

The carved wooden front of the drapery store was as old as the town itself. That alone ensured it remained. Bill would prefer to leave everything just as it stood, but he was obliged to make certain alterations for change of usage. Toilets with wash basins were becoming fashionable in some bigger towns. He would locate his toilets in the yard. There would be no bad smells inside the premises. He painted 'Bill Flanagan's Pub' in gold letters over the front. It wasn't a perfect job, like it was 'sliding', but he said it depended on how you looked at it. 'You might be straight going in, but you'll be crooked coming out,' that's the message there,' he quipped.

Everyone knew Kelly's Drapery Store in town; outside this building couples had met up for dates down through the years. Now it was a pub, a warmer spot to await the arrival of your loved one, even though it was still a rare occurrence for women to enter bars alone. That was one of the reasons why 'snugs' were used as private drinking spots in some premises.

Bill had plans for changing that tradition. His place would be female friendly. He would hang big advertising mirrors on the walls, to look into all night, if they didn't mind going outside for a pee. His only stipulation was, don't mention 'paper' to him.

Kelly's store wasn't as relevant to the town's history as the rebel soldier with his rifle raised. The statue on the fair green was one of their own. It stood near an old yew tree that had grown for three hundred years. With its own troubled history, there wasn't much happening around Cody's Cross this tree didn't witness. The statue had been erected by the hardware store. Politicians spoke after mass on Sundays in his gallant company, as if they were part of it all too, roaring their garbled account of Irish history, that called on people to honour dead heroes, and shape a better Ireland.

And they spoke more encouraging words for their listeners: 'It will benefit you all in the long run.' That line hung over them, like a promise made from heaven.

Vote No 1… 'It might be one of you that needed me'.

Bill was excited when the pub opened. There wasn't a rowdy person on the premises to spoil that memorable occasion; swilling porter and singing songs into the early hours. Not a fist fight in sight.

That particular easy-going mood was too good to last.

His first customer the next day was Ned Goat; subject of distasteful tales, with a stink of goat coming from him. The last person you wanted around the place.

Bill was a little amused at first; he knew a set up. His workmates were up for the craic, at his expense, payback time arrived early. You could be sure. They weren't going to miss how it played out, either.

Bill's mood dipped when Ned made a sudden move for the counter. 'Oh no don't, sit over near the door Ned, leave it open, so you can look out at the sunshine. I'm cleaning up here.'

'No sunshine, it's freezing out there,' Ned said sharply, picking up on this blatant disregard for his custom. It wasn't the first time he had been subject to rough treatment in this town. He knew all about it.

'Leave the door open anyway to get rid of the smell,' the

barman ordered, remembering the crew threatening to send this plague into the pub. It was no surprise that the rogues had kept their word. Bill knew they were hiding nearby, to document events for posterity, especially if Ned resisted.

He was a notorious old scrapper who could get physical if manhandled in any way. That's when they'd enjoy the craic, fighting with Stinky, who'd take a grip on the door jamb, holding his ground, going nowhere; defying all odds to shift him.

Opening day folklore in the making; but Bill wasn't going to get caught in that trap, if he could avoid it.

'Why am I so far away from the bar Bill?' Ned asked with a hostile frown twisting his sagging features.

'Because you smell of buck goat that's why, stay there. Or you'll get no porter from me.'

He poured the glass of dark stuff from a wooden keg on the counter before disappearing, hoping he'd be gone when he came back. How long would he sit there with the wind blowing in, freezing the arse of him? And porter that tasted like piss with no creamy head on it, to give him the shits.

Ned had his cap pulled down tight, making his grey moustached face seem shorter. He muttered about getting this treatment. Said he'd never put his foot in the place again. Bill would like to have heard that promise, if he was anywhere near him.

When Hanna came home, she was surprised to see Ned holding a glass in his hand. Bill swore he'd never serve this man. She'd heard the stories; he hadn't washed himself for years.

She grabbed hold of Jonsie's hand, pulling him away from his clutches. That reputation for having children upon his knees was a bad one. He was far from your caring uncle. On high alert, she made a hasty retreat without opening her mouth, heading in to prepare dinner. Now she was glad of the window in the kitchen wall, a safe place to observe him.

When Bill came in, she was peeping out. 'Is he still there, Hanna?'

'Yes, stuck to the chair. That was a great night Bill, we'll do well.'

'Yeah, it was a night to remember. I'll stick on the kettle, not in any hurry out to your man. The smell would make you sick.'

She enjoyed his annoyance.

'Jonsie what are you up to there?'

The boy was so intent on what he was doing; never losing concentration. But he understood how friendly sounded.

'He's drawing ducks, Bill. I picked up that book at the market for him, when he saw a duck on the cover he wanted it. Isn't it great though, showing such an interest in drawing at his age. We might have an artist on our hands.' She laughed.

Bill looked at his son colouring the duck. He knew he'd never had crayons in his hands or seen a drawing book in his life. TV was still an absent distraction from country life.

How could the boy know to colour in yellow and black wings? The same colours on the duck, not plain yellow like the chickens he had mistakenly drowned.

'Hanna, that's strange, he only saw them a few times.

'He's ready for school now. I will talk with the teacher,' she said.

They sat down to discuss their clever son, how they would save money every week for his education, so he could have a better chance in life. Not have to struggle when he got older, like them.

They'd forgotten about everything, until they heard a commotion coming from the bar. Bill jumped up to look through the window.

'Jesus Christ, there's a donkey out there!' he said, and he ran for the door.

Bill's pals had been scheming for a long time. They had listened to his rants on the job, and wanted a bit of craic. There was a story told from earlier times that provided their inspiration. They gave Ned Goat a few bob to buy a pint of porter in Flanagan's bar, 'the morning after the night before'. They printed a square of cardboard for the counter, 'Ned's Here Now,' in black paint; but when they saw Jack the donkey walking up the street, the idea took a twist. They tied the sign to the donkey's tail. When they pushed him into the pub, he got mad as hell. Ned could see trouble brewing, so he took off.

When she heard Bill roaring, Hanna took her son with her. It was funny when she spotted the donkey's sign, 'Ned's here now'; she tried suppressing the giggles. But he spotted it. 'I can't see the joke here Hanna,' he said, grabbing the sign off the donkey's tail to fling into the street. He pushed Jack out after it. He never bothered looking for the pranksters. It was bad enough knowing they were hiding there, laughing at him.

'You two should try a day's work some time!' he roared up the street.

Jack was a tetchy customer, like his master. He lifted his tail when he was manhandled through the door, with a loud roar of protest. He let out the forlorn cry of a lonesome jackass, dumped where females never strayed, peppering the beautiful counter, and covering the antique floor with foul-smelling dung. Then he spread his hind legs, splashing the lot with foamy urine. It looked like custard. And smelled like shite.

It took them a while cleaning up.

There was tension during the whole episode. With the whiff of goat lingering too, Hanna broke up camphor balls to sprinkle around the floor, killing the smell somewhat. She took a basin of boiling water and red carbolic soap to the counter with a scrubbing brush for the hidden crevices of its carved features. The comments made about this counter on opening night were all positive. It was 'the best counter for drinking a pint you'd ever stand up against', and low enough to rest an arm on. Bill liked hearing that. He couldn't blame the donkey. The animal had been callously hijacked by desperadoes.

He'd enjoy the craic too, one day, when that was the end of it.

Mad Phil talked kindly to Shelagh the donkey on the journey to town.

They'd been together a long time. Phil knew Jack might be prowling the street. They had experienced his unwanted attention in the past; he had tried mounting Shelagh and she was helpless to resist, chained to the cart. When Jack got the urge to perform with his manhood largely exposed, there was no stopping him. It didn't seem to matter a damn if anyone was looking on.

Mad Phil shouted abuse at Ned Goat in the town about that. 'Mind yer Jack donkey, yer father was a stray buck, yer auld mother a wandering nanny, every man's 'jaunt.''

'The asylum wasn't big enough for ya madman,' the goat man

roared back at him, going up the street in the cart. He knew Phil had spent time inside the high walls, for his nerves.

Mad Phil's cousin Drover lived in one of Major Cody's estate houses, with a small field and a stone shed near the road, for minding a cart. Drover had assumed 'a right of privilege', on account of that. He kept a wary eye on everything going on in town, remembering stories from his father relating to 'skeletons in cupboards'. He was one of those 'ill will' collectors.

'No harm knowing who you're dealing with', his father advised. He let Shelagh use his field. Then Phil would shout things in the pub, and when the 'drink madness' hit him, he'd drop bombshells. Phil roared out the bad stories Drover told him to tell, so people would be fearful of what the mad man said next. He could say things they wouldn't want anyone to know about.

The blacksmith's forge at the end of the street looked like a ruin, with galvanised sheets on the side rusted and twisted. But in spite of its appearance it was a hub of activity in the town. Here a burly smith turned red hot iron into horseshoes. It gave a pleasing sound for the town dwellers. Ringing chimes sliced the silence. Smithy cooled his work in a stone trough of water hissing spits with every turn of his hand, eyeing it up for a blast in the fire again. He used long tongs to move the hot embers around, pulling hard on bellows to redden it more, beating the curved shape for a snug fit. The smell of burning hoof was never forgotten. Hot sparks flew like bullets around Smithy. You'd wonder why he wasn't hit by one of them. He jiggled the hammer for a high pitched ring off the anvil. When it stopped, ears cocked for its return. There was money made, and people fed. Market day made work for everyone and a few shillings to rattle in their pockets for another week.

Cody's Cross had many prejudices bothering it. On fair days tough men with scores to settle walked into each other deliberately. Whiskey brought the mean streak out of them. Young boys followed along to witness the melee. They all looked the same in their long coats, and peaked caps, except for Louie. He was involved in every fight, stepping in as peacemaker first, but taking sides if he chose. His bald head was a low target, regularly bloodied by belts from a blackthorn stick. But the abuse never deterred him. Something 'not right' made him that way, they said. It wasn't natural.

A red galvanized shed, the town picture hall, stood in off the street. A man called Blimey showed one film every week. He'd spent years in England working as a projectionist before setting up at home. His house was called the Steward's Mansion. A place viewed with historical contempt.

Blimey's father had been a trusted employee of the Cody estate. The big house portrayed the importance of his position; where he collected rent money for the estate every week. Now the Major took care of this task personally. He knew the cinema owner couldn't be trusted. The issue of his outstanding rent bothered him for a long time. There was some tension between them.

Blimey lived where he was born, and any notion of paying rent was never considered. He ensured there was no way of getting any rent from him either, eyeballing the Major when he tried it on. He told him he was an IRA rebel who paid English landlords no rent before shutting the door in his face. So that was the end of that.

The Major was wary of him, having been harassed by this

organisation in the past. But there was one thing he didn't know: IRA men never disclosed membership.

Annoyingly for the local priest, he wasn't getting a penny from Blimey in the collection box on Sundays. He lambasted the 'picture hall' from the pulpit. 'Hell would be waiting for those frequenting this den of iniquity'. When most of the congregation held their heads down in guilty shame, the priest felt satisfied.

They said it was too much competition for his 'show' in the chapel. Blimey had been a Catholic before he left home, but turned Protestant in England. He was one of them now. Blimey hated the priest, but there was only room for one principal act in town. The pictures were moved to Sunday night when mass was long over.

This priest was noted for another kind of sincere devotion; gambling on racehorses. This topic was never raised by any right-minded person. A miffed clergyman could do a lot of damage.

The priest never missed a race meeting anywhere in the country. His travelling companion was the local schoolmaster, one of the very few people in town with a car. And Rasp always assumed a 'holier than thou' attitude, driving the priest around. 'God Bless' was his chosen words for dismissing you. It sounded right coming from the priest's friend. When you were in with the clergy, you could say anything you wanted; nothing if you choose. And promise what you didn't have. This priestly code of indifference was a sure way of getting there, wherever it was.

Jonsie loved market day, when the street was different. It was so enjoyable with everyone laughing with each other. His mother took him around several times during the day. She missed not knowing what was going on. Familiar faces would do her heart a power of good. Some things she didn't like weren't allowed to register. 'Such is life,' she'd say, 'such is life'. And then go on to talk about the weather. He soon learned that bad news was 'such is life' with a sudden change in weather conditions. Even a small fellow that's listening learns when it doesn't sound right.

She wore a long flowing dress for the day. He watched how she fixed it in front of the kitchen mirror with careful finger plucking till it suited her taste. Everyone commented favourably on it, all day after that.

Jonsie listened as people said nice things. It made him happy when he saw everyone talking with her. Up and down the street on both sides, big spoked wheels propped up red and blue carts. They were backed into the pavement, the shafts placed side by side on the ground, left sticking out on the street.

Some of these carts had piglets for sale bedded in straw, young suck calves as well, but never a goat, they weren't good enough for that special treatment. They were tied to cartwheels to bleat loudly for this harsh treatment. It wasn't much fun being a goat.

Jonsie felt sorry for them. That's why he started minding them. Even so, he was totally absorbed with all that was going on, until an unfortunate meeting with this 'nose-in-the-air' person took a bad twist, to ruin a perfect day.

This lady was noted for assuming opinions above her station in life. She held on to a little girl's hand, in a white dress. Jonsie knew all about this one's antics, so he watched her very closely. She was subject to 'sudden' change. Hanna tried talking to her mother. But 'Nose-in-the-Air' always took charge of everything.

'Mrs Flanagan, we are having communion and I wish it was over. It's been a long day since six o'clock this morning getting this young lady looking so well, I can assure you.'

'Ohoo, you poor thing, you must be exhausted.'

Hanna consoled, in her comforting manner. Nose-in-the-Air wished for more of this kind understanding. 'Show her how good everyone's been to you dear, show her.'

She instructed the girl, accepting cash donations for communion; her hand reached out for Hanna to respond in kind. Her money stuck under the boy's nose. Hanna opened her purse and took out a silver shilling to place with the rest. It was a generous donation, as sixpence was usual. But Hanna was decent.

'Crossing your hand with silver will bring you lots of good luck for the future,' she told the girl sweetly.

While her mother thanked Hanna, the girl turned her attention to Jonsie. She didn't like him because he was a 'country bumpkin'. She bit his arm once at school to make him cry, but he didn't, and that annoyed her. She reached out her hand to let him see how much money she had now, making him jealous. He remembered the dog knocking his milk bottle from his hand, so he gave the money a slap, and she recoiled in horror, looking at it scattered on the ground. When her heels struck the cart shafts behind her, she fell back, sprawled on the dirt.

The young fellow couldn't stop laughing at her predicament.

Her mother shouted angrily; he was trying to steal her child's 'communion money', she saw him knocking her over. He was a bully boy. Everyone in the whole town knew about that. Hanna wasn't pleased, hearing her son bad mouthed. However, the importance of communion dictated they go inside.

To see about cleaning the dress, if only the rough stuff was removed, they agreed. So they went into the kitchen. A further examination revealed that the dress was in need of a professional cleaning. It started them wondering where it would go from there. But Nose-in-the-Air just wanted to gossip. The woman that ran the drapery store, Miss Kelly, was the topic of her conversation. Her mother was very friendly with her. Then she went on to relate the scandal that had kept them going years ago, something Hanna knew very little about.

The sadness she felt hearing about these past events changed Hanna's mind about things. She had genuine concern for what the old lady had gone through. It was as if she had 'only just' got to know her. She blamed herself for being selfish. Hanna made some meaningful decisions. There wouldn't be any more animosity towards this woman who had suffered enough in life already. She promised to give Miss Kelly more respect, so she could have peace for the rest of her days.

Bill was busy cleaning up the back yard at the pub. It was safely walled, with small sheds squaring it in. The place would be perfect for kids to play.

He had Jonsie's rocking horse outside the kitchen window already. A big iron gate at the back opened into a wood, with a small lake in the middle. No one knew where the water came from, as there was no river running into it. So it was regarded with suspicion; local legend said it had no bottom to it. And deep in its darkest depths a monster lurked.

Bill remembered when he was ten, fishing with friends. They got a fright when something scary happened that could never be explained after. The wood all around got eerily silent, the birds stopped singing, and a dense mist over the water gathered into a dark foreboding cloud that wasn't going away. They tried shaking off the fear. They'd been talking about the dread of this lake. As they sat on the grassy slope, staring at the quietness of it. 'You'd never know what could happen next,' they all agreed.

A bad feeling was coming from the depths; they didn't want to be there when it arrived. They ran off roaring at the tops of their voices, 'It's coming from the lake!'

Bill put a big lock on the gate to curtail his inquisitive son, in case he drowned. He erected a 'PRIVATE' sign for customers. The bar toilets were located beside this gate.

When Hanna served up tea for Miss Kelly, she poured a cup for herself and sat on a chair beside her at the fire. This cosy room the previous household called 'the parlour'. A place for special visitors, private quarters for entertaining priests with a glass of whiskey, if they were so inclined.

It was Miss Kelly's sole domain again, and there was calmness in the house because of it. The time was right for making amends. Hanna sat quietly; there was lots of time. Now she hoped to apply some of her mother's wisdom,

'Don't impose yourself; allow her to do that to you. Be very tolerant to encourage her. It could be tough going; there will be bad feelings, but with God's help, friendship will make its presence felt. I'll say a prayer for both of you.'

It was time for healing. So Hanna sat and patiently waited.

William Thomas Flanagan & Sons Hardware Store, Funeral Undertakers, established 1824, was painted in gold lettering on a black surface. Like the pub over the street, only bigger, and much straighter. Big transactions were conducted in the yard. There were two massive solid oak gates leading in off the street.

Bill spent all his time in this yard with the horses, when he worked there. Now, as he watched the loaded wagon coming out through the gates, he felt a deep sense of sadness for his kind of work. Danny was skilfully driving the horse team from the bench seat. A task they had all learned so well, over the years. Now this pub he was stuck in had made him feel bad, from the very beginning. He couldn't tolerate all the nonsensical talk, the long-winded bar room blather, steeped in lies. So he'd changed his mind about running a bar.

He was obliged to keep this discontent hidden. They'd worked very hard to get there, and Hanna was pregnant again. He knew his father wouldn't tolerate rumblings of discontent. There was nowhere else to go now.

Bill knew the years spent in the trading store were good times. There was enough to keep him occupied. And at that time, he could change his day around: take the horse delivery out while Danny worked the store with Hanna. Nothing seemed to change much. He wasn't away from everything, like now. There was a constant reminder in this place, looking out at Danny, through the bar window. When he thought about it, it didn't make sense.

'What you want isn't always what you need,' he said.

Hanna was getting worried about him. The Gardaí were trying

to catch him for after-hours drinking. If he was caught a few times, he'd lose his bar licence in court. Things were turning very sour indeed. He was depending a lot on after-hours drinking to pay the bills. Some of his customers made this illegal drinking activity difficult to carry out. They thought it was funny, but it was very stressful on Bill, something he could well do without.

'The place must be kept quiet after hours,' he pleaded with them, hoping they would listen and cooperate. But that made them laugh even more; they were enjoying the craic. He was full of fun when he was out on the town himself. Now he'd turned into this 'lawful landlord person,' they roared. He was hilarious, you couldn't make it up, they said.

Garda Nelson made the rounds diligently, his dark uniform blending with shadows, observing, before pouncing. If the moon wasn't bright Bill couldn't see him until it was too late. All he could do was keep the bar quiet, and it full of characters with a craic agenda. There was no consideration at all for an anxious bar owner trying to make an 'honest' living.

'Ye shower of bastards!' he raged at them. 'Why did your mothers bother having ye?' he fumed.

Garda Nelson knew he was always watched. Sometimes he'd stroll past the bar door with his arms folded behind his back, then double back suddenly to put his eyes to the slit the bar owner was looking through. They were eyeball to eyeball for a second. This shock treatment always made the Garda's night. Even if he didn't get him, he was close. It was very tense when it shook him. The guard liked that part best - torture.

The fire was burning warmly in the barracks when Nelson

returned. He saw Muldoon had done no work, and he resented that. He was aware his fellow guard was on friendly terms with the bar owner, and he was highly suspicious of that connection.

'This Bill Flanagan is a slippery chancer,' he ventured to say. 'Catching him would be a feather in my cap.'

He said that for a reaction. But there was none from Muldoon. Nelson took note of his discomfort hearing it. He'd been forewarned. The superintendent had instructed him to keep an eye on Flanagan's bar. It was noted for after-hours.

But Nelson was doubtful about Muldoon's commitment to the cause. He'd been in town a long time, and he'd made friends. Feeding him occasional false information might expose collaboration between him and this renegade bar owner.

Muldoon's time for promotion had passed. He'd know which of them qualified for Sergeant, and he wouldn't be foolish enough to double-cross his new boss, would he?

Nelson was confident that he'd make Sergeant. It was in him, his father had been one. All the attributes were there. He was suspicious of everyone, and that was the hallmark of a great Sergeant.

There wasn't a person around to occupy Bill's fuzzy thinking. He'd ask his father if he could do Danny's job, while the wagon driver, with such a placid temperament, might like doing barman for a while. Anything to get out of the boring pub he so disliked.

WT wouldn't listen to it. 'You're either a publican or you're not,' he advised, cutting him short. He was irritated that Bill found it so difficult to settle. He'd been scheming for a long time about a hotel on this spot, with space for twelve bedrooms at the back; a little goldmine. There were certain factors necessary to remain in place. It was crucial to have a clean bar licence to reflect the integrity of a licensed premises proprietor.

Anytime WT thought about family, prospects for his successor were tight. The whole thing would flounder if he hadn't someone of his own ilk taking over. His two sons were very different. Tom thought he was an opera singer, and working in a hardware store wasn't good enough for him. That left him stuck with this unsettled publican who harboured a notion of quitting. These plans for converting the pub into a hotel were exciting, but they must remain hidden for longer.

Bill knew after his last brief chat with his father that he'd have to soldier on. He wondered if Tom would prefer a pub to sing in. And he'd try convincing his wife of the problem with their son.

'Look, he lives in a world of his own making, Hanna. It's looking like the boy will finish up with the pick and shovel; he has brains for nothing else. He took every opportunity to give out about his son talking to her. But she was way ahead of him.

'We shall see about that, Bill.' That wisdom received no answer. Hanna had his measure.

CHAPTER 3

Jonsie was growing into a strong young fellow. All these energetic pursuits kept his muscles exercised and his mind active, for certain things. Learning from books wasn't one of them. He went to school because he had to, but never listened. He couldn't wait for three o'clock to get away from it. Then he had a long evening, to look after the more important things in his life that kept him so occupied. He'd taken over a few sheds behind the pub to house his animals. There were kid goats to sell. He gave them slops of beer, leftovers. That was supposed to fatten them up in a hurry; it turned out disastrous in the end.

He saw how Jack the donkey ate dandelions, so he gathered some for the goats. He was feeding three. After a month he'd sell them on to Ned the goat dealer for threepence each. The money went in his savings box; he wanted to buy a pony. He'd begun to breed rabbits. It was a very busy operation now. But there was another special interest. He'd discovered where the keys for the back gate were hidden. When his parents were occupied in the bar, and he was supposedly confined to the yard with his animals, he'd head out around the lake. A place like the big river, where he was forbidden to go; his little dog Trotsie faithfully followed him everywhere he went.

He felt a connection to the place. The calm lake reflected the dark silhouettes of majestic pine trees on its surface, standing like sentries all around. There was safety in this quiet place. You could learn everything you needed to know in peace, without anybody telling you what to do. When he climbed a tree near the water, he talked to the lake, and told it many secret things. It would always be there for him. He hid the key in a safer place, so nobody else would find it.

When he was fifteen he could do anything he wanted without them saying it was wrong. Blaming him because they couldn't see it, the way he did. Boxer said fifteen was when he'd become a man. He was that age when he went to London for an adventure.

Jonsie listened attentively to everything Boxer said. He had years left to spend waiting for it, and it sounded like a whole lifetime. But 'adventure' had a magical ring to it. So he listened.

One day something very bad happened.

He left for the lake with Trotsie on his heels. The dog always disappeared sniffing out rabbit holes. When he reached the back gate on his way home, he found him lying there; dead. He had got trapped by the neck under the gate.

He sobbed, and pitiful tears flowed down his cheeks when he carried him into the kitchen. But there was no one there except the old one. When she saw the dog, she said it low, so no one else could hear. 'You did it again, murderer.'

Jonsie ran back out to the yard. He took a spade from the shed and went to dig a grave, in the special spot near the water he could see from the tree. A place no one else would find. This quiet resting place, for the only friend he ever had.

He made one of his well-considered promises to the lake. It was like a code of behaviour he respected for himself to honour, one that could never be broken. That's why it came out of him so solemnly. He was very emotionally connected with its meaning.

'I'll never let them change the way I am, never.'

At the end of the summer, when all the football games were played out, the town team won a few games in a row, something that hadn't happened before. Bill, a former player, thought it a good time to raise some money for the club. They were on a roll, ready to believe in anything.

He knew the craic must carry on into the early hours, like his opening night, to ensure he got a good pay night in the cash till. There was a possibility of the Gardaí raiding him, so that was the first thing to sort out. It was risky to chance anything now. That Nelson bastard had ruined the whole show.

He called out a friendly greeting to Garda Muldoon; he'd been watching him coming down the street. He was ready for him.

'Good man Pat, warm sort of a day that, would you like a beer?'

Muldoon walked into the bar without breaking his stride, putting his police cap on the counter. In time-honoured ritual, the badge faced out to the empty bar, indicating that he was still on duty.

'Yes Bill, I'll have one.' And he sat gingerly up at the counter.

'I'd say you Miss Sergeant Murphy, Pat, he was a good friend of everyone in the town. It will be hard to replace him.'

The Garda scratched his face, with his jaw to one side. He knew this fellow didn't give a damn about Murphy. He was always looking for information. He'd throw him of balance.

Muldoon took a gulp of beer before rushing him with a quick one. 'And what about my new partner Garda Nelson, I'm sure you have opinions about him yourself, eh Bill?'

That statement was a bit full on for Bill's liking. Muldoon was talking like he was interrogating him.

'He called me a sly old fox not so long ago. That wasn't nice, was it Pat; with children to bring up, here in the town.'

'Depends what evidence he had to substantiate the claim, he might be on to something. Or he wouldn't have said it, I'm sure.'

Bill stared hard at him. Even sitting at the bar, he sounded like a Garda on duty. Muldoon wouldn't be wandering too far off track. They were all the same.

Bill started talking about the weather, a strained discussion. That lasted until he finished the beer. When he was getting off the bar stool, he smiled knowingly at Bill. It was the hopeful sign for a desperate bar owner trying to make a few extra bob.

'Friday week Pat, the football lads are having a fundraiser. Will you be working the town that night? This Nelson stalks the place like a fox after chickens, when he's on.'

'You're asking if I'm working that Friday, I think so.'

'You'd be welcome in for a pint to wish the lads well,' Bill assured him, knowing all was good.

'We must try to support the local team anyway we can, Pat. Sergeant Murphy had a great way with him; he always put the community first. Hope our new man, Nelson, follows in his footsteps. Everyone will have a good word to say about him, like they have for you, good luck to you now. Give my regards to your dear wife.'

Hanna was very pleased with Miss Kelly's progress. She wasn't as stooped anymore, looking ten years younger.

It had been tough going, when she couldn't get through to her. She could have abandoned the task. But she knew to persevere. Wearing lipstick now with a nice red smile, it was worth getting to know the real Miss Kelly.

They were sitting together at the fire one day, when for no apparent reason she took hold of Hanna's hand firmly. 'Call me Mary all the time,' she whispered.

'Will you call me Hanna?' she asked.

'I know your lovely name, dear,' she replied softly.

When her mother volunteered to help, Hanna was delighted. So she planned afternoon tea especially for them. Hanna sat listening when they discussed the fashion shop, as if it was still going on. It was obvious the ladies were warming to each other, fond memories connecting them once again.

After tea, they continued talking in the same breath and Hanna heard more tales about that time. The story she'd heard on market day, from 'Nose-in-the-Air,' was only a short version. This personally related full account was riveting.

Mary admitted that she was mesmerised by the charms of a salesman in her shop, a flashy type, and this besotted young woman couldn't see through him and his three-piece suit and watch and chain dangling from his waistcoat pocket. The way he dressed reminded her of men she had met socialising in Manhattan.

Mary's dull existence became livelier then. She started applying makeup with more careful attention and rediscovered the fun girl she had lost in New York. Her cousin listened to her travel stories enviously; she longed for an escape from the boring town as well.

When Mary's fiancé invited her to the awful Freddy Brown's Pub, full of big spiders, she refused point blank to go near the place. She entrusted her wayward cousin to accompany him instead.

On her wedding day, Mary was the happiest woman in the world. She knew what her bridesmaid wanted. There was a special present passed on to her and she hadn't seen her since. Too busy getting ready for the big day.

Mary had written to the department store in New York and secured employment for her star-struck cousin. Her fare was saved, with enough cash to keep her going.

She knew how tough it could be in New York City, knowing nobody. She wanted to see how much pleasure it gave her after the wedding. Then she became aware of the great deception this unscrupulous girl had brought on her. On the very day she was being a bridesmaid, she absconded to Gretna Green in Scotland for a hasty coupling with Mary's future husband, a scandal she could never live down. She went on a downward spiral from that awful day. This predicament of being 'left on the shelf' invaded her soul. And she became convinced that everyone in the whole parish was laughing at her. The shame of being 'stood up' would last her lifetime.

Bill was delighted about the upcoming footballer's party. He'd everything covered for this sure money spinner. His brother Tom was lined up to sing a few songs. The locals enjoyed him, but Tom wasn't flattered by their phony enthusiasm. He was a tenor in the musical society, a veteran of many performances, and he always dressed for the occasion in his blue suit, white shirt and blue polka-dotted tie. A quiet man usually, but on stage, he came out of himself. 'Vulgar gyrating', they said, but forgave him, because he was religious.

Pretending he was a rock and roll star got to him. Bill was sure he'd like his own singing lounge. With the bar filling up, he called Danny to relate details of the gate keys' precise location. 'So there would be no slip ups,' he whispered.

'Listen to me, if a Garda knocks on the door, open the gate at the back immediately; get the crowd out into the lane while I stall him at the front. No problem, Muldoon is on duty tonight. It won't be hard to manage him. He'll go along with everything.'

About 2 am, the night was going full blast. Tom hushed everyone for 'Danny Boy', a bit of calm. But they applauded. Bill did his best to control them. He told Tom it was too late for the rock stuff. He didn't want to dampen it either, they might leave early.

Bicycles stacked outside, against the pub wall, told the story. The country boys were in there. The top Garda was on to it, with a bad-tempered grunt, making some sound for his hunting face.

The door knocker got a loud bang, and that had a sobering effect, on some of them. The rest geared up to relish the tenseness of the situation. This was mighty craic. How could you miss it?

When Bill opened the door, Garda Nelson confronted him, standing square, with that 'you're caught' attitude. 'Gardaí on duty!' he roared as if he was miles away. 'You have an illegal gathering on the premises. I will talk to everyone. People on licensed premises after hours are going down in my book.' He took the black book out of his top pocket.

Pushing past Bill, he found that all that remained inside the pub was cigarette smoke empty glasses. 'See, Garda Nelson,' Bill smirked, 'not a sinner in the place, we were just about to clean up after a football party. And that ended on the dot of closing time. The missus made tea for me and Danny; we chatted for too long after. Sorry for wasting your time Garda you have a lot to do.'

Out in the yard there was panic, because Danny couldn't find the gate keys. Nelson soon discovered where the patrons were cornered. He began writing names in his book. There were no false names passed over on him. He knew them all. He could see some religious people; they would be mortified, caught in a public house in the middle of the night. It wasn't going to enhance his image in the community. But that wouldn't bother a good sergeant. 'After hours drinking' had an unfortunate ring to it. Decent people didn't do that. It would always be remembered as the night he did the dirt on them. They would never forget, as they stood waiting in the cold, anxiously.

Nelson was new; he didn't understand how everything worked. There would be favours sought and promises made. The elections surfaced in times like this. And the 'brown envelope' would pass to the greedy clutches of a taker. There was a fixer everywhere.

In time-honoured tradition wonders worked and no one knew how it happened. But 'big shots' must escape wrongdoing.

Garda Nelson knew they would pick up their ears in Dublin when they heard of this successful operation. The new sergeant in waiting felt the stripes on his arm already. And the raid should keep Bill Flanagan quiet for a while.

Boxer spent his time sipping pints of porter. Everyone said he must have a great tolerance for alcohol, because he never got drunk. He sat quietly smiling, listening to stories from around the lake. The boy's simple take on life brought him back to his own time. He was delighted the young lad was so in tune with nature.

Boxer knew it was important to learn about the real world too. A young fellow, not fond of listening, would find the journey tougher. Embellished tales carefully told might guide his way.

Hanna had to coax him to school, on that first day, but the minute he went into the building, he hated the place, and didn't want to play boring games in the schoolyard either.

Some of the older boys lined him up for special treatment, 'a country boy with nothing to say'. Maybe he had an opinion of himself. Because his parents owned a pub he might think he was somebody. They said things to rile him, but it didn't work. It was bound to get difficult when they found out he wasn't afraid of them. And if it came down to a fist fight, that was okay too.

The first class teacher was a serene lady, rarely raising her voice in anger, or inflicting corporal punishment on anyone. When she wasn't getting satisfactory results, she coaxed her pupils with the patience of a caring mother. All the kids loved her for that.

But he got a rude awakening in another classroom. The learning environment deteriorated, and the person in charge of delivering the message was on the wrong page. This teacher was a thin man with piercing eyes. He got the nickname Rasp, and it stuck. His long red nose twitched irritably when he talked. If you were self-conscious, you might think there was a smell from you.

He lifted boys from their seats by the lock of hair at their ears. It didn't take long before Jonsie was focus of his attention. Another one that didn't do what he was told. He took into the abuse with perverse relish. Like a demon from hell he never stopped until he got tired. For those that suffered, he wasn't tired often enough. He picked on the same ones all the time. So it was personal.

The whole class was upset by Rasp's treatment of two brothers. How he beat them was frightening to witness and demoralising for those quiet lads on the receiving end. They never deserved it. The boys knew what was coming. He'd elicit some response that drove him into frenzy, slapping the boy's head until he was dizzy.

One of them had a cyst inside his top lip. It gave the impression he was laughing when he was just grimacing. It was disrespectful to the teacher's eyes. That spurred him to beat the boys until he got tired. Neither of these proud young men ever shed a tear. Unlike their tormenter, they were of noble character. The teacher was flawed, deficient in character. He would break them, if he could reduce them to tears; that humiliation was what Psycho Rasp must have craved most.

He never got it from this pair of faithful brothers. There is always a special character in real ones, to help them cope. Afterwards, they'd sit together, red faced, battered and embarrassed; powerful natures dented yet again by a bad attitude. These boys would always be respected for the way they coped with this cruel abuse. Would it affect them negatively?

Over sixty years later, a long way from home; I sat in the waiting room of a doctor's surgery. There was one other patient. One of life's amazing coincidences occurred then. He was the boy with the cyst under his top lip. There was a well-trimmed moustache there now. We got talking and discussed the teacher. He confided he'd only forgiven 'Rasp' a few years earlier. His brother had had difficulty with it all his life. They lived in the USA now. It was a great privilege to meet up with him, and it prompted these reflections. Someone will surely know about them still.

Jonsie was completely taken over with the monthly horse fair on the green. Owners stood holding reins, selling to anyone that listened. Ennis was a wiry middle-aged horse dealer with a feather in the crown of his trilby hat. Everyone knew him by sight. It was usual for horse dealing men to have a nickname, and some of these names were informative. Like the nickname 'Bad News' given to one crooked dealer. 'Moonlight Flit' was another one.

Fair day transactions were always dodgy. There were wrong ones everywhere. That's why they were there. If they were any good they'd keep them at home. 'How do you know a good horse?' one dealer asked another dealer over a pint. 'The one that makes the most money for you,' he replied, before sinking the porter in one go. Just like that. 'You don't have to know anything if you're saying nothing.' Not much more to know about horses so.

Decent men at home, dealers sold horses to support their families. They were good doing a tough job; it wasn't possible to have a sound horse for sale all the time. You had to be observant. It was all about 'a nod is as good as a wink.'

One day Ennis put Jonsie to sit in the dipped back of a quiet old cart pony. He was trying to sell it to a toff couple, for their son. Anyone wearing fancy clothes was seen as a toff. And the seasoned dealer grinned at the thought of taking them. But they were very cautious with their money and didn't trust horse dealers. So they didn't believe what this shifty dealer was telling them. The pony was 'very quiet to ride'? He might be a nasty bucker when they took him home and the tranquilizer wore off. He could do damage to their son.

When they refused to chance their precious son on his back, Ennis asked the publican's son in desperation. These toffs looked like victims. He couldn't let them go. He walked the pony around in circles, with Jonsie on his back. It was a comfortable feeling for the boy, like sitting on his rocking horse, only better. When the dealer saw how steady he was on the pony, he handed the reins to the man, and let him walk off on his own; a real horseman. But it was the wife that looked after the horses.

He explained, 'I run the shop at home'.

Toffs were easy to predict. They could read how it's done in books. But nobody ever fell off a book. This trade was about experience. Ennis had heard it all before. And she was at it again. The wife was trying to make him sound like a liar.

She enquired if the pony had done much hunting. With a sniff of her nose, she said she was sure he hadn't. Ennis knew the cart pony wouldn't pass as a hunter, not even with the help of all the angles in heaven and all the lying dealers in hell. She was looking for a way of pulling back from doing a deal. And this wily dealer saw a weakness, she was afraid she'd buy, over halfway there. The odds were on his side. One like this could always be turned over.

He leaned towards her, with true sincerity dripping from his boozy eyes, and roared, 'No. He's never been out hunting yet, but he'd love to go. He told me so himself, not so long ago.' There was knowledge there.

Because she didn't know what to say to that, she finished up buying the pony. Then there was haggling over the 'luck penny'. She insisted Ennis should give the 'young jockey' a threepenny bit to regain control of the deal. She had almost married a horse dealer once, until her father found out about it. So not only was Jonsie treated to his first real horse ride, he was paid good money for enjoying it. Another lesson registered.

Bill stacked cases of empty bottles on the sidewalk. Calling out to Garda Muldoon, he waited for him to cross the street. 'Well Pat, that's a nice sunny day we're having.'

'Come off the old chat Bill, I know what you're thinking.'

'Then you know Nelson took names here. The same night you told me you'd be working.'

'Bill, he locked me in the cell.'

The bar owner looked for the lie, but couldn't see it. 'Locked you in the cell?'

'He ordered me to clean up the place for visitors. And locked the door behind me, saying it was all a big mistake when he arrived back. I know it wasn't. That's all I can say.'

When he turned to walk away, Bill called him back. 'I believe you Pat, this is a dangerous man to have in our town.'

'He will be Sergeant soon, I've seen the letter, he held it under my nose, and he can order me to raid you any night. You must be careful, you've been caught already, twice more, your licence is gone, and all you're left with is an empty drapery store. You're a hard-working man. I wouldn't want anything bad happen you Bill. Take it easy.'

Bill said nothing. He knew a decent man when he met one. Nelson promoted to Sergeant was an advance warning though.

The Politician said as much one day, with a sly wink. 'Nelson was sent to Cody's Cross just to catch you.'

Bill wanted his father to pressure the Politician and get Nelson promoted to an offshore island, where they'd drown him if he didn't toe the line.

When Hanna arrived with a pot of tea she was amused by Mary enjoying herself so much, with Danny doing all the talking. She wanted to hear it all over again, for the umpteenth time.

'The horse stumbled, Mary, if I hadn't put my arms around you, you'd have hit the ground. I didn't think I'd get into such trouble for trying to keep you safe.' He laughed. 'I could have lost my job for laying a hand on you.'

Hanna had never heard Miss Kelly laugh so much before, and she wanted to encourage it. Since they had moved into town he'd become a regular caller. He lived down the street in the same house he was born in. He took the Kelly's to mass in the trap on Sundays over the years. It was Danny who explained Jonsie's mistake, telling Miss Kelly all about the young ducks swimming on the flooded road. She was still angry, but she asked him to get her a duck colouring book and crayons, one yellow and one black, insisting all this must be carried out in secret. One day when the couple were busy, she showed Jonsie how to colour in ducks. 'This is our secret,' she warned him.

When Hanna found out, she was amazed it was kept so quiet. "There's a secret organisation in the house!' She giggled. 'Wasn't it funny Bill, we thought Jonsie had the artist urge in his veins. But she was tutoring him all the time, when we were busy. She must have felt guilty for hitting him.'

'Don't mind it Hanna, everything happens for a reason. We must encourage Danny. He knows all those stories to make her happy. Keeping her occupied would help us. Of course, she was good to me when I was young. She wouldn't have been invited to live with us otherwise. It's great to see you two getting on so well now. Long may it last. But we need more help, Hanna. You have enough on your plate with two children and another on the way. I'll talk to Danny about bar work, the customers like him. You needn't go in there anymore. It's not your cup of tea, I know. You don't like it Hanna, and I don't blame you for that.'

They'd reassembled the kitchen from their previous home. It was much better with the electric light. No more oil lamps and candles. The old dresser, with the turf fire blazing away, remained a heartfelt sight. She was right; a cosy kitchen would always be the hub of the home. Electrification was essential in houses, television a necessity. They were on the waiting list for a coin box telephone in the pub. Her mother had a phone; she'd like to keep in touch. Good things were coming, slowly.

In the hardware store Tom applied himself diligently to his customers' requirements. He was tuning his throat for sweeter notes. Singing came naturally to him. There was a crowd turning up to hear him on weekends, but he had expected that.

Songs he sang were 'ordinary' compared to his classical range.

He wouldn't be singing any of those in a pub. If he had his own singing lounge, he could stop working in the dreary old hardware store and become famous, as he'd always dreamed. But with no money, he was stuck in a rut.

His fiancée kept saying he had the Flanagan business calling. 'You are the eldest son; the home place is rightfully yours.' But a singing lounge was all he could imagine.

WT Flanagan was a tough man to live with. They said his wife jumped into the river to get away from him. The fast-flowing water took her while she laughed up at the moon. They whispered, 'she was full of wine at the time.'

This sudden death troubled everyone, and it was much speculated about, in whispered tones, always. The history of events would vary; some stories relating to that sad event should never be told. Bad people made accusations.

There was an undercurrent of religious bigotry throughout the community. The haters pulled out their swords for defending God before they thought about saving Man.

One day, Rasp the teacher was giving his Christian doctrine class. The big blue Catholic Apologetics book lay open in front of him. Rasp drooled out the scripture reverently, like he had witnessed it. 'Pontius Pilate, the Roman governor, condemned Jesus Christ to death at the desire of the Jews.'

Jonsie liked Christian doctrine because there were soldiers in it. The Romans wore big helmets and swords. He wondered if Jews were like Indians that fought back with bow and arrows when they were attacked. Indians were very brave warriors. Boxer told him all about them. So he was excited putting his hand up.

'Who were the Jews, sir?' He asked.

The teacher pulled him over to slap his ears. He had his hand cupped, for the deafening effect. Then he wrote these words on the blackboard:

'Don't ask about Jews.'

He shouted, repeating the scrawled words on the blackboard. 'They're all dead now, the Germans killed them all.'

The teacher tied him in the desk with twine.

He had plenty of time to read the date on the blackboard, 5/5/1955. He was eleven, and he'd never forget the humiliation. He wouldn't be asking questions from 'teachers' ever again, and he lost faith in all kinds of religious instruction after that.

There was something not quite right with it; things with no answers were accepted as mysteries. Jonsie saw 'mysteries' like a lake with no bottom. Something bad lurked there, and it might make a visit, when you didn't ask.

Working for Ennis the horse dealer was much better fun. The old boy understood him; it seemed, laughing at his antics, a bit like himself when he was young. And he was selling more ponies with this lad around him. Some people thought it was his son, and for a roving horse dealer that never planted any roots he was okay with that. It might seem someone liked him, once.

Jonsie learned to ride a horse the hard way. When the dealer sold one he purchased another. He kept his stock fresh, with some money left to 'keep the show on the road'. He kept saying that. The boy was very happy doing this job, it didn't feel like work.

Love for the horse came from deep inside. That very first

flooded road trip made a lasting impression on him. He perceived the horse as a magical creature that could keep you safe. But this road galloping madness went down badly in the house. They were telling Bill in the bar that Jonsie was travelling the road like he was in the Grand National.

'You couldn't catch him on a racing bicycle', they joked.

His mother worried about him, and his father constantly gave out about injuries. Falling off horses on that tarred road wouldn't be good for playing football. He'd shout at the boy.

But Jonsie rode the ponies bareback for three miles to the dealer's and let them out in a field. Then he'd run back to the fair, and get another one. It went on for the whole day. Ennis paid threepence for every delivery. He knew when people saw a young fellow on a pony that was quiet to ride it was a big help selling them on for children.

He had dreams of owning his own pony. Threepence was a nice little coin with square sides, for his savings box. It was safely cemented to the floor of the shed. The horse dealer treated him with respect. They formed a trusting relationship, like a considerate father and an attentive son. And he was learning all about horses.

Bill lost interest in what his son was doing. He regularly complained that he was too wild to control, because he'd listen to nobody.

An American couple, recent arrivals in town, were new customers in his bar. This woman's ability to capture the limelight was talked about. It was to do with what she wore, or maybe what she didn't wear. But there was no doubt in her mind that she was very enticing.

The gossip woman Nose-in-the-Air included her in the stories. Much exaggerated accounts of sexy happenings had the wives simmering. And she couldn't wait to inform Hanna. But she was ready for her annoyance, with a curt reply. 'We shouldn't be bothered about what men do, they will always be boys. I couldn't listen to hear about their stupid antics.'

CHAPTER 4

Hanna talked with Danny more often. He attended mass every day for his mother. It was difficult for her when he was growing up. They had the same shame to live in a small town where everything was common knowledge. Their tidy little house was at the end of the street, near the forge. The yellow rose bushes were either side of the front door still, in that sunny spot, planted so long ago with prayers, for the return of a lost child. The prayers were answered, eventually.

Hanna remembered hearing about Bill's mother's untimely death. There was a hint of scandal, depending on which version you heard. A séance with Drover was talked about. Not many people knew about that. She was determined to get to the bottom of it. It was said that Danny knew everything.

Taking her lifeless body from the river must have been a very troubling time. Anything other than the weather, or horses, was of little interest to him. Why then, she wondered, did he have long chats, sometimes in whispers, with Miss Kelly? She could hear some of their conversation when she was making tea.

It gave her satisfaction seeing the elderly lady's improvement.

She could imagine her devastation, left sitting alone in her wedding dress. The man she loved on his way to Scotland to marry her bridesmaid. And that was the end of it.

Whenever she struggled to cope with Miss Kelly's depression that thought kept her going. She was there for her now, no matter what happened. How she longed to see that famous wedding dress. Bill said it was stored in a big cardboard box under the bed, hidden from view, 'like everything else about her'.

Hanna chastised him for that unkindness, and all the poor woman went through. It was comforting she required now.

The teacher intensified his dislike of Jonsie and asked questions from the religious book to catch him out. When he didn't know the answers, Rasp ordered him to learn it during lunch break. He always had a cynical twist to his mouth, asking him the same question again. He'd never got a proper answer. That set him off, glaring at him first to let the rage build. His daughters hung their heads, dreading the floor show. Jonsie was always ready to resist. But teacher warned him first. 'I'm going to take down your trousers, you disobedient little brat!'

White froth congealed on the corners of his tormented mouth as he struggled to remove the short trousers while his victim wrestled furiously, kicking up at him from the floor.

He was terrified the girls would see he wore no underpants and was urinating on his legs to make him stop. It could be punishment for being no good on his tin whistle. The teacher had arranged for all the boys to have tin whistle lessons. They formed a band to play on the street. Jonsie was in the middle of them without a clue in his head, or a note coming from his flying fingers. No one would know any different.

He got away with it, until he was caught. Rasp could see he was out of synch with the rest of them. He stood behind him with his ear cocked, listening. All that came back was silence. Not a note from his most troublesome pupil.

The teacher sucked on his pipe furiously. People came out to hear the band for the first time; if they saw this play-acting, it would be bad for the school image and the end of the whistle band.

Jonsie had it figured out how not to get caught. If you blew into the whistle when you didn't know anything about it, everyone could hear you were no good at it. If you didn't blow at all, no one knew the difference.

When the teacher stared into his face, Jonsie gave him a cheeky wink, letting him know 'all was well'. There would be no bum notes played, his fingers fluttering, like he was good at it. He was sure of one thing, his trousers were going nowhere on this occasion. The street was packed with people and Rasp wasn't that far gone, yet.

As the months passed by Jonsie became more withdrawn. After dumping his school bag, he went round the lake. The circle of trees was called the Twelve Apostles. Here he'd plan an 'adventure' over to the other side. It wouldn't take long to build a 'raft' for the voyage. There were long beer cases and a good linen sheet to 'post sail' on the handle of a yard brush. He'd been collecting, since he figured it out.

From his perch in the forked tree, he cast his woes on the lake. He wanted to live over there, where Rasp couldn't get near him again. And he didn't plan on returning until he was too old for school. He could see the sunny hill across the lake was a peaceful place. There were never animals grazing the land, so he made plans for a look.

He couldn't tell his mother what was happening to him at school. How was she to know if he deserved it or not? His father talked to the teacher in the bar occasionally. He saw them laughing. So he wasn't going to mention school at home. Maybe his parents would find out he was no good at learning, and they would be ashamed of him.

The whole thing was troubling the boy so much that he wasn't looking after his animals properly, like he always did. Bill took over possession of the little bicycle shop next door to the pub. The bar was doing well, so it was a good investment.

Then one day, he heard a troubling tale. He got a visit from a local fisherman concerning Jonsie. He told him he was fishing at the lake when he heard shouting. In a deep part near the Twelve Apostles, he found Jonsie struggling in the water, out of his depth. And he couldn't swim. This man was wearing waders up to his waist and with the aid of his stout fishing pole he hauled him in safely.

There was a beer case with a makeshift sail fixed to it sinking beside the boy. Another few seconds, he would have been gone. The boy told him he'd built a raft to sail over the lake, and named Rasp as the reason why he wanted to get there. The man advised his father to investigate the teacher's behaviour. And it might be time to find something useful to occupy his son. He had far too much energy.

Time to rein in; Bill said that one very low indeed.

When Bill looked out the pub window, he saw two familiar

customers having a loud barraging exchange on the street. His father's tone was insulting, peppered with vulgar words, while his companion tried to pacify him with contrived kindness of a demeaning nature. It was always a battle of wits between these two; which was an axe and which the sword. The Politician was heavy going, but Bill knew well there was always a bit of comedy in this act, if you were up for hearing it.

Flash, the politician, had pulled into the hardware store an hour earlier. He couldn't be bothered talking to people. They were always looking for something. Putting in an appearance should be enough to get support. He had been a long time 'in power' now. He took a bottle to spray between his trousers legs; he was blighted with the curse of 'spontaneous flagellation,' another reason for keeping on the move. He swore at the driver for coughing and spluttering about his allergy to aftershave. How was he to know it was the farts? 'If you don't shut up you'll get nothing at the week end.'

Because he was related through marriage, he didn't always get paid. The honour of being close to government should be enough. Flash read the letter again; he did a long fart before getting out of the car, to put manners on the driver.

WT was soon telling him about a shop he could have for an election office. It was rent free if everything else fell into place. 'There's the problem' he said, tapping the letter in his hand, so the driver heard how easy he had figured it all out. 'See here, he wants something, no free spin in WT Flanagan's hearse. Sit here quietly, do you hear me? There are papers on the back seat there. Make sure you mind them; its private government correspondence.'

When he walked in the door, WT bellowed out excitedly, 'Will you look at this bollox, running around after me again. He'll only get votes if he takes good care of us. The people around here can't be forgotten. There are several wasters lining up for the top job, but none of them could equal our own bollox here.'

The customers laughed at WTs disrespectful rhetoric. 'Bollox' was an Irish word for correctly describing 'idiot with no knowledge'. But one must be careful; something might come up someday so you'd need him, getting you what you wanted, if he was kept sweet. The politician's rapid handshake got him moving past everyone in a hurry, without hearing any of it. Just so they could see him nodding his head, as if he was listening. Election time was rife for making demands. They were all pretending to be his.

Flash knew WT had the ear of people. That was the only reason he tolerated him. He'd promise everything, without knowing what everything was. The clever ones knew it was all nonsense, but there weren't enough of them. The easily led ones would do what they were told. And they could boast how well they knew him after he'd given them the feeling he was there for them. That, Flash learned, was the hallmark of a great politician.

Old man Flanagan could swing votes his way. Of course he would demand some kind of favour in return. That's why he wrote the letter to his office. Flash would listen carefully, aware of the store owner's ambitions to open a hotel. He would toe the line, to get his hotel planning permission granted. Flash knew well how to play him, so he could say what he liked. The bottom line was all about wielding 'power 'to influence everything going on. And he was the only one with 'power' in this gathering.

After the politician had shaken hands with everyone, he was invited for a drink, over the street. In the pub, well informed revelations spilled from his mouth. His self-importance made false promises; there was something in it for everyone, he insisted. He'd been repeating this stuff so long now he even believed it himself.

Bill listened to them for a while without making any comment, getting the drift of where it was going. He surveyed the two pompous gentlemen standing at his counter coolly. If he didn't know them, he'd think they were decent people, looking for kindness in each other, not trying to express some form of a nasty put down to get one over. Which was the case?

Flash had his phoney voice switched on high volume for the occasion. He was trying to hide his common way of speaking with a new invention, the word 'actually', which meant nothing but sounded great. It provided a gap for abstract thought; you might understand how little it meant if you heard it right. But there was something about it that conferred power on the speaker. This word that someone who thought they knew something constantly used.

'Actually, when I open a clinic here, I'll get you the agency for Raleigh bicycles and Bush radios. Your father tells me you're modernising the cycle store, actually. There's a new development scheme going forward, actually. Grants, it's called,' he said with a wink.

Bill cut in impatiently, to modernise the conversation slightly. 'This new Garda in town is a proper nuisance. I'll tell you, he could block your election office if he took it into his head.'

'Now what law would that break? He mustn't be one of ours actually; I don't like the sound of him at all, where is he from?' Flash said, a scowl puckering his thick lips.

Then Bill mentioned this bastard was targeting him, and his licence could be in jeopardy. And worse still he was going on to become a sergeant. Could Flash do anything about the problem?

'I will get rid of this fellow for you, actually. But it won't be easy. If you could find something to discredit him, that would help. Would he take advantage of women?' he enquired seriously.

When Bill told him how he had locked Garda Muldoon in a cell one night, the politician got very interested in that. 'That's a bad one actually, a mental distraction there. He might be better off where there are not too many people around him.'

He drank the whiskey in one go, as did WT, who'd been listening. They'd soon see what this politician was made of.

'Good man Flash, you'll do it for me too won't you.' He walloped his back in appreciation, almost knocking him over.

'There could be another explanation,' Bill suggested, wiping the counter in front of them. Flash was hoping the problem was solved. 'That incident with Muldoon in the cell might have a more sinister angle to it,' the barman remarked.

'Bejesus I see,' said WT.

'Republican sympathiser in the Gardaí, is it?' Flash said.

The politician was switched on again. He might hear some useful information for the Garda inspector. These Flanagan's had a statue erected to one of their rebellious kin on the green, so he'd be careful what he said. You never know where you're talking.'

WT enquired about that word 'sinister'. 'What's it supposed to mean? Tell us Bill.'

'Nelson might want to try something different, but he was too busy taking names of decent people here. He didn't have time for pleasure on the job, raping poor Muldoon in the cell.'

The old boys' mouths were left hanging open.

'Jesus, I've heard it all now,' said WT.

The politician was shocked. 'He's a playboy. I never saw one of them before. I didn't think there were any around here.'

WT added his caring comment. 'There were no women molested in the barracks so.'

Flash bared his teeth. This subject he was uncomfortable with.

'This Nelson fellow shouldn't be in the town at all.' He hoped to end the speculation, saying that.

Bill stared out of the window; he was thinking about his mother. He remembered her telling him how she had found his father in bed with the maid. 'You're Uncle Danny knows it all', she whispered. The first time he had heard of the wagon master's connection to his family. He was watching him standing at the yard gate; he looked for some resemblance to his father. There was none. He blamed his father for his mother's demise. He was too young to understand. The remorse of failing her always came back to him.

Looking over at the hardware store gave him a lump in his throat. He wondered if his father had stuck him in the pub to get rid of him, because he wasn't dependable. He'd heard what Tom's woman said in the bar one night, with a few gins too many in her, trying to impress Nose-in-the-Air. She said it as if she knew what she was talking about.

'When I'm working full time in the store with my husband, we can plan shopping trips to Dublin,' she promised her.

Bills private nickname for Tom's woman was 'Peril' – a devious character that needed watching. He knew about her past antics. You hear everything going on, in a pub. The bad stuff gets special consideration. She was the topic of some conversations already with this strong sense of immoral behaviour going down her way.

Rasp the schoolteacher had a special interest in history. Noted for his dislike of Protestant people, he hinted at some past connection to freedom fighters. He invited an old rebel into school, under the pretext of teaching the boys how to play tin whistle. He'd talk up a United Ireland for a while. And Rasp would point out the window during the lesson. 'Those people were left here to watch over us by the English, to keep Catholics down where they put them.'

The class got intense when it involved naming. Rasp couldn't refrain from his menacing way. 'Protestants should be sent home to England, their tails between their legs, that Union Jack flag of theirs along with them.'

There were chills in the classroom as he'd tell his contorted version of history. The boys listened quietly. He was easier to ignore when he stared out of the window.

'Those people over there would get no peace in my day. Especially with snow on the ground,' he smirked. 'Get out there and pelt the living daylights out of them. Let them see who's in charge here now.'

The boys had only one thing in their minds: 'Get the Protestants!' They pelted them with snowballs from all directions.

Jonsie was as hostile as the rest of them, until he saw the girl falling in the snow with a long thick plait bouncing off her shoulder. She had tried protecting her friend again. He remembered how fearless she was the last time, her eyes glaring at him. She'd fight for her rights. The boy pelting her was bigger than him. He shouldered him hard, knocking him down in the snow, and got a box in the eye for that. He shouted after the girl. 'I'm sorry.'

When he saw her looking back, he quietly vowed he'd never do it again. Something in his soul felt strongly how wrong it was. Jonsie knew religion was mixed up with bad feeling. And it couldn't ever be right, on account of that alone.

The lies only made things worse. These people were just like him. His sisters were the same as their sisters. Why couldn't they all be friends? If religion was making this badness sound right, then religion was all wrong. He was sure of that, more than anything else now. And he was always acutely aware of this hidden bias.

He reached down and took a handful of snow for his throbbing eye. Boxer was a good fighter in his time, they said. He'd ask him for some instruction.

When he arrived home, his father took a look at him with a big grin on his face, not a bit sorry for him.

'How did you get the black eye, Jonsie?'

'A girl hit me, Daddy.'

'And what were you doing to her?'

'Throwing snowballs.'

He ran in to tell his mother the same story; if he said a boy hit him, it would come down to a fight. But if it was a girl, it sounded like a lie. Lies were great for keeping truth secret.

Bill sat down for a chat with Hanna that same night, everyone in bed and his head full of troubled things. Hanna was concerned about a fraught relationship developing between father and son.

She'd witnessed it going on. She held her tea cupped in her hands, sitting across from him expectantly.

'Now Hanna, this black eye he arrived in with from school was not the work of any girl. There is something else going on here, and we must know more about that. What's troubling me is what he's hiding. Doesn't he always come out with what he's doing? He's been acting strangely secretive for a long time. It can't all be 'just growing up', can it, tell me. We have to find out.

'I don't notice anything different Bill, so busy with the girls, he seems happy out the back with his animals. I know he loves being around that lake. He always seems to be doing good things. Maybe I'm missing something.'

'I didn't want to trouble you about this. It's long over now. He made a boat from a beer case. You need to hear what he gets up to, Hanna.'

He told her the whole story of their son's sailing adventure. How he was able to make this contraption that would never float on water, it had so many holes in it.

'His teacher was in for a few pints the other night. I asked him how he was doing at school. He said, first he refused to learn Christian Doctrine. And then he refused to learn anything.'

'He was traumatised when his money was stolen, Bill.'

'Yes we all know its Ned Goat, it will be sorted when it's right. There are a few of the boys lining up to settle that score. Hanna, I think it's time we all sat down for a chat. He didn't get that black eye from falling off a pony. We should know the real story, so we can do something about it. I'm going to talk with this teacher again. I don't like the man, but I need to know all about our son.

Teachers a good place to start.'

'Maybe Jonsie should be included in the meeting as well,' she suggested.

'I don't know about that; he might go into his shell. Let's think about it first. We must talk with him soon though. Hanna, I have a good story about him, told to me by a farmer at the fair. I almost forgot about it. So I'll tell you now.

'He praised Jonsie for helping his daughter in distress. She was laden down with bags of groceries in the town, waiting for a lift in a cart home. Smithy was shoeing her neighbour's horse. Two young brats on the street urinated in a tin to throw on her. When Jonsie saw that, he confronted them. And they weren't long skipping off I'll tell you.

'He walked her out the road until she felt safe. Then he told her anytime she was afraid in town, he'd be in his father's pub. He promised to help her, if they ever bothered her again. But he'd make sure they wouldn't and told her not to be afraid coming into the town. A nice gesture, the farmer said.

'He was very appreciative, Hanna. The boy's kindness well noted. I was meaning to tell you but I forgot. If it was bad, I'd remember it quicker I suppose.'

The sequel to that event played out over thirty years later. It was a very wet summer and impossible to get hay. I was looking for it everywhere, worried for the horses. Then one day, this couple arrived with a lorry load of loose hay. They said they had saved it from their field especially for me. They didn't want any money for it. She told me about that day when we were both young and I rescued her from thugs attacking her in the town. The woman was that girl grown up. She lived a few miles away from me now. Someone told her of my plight, and she was bound to repay that long ago act of human kindness. The moment was kindly and the wonder made us cry. A good turn comes back when you need it too.

'There's good in that young fellow,' Bill said, 'but he's prone to mistakes with this reckless streak. It often seems he knows no fear. If that's the case I hope the luck stays with him. We must keep an eye in case we lose him. He sails very close to the wind, as we already know. I was never that bad in my day. Are your crowd all the full shilling?'

Hanna made a playful slap at him, taking his hand across the table; she was very worried about their son. She'd make it sound better, for the sake of calm.

'He's like you Bill. This adventurous streak will fade away when he gets older. He'll find that girls will occupy his time. It's called growing up – didn't we all have to do it? How many times did we get it wrong, when we were learning? We didn't even know we were learning half the time. It just came over us, like a bad idea. How come there was no such thing as good ideas?'

She laughed at how silly it all sounded, this 'growing up'. Good ideas were hard to come by.

'He's in a different world Hanna, thinks he knows more than we do. That can't be right, can it? How does he spend time looking at animals, and the lake he tells Danny and Boxer all about? We were scared to go near there as kids. We got an awful fright. He's always down there. What's wrong with him? Would he be mad, do you think?'

'Oh come on now, we can't start thinking like that about our Jonsie, How could there be anything wrong with him? He was always different, Bill.'

'I get embarrassed in the bar when I'm asked about him. They're laughing, as if he's not right in the head. Boxer won't let anyone say a bad word about him and Danny's the same way. A special young lad he says. I wish I knew. I could sleep better. Unless I see something special from him soon, I'll be getting him off to boarding school, where they can keep tabs on him.

'I hope he hasn't taken after his Uncle Tom, he's away with the fairies, with that opera singing he talks about. He's one we have to sort out. WT said he's taking up valuable space. My father makes you a very bad case, if he takes a pick on you. How are the girls doing at school, are there any problems there?'

'No, they love school, Bill.'

'I haven't been much help to you with everything happening Hanna. It seems to be getting a lot busier these days.'

He folded his arms around her waist for a tender cuddle. Love kept them strong for each other; there was love in the kiss. It reassured them all was well. This parenting duty was a very demanding task. There was never enough time for anything else. And they started giggling like teenagers when they told each other secret things, how much they missed these impromptu romantic interludes. The problem with Miss Kelly listening to creaky beds was no more. They fixed the bed. All was well.

Friends make excuses for friends they love.

CHAPTER 5

Danny was chortling, reminding Miss Kelly of a funny story from long ago. Hanna was enjoying the morning tea break with them. She sat quietly, marvelling at the change in her. It was good to see this elderly lady laugh so heartily. The best influence on Mary's gradual rise from the depths was Danny. He brought her back to where she liked to be. Now she was ready to reminisce.

Hanna waited to hear about times gone by. She talked about a day she'd never forget. She was excited, opening her new shop. All the fashion-conscious ladies wanted to see her American dresses. They came in numbers on opening day, all suitably attired for the occasion. She was delighted to see them.

Then the bad smell turned up in their midst. Someone had told Ned Goat there were men's jeans on sale. He wanted to buy a pair. He would revel in the company of ladies. They took it good humouredly for a short time. What could they do, put up with the smell, or leave? And after a while most of them did.

The event turned out good for business though. Word spread about opening day and people wanted to see the place, so they could envisage it properly for themselves, as if they were there.

She had been open a few months when the scandal whispering began. There was something going on between her and WT Flanagan. She couldn't live it down. It was, she remembered, the beginning of her downfall, in the place she had loved growing up in.

WT gave everyone a far more exciting angle on the tale, and she was branded with exhibiting 'low morals' that she had acquired in America. That episode might have influenced her disastrous marriage attempt. Nobody wanted a second-hand woman, it seemed. 'She got what she deserved in the end' they said.

'It's the way of the world' Miss Kelly whispered, her lips slightly quivering, and she took time out for some composure. That's when Hanna excused herself quietly, to make a pot of tea.

Mary Kelly had an interest in Betty Flanagan's sudden demise, and she wondered over the years if her death had anything to do with her own dreadful experience. That horror could have taken place yesterday; it was still so fresh in her memory.

'I often wondered about Betty's death Danny?' she said calmly, looking at him.

The old lady sensed Danny had things bothering him too. Was there any way he could have prevented it happening? That thought had occurred to him over the years.

'Yes Mary, we detoured to the bridge. I remember her sadness in the days leading up to it. I drove her around and saw what was going on, but I kept it to myself. She was fond of a cup of that specially brewed tea Drover makes. I still can't imagine what she had in common with that fellow. It could be some spiritual connection she believed he had with the yew tree. He was telling her all sorts of stories, you can be sure. I sat waiting outside, in the trap. Not deemed good enough company, I suppose. That Drover's a sinister boy, let me tell you. He chooses his company with benefit in mind. Everyone must have a place in his purpose; otherwise they are of no interest. Betty had her last cup of tea that night with him, just before the tragic turn of events. You can imagine yourselves.

'She'd been to the Chapel earlier, saying a few prayers for forgiveness, she told me, as if she had done something improper. There was a bit of fun in her to be sure. She had a mind to explore matters for her own peace of mind; she often mentioned that. But I know she didn't jump into the river to drown herself, as the story was told. There was a full moon. She fell in, looking up at it. She kicked off her shoes and jumped up on the bridge for a dance. I heard her shout it just before she fell. 'I'll have to dance with 'my man in the moon'.

Miss Kelly interrupted him. 'Danny, you know WT attacked me against my will.'

'Yes Mary, I do.'

Danny replied without flinching, 'sure, haven't we discussed it several times over the years?'

Mary took solace from the response; there was something to talk about now. And it was so refreshing to have this young woman Hanna privy to some real events. She'd tell the true story forever after. Everyone would believe her. And she would be scandal free.

'I would like a little sherry to sip,' she said, looking over. 'Talking is not something I do very often. I have something on my mind that will not come easy, a small sherry might help me talk more about things.'

'Oh yes of course!' Hanna jumped up, her hands trembling. Rushing into the kitchen, with a red face, she wasn't gone long.

Mary just carried on. 'Betty liked two dresses in my shop, but she was too shy to try them on. She was reluctant to remove her clothes in case anyone came in. So I suggested I'd bring them over to her living room, when I closed up that evening. When I got there, the door was opened by a nervous teenage girl. She wasn't inclined to make eye contact; I noticed that because it's the first thing they tell you, in Manhattan; keeping eye contact makes customers feel confident in you.

'Mr WT Flanagan was sitting on a couch with a table in front of him and whiskey on it. He didn't have the respect to rise for a lady, as most men worth their salt would do; it should have been an early indicator for me that this particular individual was no gentleman. Yes indeed, no gentleman whatsoever.

'He patted the couch, smiling, to get me sit down. I enquired for the whereabouts of his wife, which he brushed aside flippantly. When he slapped the couch harder I felt obliged to take my seat. It was his house after all. I was a neighbour from over the street, visiting his wife.

'He began rubbing my hand, like it was cold, a big fire blazing away on the hearth. I though he was making a kindly gesture. Suddenly he lunged at me with his stinking whiskey mouth on mine. I felt sick. I was so petrified? I froze on the spot. His wife came running, hearing the commotion. She was screaming. 'WT, I can't stand you anymore!'

The desperation in her voice was pitiful. I felt so sorry for her, even in my dire circumstances. The whole room stood still;

I thought the quiet time would never end. Then she emptied her full wine glass over his head. They were shouting as I ran out the door crying. In such a hurry I forgot my dresses. First thing next morning he was over to pay, as if nothing had happened. He told me he was giving his wife both dresses, because she was so good to him. "She gets confused with too much wine," he explained. But he never apologised for assaulting me on his couch.

'Then I hired my cousin to help me out. She was the only person I had to confide in. And she told me everything that was said about me around the town. It really broke my heart hearing it. We know now the friend she turned out to be. When she took my future husband away from me that was the last straw. After a while I lost all interest.'

Her lips were quivering. Danny took her hand gently, leaning close as old friends do, and told her what she must know.

'You're hard on yourself, Mary. Betty told me the whole story. She knew it was none of your doing. WT was having a carry-on with the young one in the house; when she found them in bed together, that finished it. He paid her fare to England'.

'We can't talk about this. There are ears everywhere, those that tell him what's going on. We can't finish up in his bad books.

'Mary, nobody blamed you, that episode with WT was secret. Until she opened her big mouth and added to it. I straightened out a few of them, I can tell you. I should know you better than anyone else.'

He looked very caringly at her. Hanna saw something then. This concerned correctness. Could it ever blossom into something else? Maybe it did, and nobody noticed. Love, unlike hate, can alter course to conceal itself as part of nature's true intent.

The town was named after the Cody family. Each Major Cody had provided a personal touch, but the character remained colonial. These landed gentry were convinced that they owned everything they had pillaged. The Major was a dour individual of condescending nature. That was a common defect with them all. The fourth Major in line, since the Manor house was born.

This Saxon/Norman influence brought a mentality of suppression with them. A disregard for anything Irish was firmly planted in their attitude. The ordinary people below them were peasants. And that's where they'd stay. They'd make sure of it.

Brash family portraits adorned walls in great rooms, showing destructive plunderers, attired in military regalia, proclaiming lineage they barely owned, looking down on decent Irish people. Their ascendancy spread a trail of destruction around them. And they decorated themselves favourably for their accomplishments. Major title came from power within. A gross military inference to keep the Irish 'peasants' respectful towards them; it failed in this primary task, like everything else they tried to accomplish.

Jack the donkey would have the same entitlement to major if he was living in a big house with his peasants grovelling after him.

Drover's father told him every story he ever heard about them. The old yew tree had suffered from their indignation in the past, and it was banished from the land unceremoniously, to occupy a derelict place, long before the street arrived. Then it was the perfect location for a band of followers that preformed rituals around it.

The Major labelled the tree 'poisonous' as bad luck to cover his own folly. The curse came with it. 'Drover had tree knowledge, passed down from his father. On a full moon, he held a ritual for special people. Madness struck that way. But you'd never know them. Mad Phil urinated against the yew tree once, look how he finished up. There's more than him around, when you get to know the full story about all of them. Drover knew that.

Major Cody was the worst of them. They whispered, and everyone agreed with that. Burn the bad witch out of him, there'd be no more rent to pay. It would take one of 'his own' to do that job.

Jonsie was fully occupied with everything going on.

The milkman wasn't making his rounds in the pony and trap anymore. No longer would his hand bell ring up the street. They would all have to find another source for milk, or do without the cup of tea. That would be a fate worse than death itself.

Bill bought a cow at the fair, and Jonsie was given instruction on how to milk her. Every morning he got up at seven to ride his bike a few miles. He carried milk home on the handlebar, with a lid on the bucket, so it wouldn't spill. Then after breakfast he cycled out past the cow field again, on his way to school. There was no time wasting on this tight schedule.

Only once did he fail to deliver the milk. It would never happen again. He tried blaming mad Phil for that, but it was his own timing that let him down on the day. They all said he was lucky he wasn't killed.

That day he came upon a donkey cart in the middle of the road. Mad Phil sat in the back, with his peaked cap turned up, and a clay pipe gripped in his gums, puffing away, oblivious. Just as he was passing the cart, Jonsie cut in front, to frighten him. That was all he remembered, landing with his bike on top of him in the ditch.

He didn't realise the donkey was having a little trot. The cart kept on going; it never took a puff out of him. He was Mad Phil. But it finished the milk delivery that morning. Bill was furious about not having any milk for his tea.

Mad Phil called into the pub later the same day to talk about his son. He said the boy was 'flying on the road like a madman'. And that statement, from a real madman, annoyed Bill more than anything else.

Bill heard the story about 'this Rasp bastard', as he referred to the schoolmaster now. And he couldn't believe what he was doing to his boy. The thoughts of his son tied to the desk like a condemned criminal, ridiculed by classmates, got through to him. He could imagine how frightened he must be when he tried removing his trousers in front of his daughters.

Bill promised revenge and made plans. He called for the assistance of his two cronies. The brothers were always available for the craic. Rasp didn't know them personally.

They were Protestants and that was better. It might seem like an outside job. The 'Prods' were at it again.

The teacher thought the message he had received was about her son. Hanna's name was on the note. Rasp had spruced himself up; she was a fine-looking woman. And he would like to impress.

She of course, knew absolutely nothing about the arranged meeting or any reception meticulously planned. Hanna was away visiting her mother when it all took place, thankfully.

Rasp stepped into the bar dressed to kill, a flowery cravat around his neck. It gave him a feeling of importance. People in the town were saying only bolloxes wore cravats. Bill stood ready behind the counter, listening to him. He heard the teacher say it was a long time since he'd had a good pint. Then he put a pint of porter in front of him, almost flat. It was loaded discreetly with a super charge. They had agreed at the planning stage, it would take industrial liquid paraffin laxative, for the perfect job.

The toilet door was far away. The two boys were close by looking after it. All three shared a knowing wink when this back door was locked. The stage was set for action. Rasp was giving a few political views that nobody wanted to hear. Blast off was on everyone's mind, how soon it would happen. And the boys were laughing.

Bill asked him a lethally loaded question. 'Are you still driving the priest around on those big gambling excursions, Master?'

The teacher chooses not to answer. Holding himself stiff to resist the question made him fart. That sounded off a gushy flow, and he ran for the toilet with a petrified look on his face. Total deposit delivered on time, already. They escorted him out the back like two concerned gentlemen. He was humiliated responding to their instruction.

'Step out of the trousers master; we'll have this little accident sorted for you, in no time. Don't be embarrassed; we'll tell nobody, you must have eaten something that didn't agree with you, sardines maybe. They're very oily, you know, master. Take your underpants off master, destroyed as well master,' one of the assistants suggested respectfully.

Bill handed over a bucket of cold water to his eager helpers. When teacher removed his underpants he was drenched with two full buckets; one for the privates, in the frontal area, and the other for a tougher job, the back exit department, got a bucket as well. One of them pulled off his cravat to wipe his ass with. And then they stuck it into his top pocket for effect. Memories were made of this.

Bill shouted into the yard at him, 'Now you know what's it's like to have your trousers removed, you degenerate. You were abusing my son for a long time before we took him out of your school. You tied a little boy to his desk to demoralize him in front of his classmates. Your job as a teacher of children is to give them confidence. You tried breaking my boy's will. In that you failed, he's made of tougher stuff than you. Don't come into this pub anymore. I'll throw you out the door.'

The teacher got the wet trousers back on him. He made some feeble attempt to go inside the bar. Bill blocked his way.

'Did you not hear what I said, don't come in here again? I'll let you out the back gate; make your way home along the lane. So no one will see you. The fresh air will dry you out.'

WT's never-ending scheming would become more focused from now on. There were ambitions to take up his time. He'd have to find some interesting alternative; a hotel was next, to suit a man of his standing. Brooding how to get the politician to help out more, that question occupied his thoughts all the time now.

He regretted putting the pub in Bill's name, but he'd threatened to go to England if he didn't. So he had some work to do with his next plan. The whole site would be required.

The lack of any hotel facility in Cody's Cross must be dealt with as an urgent requirement. It was 'grant' time again, there were loopholes to find. The town committee meetings would be taken up with it from now on. WT would make sure of that.

It was important for them to remember what they were supporting, and why. They all stood to benefit one way or the other. But it must be delivered subtly.

Flash the politician swore he was working on it. WT told him if he got planning, he'd get elected again. The big river was promoted as a tourist destination all over America. Times were moving on and WT was moving with them. He knew the money was coming. He advised Flash not to get left behind.

He hired a bicycle mechanic to carry out repairs in the little shop next to the pub. This man Dennis had worked for the previous owner, and people trusted him. He was a grumpy, silent man who wasn't fond of washing himself. He came out of retirement at Bill's request.

Dennis didn't mind. Backing horses and drinking pints next door wouldn't change.

Bill assured him he could still wander in any time he liked. He even volunteered to open an account for him in the bar book, so he could have the price of his drinks deducted from his weekly salary. He wouldn't need to carry cash on him anymore. It all sounded good to Dennis, in the caring way it was put to him.

He was a great bicycle mechanic and understood everything, but never needed to keep an account of money. It just wasn't his way.

Bill asked Boxer to instruct his son in self-defence. Hanna was not as enthusiastic about this, so he explained why their son must be able to take care of himself. 'No good being strong', he told her, 'unless you can defend yourself. We know all about the bullying he's been subjected to now. We cannot let this kind of thing happen again. It would destroy the young lad's self-belief. Boxer is a well-travelled man, with experience in life. Jonsie will benefit from his good advice. It might stand to him later. I'm making sure he's able to defend himself, next time someone hits him. Mark my words, Hanna; it will make a man of him.'

The gym Boxer set up in the store was very basic. The punch bag was a sack of wet sawdust, weights were empty beer barrels. Boxer was making a fighter out of him. He assured Bill it would be difficult to blacken his eye now. The young lad told him he liked his new school. But there was an attempt made at bullying him, in the beginning. When he was nicknamed 'townie', country boys knew they were soft. The fight was looming.

He got a punch in the face for nothing, one day. This big red-haired thug wanted to fight. He was noted for throwing a false one. It didn't last long, as like all cowards he recoiled after getting a few punches. He turned his back to Jonsie with his head down, and then got a good kick up the behind. There was a loud cheer when that happened, a big put down. To a place he wouldn't be rising up from, ever again.

He'd guaranteed safe passage through school; the boys looked up to him. They'd always been afraid of ginger, now they had someone to stand against him. The girls took a shine to him as well. Townie could be a country boy when he had to. He was quiet, they liked that about him. Everyone played happily together after that, with more laughter ringing in the schoolyard, than ever before.

His father bought an old bike for him, with a job in mind.

Jonsie was paying him back for it, milking the cow every morning. Because he had a faster way of getting around, he found more things to do. Dennis encouraged him to learn the bike fixing trade. 'Watch what I do, and then you can do it.'

He'd been looking at him putting bicycles together for a while. The man was delighted and wanted to encourage it. So he told him he should build his own bike.

He gave the young fellow an old frame to start him off. It was called a High Nellie; noted for its wide U in the centre, so ladies with long skirts could mount easily, big wide handlebars for a reliable feel, to balance properly.

'It was well made to suit itself', he said, like he knew something about it.

This bicycle frame had nothing on it, and looked like its days were numbered. Dennis recited poetry Jonsie didn't understand, but it sounded nice the way he said it. 'Beauty is in the eye of the beholder, necessity is the father of invention'. He advised him to build a strong bike, to pull a little cart for carrying his stuff around. He would have to wait for discarded parts, but there would be some with a few years left in them yet.

The boy took the frame away with him, over his shoulder.

One morning he discovered four new born rabbits in the shed. Sadly they were all dead. He buried them near his dog.

The old one whispered 'murderer' when he cried for his rabbits. He began to think differently after that. Should rabbits be held prisoner, when they loved being free? Like him?

He released the old pair in the wood where he had caught them. No captivity anymore. The goats would be next. Dennis said

Ned ate them. Thoughts of that happening to his pets made him sick. He hated the goat man more than ever now. They were all saying he had stolen his savings from the box on the floor. When Ennis heard about the theft it made him angry. He promised to keep the coloured filly safe until he was ready. 'Keep saving your money,' he said, something will turn up.

Jonsie felt there was something about the coloured pony. He liked her from the word go. He had experience galloping them. This one was special. She was careful and tough, and didn't want to stop running. That was the best sign, a clever girl our Ruby.

The long stretch up the castle hill, down the other side, she took without giving off the wheezing sound of bad wind. When they reached the dealer's place, she ran into the yard at full pelt. She still had it in her. But he was taken clean of her bare back by a clothes line. When she felt his weight gone, she stopped to look back at him on the ground. She knew when to wait. He wouldn't tell anybody about this, especially Ennis. He mightn't be able to resist, dealers were dealers, and good horses were rare. It was the quality inside that counted for most; the one hard to see. It's always there in people that change for good.

But his focus now was on building the bike.

The big frame had no handlebars, wheels, or saddle. There was nothing in the centre for holding pedals. It had a long way to go. Dennis would look after him, Boxer's drinking pal and they were always on his side. He'd soon give him two wheels to fit a High Nellie.

Jonsie took into the wheels using sandpaper to remove the rust, and then he patiently painted them with aluminium paint. They looked like the real thing, from a distance. The bike's 'image' was greatly improved, and it was easier to stay interested in it now.

The thing looked like it was taking shape.

He took an interest in Gaelic football, but his endeavours ended abruptly at a trial match for the town schoolboy team. Rasp was the main man in charge, a self-appointed team coach selector who had never played the game. He reprimanded Jonsie viciously after this trial game. The boy would suffer more humiliation in front of his team mates. He shouted it out loud with personal memories to spur him on. 'You're never going to make a footballer Flanagan, give it up'.

The young lad walked off the pitch with his head down. One day, he swore he'd settle with him for sure.

When he went training with the country lads, it was a different world. Everyone worked together. The sessions were monitored by retired players who knew what they were talking about. Under their tuition he became a fixture on the school team at full back, with special instructions, to mind the goalkeeper. He felt a pride in this team; he never had that with the town outfit.

Hanna heard what had happened to the teacher in her absence. They had got their message across to the poor man. According to reports, it was one he would never forget. But there was nobody up for telling her about it. She couldn't embarrass Danny by asking him.

Her son's abuse in school was very worrying. What Bill described as an act of cruelty couldn't be tolerated. She favoured the country school, the same one she had attended. At least he would be safe there. Her two girls were no trouble. They were quiet kids with all the requirements and interests of girls their age, children she could be proud off. But she was very proud of her son too. And she well understood his sensitive nature, how his vigour for life, this 'free abandonment' landed him in so much trouble.

Bill was sullen. Any issue with his son was enough to set him off. She was trying to keep the young lad's exploits away from him. Sometimes it took a bit of doing. There was never a dull moment.

Hanna was delighted when the friendship in the parlour became routine. Danny didn't put her out; he washed and tidied after their chats. So she wanted to compliment him. It backfired badly. 'You're just like another woman in the house,' she said.

He wasn't pleased hearing that. He scowled, put his head down, turning away from her. The first time she had witnessed a change in the man. It was very odd. She wouldn't be saying anything like that to him ever again. And it made her wonder.

He worked part-time in the bar, arriving early, for his chat with Mary. She looked forward to it. They were like two old school pals, sharing happy, sometimes sad memories from their youth. They were that comfortable in each other's company. What was wrong with him?

Hanna fantasised about how wonderful it would be if they were allowed to fall in love when they were young. Not hounded apart, when her tyrannical father couldn't tolerate him for his daughter.

His pedigree was so questionable. Danny had been brought up by a caring single mother, when this predicament was still harshly judged upon. She refused to take the boat to England for an abortion and the whole trip paid for her. She had her child at home. When interested parties used their influence, the child was taken into an orphanage. She fought a long battle, to have him returned.

The midwife at baby Danny's delivery was paid by Bill's grandfather. Not a charitable man by all accounts.

'Remember this,' Danny whispered. 'WT didn't get his passion for ladies off a whitethorn bush. His father was mad after the women as well.'

Danny's slow drawl pulled her back into the story again. His mother worked as a maid for WT's father as a teenager, there was intimacy between them that resulted in pregnancy.

She told her son all about it when he was fifteen. Danny was WT Flanagan's half-brother.

'Let sleeping dogs lie, it's better that way,' he said with a consoling look on his face.

Miss Kelly remembered her mother talking about Danny to her father. That curt exchange between them had made a lasting impression on her at the time.

'Indeed he's anything but a home boy; he's your friend Flanagan the hardware's son and that poor abandoned girl.'

Danny interrupted her. 'My father didn't want anything to do with me. He claimed my mother was a tinker, so he got me into an orphanage. She never gave up trying to get me out. It took five years. He provided me with work to keep the scandal quiet. Some people knew, but none were inclined to talk.

'The fact is, WT has no knowledge of my connection to him. Who'd have the nerve to tell him about that, I wonder?' Danny gave a muffled embarrassed cough, and continued talking, as if the story wasn't about him anymore.

'The priest acting under old boss Flanagan's influence had

the child sent to an orphanage. In part to discourage more fallen women, as the religious called them, from having children outside wedlock. The child was badly treated, like all those that finished up in this so-called reformatory school.

'Reform them for what?'

The religious orders sometimes attract a type of predatory creature, depraved connivers, carrying out harmful things on innocent souls. While they preached about saving them, it's a kind of tricky-the-loop hypocrisy, religion holds over them. The boy was dressed in girl's clothes that demoralised him.

Jonsie never missed a day, seeing if there was anything for his bike. Dennis was true to his word. He'd put some necessary part aside for the boy. He was impressed with this determination to see it through. But there was a long wait for handlebars.

Dennis explained that they were a special kind. Not many people with 'high nellies' had reason to replace sturdy handlebars, so, for the young boy who'd waited long enough, it was time to change the original design somewhat. It happened by chance. When he noticed a shiny pair of new looking handlebars dumped in a corner. He picked them up excitedly. But the bicycle mechanic ruled the idea out of order immediately, looking at him, bemused. 'Those handlebars are off a racing bike son, no good.'

Jonsie persisted. Dennis relented and fixed them on the bike to let him see how bad it looked. The boy asked him to turn them the other way up. They looked more like you were driving a horse this way.

'Now you're in the circus,' the mechanic announced, before

going back to what he was doing, laughing. And he shook his head from side to side.

When Bill heard about the High Nellie with the racing handlebars the wrong way up he had to see it. He found it so funny; he took Hanna out the back for a laugh as well. It was a real original.

WT dropped in for a whiskey, and he was entertained by the sight of this old model too. Boxer heard the story from Dennis. It was soon talk of the town. Everyone was sniggering, calling into the pub for a look. They called it 'Methuselah', after Noah's grandfather.

Bill said it was so good for business it should be hung on the wall like a picture of the Pope. 'They might even pay to see it.'

He knew for sure now the young fellow was mad in the head. How could anyone normal think like that? But the strange thing was that no one mentioned the bicycle to the boy, not wanting to cast a slight on this young lad's dream, even if it was a mad one; 'mad people are very special,' some of them said. Didn't the old yew tree know all about them?

Then, a few months later, a sequel to this bike episode unfolded. It was neither planned nor promised, it just happened by chance.

And it must be absolutely correct; to show that sometimes good things come to life by accident. It sounds like a perfect song title for disbelievers. And the sequel's okay too. 'Designers don't do things well enough.'

This day in question started off a like a Western film. The sun was beaming down on a quiet lazy street and everyone was in the shade when mad Phil arrived in town. He drove the old rattling cart down the empty street, past the pub, to unhitch at Drovers field. The way it always was. Shelagh could tumble on the grass, after her journey. Then she could eat her fill. He patted her quietly on the neck before leaving. When he collected the groceries he headed over for a few pints.

Sitting up at the bar, he was telling Bill he was buying a bicycle in the shop next door. 'Drover put the idea in my head'. He complained about it, telling the barman some of his woes.

'I was giving Dennis five pounds, he'd take nothing less than a tenner,' he shouted. 'So I told him where to stick it.'

Phil was cutting tobacco in his hand to fill a white clay pipe. Jonsie sat quietly, taking it all in.

Phil tapped the pipe in the palm of his hand, and it broke in two. He made a go for the hardware store immediately to buy another one, but Bill reacted very quickly. He knew if Phil left the pub, the idea of buying a bike might leave him too. He took a roll of clear sticky tape from under the counter, and proceeded to wrap a generous amount around the broken shank of the pipe, to hold it together. There was a few quid to be made from this mad man, he thought. Keeping him focused was the challenge. So he didn't want him leaving.

He handed the pipe back to him 'as good as new', he said.

When Phil lit the pipe everything was back on track. But he had a few things to get off his chest first, with porter spurring him on. He related more of his heavy tales to the uninterested barman.

'Shelagh doesn't like the journey anymore, she's tired travelling.' He shook his head sadly, thinking about it made him quiet for a while.

Bill wasn't familiar with Phil's marital status, so he chose the caring words of a cunning barman with a hidden agenda. 'Aha, that's a pity Phil. There's a woman's shop up the street. Why don't you buy her a new coat? She'd come in here more often then, I'd say.'

He didn't like the way mad Phil, a single man, looked at him. 'She wouldn't come near this pub!' he roared.

'She mustn't be a drinker so,' Bill said, looking at the mad man. You could get fearful of the bastard. He wiped the counter furiously in front of him.

'How could my old girl do without a tumble in Drovers field?' Phil said, with hostility towards the bar owner.

'Ohooo right, I see.' Bill said cursing himself for asking. This could be a hard-earned tenner. But then to his absolute horror he saw the pipe slowly descending down the old boy's coat. And it was tipping its head sideways, as if saying goodbye. The tape was softening and the head was dropping in slow motion. Phil hadn't seen the sparks falling on his coat, yet. Bill could see the whole lot going up in flames. He grabbed a shilling from the till, shouting, 'Keep an eye Jonsie I'm getting him a pipe.'

He took off, running like hell across the street.

It happened nice and easy just then, matter of fact in its way. Jonsie told Phil he'd sell him a bike for a fiver. Enough said.

When Mad Phil saw the High Nellie, he liked the look of it. The young lad pointed out obvious benefits to him. 'Mr Phil,' he said innocently, hoping he wouldn't remember being sideswiped on the road. 'This bicycle is good for you, like driving a donkey and cart. See, handlebars close together, same as holding the reins.

It can pull a small cart for groceries, look at my one there.'

Phil took a big step backwards to look at everything right, with his excitement rising. He could see the High Nellie was mad too. 'Be Christ, a fiver you say, I have enough of it now.'

He slapped his hand hard against his thigh and shouted, 'Deal!' It was all over the minute he handed him the fiver.

Then Jonsie had a problem; the fastest way to get rid of him. He opened the back gate to let him out, shaking with excitement. 'Go right Mr Phil; it goes up to the green for your cart.' Then he locked the gate hurriedly in case he changed his mind. His heart pounded for the fiver in his pocket, the most money he'd ever had.

When he went back inside, his father was cursing Phil for wasting his day. He wondered how he had got caught up with him, knowing the way he was. He blamed his son for it all.

'Did I tell you, keep an eye on him? Where is he now?'

'He ran out the door laughing, like he always does,' Jonsie told him.

Bill went for a look; he wasn't to be seen; maybe in dealing for the bike again. No, he wasn't there either. Dennis never saw him.

Jonsie knew things were going very wrong when Phil came cycling up the street puffing his pipe, without a care in the world, his hands close together, like he was praying. It didn't feel like a blessing anymore though. He'd taken the left turn to the forge. If he went right, the bike would be on the cart and he'd be on his way home by now. That's how it was supposed to be.

Bill glared at his son, the clay pipe still clutched in his hand; he'd paid for it with his own money. And he didn't even smoke.

'Come 'ere Phil,' he shouted. The old boy stepped gingerly off the High Nellie, like he was born on it. Bill would have been better pleased if he had fallen off it.

'I bought this pipe for you Phil. It cost me a shilling.' He was hoping to get his money back.

'There yar Mr Flanagan sir, thank ya very much.' He put the clay pipe in an outside pocket, carefully. 'I always likes a lucky penny with me deal, ya know.'

He laughed getting back up on the bike again, leaving them standing there. Bill nodded to his son. The fun had just left the scene. And it wasn't on a bike. 'Come inside, it's time me and you had a little chat about things. There are rules in business dealings, not like the horses. And we all have manners with them. I want to tell you how it works around here. If you're joining the sales department, there are things you must know. Commission on sales are first up for discussion.'

Jonsie had the sinking feeling again that comes with a loss.

Someone told WT about the craic in the pub across the street, and he went for a whiskey. This comedy between his son and grandson was worth hearing. When he sat down in the bar to enjoy the fun, he listened quietly. Bill was telling how it was, laying down the law, if you like.

'Now Jonsie, tell me how much you got for that heap of shit the madman rode off on. He'll probably get killed of it before he gets home. I know you won't tell me a lie, when you're caught. You're an honest young fellow behind it all.' He praised him first.

Jonsie handed over the five-pound note, very reluctantly.

'A fiver, now let's see how much money you're entitled to out of this deal. There are expenses to cover here. It's not all a free load.'

Bill was revelling in this talk. He could see his father waiting for something to happen. This bike deal was bound to impress him.

'All parts came from next door. Dennis did most of the work. You sanded and painted it Jonsie, isn't that right?' He was loud.

'Yes, but the parts were second hand, Dennis gave me them for free.'

He tried making little of it. But Bill was seeing it differently.

'Phil didn't look at the parts, did he, you cheeky little brat? You took my customer for your own financial gain, same as the boss does here.' He nodded the insult in WT's direction. 'I don't get much financial gain from him either, and I earn it all the hard way. It's going on long enough. Now you're at it as well. Jonsie, you did an underhand deal. That's not fair trading. It's not the same as horse dealing, there is honesty in business. You must understand that, if you're doing it right, to start off with. I'll let the boss explain how it works.'

WT hadn't planned on saying anything. His father had a saying to suit this predicament. 'When you're going to say something, say nothing' was his favourite.

'Oh what I have to say is simple, buy it, sell it, that's it all done and dusted, there is no need for complications. Or making them either. The best result is when the moneys in your pocket. Young Jonsie here won, that shouldn't make him a loser. Leave him the fiver, the best of good luck to him. Let him make it into a tenner. That's all I have to say,' he said.

Bill was annoyed that he never mentioned loyalty; he didn't have any either, so how could he say it? He only saw the fiver.

'Jonsie, what were you going to do with all the money?' he asked.

The boy told them about the dealer's coloured pony, for ten pounds. Bill declared he'd keep the fiver safe 'until we see who gets what', sticking it in his pocket. Jonsie ran out the door to head for the lake. There was no money left for his pony. Why did everything always go wrong on him?

WT had a few words for Bill. 'I'll give you the tenner to buy the pony from Ennis. He might take eight, when it's for the boy. He'd charge more if I was buying. Ask him for a good luck penny for your trouble. Everyone gets money out of it that way, right?'

Bill never answered. His old man was still talking. 'I want to keep my eye on things, see what plans he has for this pony. Don't be too hard on him, you'll ruin him. That would be a pity. We must encourage him, Bill. You were like him, and you've done all right for yourself, and I think there's more in you yet.'

Then he walked out the door whistling.

WT had being thinking about Mrs Wilson's property for a very long time. He would have to be careful though; a wily old girl was she, clever enough to suspect another motive. Her husband, Dr Wilson, had been a general practitioner for over forty years. They weren't blessed with the gift of children. There might be a void in her life. And she could take a liking to Jonsie with the pony.

Now that would be just perfect. He'd pop over for a chat, a private glance at her sites. She was always a very welcoming lady.

He took the brass knocker in his hand, and gave the door a bang. Mrs Wilson opened it rather quickly. She sensed trouble.

'Do you think I'm deaf, Flanagan? You had better come in,

what's the matter with you, there's no doctor here anymore, 'are you having a heart attack? I fear you're outside my line of medical expertise. Come into the kitchen, I'm baking. You're not going to ruin my bread, talking nonsense at the door.'

'Thank you Susan. Oh my, I haven't been in this house for so long, the memories, Christmas parties you invited me and poor Betty, God rest her soul, back in the days when we were all so young, and full of devilment.'

'Ah it's not that long ago WT, age is in the mind, as my dear mother used to say. Would you like a cup of tea with a hot buttered scone and blackberry jam, or a nice drop of whiskey?

'Susan, I'll have the lot, glass of whiskey up first, please.

I want to discuss something with you, a very good pony, that might take up a little of your time, and a lot of your interest'

WT didn't miss her faint smile at the mention of horses. It never left them. So he told her all about this pony the boy had, a born horseman in his opinion. He related the bike story with mad Phil, and the competition for business with Bill. It was a perfect warm-up topic for him to talk about. Susan had to sit down at the table laughing.

'The thing is, Susan, we don't have a convenient field for the pony. He must become a good horseman. If only you had the inclination to help out, you might enjoy this new interest. And we all know you're the best horsewoman ever was, in these parts. Sure everyone in the country knows that. Danny would be on standby to help anytime, if needed. We can agree the rent is paid in cash. Let's help him get into the horses, see if it's in him.'

There were a few issues for her to consider. She talked seriously.

'Young people must be encouraged when they are interested in horses. I could try it for a while to see how it goes.'

They discussed a deal that wouldn't be permanent. If it worked out well, it could continue. They agreed in time honoured fashion, a strong handshake. With the eyeball to eyeball look. Susan knew she couldn't trust him as far as she'd throw him. Both of them knew who they were dealing with.

He asked permission, walking the field, checking the boundary fence and examining drinking water. In case Danny was required to do some work, he explained. Making sure everything was safe for a pony. Susan watched out the window after him, wondering.

But when WT got into the field, his mind was miles away from horses. The bigger picture included new houses for sale. He hadn't decided on how many he'd build yet. This was the best location to live in the county, another of his secret projects.

He stared towards the far corner of the field, at the big chestnut tree perched over the river. Betty had danced the last waltz over there. He wondered if she did it on purpose. Wine made her head giddy. She'd find a reason from all the troubles they had.

He headed towards the tree, memories filling his head. Everything didn't seem that much older, his gaze lingering.

The wooden seat under the tree was long gone. They'd made plans sitting there, promise of a dream home, built beside the river she loved. He'd carved their names on the tree. And they were still there, in a heart, with an arrow piercing the centre. It brought him back to better times. He sobbed when those carefree times overcame him. And when he leaned forward, with his hands on the tree, he called out her name. 'Betty, I miss you so.'

Somebody else heard that. And it pleased her so much.

She was standing behind him, listening to everything he said about her sister in law. Susan knew the real story, how their love life had played out. They were quarrelsome, trading insults in anger. Make up, love you, hate you, did it for them. It would have been interesting to see them grow old together, when they were worn out squabbling and they could appreciate each other more. They were nearly the same.

She spoke out loud, as if she'd just arrived on the scene. 'The chestnut's waiting for flowers,' she said, waiting, nothing, only more waiting.

It wouldn't be fitting for this proud man, caught in a tender moment. His ruthless cavalier style suited him better. She turned for home. Best let him find peace with himself. He might need it.

WT was in charge again. He was thinking how this game would play out. Susan was going to get a well behaved twelve-year-old to mother. When he required a few stables, she might agree to sell it. This must be all about the boy's pony. In the meantime there were his contacts to manipulate, now that he had something to talk about. There were obstacles, he could see them.

Flash the politician obtained information to fool voters into thinking it was all his hard work. His man in the council gave him details of jobs planned for the coming year, a breakdown of their relevance to his constituents. He'd call around to their houses when he knew they had visitors to let them know he was working on these problems for them. A double whammy he called it, the visitors brought news of his good work with them.

'It's on the way,' he'd say, winking at them, he couldn't describe it, because he never saw it. And he didn't care that much, either.

He never listened intently about it when they were telling him, but it was there like a blur on his mind.

When the job was finally delivered, Flash turned up on the doorstep for the praise. That's what got him elected. A careful man, he wouldn't have made it so far if he wasn't sneaky as well.

WT knew how to handle him. He'd been working him over for years. There were skeletons in everyone's cupboard. A lot of things can get caught in a tangle, with sins of the flesh. Flash, just like the rest of them, wandered.

Jonsie was breathless, looking at his pony in the stable, her mane and tail plaited like he'd never seen before. He knew the doctor's wife did it all on her own, when he held out his hand in grateful thanks. She took hold of it with the same enthusiasm. There was a bond instantly made then. The old boy was looking at this display of respect for Mrs Wilson.

'Hey,' he called out, 'I bought the pony for you, Jonsie.'

But that didn't matter now. Good things happen for a reason.

When Mrs Wilson tacked up, he was mounted on a saddle for the first time. He would learn how to ride a horse properly, under her tuition. Her old riding boots would fit him and there were riding breeches lying around too. His mother could make them bigger for him. Jonsie didn't care who owned them.

Danny found out that Ned Goat had robbed the young lad's savings box for sure. It took a bit of time to get Mr Whyte in the paper shop to talk about it. He was a very timid man who was reluctant to get involved in other people's business. Controversy was not on his list at all. But because he respected Danny, he admitted changing all the threepence pieces for the goat man. He was saving up his goat money, that's what he told Mr Whyte in the shop, pocketing over three pounds he exchanged for the coins.

'I 'apologize for doing the wrong thing Danny, I didn't know,' Mr Whyte said.

The wagon master reassured the kind newsagent that it was none of his doing, how could he possibly know what was going on with them? Everyone knew he never left the house, minding his wife.

When Danny told Bill that story, the publican was very angry. 'It's a long road that hasn't a turn Danny; someday our paths will cross again. I will never forget what that rotten bastard did to my son.' Everything changed when Bill took things personally. 'I'll get him good, when I get the chance.'

The fight was in him with the temper up. And there was no doubt that he meant every word of it.

CHAPTER 6

Jonsie was boxing, horse riding, and hadn't time for small animals anymore. Everything was big now. He was still milking the cow every morning before school and playing Gaelic football with the team. Boxer told him he was ready to fight in the ring, but there was no boxing club anywhere near Cody's Cross. And he wasn't bothered about boxing anyway. It wasn't one of his interests, like horses.

The more time he spent with Mrs Wilson, the more settled he became. He was right about the horse's receptive brain. Susan agreed with him. He called his pony Ruby. Susan was riding for exercise, teaching the pony to accept direction from her legs. Then it was an easier task instructing her pupil, when the pony knew how it was done. They could learn with each other.

His visits to the lake were not as frequent. But when he had something bothering him, he headed straight for the tree. It was great having this place to go when it was time to be alone.

Mrs Wilson listened to his stories with interest. She was learning more about him. She said this lake retreat was like doing yoga. He liked that word, but didn't know what it meant. That's how she started improving his concentration, listening to her talk about yoga. She was somewhat bemused when he said that he knew about it already, but didn't know the name for it.

She never put pressure on him. Just advised that he enjoyed his time with the horse, to learn their way, and she advised that he should get the 'deep feeling' for them first. Understand about their natural instincts. Be aware of their needs. And treat them with respect.

She explained about their herd instinct very carefully, so it was all correct from the beginning. He'd communicate with the horse on a natural level. That would benefit both of them.

When she invited him to accompany her to the Christmas party, Jonsie was delighted. Catholics weren't regular visitors to the Protestant Hall, as some unwritten code of behaviour from years gone by still prevailed. He knew he would have to get dressed up. That wasn't something he did very often. His mother was in charge of getting him ready. At the end of a tough battle she'd just finished washing his hair; the hardest part of this endurance test was over for her.

She gave him instructions to wear his white shirt, but short trousers were a problem for him now. He'd started wearing long trousers with the horse riding, so he should be wearing long trousers all the time, he complained.

Hanna wouldn't hear of it. It wasn't going to become a topic of conversation, either. 'This is a Christmas party, not a graduation ball.' That was that. She'd hand-knitted a navy jumper and he liked wearing it. There were some reservations about the red tie. When she explained that Santa Claus would be in red too, that nearly finished it off altogether. He wasn't aware it was a 'little children's party'. He thought it was for big people. He felt more grown up now, a 'real' horseman. Children were a hassle for him. There was no way he'd keep up that pretence about Santa Claus anymore, down chimneys and all that nonsense talk. He'd found out all about it. That created another problem. He didn't want to hide anything from Mrs Wilson. That was very important.

He asked her if it was okay going to the party when he didn't believe in Santa Claus anymore. When she laughed heartily, he thought she'd enjoy hearing the real story. He told her about surprising his mother, doing her Santa toy delivery, something she loved doing. She was only a big child herself. Sneaking into his room thinking he believed. He was only pretending for the presents.

That Christmas time his mind was made up; it would be the end of the acting. He couldn't be bothered playing the game anymore. Christmas Eve, he'd stayed awake all night waiting to catch her. When she opened the door for a peep, he'd snored loudly, to let her hear he was asleep. Then he spoke out sombrely in the dark, as she quietly left the presents on the end of his bed. 'Just who do you think you're fooling, Hanna Flanagan, pretending you're me?' He said it in an old voice, like Santa.

Hanna took into a fit of laughing, for being caught. Of course she knew he was a Santa Claus denier. But she wanted to keep it going for longer, if only to enjoy the dressing up part, for her. He was a sneaky little brat, for catching her.

Now Jonsie must help to keep the girls believing in Santa Claus. They were too young to have Christmas spoiled on them. She complained about the nuisance of boys, always doing the wrong thing, when girls were so easy about everything. They'd go along with anything, and try to do what they were told, for peace. 'That's the bad luck we women were born with, right there. We're still putting up with men's bad antics, just for the sake of peace.' She often scolded him to get even for that surprise on her.

Jonsie knew a few people at the party, from the town, but there was no one he'd know well enough to talk with. Rev Steele with his high pitched voice, he saw him on the street. He was 'proper religion' kind to everyone, no matter what faith they worshipped. He liked him a lot, but he didn't know him either. These Protestants kept themselves separate, even in close confines.

A few others he recognised but couldn't name. They were frosty towards him. He saw how religious prejudice played out first hand. He felt a strong resentment to his presence in the hall. Darkness came down on him. How could it be so?

When Santa Claus arrived, the children went wild. The old man in red sat down on a chair, with this big bag of presents lying open beside him. They lined up in orderly fashion for a gift. Jonsie's heart fell when he realised what was expected of him. This was something he didn't want to do. He was one of the tallest at the party and this Catholic stuff made him feel self-conscious. And he didn't believe in it, so he couldn't pretend.

He moved closer to Susan, who was in conversation with a woman talking loudly. Mrs Wilson appeared shocked. This woman of about her own age was scolding her in no uncertain terms. She wasn't concerned about who heard her. In fact she seemed pleased they did. 'He's a Catholic boy Susan, he shouldn't even be here. The money for these presents was collected from Protestant people, with children at the school. This young boy from the pub is one of the gang that attacks our kids. Hurls abuse with foul language in their direction. He's the last person the kids want to see at their Christmas party. Someone is bringing up a pupil he attacked, to identify him. Then he must be removed from the hall immediately. We don't trouble Catholics with our presence. We wouldn't have the audacity to show up at one of their private functions. This occasion will not take precedence, for unmannerly intrusion, Susan. I can promise you that.'

She'd got more animated as she went on. It left Mrs Wilson speechless. Her hands were shaking. Jonsie felt panicked and wanted to run out the door, but he couldn't. That would be abandoning her. So they sat there, staring ahead, without saying a word.

'We're like condemned thieves, waiting to hear our fate,' Mrs Wilson said, her hands still shaking. But it made them laugh. The aggressive woman arrived back, dragging two reluctant girls after her. This drama was being observed by adults, but not one of them came forward to support the local doctor's wife. A caring midwife, present at most of their first days on this earth, this woman of great character, that happened to be one of their own. Abandoned and left to her fate. What price is belief now?

'Isn't this the Catholic brat that pelted you and your little sister with snowballs? Wasn't it him that chased after the van when you were terrified? Didn't he call you bad names just because of your sincere religious beliefs? Take a good look at him, sitting there beside Mrs Wilson, as if he's a saint. You know the real story. Tell us all about it.'

Jonsie was surprised to see the girl with the long plait brought before them. He fretted about what she might say. Mrs Wilson was going to hear the bad news. She'd be disgraced in front of her own people. He caused it. That was the worst part.

But the girl with the long plait had a good memory. She didn't like what was being said, and remembered the look on his face when he said he was sorry. She knew he had meant it. This woman was embarrassing her in front of everybody. Taking her little sister's hand she confidently approached Mrs Wilson. Her mother always said that the doctor's wife was a nice lady. She looked up to her and wanted to tell her exactly what happened last time she saw this boy during the snowy weather. 'He saved us,' she said simply, pointing directly at him.

This little girl was from a noble family, and she went on to tell Susan the true story. It was as if she was reading from a book, precise and clear.

Jonsie listened to what she said in such detail; it was riveting for the quiet onlookers. They had gathered in to hear every word she said. He could see again how he remembered her. This calm voice was describing correctly everything that had happened on the day in precise detail. Everyone knew it was true words spoken. The character of this little girl was undeniably honest.

Susan regained her composure immediately. Turning her legendary sharp tongue on the source of her discomfort, she knew the name, but refused to give her any recognition for her unkind words. There were people that didn't care about knowing true facts. She was one of them.

That bad mouth would have manners put on her.

'Now my dear, you have made scandalous accusations against my friend here that have proven completely unfounded. Not only that, you have tarnished the name of a special young man who came to the girl's assistance when he perceived a wrong. This young lady gave a flawless account. She said this boy was a hero for her and her sister. He is entitled to some respect. I think an apology is required, to prevent a miscarriage of justice at your hands. I'm sure you wouldn't want to harm a youngster when you think so much about them.'

It didn't look as if the woman had any intention of making amends, though she knew the girl's story was believed by everyone standing around them. She scowled, and her face had ignorance all over it. The gathered community had turned their opinion against her. Now they turned their backs on her too.

She growled 'Sorry' in Jonsie's direction, but she didn't mean it. Head down, she left the hall as quickly as her legs could carry her. He would have preferred an apology for Mrs Wilson instead.

But real ladies never seek apology. When the sisters queued in front of him, Jonsie stood beside them. When Santa gave him a bag of sweets, he gave them to the little sister. But it was to the girl with the long plait he said 'thank you very much'. He wasn't surprised when she didn't reply, but she smiled, walking away.

Mrs Wilson was watching this interaction closely and wanted to know why he had given sweets to the younger girl. He said she had got really scared when they were attacked. She gets a present. The other girl was very strong, minding her. She got first prize.

This incident highlights the bigotry consciously adhered to. Time failed to redress this imbalance, which would always remain a disabling factor when more important cooperation was required. The historical errors of the fathers plagued their sons. It shouldn't even make sense. But for misguided thinking, it always would, prisoners of ignorance; Christians both, with pasts not forgotten. They were still poisoned by difference, to remain tormented souls.

Jonsie got a new pair of football boots for his birthday.

His father was listening to the men in the bar saying he was a promising Gaelic footballer. It was a game Bill played, but in spite of his best efforts, he had never excelled. His reputation was that of a good club footballer. However, if his son was better, he'd like that. The new boots indicated his ambition for the boy's future.

WT pointed out to Bill the benefit of having a son playing football. If he worked in the bar, the players would call in for a chat. Then the supporters would flock in to be with them. In the absence of a clubhouse, Flanagan's bar would be perfect. He knew what he was aiming for and was determined to get it.

Boxer told him Jonsie showed promise as a fighter. He'd been sparring with him, amazed at the power of his right-hand punch. It took him by surprise a few times. But Bill could see how boxing could interfere with his son's football. This trade-off was not one he was prepared to contemplate. Business was business. He gave instructions to get the boy focused into football. He was old enough if he was good enough.

Hanna was pleased to hear about the end of this rough boxing game, so her prayers were answered. She thought it would lead him down the wrong path. There was no need to equip her volatile son with a great defence, just in case it might be used for a sudden attack.

'You'd never know. Such is life,' she'd fretted.

When Bill opened the bar door early for fair day business, he stood watching the motley crew roll into town. The 'standing sites' were passed down in families as if they were their own. Nobody would move in on another person's pitch. It was an unspoken code of conduct. The man that pitched up outside Flanagan's pub was called Louie; someone to watch with drink in him. He was a short, broad-shouldered man with a thick rim of curly black hair around his bald skull like a monk. His head was scarred from wallops of sticks over the years.

Whenever he had sold his pigs, he headed straight for the pub. There was always someone looking to do him over, and as the day wore on they inevitably found him. He carried a blackthorn stick. It had a heavy round knob for a grip, when held half way down; it became a club for fighting with, known in Irish as a shillelagh. Louie was hard to beat, when he got the first crack in with his stick. He was false; you'd get a wallop for nothing when you wouldn't be expecting it. The drink always told him what to do next.

It was fair day when men from different parishes met up in town. They had scores to settle from previous altercations. Sometimes arranged, they were called 'faction fights'. When everyone was full of drink, it became natural to do battle, and they went looking for each other.

It was great fun for the young boys in the town. They knew the fighters by sight. One tall white-faced man with a black hat and a long dark coat took several wallops to the head one time. The onlookers didn't know how he was still standing, until he slipped on cow dung after making a swipe at someone, and his hat fell off. He had a scooped out head of cabbage jammed down under the hat. He'd come to town prepared for action, and he wasn't the only one.

These men wouldn't tolerate any bad intent from each other. It could kick off with a dirty look, or the wrong word spoken. They were always watching for it; that might be the real reason they were there. It was a bad fair day if they weren't.

The newly promoted Sgt Nelson with his sidekick Garda Muldoon walked down the street with the nervous expectancy of cops patrolling Times Square, it could kick off that quick.

'A gathering where lunatics drank too much whiskey,' was Sgt Nelson's way of describing it. He hated fair days. When they carried batons on their belts, they never smiled; just a grin from Muldoon if he knew someone well. Nelson never displayed any emotion and had a white face on him 'like a corpse', they said. 'They'd scare nobody, except themselves.'

Bill was wary of Louie; he could turn into a wrong one very quick. He was subject to 'sudden change' under the influence of alcohol, when the devil took possession of him. Then he thought he was great.

'Morning Louie', Bill said, watching him unhitch the pony. He made a complicated looking knot on the rope around the pony's neck that aroused his curiosity. He'd remarked on it once before.

'That's a fancy looking knot, Louie.'

'When he gets out from under the cart he thinks he's free for the day. He could take off, it's hard to hold him, but when this slip knot tightens on his neck, he'll go nowhere Bill, believe you me. I learned it on a ship. The hangman's knot it's called.'

He went sauntering off up the street to Duffy's yard, the subdued pony stepping politely alongside him. This yard held animals safe; they'd get hay for a shilling, and the owner got a meal for two shillings. Duffy's wife fried herrings with potatoes all day. The men could eat at any time. Sometimes they had it for breakfast, after they'd walked animals on the road for many miles, in the middle of the night.

About three o'clock in the afternoon, things started happening. Louie sold his pigs. And he headed straight into Flanagan's pub, where he talked to Bill like a nice person. After a few whiskeys on top of the pints he received different messages when the change in mood came over him. He was talking about 'bastards' that bothered him. They didn't like him. He'd settle them for that.

Someone ran into the bar to make trouble, saying Ned was selling goats out of his cart. That was it. He reached down for a grip of his stick first before charging out the door, bellowing like a madman. Ned had two she goats for sale in the cart. They would provide milk for someone that couldn't afford to feed a cow.

He'd spotted the empty cart and Louie wouldn't be around until evening time. He'd have the goats sold by then and nobody would be any wiser. But he never thought Louie would come charging out the door for a look at his newly painted cart. That was enough. Selling goats was a big climb down from dealing in pigs.

Louie threw a drunken punch at him. Ned was quicker; the bald head was within reach, so he let him have it. The goat man could handle a stick too. You could hear the roars of Louie all down the street, his head on the receiving end of a few wallops from a stick.

Bill wouldn't lift his hand to stop it. He was just a spectator, same as the rest of them, watching the action. This bastard had stolen his son's money not so long ago, he remembered. He couldn't stop thinking about that, wishing Louie would give him a good walloping with his blackthorn stick. Ned had never been confronted about the robbery. That needed sorting.

As WT always said, 'the time comes around to make things right.'

The guards arrived, puffing as if they were miles away. The Sergeant could see the bald fellow was bloodied. The goat man would be in trouble here. A night in a cell would solve the problem for the time being. There would hardly be charges.

'You are a witness to this assault, Mr Flanagan. I will take a statement from you later.'

'Don't think so Sergeant, I witnessed nothing.'

Sgt Nelson eyed Bill with contempt. This was payback for catching him after hours. The Sergeant felt the law was being disrespected again, and he didn't like it. He looked straight at him with some animosity when he talked.

'Mr Flanagan, I'm going to leave this incident unreported. There will be another time, I have no doubt.'

'That's okay Sergeant. See that statue of the rifleman on the green? That's my Uncle Sean, God rests him. He shot a policeman for taking unwarranted interest in my family. Keep safe Sergeant; this is a small town, full of history, with a long memory. We don't like people in uniforms threatening us here.'

The man in uniform marched Ned Goat off to the barracks. He would be doing something positive about this publican that showed no respect for law and order. It was always in his head.

Jonsie lay awake in bed all night. He couldn't sleep thinking about losing the half-crown Ennis gave him at the fair. It must have fallen out of his pocket when he was dumped off a bucking pony.

As soon as daylight came in through the curtains he dressed himself hurriedly and went quietly out the front door. He went straight to the spot where he had landed on the grass. After feeling around with his fingers, he found the silver coin with the horse figure on it. And he was delighted.

Then he saw something on Ned Goat's gate. He thought it was a bundle of old clothes. He got some fright when he saw it was the old boy himself on the end of a rope, the droopy grey moustache distorting a bloated face he barely recognised. He ran for home as fast as he could.

His father was in the kitchen when he arrived in. When Bill heard the story, he brought his son back up the street. He pointed to a chair standing upright against the gate. 'He must have jumped off that chair, Jonsie.'

He took a big knife from the house to cut the body down. The early morning light was bad and the knot tight, but he cut through it, and carried the body inside. He laid him out on the floor. 'Some foul deed on Ned Goat,' he accused Sgt Nelson. 'When you arrested him on the street, you assumed a duty of care to look after him. Everyone knows Ned was in your custody. There's a mystery here. Someone hung him up on the gate,' Bill said confidently, suggesting he might have questions to answer. 'Who was the last person, to see him alive, Sergeant?'

He smirked, and felt good incriminating the Garda. Even a suggestion was enough. It should keep him quiet for a while; give him time to polish his buttons. And shine the boots.

Jonsie needed work on his ball-handling skills, that crucial element in the Gaelic football game. Backs and forwards was good practice in the schoolyard. It could get fierce, with no referee keeping order. The toilets had no running water. A lack of knowledge of how these toilets were maintained caused a problem on this occasion. The doors at the back were hanging open, like they were being cleaned out for the summer holidays. The galvanised floor looked spotlessly clean, from a short distance.

Two coats were placed on the grass for goalposts in time honoured tradition. There were six backs and six forwards, no goalkeeper available. But just as it was about to kick off, a young boy strolled into the yard with his red plastic shovel swinging in his hand. Someone said, 'let's stick Jim in the goals, he's better than nothing' and another one said, 'he'd get killed'.

Football wouldn't be Jim's choice for afternoon entertainment. He had never played the game, too fragile to learn, a white faced lad with wire glasses and a bad habit of chewing his tongue at the side of his mouth. It could be cut in two with an elbow tackle. This little fellow was absent minded to the real world. Having him playing as goalie, a very physical position, was clearly the wrong choice.

Jonsie intervened for the young lad's safety. It was a forgone conclusion what would happen. He wouldn't have a clue about any defensive moves to protect himself.

'Jim,' he shouted at him, 'Jim, go over to clean out the toilets with your shovel. You don't want to play any football today.'

The young lad headed off to do what he was told. The game was about to start when a scream turned all heads towards the toilets. Jim was up to his chest in it, and the smell was sickening.

Jonsie dragged the youngster out and he ran for home, with the contents dripping off him. Rumour spread afterwards that a perfume salesman was doing business with his father in the chemist shop when he arrived, and he left in a hurry. Jim told the story about being 'thrown into the toilet' to protect himself and that version of events was accepted as truth around the small town.

Everyone knew Flanagan's son was a trouble maker. The bad mouths loved the story and added to it. 'He threw the lad into the toilets deliberately to drown him,' they said. This was the thanks Jonsie got for trying to do the right thing. It would unfortunately form a pattern of lies the rest of his entire life. Until one day.

Next day Bill had a note delivered from the priest. It requested the presence of his son in the chapel at six o clock. Jonsie told his parents the whole story of what had happened in the schoolyard and they were horrified. They assumed the priest wanted to hear about it from a witness, to make everything safer for children. That was typical to get them at it.

When the boy met up with the stern-faced priest, he didn't give him a chance to explain. The reverend gentleman had heard it already. Jim's story was taken as a detailed version of true events, not a lie to cover up his mistake. He said he was pushed into the toilet.

The priest told Jonsie he was a blackguard, taking his blackthorn stick to beat him. A warm-up for six slaps on each hand left them numb. The pain made him cry. He'd never want anyone to see that. The priest must have been bloated with pleasure after.

The mental trauma was tough for Jonsie to deal with. It would never occur to him to do such a thing. That cowardly instinct for torturous acts was never in him. They were always the domain of the bully boy. Jim must have known he hadn't been thrown into the toilet. So he had his own reasoning to deal with.

Jonsie wasn't within five yards of him when he stepped into it. But he was there to pull him out. It would become more damning the longer it travelled.

Jim would always stick to his version of events. Forty years later, he'd finally admit the true story, in even more extraordinary circumstances on a mountain in Connemara. That story will be told with this incident in mind.

Bill was very angry when he found out about the beating.

Hanna tried talking to him as usual, saying 'let it pass'. How could he go up to the priest's house to confront him? It could finish up anywhere, she said. Bill listened to her but he'd never forget. 'This brutality with children, I'm convinced they're all at it,' he complained bitterly to her. They should be exposed.

That led into talk of sending their son to boarding school. 'It would get him away, until all this trouble was in the past,' said Bill. Hanna listened to his reasoning. She was all for it, to keep him safe.

'We'll find out if he has any brains Hanna. I'm fed up hearing from everyone how smart he is. Then in another breath they say he's an idiot. Then he turns to do the stupidest things. I can't start asking men in the bar what their sons are like. It might get out that he's not the full shilling. That's the last thing we want, isn't it? I believe his schoolyard version of the story. There's one thing only that I can always be sure off with him, his honesty. That's all he has, honesty, and strength with a kindness that makes him soft-hearted. He's a strange mix. It's bound to be tough going. He listens to WT and talks all about the pony now. But my father would do some job on him if he got into it. He would relish the opportunity to make him like himself. Another WT. Sure he tried it on me. That's why we finished up in the Turlough when we got married, to escape his clutches, don't you remember? He mustn't get his hands on Jonsie. I will do anything to stop that happening. All this tricking he's doing to make money is straight out of my father's book of scheming. He's putting ideas in his head, and he's far too young for that serious business nonsense. Let's get him off to boarding school.'

'Oh Bill, he has a lot going on in his head. He's never had time to be a little boy.'

'Yes Hanna, maybe boarding school with lots of boys his own age would take him out of himself. He hasn't any friends around here. I can't figure out that remote behaviour either. I had lots of friends growing up, in this town, something missing in Jonsie.'

'Right Bill, Let's get a letter off to that college in the west. We only have a few months; we can discuss costs, see if we can manage it.'

'Carry on as usual; we will let him know soon enough Hanna.'

WT was struggling to get the hardware store closed for the night.

Saturday was late, ten on the wall clock. Tom was getting his throat exercised before he left. He irritated the old man no matter what he did. But there was something else catching WT's eye. A new blow-in to town, an American, was holding up the whole show. He'd never get away with it in the states. They'd throw you out of a funeral parlour over there, when time was up; he'd heard that from visitors.

This tall man about his own age, known locally as the Yank, was in deep conversation with Susan Wilson. WT walked down the shop to speed up their conversation. In a nice polite way, of course; Mrs Wilson was very posh. It would be proper to keep her away from this loud, annoying bollox. WT had taken a strong dislike to his attitude already.

But that chance meeting led to the three of them going over to the pub for a drink, in true Irish style. The Yank was already a customer, but it was Mrs Wilson's first visit to the pub. And she was saying nice things about it to the boss.

The three new-found drinking partners sat around a table in some initial discomfort with each other's company. They were all different in their way, struggling to make conversation. A few drinks would loosen their tongues, as they settled with each other's company.

Susan was the first one to speak out loud. 'My word, you never lost the character of this beautiful old store when you changed usage Bill,' she said, when he delivered her glass of port wine. WT had his regular 'small Irish whiskey', the Yank opted for a double brandy, straight up, he said confidently. As if he drank it all the time. The sound of that 'big hit' instantly registered. It was commonly known as a victim's turn; a double brandy. One you asked for when you weren't intent on paying. WT eyeballed him through bushy eyebrows, high alert time arrived early. He was conscious about people buying their round. The fact that he was a bit tight-fisted himself highlighted the seriousness of this intent. But as well as the price of his drink, WT could see another annoyance. He was trying to make friends with Mrs Wilson. And he was calling her Susan. She must be feeling like the cat among the pigeons. WT was surprised at her, laughing with him. 'Some of these women don't know what end of them is up', well-worn words he liked repeating.

Every time he started talking to her seriously about his grandson Jonsie the Yank cut in, distracting her from what he was saying. He had no manners.

WT emptied his whiskey glass in one gulp, with pure annoyance. He eyed the Yank's half-full glass and saw lipstick on Susan's. He shouted at his son to get the Yank's attention focused on the serious business of ordering a round, and paying for it. And he didn't care if anyone took offence or not.

'Bill, make that a double Irish this time like our friend here.' His little finger and thumb were wide apart, indicating a double. Nothing registered with the Yank. He was telling her his team had the best quarterback in American football.

Susan made a calculated break for it, her loud voice edged with personal knowledge and a good bit of devilment in there too.

'WT, were you a good player in your day?' she said. 'But I don't remember hearing much about your triumphs on the football field. Maybe your other interests were more demanding. Like the chess!'

She roared that out like a 'horsey Hilda', knowing he wouldn't know a chess board if he sat on it. Susan was hard of hearing in crowds; loudspeakers at horse shows had done that to her.

WT looked like he'd done something in his trousers. He had never been on a football pitch in his life and knew nothing about 'chess.

She looked over at him. A power feeling came over her then, when she saw him silenced, his jaw left hanging open like that. That was a win. She giggled to herself. Betty always told her he was more thrilling than scary. She admitted to enjoying some of his antics. Long as there was a good end to it. His predictability made him easy to catch with a counter punch. Susan could play games too. He always expected to get what he was after, let it be business or pleasure. They were all the same name, in WTs game.

She was fascinated by his wayward take on life. That refused to stay hidden for long. Betty always maintained, 'he's no better or worse than most men, seeing no harm in pursuing their natural instincts. Best friend you could have when you needed one, that's what counts most.'

Bill couldn't look at his father. He was laughing so much his shoulders were shaking. He knew how miserable his old man was feeling. Oho boy, he deserved getting some of his own back.

All glasses were empty again, and still no cash for the till. If nobody was paying up, encouragement was necessary, so he pushed it a bit. 'I can't hear with the noise, did someone order more drinks here, same again?'

WT listened to their conversation. Yank had moved on to some cultural interest, sounding pleased at finding a fellow art lover. It might be his first time to meet one, WT reckoned. He had answers to things he didn't know about. The more he heard, the sicker he got of him. The Yank boomed loud with his brandy doing the talking.

'There is nobody around this damn place that I can discuss the 'love of art' with, Susan. I want to take you to an art auction some weekend, if you'd care to come along for the ride.'

On hearing that proposition WT wanted him thrown out of the pub. He told Bill. 'You should give this bollox the door, talking like that to a lady, do you know what he said? He only just met her and he's calling her Susan. Now he wants to ride her in the car at some auction or other. The cheek of him, I've heard it all tonight, I can tell you that. What's the world coming to? I don't know.'

'I said, is it the same again folks.' Bill roared over him. Then the barman's well-timed pause, pay up or shut up, especially crafted for separating the sheep from the lambs.

Some movement was expected. He stood looking at them. If he opened his mouth, he'd collapse laughing. Bill knew the American terminology. A 'lift' in the car, was called a 'ride' in New York. His father hadn't a clue of this lingo. To him it was all the real deal, a ride was a ride. No matter whom you got it from.

His 'riding' days in the car were well documented. It made sense no other way. So there was genuine concern there for his good friend Susan, and the ride she shouldn't be getting from the Yank. Something WT could never condone? Wherever this bit of action was going to take place it was likely in the car. Surely the doctor's wife wasn't that far gone yet. WT wanted to protect her from him.

The Yank picked up on the uneasy feel of bartender presence. He wasn't biting though. It was just another play in a tight game. Then he delivered the cameo drivel of a 'likely dodger' fan.

'I want to thank you, Mr Flanagan, for buying the drinks. It was good of you, inviting me to talk with this lovely lady Susan. I'll just go with a small beer this time to wash the brandy down. Before I head for home, I wasn't planning a trip to the bar. So I neglected to bring dollars with me tonight, next time for sure.'

Everyone's eyes turned on WT. Reaching his hand down deliberately as if opening his fly he felt for his pocket flap one button. He withdrew a big bundle slowly, to let the Yank see what it took to stay in charge here. He peeled off a twenty-pound note with a dramatic gesture, for his son. He said in a loud voice, 'Give the Yank the schoolmaster's drink on me, will you?'

Bill knew the scathing tone, the seriousness of its intent. But the schoolmaster reprimand was a once off. It wouldn't be fair to Mrs Wilson, having the Yank with suspect bowel movements beside her all night. His father, however, would revel in such an event.

Next day, Bill got out of bed early, for an important meeting. Hanna told him they called into the pub in the early morning, last time. He'd make sure the place hadn't got the scattered remnants look of a boozing session late into the night before. There was no point drawing the scorn of Sgt Nelson. He'd have done a good job ridiculing him to this Dublin detective already.

Bill wanted to come across as a decent man, a reliable witness. Not the carefree chancer running an illegal drinking haunt. If there was a detective on the job, things must be serious.

He hadn't the door open ten minutes before they were on the premises. Sgt Nelson was in the new uniform.

Detective Crotty got straight to the point. He whipped out his notebook, sitting down at a table. Bill took a seat in front of him. Nelson stood at the side, his arms folded, like an umpire at a football game.

'Mr Flanagan, I'm expected back in the Capital before lunch. I missed you yesterday. I'm Detective Crotty, you know your local police officer, also on duty here today, Sgt Nelson.'

There was no exchange of pleasantries between two local men.

'Morning Detective, welcome to this part of the country.'

Bill reached out his hand, but it was ignored. And that, he considered, was how proceedings were intended to continue, cold and distant. Respect had no part in this coming together.

Bill eyed up this character in the shabby suit, but that wasn't giving much away. His whole demeanour was official boredom; a plain clothes policeman with a job to do.

This Dublin detective must surely have figured a suicidal escape was most likely. A town you'd die to get away from in a hurry.

But there was a body moved illegally. The Gardaí knew who had shifted it. This countryman, with his flat cap, squared jawline, awkward trousers and ordinary touch made common sense of the yokel type in his appearance. The detective wasn't going to waste his time; this fellow's reputation travelled before him.

Sgt Nelson had filled him in on a few matters and it wasn't pleasant listening. Threatening behaviour to police officers was an assault on them all. Nelson was an old friend from the depot. This Flanagan would only heed issues implicating him.

Crotty wanted to give him a few negatives to think about. It might teach him some respect for the law, in future.

'There are a few things that I must clear up first, regarding your input into the victim's life history before his sudden demise, Mr Flanagan. To get it all out in the open, we must go back, to go forward. You've had bad encounters with the victim in the past.'

'I had no bad encounters with him. Who said that?'

'Okay sir, I will relate some information provided by Sgt Nelson here, you can qualify or contradict what you see fit. He has every word of it documented on a file in the barracks. I read it through again this morning. There are some relevant events from the victim's past. We must examine them more closely. In this way we can evaluate his frame of mind; his response to certain issues might be negatively influenced, particularly any demeaning treatment to unbalance him, when making life and death choices. Sometimes blame comes forward from far back. Now, do you understand that sir, before we proceed?'

Bill nodded, at the nonsensical sound of the whole thing.

'Your first negative contact with the man known as Ned Goat was the morning of your pub opening, isn't that right? On that occasion you physically evicted the victim's property and his person from your premises in a very confrontational manner. You forbade him from gaining entry, to your public house thereafter.'

'That's right' Bill interjected, 'I barred him, my entitlement.'

The detective continued talking. 'When an altercation took place with the victim and another person outside your property, you refused Sgt Nelson's request to provide a witness statement. That was your right. Even though the deceased might benefit from your account, you refused. He was attacked, you watched, and said nothing. Were you thinking about the alleged theft of your son's savings money, I wonder?'

'Wait for a minute, what's this all about? It seems as if I'm being accused here. Is this a set up? Is Nelson here out to get me?'

'The theft of your son's savings was the final straw. You were repeatedly heard swearing in front of witnesses that you'd kill him.'

'Look, look here, Ned finished up hanging from a gate when he was supposed to be safe, locked up in a cell. Sgt Nelson was minding him; he had the last known contact with him. What's all this to do with me?'

The detective's smile broadened, lying back in the chair. 'You were driving early that morning, weren't you Bill, in your father's red van. You had a friend with you, a friend with a bandage, the only one in the town, someone that wouldn't hesitate to hang the goat man from his own gate, if his company encouraged him. This Louie man shouted at him on the street too, he'd kill him, same as you. Now that's two of you, partners in crime with the same stated intent. Bill, you know what I'm getting at here, doesn't it seem like a team effort, what do you think? The two of you did a job on him.'

The detective stared hard at him, before continuing. 'Because you are one of the team, and your partner in crime Louie was bandaged. He was very easy to identify, even in bad light. Both you and Louie were seen driving that morning, just at the light of dawn. The Sergeant here has the vehicle number. There is no other way of summing this one up. Murder, he grinned. Did you meet Ned Goat when the Sergeant here released him, to feed his donkey? Come on now. Admit it to save a long enquiry. The two of you waylaid poor Ned, and put an end to him.'

Bill tried explaining. 'Drover is the only person that parades the town that early, was it him that told you this nonsense? He should stick to driving cattle, and drinking funny tea. Or so I'm told. I was taking my son off to boarding school later that same morning. I went over to the yard to get my father's van. Horses don't like the noise from a motor engine; they could spook and hurt themselves, I had to take it out early. I discovered Louie in a drunken slumber, lying on a pile of straw in his cart. It was wet, and I offered to drive him home. The decent thing to do, it's only a few miles away. I went back up to bed when I came home. It didn't do me much good. I had to get up again soon after, when my son came home crying about Ned Goat on the gate. That's all I have to say.'

Crotty sensed he was rattled.

'Your son said you were in the kitchen when he came in that morning. Why are you lying, Bill? You were not in bed. You were standing up making tea in the kitchen, after the deed. And why did you cut a dead man down? What reason did you have for destroying evidence by carrying him all the way into his house? And you ruined the knot. Or was it your partner Louie? No, he wouldn't be tall enough, unless he stepped up on a chair. The legs were driven deep into the ground. There were two people on the chair. The victim's weight wouldn't have driven it down on its own. Any interference with a suspicious death is a very serious breach of the law. That could result in a jail sentence.

'It will take a while, but you might be wise to seek the advice of a good solicitor. We will call and have a chat with you on another occasion; when you're better prepared, there are legal matters to consider as well. And some new leads to follow up on, then we will reach a conclusion, an arrest most probably. Now do you have any questions before I point my nose for Dublin?'

'Yes, why do I need a solicitor?'

'Mr Flanagan, you're the one that removed the corpse, and that must jeopardise the scene of the crime. There's only one reason why this act could occur; hiding evidence. That would only be carried out by a guilty party. Sure that's obvious, isn't it?'

'I was just keeping the body away from frightening kids going to school. My son was traumatised by the sight of him. I didn't see any harm in it; if I did I would never have touched him. How was I to know it was the wrong thing to do? I never saw anything like it happening around here before.'

Detective Crotty flashed the tight smile again. 'That's what I'm saying. Get a solicitor to explain it all to you properly. Tell him the whole story, including why your van was parked for such a long time doing a few minutes' work in Duffy's yard.'

'I was waiting for Louie to feed his pony.'

'You never mentioned parking, did you forget? Get it right next time we meet up. It could be a more serious discussion then.'

Bill looked at Nelson when he was leaving. The Sergeant was having a smile to himself. He wondered if Louie came across Ned Goat, by chance, and did him in. He was capable of it. That could easily implicate him, if drover the informer saw him in the bandaged man's company. What could he do about that?

Detective Crotty was having a laugh in the barracks afterwards.

For Sgt Nelson it was great payback for all the annoyance. At the very least there was manners put on the bold bar owner. They agreed on a job well done. Ned Goat had taken his own life on the morning of his release. That's how it looked to them. The Sergeant had recruited the assistance of Sam Crotty when he had a few days off. They had known each other for many years. The plan was to give the unruly bar owner the fright of his life.

'He's threatened me on a few occasions, Sam. On one instance he inferred the use of a firearm.'

The detective was sure it was the proper thing to do under the circumstances. Bill needed that lesson, because he shouldn't have interfered with the body. 'But we don't have to bother anyone with all that. Too much paperwork, and if you didn't do it properly there'd be an inquiry. And we don't want to get stuck in anything like that either, isn't that right, Nelson?'

The Sergeant wasn't sure about that, but he nodded his head in agreement. What if there was a case to answer?

They were both pleased with their morning's work. It would be the talk of the barracks when he got back to Dublin. Crotty knew that grilling in the pub would keep Bill Flanagan in a respectful state of mind towards the local Gardaí for a while. He might be more careful about closing time in future. They shook hands before the detective left the station. It was good making contact with an old friend. They would meet up again, no doubt about that. Proceedings would be ongoing.

CHAPTER 7

Jonsie had endured a long, gloomy drive before his worst fears were realised. The grey stone building was stark. His first thought was jail; he would be five years rotting here. Two tall white pillars, either side of the door, were ringed and fluted for that important ecclesiastical presence. They had their hands on him now. That's all he could think about.

His father never spoke a word getting out of the van. He marched towards the big brown door purposefully, his eyes fixed on the brass bell. But something made him turn back, after ringing it, scratching his jaw; he opened the van door.

'This is some place, Jonsie, like a luxury hotel, I could do with a holiday here myself. I can tell you that much.'

'Why don't you stay here, I won't mind.'

Then one side of the brown door eased open. After a brief conversation he entered the building.

The boy took stock of his surroundings. There were tennis courts behind a high wire-mesh fence and four handball alleys, near a football pitch. There were small lime trees, tidily spaced in a line along a tarmac path to nowhere. The lawns were all carefully manicured; even the grass was subject to restrain. He stared at a long two-storey building with big windows along the bottom. There were smaller windows along the top. It might be a greenhouse, but nothing would ever grow there. He could feel the cold chills coming over him already.

The door opened again. His father came out laughing, raising his hand to beckon his son over, urgently. Jonsie swore loudly getting out of the van.

The bald red-faced priest wore a black gown, buttoned from the white collar to the ground, and he had a prayer book in his hand. He seemed jovial, with a big grin and the longest, whitest teeth the new student had ever seen. That should have been cold warning. Sharks had teeth like that.

When his father introduced them, they shook hands. And the priest was laughing out loud, sounding like a real nice person.

Bill helped him lift the big wooden trunk out on the ground. And then he turned abruptly, to give his son a strong convincing handshake. That deceiver's grip, one hand on top of the other, to say 'you're well regarded' or 'done up to the two eyes' in horse dealing chat. Jonsie knew there and then he'd been sold a dud.

Bill got into the van in a hurry to disappear out the gate without looking back. No wave goodbye, a marked difference between 'I'll miss you' and 'I'm glad to get rid of you'.

When he left, there was a sudden change in attitude from the 'pope's person'.

'Could you give me a lift with my trunk, father?'

'How dare you, Flanagan?' He moved in, taking the hair locks at his ear in a pinch for a nasty pull. It was teacher Rasp's favourite grip. They must have attended the same school of persecution sometime in the past. He saw the holy man strip his teeth. The 'shark' whacked him hard with his hand, on the back of the head, shouting at him.

'That foul language I heard from you has no place here, Flanagan. Now go off and find someone to help you.'

Jonsie looked towards the big iron gates. The best help was out through there. He knew that, and not an hour in the joint yet.

With a swish of the long black robe, the priest left him standing there, dazed. His stomach froze. Bad memories came back. In those few minutes he'd found out the worst, and he made one of his 'special' promises that lasted forever. The words were dead cold.

'I swear I'll never learn here, nobody will make me.'

He looked at the priest, walking around the tarmac maze of lime tree folly, reading from his prayer book, the way a 'saint' should be. The heavy trunk could sit there; he didn't care if it rained again.

When he walked the long corridor he came to a yard full of boisterous lads. He found a wall to stand against. Some older boys greeted each other, pushing roughly. Other sedate types were different in their way, almost shyly greeting each other, wriggling like nervous bookworms. The strong boarding school ethos, making friends for life, was hard work in the making.

He saw this young lad standing near him and chanced a word. 'Is this your first day too?'

'Yeah, I'm afraid it is.'

Jonsie would spend all day in this fellow sufferer's company. He was called Timer, a nickname, he explained. And it had absolutely nothing to do with good timekeeping practices. He proved to be a lot stronger than he looked.

They parked the trunk on a rack, in a crowded 'boots room'. Two new-found friends headed off to find their sleeping quarters. Timer led him back down the long corridor, into a small stairwell.

'That's the dormitory up there Jonsie, forty beds, enough for all us first years. But there's something else to see down here first.'

They went into a small yard with a high wall facing the road. There was a nice building here, made up in stone, with two louvred huts on the roof top, like beehives. Timer explained that these back toilets were the centre of all the action. The cigarettes arrived in over the wall, fish and chips too. He boasted of his card-playing skills. His brother had been here the previous year and his reputation lived on. Honest Harry was his nickname, a card shark. Timer was planning on taking over his mantle. His brother told him there was a fortune to be made. Some of these country boys had never seen the three-card trick before, he said gleefully.

Jonsie listened bemused. He had seen it.

The staircase led up to a dormitory, the full length of the long red corridor underneath. The small windows were the ones he had looked up at earlier. Now the room seemed enormous, twenty beds lined up on either side. Timer had selected the second bed from the end. He took his pyjamas off the next bed. He offered Jonsie the last one against the wall, the quietest place in the dormitory, to spend the night talking, without being heard. 'It's great, I'd sleep there,' he said.

Timer couldn't hide his excitement. 'I took this bed knowing that a solitary figure would look for the end one. That has to be you. The rest of the boys would have paired off and got beds beside each other, that's how it works out. You stuck out like a lost sheep out there against the wall, that's what I bring to the table, sound survival instincts. It's in my own interest,' he said. 'We're stuck with each other now for better or worse. Don't fall out with me, or I'll turn my back and fart at you all night. Timer knows how to strike.

'Welcome to my end of the living quarters Jonsie, I hope we always get on as well, there could be a bright future for us.'

'You'd never know Timer. You'd never know.'

Jonsie was enjoying this. Small in stature, there was something mad about Timer. He would be great company. Jonsie thought a small moustache would fit his face perfectly, like a warning, to take the innocent look off him and keep you on your guard. He had this deadly feel to him.

They lay down on their respective beds, to try them out. Like sleeping on a plank, they agreed. They laughed at how things had turned out. Now, there were two of them, trying to make the best of it. Or the worst, whichever one came along their way.

The next big event was tea time and Jonsie was starving. They got to sit at the same table, for eight pupils. Timer had been forewarned about the rush for chairs. They were sitting next to each other waiting for someone to talk. An older boy announced he was the Prefect in charge of their table, and gave instructions on how things were expected to work. Everyone listened respectfully, learning how to conduct themselves in future. Then they queued to collect hot plates from a person who never even looked at them. They might as well have been not there at all.

Two sausages and a fried egg, and there was a big spoonful of beans poured on the plate by the 'chef'. 'Toast,' he shouted, pointing to a basket of cold toast. You could take what you wanted, if you were quick enough to get it.

The conversation at the table struggled for survival. Nobody was giving anything away; sounds of knives scraping beans off plates grated on the loneliness of these young fellows, far from home. They missed their mothers.

Jonsie was watching the priest going around the hall with some purpose, like he was exercising. It was the same character that had walloped the head of him earlier in the day. He kept his eye on him, with his hands folded behind his back, watching everything. Occasionally that insipid smile split the grim red face. He must be having the occasional funny memory too.

He asked Timer about him. 'That's Nasser, the dean in charge of all the boys in the college, a jailer. Hell will never be full till he's in it, the fucker. He's our tormenter for as long as we're here. This fellow beats people wherever he likes. In front of your mother if he wanted to. Don't draw him on you, he enjoys his work.'

'Too late for that Timer, he's nailed me already.' He whispered his experience at Nasser's hands.

From that day on these new school friends would become inseparable. What they had in common was a dislike for confinement and a total lack of interest in learning from books. They sat at the back of the classroom, providing readymade targets for a tyrannical regime, particularly vulnerable to the whims of a psycho called Nasser. He'd relish the challenge of getting more victims, no doubt about that. It was like serving a jail sentence, with hard labour. For something you didn't do.

CHAPTER 8

WT was in one of his more depressed moods. He couldn't handle customer demands. He'd been doing a lot of thinking and his recent resentment surfaced, as a result.

Jealousy of the American consumed him. This fellow that nobody seemed to know anything about was taking over. He'd watched his performance with Susan Wilson in the bar that first night with pure envy. That bloody Yank had a 'straight in' style, much favoured by WT himself. The deadly touch was in him, all right.

But there was something else there that didn't come across easy, and WT couldn't see it as clearly. All he knew was this Yank chap must be kept under observation. The town was only big enough for one of them. And he was sure of one thing; he was the man with all the money. That's what made the difference. The double brandy issue had put the tin hat on it. He had taken him for a sucker, making him pay; WT wouldn't forget. And chasing local women made matters worse; this fellow had hustled a date with Susan Wilson. Nobody got that, but he was slick. On the pretext of some art auction. She with the giggly head on her after one glass of wine, sitting there looking at him when he mentioned a 'ride' in the car. WT never imagined she was that far advanced in her thinking, but you could never tell with them when it came right down to it. What they'd be thinking was their own business. She'd never mentioned art before, either. Maybe she was lining up a bit of fun for herself at last. That was WT's considered opinion anyway. And he should know.

This Yankee man had her talked into an overnight frolic in Dublin. That reminded him of his nights roaming the city. But this fellow could be a dangerous man, if he could manoeuvre his way into a clever woman's trust, as he had done with Susan. He was lethal. WT heard that he was a 'good builder' in America. Now if that wasn't a warning in advance, what was? He had picked up on it straight away. His eye was on him, and what he was up to.

Mrs Wilson had left her paint on the counter. Was it a sign she might be forgetful, an easy target? Things were getting serious so.

WT picked up the paint tin when he was leaving. Danny was walking across the yard when he shouted at him. Turning to have a word, he wondered if WT knew the connection. Not once in his life did Danny get the impression he knew the truth. So for his part, the secret was well minded.

In fact, he forgot about it when he talked with his boss. WT got straight to the point.

'I've seen you talking to this Yank a few times. What's he doing around here?'

Danny had watched the drama unfold with the three of them in the bar when WT lost control of the show. He was getting old and insecure in himself. He felt sad for this great character, adjusting to the painful awareness of elderly years, losing a few rounds every so often now.

'He's a wealthy man WT, retired from his construction business in America to live a quiet life. He likes it around here, so he says. He was building private houses in America; now he wants to do the same in Cody's Cross. He's interested in purchasing land near the water with a nice view, for retired Americans. That's what he told me anyway. It will be good for the town. He's a very enterprising man, bit like you.'

That comparison was not appreciated by the bewildered WT.

'View of the water, you say. Did he mention any particular water?'

'No, sure it's full of water around here, isn't that what we're famous for, water? Probably some lake shore he's spotted I suppose. These builders have an eye for the best site to secure their investment. It might give people badly needed jobs in this area. If he ever got it off the ground, you never know, do you.'

Danny knew well that WT was absorbing that loaded information.

He enquired about any personal knowledge of the American, but Danny wasn't going to volunteer any of that yet. He knew WT was hot on the Yank's case now, so he wouldn't say anything that harmed the American. Danny had great respect for where he was coming from. It was all about some things that had happened a long time ago, when everybody was young. But he was going to enjoy this saga playing out.

There was a quiet unease settling over WT though. And it all came from this Yank who proposed building houses on his patch.

He wondered where he wanted to build them. And the old boy knew the answer to that, he didn't have to guess. 'With a clear view of the water,' he had told Danny. Well if he was any good at all, he was talking about his water.

The store closed early on Sundays, an hour after last mass. WT knew the routine in Dr Wilson's house better than anyone. She would be cooking delicious roast beef at two o' clock. The can of paint would provide his lunch.

Susan was busy in her kitchen. A small joint of beef, served with Yorkshire pudding and marrow fat peas, swimming in gravy. She was looking forward to it. But then the worst happened; the door knocker banged with the urgency of unwanted intrusion.

She didn't bother removing her apron.

'Oh damn, it's you.'

'Good afternoon, Susan.'

'It's lunchtime WT, as you surely know. Come in, it looks like I'm having company with my beef.'

She took the tin from his outstretched hand. 'Thanks for delivering my paint. I'm getting forgetful.'

WT didn't use the armchair; he hung his coat on the back of a tall chair and sat down at the only place made up on the table. Susan set another place, opposite him. And they chatted about the state of the country, and some news items from abroad. She was well up to date with those. Not WTs favourite topic, so he had to listen a lot when he couldn't say much. Susan was watching him wolfing it down. It pleased her to see him enjoy her cooking. Her dear departed husband had loved his roast beef too.

'You must have smelt the roast cooking at the shop,' she said.

'Yes I had a fair idea it would be ready for me.'

They laughed.

"Would you have tea or coffee at the fire? I have a nice slice of lemon cake, if you'd like some of that. With a dollop of cream, I'm sure.'

'I'll give it all a shot, Susan.'

When they had everything finished off, she produced two crystal glasses of special liqueur, Irish whiskey. It was like cream to a cat. WT was delighted with his good fortune.

He was soon reminiscing, saying how pleased he was seeing her enjoying a night out. She should do it more often. He would be there to escort her home if need be. But she would never be that reckless.

WT went on to say how it would be an opportunity to talk about Jonsie's future progress with the horses. That's if college didn't take it all out of his head. And if he could suggest respectfully, she had been in mourning long enough. Dr Edmund wouldn't have wanted her stuck in the house all the time. He was a man that enjoyed the occasional social interaction himself. A few drinks in the local pub, among friends, were no harm at all, WT assured her kindly. She'd be only across the street from her own front door, as soon as she felt like going home, he added.

Susan was sitting quietly sipping her drink listening to him; she could almost believe those words. She hoped he wasn't taking an unhealthy interest in her, if she could be so bold as to imagine that scenario. He would get a stern rebuke, with a good telling off. She would keep her eyes open and her thoughts clear.

He seemed to be changing course though, in his mature years. Because, since he'd started visiting her place with his grandson, she'd noticed a difference in him. He might be mellowing; he'd left it late enough. There was also that incident she couldn't get out of her head; that poignant moment when she had found him having a little cry for his wife in the field. She was so struck by the moment that she had cried too, thinking how her dear friend Betty would love looking down on that romantic scene.

Prior to that, she would never have thought of him shedding a tear for anything, except money. Maybe his disposition in life was misunderstood, in some ways. There was more than one WT. She saw a lonely man behind it all; except he didn't know exactly what he was lonely for. And she'd be keeping it all to herself.

'I must say WT, that American is interesting isn't he. I discovered he's our age, but my word he's fit, not an ounce of fat on him. I wonder what he does that keeps him so healthy. He moves around a lot, I suppose.'

She noticed her guest gathering his stomach in fast and struggled to supress a giggle in front of him; she looked for that reaction, just to see if he was switched on. The old martyr still had a competitive streak in him. Bless his dear soul.

Susan enjoyed that little bit of theatre. She wasn't surprised he didn't like the Yank. Boys would always be boys when it came down to basics. Weren't they enjoyable to observe, when you got older, and knew not to take them so seriously. Every girl must learn to master the boyish language, to further her own objectives. Their actions were based on getting what they want, but were easily countered by a promise of everything later, the long wait.

WT was brooding, holding the glass in his hand. 'Dangerous, I'd say Susan, don't have much to do with that playboy. You'd never know what he'd be thinking.'

She was annoyed by that reprimand, telling her what to do. The old scoundrel might think he could control her for some reason.

'Oh I don't know, he seems quite harmless to me,' she replied very casually.

The old boy sucked air in noisily through his teeth. This thing women had for accepting everything at face value was their undoing; their demise was invariably hastened every time they acted rashly upon it. Another thing; they'd listen to no one.

'Susan, he never put his hand in his pocket, to pay for a drink, Jesus he's mean for a start. You know what they're like yourself, I don't have to explain it to you. People like him have been scorned for as long as we've known each other. Your husband was a decent man and he hated meanness. It's everyone's duty to accept responsibility for their situation, to pay their way.'

'Well that American gentleman, whatever his name is, was decent enough to invite me to an art exhibition in Dublin shortly. I'm tempted to take him up on his offer; I could stay overnight with my dear sister Robyn, and her husband Stanley. They live in my old family home in Rathgar, you know. Its three storeys in a Georgian setting, with lawns and tennis courts and a giant pond with trees all over the grounds; I shall contact her first thing tomorrow morning to see if she'll have me. She's quite independent, you know, you couldn't just walk in on her with a tin of paint in your hand. Not even if you were going to paint the whole place for nothing.'

She laughed at her own humour, but her guest wasn't amused.

WT was hearing it all bad. Never in a million years would he have thought Susan Wilson could think this way. She hadn't understood him properly in the pub with all the noise going on. But she must hear the truth. It was his duty to say it, for old time's sake.

'Look, he wants to 'ride' you in the car, he told you didn't he?'

'What? How dare you Flanagan, that's uncalled for, you're an old scoundrel, that's your stock in trade. I've heard all about you. The American is a decent man. I wouldn't travel with you, not even if you were being driven to the funeral home bolted into a coffin; you're a dangerous old boy, dead or alive.'

And then, for some unknown reason, notwithstanding the insulting insinuations, the two dear old friends laughed heartily at that unflattering image of the last day for the legendary WT.

This liquor Irish whiskey was great stuff. They topped it up again.

'Susan, we go back many years. This man's a blow-in, and no one knows anything about him. I'm only trying to make sure he doesn't take advantage of you. That's all.'

'Advantage of me? Let me get this right, are you trying to tell me you're worried about my chastity? Because if that's it, lay off. It's my chastity, WT. I will do what I like with it. Always did. But of course I was always committed to one person. And I shall always be faithful to my dear Edmund, when I still want to.'

He looked at her. He knew her morals were never in doubt; he had weighed her up as a waste of time years earlier. Was she starting to wobble now, he wondered? So he must say it out straight, with respect; from one old friend to another.

'Well, I knew you wouldn't be on for 'the ride' in the car. That was a pretty insulting suggestion to a lady of your standing, Susan. The man has no class. I'll wager little interest in art either.'

Susan looked across at this man she'd known for so long, but never knew at all. She thought about New York and how they talked over there. She considered the mental state of this character before her, with his comically serious perceptions. His wily cleverness continuously rescued him from harm's way. He was a remarkable survivor, and she understood where he was coming from, and knew exactly where he thought he was going. He was after her sites along the river. So, too, was the American. She knew all that.

Surely there must be an opportunity here for her. She could out-think the best of men. Let them watch each other if they want, and lose sight of her in the process.

There were things she wanted. Her big garden of flowers was a long time coming. There was a fresh smell of roses in the air; time to buy gardening gloves. She smiled pleasingly to herself, thinking about that.

Her dear departed friend Betty would like her to give him something nice to eat occasionally. In spite of all those negative rumours about their relationship, she knew the real story.

'Would you care for a small dram of liquor, WT?' she enquired politely.

He pushed his shoes off discreetly, hearing that. Mrs Wilson smiled when she saw it.

CHAPTER 9

Jonsie was devastated when he discovered that Timer had left the college. A young lad said his friend had gone to a hotel management school in Glasgow. That was the end of it, after one year. He felt alone in the place without him, having nightmares every time he put his head down to sleep; the goat man hanging on the gate was a regular visitor. He'd wake up in a sweat. How would he cope with it now? There were a few psychopaths here. He remembered one of them had hit Timer a nasty blow on the nose with a piece of wood.

This middle-aged teacher was tall in stature, with a well-toned physique. He'd been a boxer in the past, and had a split personality. He moved around the classroom on his toes, dodging and weaving, like he'd won a few fights, wearing an expensive sports jacket, a starched white shirt, and a striped college tie. He looked the part, but he often felt different when a rush of madness hit him. He became someone else; it all happened very quickly.

He was a proper gentleman in appearance, and those adoring elderly ladies he fawned over in the shops, would never have imagined his behaviour when sudden change came over him.

He always coughed into his closed fist first; a signal for action. Standing before them, he'd clear his throat, straightening his shoulders, looking down on them with a scary look in his piercing eyes. He used a pointer for the blackboard, from a chair in the teacher's room, and it could also work as a weapon. When some form of insane release let a pure lunatic out, to cause terror amongst them, if you could run, you would. But you couldn't. So you froze instead, waiting for the worst to happen.

Jonsie and Timer were sitting back against the wall one day when his mood changed, mid-sentence; boys frowning could trigger him. He made his way down the back to continue his lecture. Timer, sitting on the outside, was partial to deep frowns of misunderstanding. When he got nervous, he put his finger up his nose. The maniac went for it. He'd been watching Timer, the pointer dangling between his thick fingers. He stood slyly by, with his back to the wall, priming himself, before suddenly letting go, right across the bridge of Timer's nose. Timer might have been blinded if it had gone wrong, or his nose could have been broken.

"Look up at the light!' he'd roar at a terrified pupil. Then the slap on the jaw followed. He knew to pull it from doing too much damage. He was an ex-boxer after all. Maybe he never won many fights in his time; bullies don't.

How could Nasser the priest not know he was wrong? Why didn't he consider, that some religious colleagues would abhor his actions? He walked around reading his gospels like a devout person. What God did he think would condone his behaviour? Some of these phoney reverend gentlemen should be burned at the stake for all the damage they caused to innocence.

Timer had used a folded table at the back toilets while he was there. He'd set himself up as a card sharp, playing games of twenty-five for money. There was always a poker game ready, if anyone had more cash. He'd order fish and chips from the local café with the winnings. They worked as a team, making enough money to keep them going. It was Jonsie's job to keep watch for Nasser. That job alone was risky, for letting him see you.

The scary Dean knew what was going on, but he had to catch somebody in the act. That was his challenge. This predator swished around in his black robe and white purified collar hunting for victims. You didn't want to meet up with him. The back toilets were his favoured destination when he searched for smokers. He left his victims dazed with the blows he struck on their heads. This man was responsible for shaping character. His calling in life was as a sadistic brute getting pleasure doling out punishment to frightened young boys. Hell was waiting for him, no doubt. If he'd read the religious book correctly, and taken it all in, he'd expect that. But when you're badly screwed up you can think of nothing good to do. Fortunately they weren't all that bad.

Jonsie was victimised by Nasser from the word go. They watched each other with the same wariness, predator and prey. The priest took an unhealthy interest in Timer as well.

These two boys were always up to some harmless stuff. They set about playing pranks on other students for their amusement. Bullying was never part of their agenda.

Jonsie spent his time alone now, catching the football over his head, drop-kicking it off the wall in the handball alley, to take it down from the highest level coming back. He spent hours at this, moulding a great technique for catching a high ball and holding on to it. The ball spin on the return from this drop kick added to its value; it must be gripped tighter to hold on to it. That made it difficult to dispossess, developing leg muscles to reach high over the very best of them. His physical strength would help him win the ball in any crowded tussle. There was no doubt about that.

This football game would be the only positive lesson he learned at College. And he'd tutored himself. It gave him a good pair of hands for catching a ball in Gaelic football. On future occasions he'd excel in all company, using this well-honed technique.

Thankfully there was one special priest in the dreadful college, an Irish language teacher who doubled as a football coach. Father Peadar was a tough chisel-jawed powerhouse of about thirty-five who chose to tog out with him for one-on-one sessions, showing him 'turns on full backs'. He would tell Jonsie to hit him as hard as he could, but the student always held back a little, not to hurt this priest he respected so much.

Fr Peadar asked him about it. 'I told you Joe; hit hard with your right shoulder, spin your back to drive the ball with your right boot to the corner of the net.'

'I don't like crashing into you hard, Father,' was the reply.

He didn't say 'in case I'd hurt you', but the inference hung on it.

'Make no mistake Joe, I will crash into you. When you see me in front of you, think 'I'm the Dean'. You're only getting one shot, make sure it counts. Now come on, hit me harder.'

This priest was a noted club footballer who played with hard coal miners in his native parish. He shook up his pupil when he wanted to. And he enjoyed doing it. There would never be anything false about this man. He'd let you see him coming before he hit you. What you saw was what you got. It was tough, but it was fair, always honest.

Jonsie showered for the night. He wasn't in bed ten minutes before he went into a deep sleep. It would take a lot to wake him.

The dormitory remained in lively mood after lights out. All kinds of quips went around in the darkness. The contributors were well known, no matter how they tried to disguise themselves when they copied each other's voices.

The dean's room was just outside in the hall. He'd be sneaking around searching for victims. He called around periodically every night. His mission was to get into the dormitory without being spotted. He'd hide with his black robe concealing him against a long dark clothes rack, until he identified a culprit to knock the head off him for his pleasure. That was his sole purpose.

On this occasion Jonsie was fast asleep when he got a violent awakening. Nasser was pulling his hair, shouting, 'I heard you Flanagan!'

Jonsie lashed out with a box at the blurred face of his attacker.

'You've assaulted me!' the priest roared, and he manhandled him out of bed, into the corridor, still half asleep, pushing him towards his room, known as 'the dungeon'. He'd been listening to the carry on in the dormitory for a while with this bold brat specifically in mind.

Jonsie tried explaining the mistake. 'I was fast asleep,' he implored.

Nasser held the cane, swishing it in front, watching for the fear to show on the young lad's face; listening wasn't happening.

'Put out your hand, Flanagan.'

'No I fucken won't, I was asleep.'

Nasser lashed out in a blind fury, hearing the bad language; the cane struck the boy's jaw and his cheek stung with a piercing pain. The boy unleashed a right hand punch into his mouth, and that dumped Nasser on his back. He lay on the floor whimpering like a dog, his top lip spilt and blood running down the white collar. There was satisfaction for a young fellow seeing this. He stood there for a second to look down on him. Then he turned to go out the door, leaving him there. It didn't bother him a bit.

They all wanted to know what Nasser had done. He said nothing. They would get to know soon enough. And they could put their own slant on it then. Like always. He was back in bed as if nothing happened. Not even the sting in his jaw could keep him awake. There would be no prowling by Dracula later, on this particular night. But he'd never say how he knew that.

He had another worry to bother him: what his father would think of all this. That was the scary part.

During breakfast, a priest told him he was expected in the president's rooms at midday. Jonsie never told anyone about the ructions in the dean's room. There was no one to talk with when Timer was gone, and being all alone suited him.

He knocked on the door as the bell rang twelve and that steadied him to stay strong. There were two of them at the desk. He stared at the Dean's big lip stripping the shark's teeth.

'Master Flanagan, the president started in his loud chastising voice, you have committed a dastardly act. You physically assaulted the Dean of Studies here, causing him serious injury.'

Jonsie almost laughed. The word 'dastardly' did it; because of his denture malfunction it sounded like 'bastardly act'. And when he looked at Nasser's ugly face again, he was glad he had hit the bastard. It had been coming his way for a long time. He felt good.

Joe Flanagan, the accused, was standing with his arms by his side. He wanted it over and done with. He knew he could handle anything when he took the time to analyse it all.

The president continued with his old palaver. He couldn't hide his cynical, unforgiving tone of voice.

'The Dean has made a complaint that you viciously assaulted him on two separate occasions last night. What have you got to say for yourself about that?'

'He attacked me first; he's been doing it since I got here. Why do you allow him to abuse me? What kind of a bad place is this? He beat me up first day I arrived and has never stopped since.'

The president was shocked at this retort; it was not something he'd ever heard before. So he lost the run of himself too.

'Yes... we will have to expel you from this college, a week from now. Boarding school is not for a boy with your bad manners. You will return here to this room, this time next week. It's imperative that your father attends the entire proceedings. Then he can take you home with him. We will be contacting him, don't worry. You should consider joining the Army.'

Jonsie had a week, to run 'like the hammers of hell', as his father might say, but not for home. Timer would be having a great time in Glasgow. There was one lad he'd ask to get money for him. There'd been friendly exchanges between them already. He'd been wandering around looking for him. And there he was watching a game of handball.

He sat down on the grassy hill beside him and Jonsie told him the whole story, finishing up with the shortage of cash problem.

'I need money to get away in a hurry,' he said. 'How much can we get with a collection?'

'I'll have a whip around for you; the ferry cost six pounds, meet me here at this time tomorrow. I take ten percent. I don't know how many of the lads like you, they'll keep their mouths shut, you can be sure of that.'

Jonsie got a day boy to pick up timetables of ferry sailings to Glasgow from Belfast, with all connections. He got into this mind-set without a single doubt in his head. He'd do it. As far as he was concerned, this was part of the long term plan. Hadn't he been here long enough to run away, now?

Three days later he climbed over the back toilets wall at five in the morning and hurried along a secluded narrow road to the station. He took an early bus to the northern depot of Enniskillen; there was a connection to Belfast there. He sat in the bus with his small yellow duffle bag beside him on the seat. Quietly pleased with his progress, it didn't stress him one bit. In fact he enjoyed the thrill of doing it. Calm in appearance and in mind, he moved along with the confidence of daily routine.

He was mentally prepared for a long journey, and not getting spotted in the beginning by being careful. That strategy set the tone. Some of the college priests drove around in the early morning, travelling to say mass somewhere or other, in the convent too. He didn't want to get spotted by one of them.

'The college class can kiss my ass, I have a free pass to life at last...' He laughed singing those lines. He had made them up himself. Those few words would keep him light-hearted.

There was a long trip ahead, and it was still dark. When he awoke to the sound of brakes, the bus was turning into the depot.

It was getting bright when he heard the bad news. There was no connection to the ferry on this particular day.

He made a decision to walk for the motorway, following the road signs; it was hurrying it up time again. The pressure was on to hitch a lift to the ferry. He must get there before evening.

He was thumbing on the roadside when a green car pulled up. Looking down, all he could see was a clerical collar, a sign of imminent danger. He was about to say no thanks, but the smiling young red haired priest wasn't much older than him. So he got into the front seat without thinking more about it. There was a feel of adjusting to the needs of desperation.

During the journey Jonsie would tell about his experiences in boarding school. It troubled the young priest that he blamed the religious for all his woes. When he listened, he promised it would be like a confession. Never to be repeated to anyone else.

Jonsie said he didn't want anyone to feel responsible for him getting apprehended by the police as a runaway. This kind young priest understood perfectly. When good people come along, you find their value very quick. They help just by making themselves available, if only to listen.

These two clicked more when the talk turned to Gaelic football. The priest still played for his local club team. Jonsie could see a younger version of Father Peadar. So he told him the story about the priest who togged out to play rough with the college boys. He promised to follow this priest's example. The man was taking up a teaching post in a secondary school. He hastily added that it wasn't the one Jonsie was 'doing a runner' from. That statement gave them a laugh.

As if they both thought it was an okay thing to do, the priest insisted on driving him all the way to the gangway, where you walk up onto the ferry. He had the ticket purchased for him before he knew it. Jonsie said he didn't need it, and showed him twenty-six pounds, which was the amazing sum collected for him. They were good lads at the back of it all.

'Joe, is there any way I can talk you out of what you're doing?'

'No, I'm going.'

'There must be something you want to stay in Ireland for, is there nothing you can do here anymore?'

Jonsie often wondered later in life what made him say what he did, inferring some notion of football, when he only played twice in boarding school. It was a very farfetched thought indeed.

'Yes, I would like to play for the Cavan team.'

'But you're going in the wrong direction for that one, Joe.' He was happy hearing that. 'Come back with me and I'll drive you all the way home to your town. You can pursue your football ambitions from there.'

'No, I want to have an adventure; to see where it takes me. Thank you for everything, goodbye.' He would like to give him respect by calling him 'Father', but he couldn't say that anymore. Not even for a good one.

He walked up the ship's gangway and looked back at the priest wiping his eyes with a white handkerchief. He felt sorry, and it made his tears flow too. All that pent-up emotion was pouring forth, and this kind young priest tried his best to save a lost soul. If it was a fair world, he would have succeeded. But it wasn't and he didn't. Not all priests were badly damaged. This was one of the good ones. Life doesn't always treat the best with the respect they deserve either.

Jonsie's first thought on entering the bowels of this cross-channel ferry was finding a place to be alone. He'd been advised to look for the Irish builder's labourer's lot, travelling back to Scotland. They were easy to recognise: tweed caps, long wide sideboards down their granite jaws, with a shoulder swagger displaying their arrogant attitude. They could handle any kind of rough stuff. He latched on to the end of a few like that. These men carried out this travel routine casually, like a trip to the pub. They were hardened individuals, with big weather-beaten hands carrying small bags, tied with twine, going down a wide stairwell, for more drink. He headed after them cautiously.

He ended up in a big bar room full of more hard-looking men with pints of Guinness lined up on the counter. They were roaring with laughter with each other. There was a visible absence of ladies present. They must have found a safer place to go. It was like a Wild West saloon you'd see in the pictures, but it was very real and intimidating; one of Jonsie's favourite places to be.

The long bar had a brass rail all around the bottom for putting a foot on. He located an empty chair next to a table at the very back. He'd see everything from here.

An older man with a red face and a bush of grey unkempt hair gave him his orders. It could be why he sat down beside him.

'When you're over at the bar, young fellow, get me a pint of Guinness, I'll give you the money for it. My legs are all sore again from walking.'

It was not Josie's intention to go near the bar; he never drank alcohol, and wasn't about to start now. He looked at the man and told him the truth. 'I don't drink, but I'll get your pint, when you give me the money first, to pay for it.' The man glared at him, handing over a red ten-shilling note. 'I want all my change back.' He said roughly.

He must have been done over by a young fellow before.

Jonsie got an earful of what was going on, waiting for the pint. The characters lined up at the counter were 'indigenous species' of their own making. They spoke a dialect lingo, in a garbled drivel among themselves. There were some Gaelic language expressions he knew, but he couldn't understand any of it.

They looked outdated in their appearance, with pint glasses in their rough hands, cigarettes dangling from their lips. They could talk to each other without removing them. Holding a hand ready for defensive duties must have been a primary consideration.

The brawling call rang clear in these men's ears. It could flare up with the wrong word, uttered in careless exchange. Maybe something in jest could be misinterpreted. Some of them were getting primed early. The tense atmosphere of fair day in Flanagan's pub in Cody's Cross was there; Jonsie's perceptions for hell raisers was sharp.

He was glad to sit down at the table again, to tell the old boy,

'That fellow at the counter's going to start a fight.'

'Which fight will he start? There'll be several of them, before we dock in Glasgow. The same every crossing, I've been doing it for thirty years now, never changes, singing first, fights after. Tough men, tough men I can tell you. That's why I stay away from them.'

He took a closer look at him then, leaving down his pint. 'You're young travelling on your own aren't ya?' He said accusingly, as if he'd caught him doing something wrong.

The boy didn't even register a thought. The truth spilled freely. 'No, I'm twenty, my father was a small jockey too, same as me. They thought he was ten when he was thirty. I'm going over to ride racehorses in Scotland.'

'Be Jesus Christ, so y'ar,' said the man. 'Isn't it my luck to meet you?'

The man was visibly impressed with the jockey in his company. Now everything was different. He stuck out his hand for a shake before grabbing the racing paper out of his pocket, the same one Jonsie had noticed when he sat down first. That's what had given him the whole jockey idea.

The man fumbled for a pencil in his pocket. His fortune, it seemed, was taking a turn for the best, at last. An old fortune teller had told him recently that his luck was changing. He was getting ready to believe her right now.

'We're going down the horses, me and you; you'll tell me all you know from the racing yards. Bunch of crooks, set it all up among them, isn't that right, little jockey, eh? Tell me so.'

He glared at him, in case he had the nerve to disagree with him.

'Right, sir,' replied Jonsie the jockey. He knew all about talking to trainers as well. This man was in charge of several different characters. And they all appeared agitated by the journey. He might get a careless box in the mouth from one of them.

He'd figured that filling him up with winners should keep him quiet. What else could he do? He knew the entire racing lingo from listening in the pub. And this old boy was ready to believe what the jockey said, without any questions.

By the time the ferry docked several fights had broken out. The bar staff close the shutters half way across the water and the brawling took off on its own. It left nothing to the imagination. The Wild West was only a movie; this was the real thing. And it was both thrilling and frightening all in the one go.

Jonsie was still watching it all when the police arrived to spoil everything. Some would be arrested, a night in a cell to cool them down until the next time. Then, like a bolt from the blue, the dreaded seasickness hit him. He puked straight out in front of him, a big gush, like a firehose. The old man's overcoat was treated to the entire contents. Would this surprise gift be worth all the winners when he woke up and the jockey was gone?

He moved quietly on deck for a breath of fresh air; he wouldn't be meeting him again. He'd never bet on a horse in his life, but he knew how to talk about it. Lying was all about confidence. He was beginning to understand the rules now. What rules? The ones you make up yourself, learning to tell lies are the best rules.

He walked up confidently to a man in uniform on the street.

'Sir, how do I get to Paisley Road please?'

Having read the address from Timer's letter, he was getting excited being so close. Saying the name out was empowering.

The man told him how to get there. 'Ten minutes on that bus and you're there. Ask the driver where to get off'.

Jonsie found the man's thick Glaswegian accent difficult to understand, but he got the bus number. And he thanked him. This was his first time ever in a big town, except for the few times his father had taken him to Dublin, around Christmas. Then he wouldn't let him out of the van until he held him by the hand, in case he got lost.

This traffic he was caught up in now was worse than Dublin, but he would be with his old friend Timer soon; they could laugh, recalling days in boarding school. That place where the demon priest Nasser plagued the lives of those he saw fit to torment. Timer would enjoy hearing how Jonsie had left him lying on his back with the blood pumping out of his lip, which was not sneering any more.

The bus windows were left open so the air could circulate, and a powerful, pungent smell filled the air. It could be the sea or river, smoke or something else; he wasn't sure. There was a dense mist hanging, no shift in it. Not like the dreamy mists he remembered from the horse wagon days, so far away now. This mist appeared to have no purpose in life, hanging there, waiting because it couldn't get away, resigned to its fate.

'Paisley Road next stop,' the driver shouted across in his direction, without looking over at him.

The road was very wide, and intimidating. The big Georgian houses reminded Jonsie of Dublin again, his meagre source of reference. So he'd seen the like before.

He took out Timer's letter for a look; Paisley Road, written beneath Glasgow in Timer's scrawled handwriting. That was all the information he was given. It was meant to be scant. There was no full written address, in detail.

At that dreadful moment, Jonsie realised he had no proper information about the place he was looking for. There were dozens of tall houses on both sides of the road. He was on the verge of a panic attack. But, steadying himself, he took an older way out of it. Nice and cool like the lakeside pool. 'If you cannot find your way, always ask a well-dressed man or a middle-aged woman for directions,' He'd been told, in this past innocent way of understanding worrying times.

He stopped a man passing him on the pavement. 'Excuse me sir, I have this address, but I can't understand it'.

The man took the letter, smiling. 'You have no number for this property. Paisley Road is miles long. This is only a small part of it, no help to you. Sorry, better contact the person that wrote the address.'

'That's the person I'm visiting.'

'Then you do have a problem,' he said. 'Good luck to you.' He passed on his way, with the smile intact.

Jonsie wouldn't be smiling for a while. He looked around for a bench seat, but there weren't any. He kept on walking.

'Where's the biggest street in Glasgow, sir?' he enquired of the next well-dressed man.

'Sauchiehall Street, young laddie, over there in that direction, five minutes' walk will get ye' there.'

So he got a more hopeful indicator from Glasgow's busy street. It wasn't just for passing through, on route to somewhere else.

This was a proper destination in itself. He was pleased to discover a small café on a side street corner, a homely, comforting place. He sat down just inside the window. The young girl attending her customers was older than him. He'd begun to notice things. She wore a blue apron with white stripes and a wide tartan skirt, and had a mop of flaming red hair tied back in a ponytail from her freckled face.

'Lunch is over for today sir,' she said, a pleasing curl in her tone of voice.

'Could I have something else to eat, please?'

'You can have a plate of chips, they're still hot, but the kitchen is closed.' She looked at him. 'I can cook some sausages for you though, if you're hungry. I'm not very busy at the moment.'

'Okay, I'll have the sausages and chips please.'

She was a friendly young woman with a caring manner. It was great luck to have discovered such a place.

He had a lot to think about now. Where he was going to stay and how much it would cost was his immediate concern. He ate his sausages and chips slowly. Thinking about his parents, the dreaded feeling of guilt returned to bother him again. He could visualise them around the table in tears, reading his letter. His mother would be heartbroken, and he was sorry about that. He'd written a long letter telling them everything. The hardest thing he'd ever had to do. He hoped sometime they'd understand that he was driven to it, and they would all be great friends again. He was conscious of the pain he'd caused. One day he would make it up to them. He could never have returned, expelled from school. Going home in disgrace was something he wouldn't do.

When he thanked the girl and left the café, he turned right, walking until he came to a narrow street going up a hill. He followed that street all the way to the top. There was a small church on a corner, with a little graveyard around it that wasn't being used anymore. That's what he was looking for; somewhere no one else would voluntarily go.

There was a chain on the gate, but a stone wall with wide empty cracks let him climb it easily to jump into the stillness.

Some people had left here centuries ago. It said so on the headstones. Their spirits wouldn't object to some quiet company in the moonlight. He'd be comfortable in their presence too.

The long grass fell over on its side like a windswept meadow; a scattering of poppies flared here and there, old headstones leaning in their scattered ways, forward like drunks at a party or tilted sideways, dancing a jig. He saw it like that. There was magic in this silent place of the long departed. Some of their souls would spend time alone in another world. They might be expecting someone anytime. He could feel their spirit mood around him, and it was all good down here.

A solitary tree in the corner reached for the sky. Its branches spread low, covering the best place in Glasgow for a sleep. Peaceful and calm like a lake underneath, a purpose of its own. This was some discovery, all right.

There would be reflections in this strange urban jungle too, where everything you saw didn't quite fit into the way you saw it. He'd learn it off, walking. He was sure of one thing' his main man would turn up, if he walked around for long enough. In the silent care of this departed company all around him, he gave his best belief that anything was possible. It would happen for him.

His first few days were spent learning the lie of the land. There didn't appear to be anyone looking after the church now. The banana skins and apple cores he kept together for a bin on the street. When the long grass went over he combed it out again with his fingers. He kept changing direction, and left no track. The spot under the tree was bedded with dry leaves. He scooped them around him like a blanket. The quietness brought back memories that made him feel good. He washed, after using the toilet every morning, in the café. He couldn't say the street name properly; it was Main Street in his mind now, to make things easier. The girl's name was Connie. She was like a nice quiet country girl in Ireland, caring, and wise to the ways of the world.

He told her his father called him Jonsie, because he reminded him of a famous Irish freedom fighter. The name stuck. But his real name was Joe. And straight away she said 'I like Joe best, it's more grown up'.

Not for the first time, Jonsie was at odds with Jonsie. It didn't rest easy when talking with a girl. He hoped she was seeing him in an older light. When the place emptied, she sat down for a cup of tea and wanted to know about things he didn't want to discuss. But conversation would have to stay civil because he needed someone now more than anything else. He would tell her what she liked.

'Why did you come to Glasgow from Ireland?' she enquired.

He told her about the mix-up with the address on Paisley Road. He was hoping to get the correct address from home. College was never mentioned; it made him sound too young. He was more comfortable talking about his father's pub in Ireland. All the work, the hours he put in behind the bar, the painting and cleaning he did, working hard from dawn to dusk.

He brushed off her question, 'where are you living?' waving his hand back to the general direction of the graveyard a few miles away. 'Up there beside Renfrew Street,' he replied, remembering the name of a corner he passed on his travels every day.

'Oho, gone all expensive, have we?' She mimicked something that didn't sound good, and she was continuously eyeballing him.

Quietly wondering why he made such a mess of the bathroom, she had to clean up after him every morning. The place this boy lived in must be without sanitary facilities. She saw him walking around the street, so he didn't have a job either. These Irish boys were supposed to be great workers. Her father wanted her to hire some help for cleaning the toilets, front windows, and floor. Her father wasn't able anymore with his back. He was waiting for a call to go into hospital, for a disc operation. There were several jobs for this boy; that's why she wanted to know more about her new customer. She noticed he had very little money when he was paying. He was a quiet young chap with not much to say. She felt that she could trust him.

She discussed with her father this new Irish 'customer' who sat and said nothing. He told her to offer him a job; he was bound to work cheap if he had nowhere to go.

'You could do some jobs around here,' she said casually.

Jonsie was delighted to take up the offer of meals for doing a few cleaning jobs. It would break up the day for him.

The snow fell on Glasgow with a stiff breeze carrying it from the

Highlands, an unforgiving harsh feel to it; maybe nature's way of filtering the air. But the smog was getting thicker. He didn't leave the shelter of the graveyard tree for a while. The light shoes wouldn't last a trip around the centre in heavy snow. What would he do if the only shoes he had fell off his feet?

He sat on the tree, the coat tucked around him, thinking about the past. Times he had at home with his family foremost in his mind. He missed them so much. The loneliness it brought to bear on him made him cry. The stash of fruit was gone, and all his money. Hard times were setting in. He was so numbed with cold he didn't care about anything anymore. It was time to snap out of it. He must get down to the café or he'd freeze into a ball.

He would never light a fire in the graveyard, it wasn't respectful.

He'd started doing a few jobs in the cafe. Her father was an arrogant, unpleasant man who made the girl's life miserable. She wasn't allowed out to enjoy herself. Now she was starting to talk to her new employee, with no one to communicate with either. They had that much in common.

Breakfast could be had for cleaning the toilets and washing the big window on the front. That was the arrangement, when he worked he got food. There was never any money changing hands. She couldn't afford to pay for help with the café's regular customers on holiday, she said. Anytime her father was present, she wasn't as friendly towards Jonsie. He didn't like her father, who called him some Scottish name that meant he was a child. 'Be sure to work the wee bairn hard.' He said this for his daughter's ears. It might have been to discourage any personal feelings developing between them. But there was no fear of that happening.

He'd been walking around the same circuit all morning, up one side of Main Street, down the other. The paper boy was yelling out Saturday's news. He would be keeping his eye on the matinee. When the afternoon show was finished the patrons emerged from the glittering façade of the cinema, crowding the pavement outside the door. Jonsie had been doing the rounds for weeks. He'd figured that one day he'd meet up with Timer here.

When he heard Timer's shrill, excited voice, he thought he was hearing things at first. There he was standing on the cinema step in front of him, holding court. He was hanging out with a girl who was trying desperately to get away from his attempts to kiss her, in broad daylight. Her height saved her when she arched back.

Jonsie laughed at the sight of Timer's clumsy amorous attempts. The curse of being small, he'd told him often enough in the past. With pure delight he ran towards him, shouting his name. Timer's jovial look turned to one of horror; Jonsie was the last person in the world he wanted to see.

It took longer for this to register with his friend. The true extent of this rebuff would soon be revealed to him. This was not the coming together he'd fantasised about for two whole weeks. The strong swear words used by Timer explained everything. Jonsie should have stayed at home.

He had to wait for the bus journey to Paisley road before he got a full explanation for Timer's lack of interest. This visit to Glasgow was a gross error of judgement. He proceeded to elaborate when they arrived at the flat. With his three roommates listening in, he told Jonsie how he'd been getting unwanted attention from 'that crowd' in Ireland. They were blaming him for everything. His father had threatened to stop paying his college fees.

Jonsie's father Bill was on his case too. The phone down the hall never stopped ringing for him. He talked about his son's untimely departure from school, and then accused Timer of instigating the whole thing with a letter he had written before his son absconded. By all accounts this correspondence included an invitation to dump college life and come over to Glasgow. When Timer denied all the accusations, he had Sergeant Nelson threatening to inform the police in Glasgow. They would be paying him a visit if he was sheltering a runaway from Ireland.

Timer knew one thing; he'd keep away from Jonsie. There could be no loyalty shown for memories from the past. Things were more serious now. It was full of responsibilities in this grown-up world.

'This hospital's a good place to get lost for a while,' he said. He pushed a newspaper under his nose, pointing to the advertisement in big lettering. 'Boys of fifteen required as student nurses immediately.'

'This is the perfect move for you. When you get some money together, you can do as you like. You'll have a place to hide, that's what's important now. You can't stay here any longer. There's no other way. As students, we have no money either. You won't get another job in Glasgow anyway. You have only one chance at making things right, and this is it? So go for it. You see, there's a requirement to produce ID that you're over seventeen, if you want to start working here. It's the law.'

Jonsie was always easily led by this little fellow, and he listened to his advice. He was clever enough to know that there wasn't another option available to him, but he hadn't even the bus fare to get to this hospital.

'The hospitals near here, I'll go there with you,' said Timer. 'Just to make sure you get on okay. I can do some of the talking. In fact, we'll go there tomorrow. You've just arrived and don't know any better. They might be impressed by your enthusiasm. There are a few things to do first.'

Timer immediately penned another letter to his friend Joe Flanagan in Ireland. This time the message was somewhat different. He encouraged him to travel to Glasgow, urging him to apply in person for the enclosed advertised position. He made it sound as if student nurse was the boy's long time career ambition.

Then he cut the advertisement out of the paper, so Jonsie could explain how it was specifically in pursuit of this job he'd travelled to Glasgow.

'We'll discuss the story of why you chose this profession on our way there. It'll be fresh in your head when they talk to you. Don't forget to let them see this letter. Hand it over with the envelope. The date on the front makes it all appear authentic. That advertisement has been in the paper for several weeks. The whole story fits perfectly. That's why we must use it now. Joe, I must have this letter back. I don't want it to get out there, so I can be branded again as some sort of a coaxer in chief so you could run away from school to end up in Glasgow. That's not happening. I'm in trouble enough with you already.'

Jonsie had something bothering him. He couldn't visualise what kind of a student nurse he was going to be. He wanted to hear more about it, to understand where he was going.

'Timer, what about this nurse job, what will I have to do?'

'Caring for people, like a woman nurse, except you're looking after men. It's a high security prison hospital, probably full of tough characters. That's why I'm sure they will want to take you on immediately. You have imposing size, for the job. The fact that you're Irish only adds to your appeal for this position.'

'Why is that?'

'They'll think that you're afraid of nothing. That might be another positive reason for giving you a job, as long as you convince them you rushed to Glasgow when you heard about these vacancies. If they think you're a suitable candidate, you'll get the job. So now is your time to prove your worth. And remember you set out for Glasgow immediately, when I sent you the advertisement from the newspaper. That's why I have such an interest in getting you sorted.

'It will take them a while to discover the college's bad news. By the time they find out you're a runaway you'll have a few weeks' wages under your belt. By then you might prove to be the best student nurse in the hospital, who knows? But if you're fired, don't come back here near us. You must go down to the south of England. Your father knows someone there, in Luton. He's been in contact with him already. I wrote all the details down, with his address, when your father called it out on the telephone.

'He warned me that you'd turn up here sometime, if you were that determined. Unfortunately he was correct. But don't take my attitude too much to heart; it's just the way it has to be. I cannot take risks that would draw attention to me. The constant harassment I've had to endure for the past few weeks has been relentless. It's affecting my ability to study. Naturally everybody's worrying about you back at home. I think you should give them a telephone call, soon as you can. It would be preferable to make this contact when you're far away from me. My father is threatening to pull the plug on my fees for college if I don't toe the line.'

'We haven't got a telephone at home yet, Timer.'

'Yes I know, but the Garda said you could call the barracks. You must arrange a time to talk with your parents in the station, the cops will organise them to receive the call.'

'Ok I might do that, sometime.'

'Look Flanagan, I feel bad about all this. However, this is how it must be. It's a difficult situation for us all now. You were great craic for the time we spent in college; we had some good laughs together. I will never forget those days. Long as I live.

'You're very independent, tough to hang out with. I don't think you were ever meant to be easy company. Not for the faint hearted. There's something different about you all right but right now, it's more nutter than genius. I hope it finishes up good. Run through the years your own way, but keep me out of the chase. It's bound to be a mad one. '

Now take this pen and write a letter to your parents, with the wrong address. Tell them you couldn't find me in Glasgow. Say you're looking for a job, but don't mention hospital yet. I will post the letter for you after I read it. You can crash out on the couch. It's a one night stand only set-up.'

Jonsie had a question for his only friend. 'Are you dumping me in a mental home in Glasgow, Timer?'

'Afraid so, it's the only place I can think of that suits you. There's money, a place to stay, or a graveyard with nothing, take your pick. All this annoyance around you is too much for me. You've put me in a tight spot here. Help me out will you, disappear for a while. And find yourself a better place, Joe.'

CHAPTER 10

When Sergeant Nelson informed Bill and Hanna about their son running away from boarding school, they were absolutely devastated. Nobody knew where he was. Maybe making his way home, he ventured to say. They would have to wait and see what happened next. He was speaking softly to console them. They listened to the painful account of their worst nightmare and Hanna was sobbing, her shoulders slouched. The policeman pledged his assistance anyway he could, before leaving the pub. He was helpful.

'You know where to find me,' he assured them.

Sitting in the kitchen now, they were wondering, was it something they did wrong? How could they tell anyone about this, portraying their son in such a bad light? There was shame attached to the predicament. They tried consoling each other, sobbing pitifully, and tears flowing down their cheeks. There was no strong one taking charge of things this time; they'd have to do battle together.

The boarding school refused to take responsibility. Their son was widely known to have a wild streak that made him difficult, unmanageable. It had all happened in his upbringing and that was it. There was nobody going to face down the priest's solicitors. Bill couldn't accept that he'd lost all his money. That was the worst part. He couldn't care less if his son never came home again.

The couple's way of interacting changed. They entered a spiral of disregard for each other, far removed from their usual happy go lucky way. Instead of bringing them closer together, it drove them further apart. And that distance didn't sit well with either of them. Everything became more difficult, and worst of all, the humorous eye contact between them was gone. Hanna prayed for God's help. Bill entertained his listeners spreading the wrong word: 'Flanagan's son disappeared without trace; ran away from the college they sent him to like the mad young fellow he was. He'll never be seen again'. That was only the start of it.

Bill blamed himself sometimes when he felt the pain of remorse. He had just dumped his son there, alone, at a boarding school kip where you wouldn't drop off a mongrel dog, but worst of all was the cost of it. Hundreds of pounds, he told them. They would quote his words, piling more anxiety on the story.

Then a phone call to the guard's barracks from a woman in Scotland broke the silence. And it brought some consolation. Their son was working in her café. Bill wanted to bring him back, for all the trouble he had caused.

Hanna thought otherwise. 'No, don't go near Scotland, you'd fight with him. And he'd never come home. Let's leave things as they are Bill. I'm going to write him a letter to let him know about Miss Kelly's sad passing, they were never best friends. So it won't keep him awake at night. Sgt Nelson said he can get a postal address for me. I will be very nice and understanding in the correspondence. He needs some kindness, Bill; remember he must be struggling now.'

Mr Whyte, the newsagent, told Bill he'd received correspondence from a mental hospital in Glasgow, seeking a character reference for his son, a recent employee. He thought it better to let him know.

Bill was reluctant to discuss this private topic. The kind newsagent picked up on the delicate nature of the matter quickly. There would be no mention of it anymore.

Bill told them in the bar that Jonsie was confined to a mental home in Scotland. It was the only place that could hold him. But he swore it was none of his doing. This young fellow would never do what he was told. Everyone in the whole town knew that.

'One bad thing after another, such is life,' Hanna complained. Then she found a new story, the way it really happened. Jonsie was working in a restaurant in Glasgow now, she said. He had gone over there with his college friend. They planned opening a business together when they had finished. Nobody believed her caring motherly tale. But they wouldn't upset her either. She had enough on her plate already.

There were more positive things taking shape in the town. The Yank had put a good construction crew together. There was major work being done, and the town was changing.

There were enough big strong fellows hanging around to dig foundations and mix concrete. They wouldn't cost much either. Work was scarce. He had appointed Louie as foreman, under his own strict supervision.

It was just like old times for this Yank guy. Building was part of his makeup, with more important plans in his head for the future. He had given this town a lot of consideration for a very long time. Cody's Cross was due a manly makeover. A man with a gripe could fix that. And he wouldn't be deterred from completing the task.

A well-appointed project in Mrs Wilson's field contained three individually designed bungalows on their own separate grounds. That complemented the town, with its landscaped greenery. The doctor's wife oversaw every rose bush planted, like a big spacious garden around her private house. The complex was named Dr Wilson's Close. His widow had insisted upon that before agreeing to the development plan. She had a nice modern home now, with her new-found friends either side of her. Life was good.

WT erected a wooden bench seat on the river bank in loving memory of their Betty, a wonderful caring person who had passed on prematurely. She would never be forgotten. They promised.

The complex was well maintained by Louie. He had worked on building sites in England over the years and could turn his hand to anything. This man might be a ruffian under the influence of alcohol, but sober, he was a meticulous worker. They called him 'the bull' among themselves, on account of his great strength. Blimey had employed him as a doorman in a cinema he had managed in England back in the day. But there was a serious altercation and Louie finished up in jail. He was blamed by his employer for the bad luck that followed him.

They never spoke to each other for years after. Now it was just a hostile nod of the head.

The 'town development committee' came about over a few drinks one night, when the 'three musketeers' were projecting the town's future ambitions. These residents wanted to ensure their input in any expansion, but Mrs Wilson felt the cause might be better served with more women taking an interest in the process. She was plotting to redress this imbalance in her own time.

Hanna, a fighter, would be a perfect fit. Susan placed her in high regard. And the newsagent's classy daughter was back at home.

Freddy Brown's bar was sold to pay for a private nursing home. He wouldn't sign the sales document for anything other than a Protestant buyer. He was full of religious intent to his last gasp. But it wouldn't matter what religion wiped his ass now, he had Alzheimer's. Even in the end game the take game is the make game. You can be any religion you'd like to take with you.

The Yank brought his son and wife to Ireland to manage the old pub for him. These two renegades, Mack and Molly, were more interested in exotic action than business. A childless couple in their forties, the pursuit of fun was their sole interest. Making money had eluded them so far on account of that. It might be the main reason why they were here.

It could be a short tenure.

They left Freddy Brown's old weather-beaten name over the door, a good move. But they would be running their pub differently. The only experience these two had of the licensed business involved high times spent rollicking with like-minded free-spirited types.

It was all fun and games on wayward street for these two. They didn't know what end of them was up. Or care who it was up for.

Yank fitted into the community perfectly. Like one of their own, a fine-looking man in his early sixties with short thick hair turning grey, and he seemed to have no religious prejudice, a good reason for liking him. Drover and Blimey didn't have any religion either, but no one cared, you couldn't like either of them even if you wanted to. And they wouldn't be trying to buy up the whole town, giving a few pounds to deserving people.

Mrs Wilson's old house lay sad and empty on the street now, but she was pleased to have so many good memories. And they would always be sitting over the road there, where she could see them. Now she had a beautiful garden of flowers all summer with different plant shades all winter. She was big into her rose bushes and she minded them like the children she had never had, with special names on all of them to suit their place in family life. Her neighbours kept her spirits up and times were very good.

They were known as the 'three musketeers' in the pub. Not some title she would ever have imagined getting years ago. But back then she was innocent. Now she was free to do what she liked. Susan took to this new lease of life that brought her out of herself and into the middle of everything. She was happy once again.

She was appointed as the official town development committee secretary, consulted about everything, but when it came to a vote, she was always outnumbered. Three is awkward, they agreed. 'We will have to get bigger.' But she caught them winking then.

Susan was doing some looking on her own. Hanna was lined up already, and she was looking forward to her involvement. They enjoyed an occasional social get-together for girl talk. Sunday lunch had three sitting around the table now. She didn't have to pay a butcher's bill anymore, and she enjoyed the occasion.

By this time the Yank man's real connection to the town was well known. He had an unfortunate connection to the history of Cody's Cross. There was some sympathy as well as some resentment towards him from the older inhabitants.

WT schemed about his hotel project all the time now, encouraged by the Yank; he remembered him as Riso when he was young. Back then WT admired his tenacity, given the abuse he got.

The Yank expressed interest in this enterprise, if it was all signed up legally? Statue barred contractual limit must be part of the deal, he stipulated. But there was a more ambitious secret plan in Yank's head. The land behind the forge, on the other end of the river, was not for talking about. And he made sure it stayed that way, playing it down. He never encouraged discussion about it. He saw it as his.

WT could see opportunities around this fellow, without much risk. The Yank was the perfect fall guy for the wily hardware store operator. Everything would be played with him in mind, and after some lengthy discussion a partnership was struck. They would visit the solicitor to make it proper. 'My word is my bond' would do until then. So they shook hands on the deal.

The Yank suggested the best location for a hotel was on the steward's house site. The problem was getting Blimey to move out. There must be no cash incentive offer, as he might get greedy.

They would invite Major Cody to join the development committee, win him over as a first step. Having Blimey's house and picture hall levelled to the ground was paramount. That site was big enough for a fine property, in a picturesque location overlooking the river. A dozen bedrooms would do for a start.

WT knew how to encourage the Major's interest. His troublesome tenant Blimey could be relocated where more modest accommodation might suit his bad attitude. Nothing would benefit the town like a modern hotel, and most people would be expected to support this endeavour. Already tourists were spending good money visiting the big river. It was in everyone's interest to ensure they enjoyed a memorable stay. The positive message was spread around the community. Everyone bought into the idea of town development. Flash the politician, quick to embrace positives, was reined in too. Things always get more serious when money gets moved around. Some of it could drop off in places it wasn't intended for.

When Mrs Wilson found out about Yank's poverty stricken beginning, on that trip to the art show in Dublin, she took special interest in him. He had had 'a very complicated childhood, bless him'. And she wasn't that much older than him.

Those early resentments turned him into a driven man. He explained how the shrink in America told him, 'Control your mind. We can live our dreams if we believe in what we're doing and put in the hard work'.

Yank confided in Susan about the plans he envisaged for the town, and told her all about the hotel project, so she had time to think more about it.

WT was delighted when he discovered the Yank's true identity. He'd always admired the dirty little tough guy from out the road, living where nobody cared, dumped out of his house to sleep in a ditch. His well-tuned survival instincts had helped him do well in America, with some money to back it up now, it appeared.

Judging by how he got the housing project finished on time, he was a good builder. Yank was ambitious, a trait very close to WT's heart. He was looking forward to working with him. One day they would say it was WT Flanagan who had laid the ground for a new, modern town. He had secret ambitions of becoming the first Lord Mayor of Cody's Cross. For debate at a committee meeting and he'd block any ambitions the Major displayed for the post with a cautious word in his ear. He must remember the influence he had over him; about this adventurist tryst they had had years ago. WT was there that memorable night, looking at them. They waylaid him into their little soirée, to see if he wanted to partake. But no, WT was straight as a die in all sexual activities. The sooner it was over the better, that's how he liked to perform.

The Major insisted the rented lady could ride him around the room, with a horse's saddle on his back. WT was not the game playing type. Blow the load and get on the road, fast and furious. The old stuff was the good stuff. But he was drunk enough to laugh, enjoying the whole performance, when it was carried out bare-assed in front of him. He had no problem being a spectator.

It started off tame enough, with goblets of port wine in front of the big log fire, before graduating to a steeplechase in the bedroom that should have finished up with a steward's enquiry. It wasn't this lady's first private gallop in the Major's field. She took her time fitting the saddle on him; letting him quiver with the touch of leather on his big white buttocks. When she sat in the saddle on his back, he moved around the floor on all fours whinnying like a horse. He never complained once when she whipped his buttocks, leaving red marks.

Major Cody would prefer his old riding associate WT to keep these bedroom secrets to himself. The Major was conscious of his image now; he hoped to get appointed Lord Mayor of the town called after his family name. He'd be in a better position there to scrutinize all offers for any development to his own property. If the right project came along, his financial worries would end. That was the main interest he had in town development.

WT was living in comfort, plotting the future, realising plans he had before Yank came to town; they were a clear possibility now. It seemed all he had to do was encourage him.

He looked out the window at the chestnut tree. 'WT loves Betty', the wood carving said. It was true to this day. A sturdy bench seat was in the same spot under it again, like it used to be.

To double the population of Cody's Cross in a few years, that was the town development's aim. There was a mobile bank service calling to the town now, every Friday. And to Mrs Wilson's sheer delight the manager was a young lady about Lucy's age. As it unfortunately transpired, age was their only resemblance.

There were people with bank accounts now who had never even stood in a bank before. Mrs Wilson had secured her dream home with the 'field deal'. She wasn't such a soft touch when it came to negotiating her plan. She confided in her new friend the bank manager, a religious lady, but more gossipmonger than holy night.

WT liked Hanna, his daughter-in-law, and she would be a perfect addition to the committee. She wouldn't go against her husband's father. Family values were first in order, he was sure.

Susan was alarmed sometimes by the sound of intrigue emanating from some of these town development meetings. Although her concerns were somewhat allayed by Major Cody joining the fold. He was an honest broker, in her opinion, and essential to future developments; a cultured man's input should be honourable. He gave the whole organization the credibility that only upper class can bring. She was convinced about that.

WT approached the Major to chair the new 'town development committee'. The military officer was well capable of grabbing any opportunity he could; with his firm conviction, they were all peasants he could exploit. But he was never part of military intel-corps, as he frequently fantasised. A low ranking signals outfit, based at home, was as far as he got. But if you asked him about his army achievements, you'd get loaded with intelligence intrigue. His imagination knew no bounds, a bit like Mack from Freddie's pub, only in a worse accent.

Getting rid of the troublesome picture hall proprietor would be high on the Major's list. The estate was badly in need of funds, and demand was bound to increase for his holdings. That potential financial bonanza could present some of his fellow committee members with opportunity as well.

Yank cautioned them about the Major's 'false respectability'. Susan was prepared to change things around. Her way for getting things done had a ruthless edge to it, in spite of her nice way. She was precise and very patient, a deadly combination. Hanna wasn't far behind with that considered approach of hers, in tune with everything going on. She was very pleased that Sergeant Nelson and her husband had become more respectful towards each other. Since the trouble with their son had first begun, things had settled when concern took hold. Caring had replaced glaring, for the time being, at least.

The Politician was taking credit for things. Getting the mobile bank to the town, his girlfriend was the new manager. The hurried phone installation in the pub was down to him too. There was a waiting list of a few years. He wanted to impress Yank more than anyone else, as he knew about future plans. Things were starting to look up for him. It was time to change his car. He'd let the garage owner know that luck had come to him as well. There was a bit in it for everyone, as he always promised them, if they voted for him. The promise was kept this time.

Drover called on 'mystical powers' when he got into it. His witchery palaver was full of superstitious beliefs. Specially tailored for vulnerable minds, to carry the magic of olden times, the departed were still there, he'd say. With scores left unsettled, troubled souls roamed freely. Religion had them scared of the hereafter. But he said it was 'here now.' Time to make amends. He was there to save them from hell; Drover knew the story.

Everyone should communicate with the souls departed. There were only a few special people chosen. They attended tea drinking 'affairs' in his house, where they listened spellbound to his ramblings. They believed him. Some of his old stories were true.

The 'curse of the yew tree' was one of those. Long ago, the Major's favourite horse had dropped dead after chewing on the yew tree's bark; Drover told them all about it. 'The bull went berserk after chewing on it; he attacked my grandfather, trying to kill him.'

The Major was consumed with rage about this 'bad luck' tree. So he banished it off the estate. He got them to build a big stone wall to cut the field off. It was destined to become part of the town instead. 'That's how the Cody's Cross curse came about, and it still resides here among us,' Drover said. 'Rituals under the devil's lair', they whispered. In times of woe, they blamed it for sheltering them. The bad luck that came upon them was part of the yew tree curse. And it was blamed for all their misfortune.

Drover was the sole keeper of this cursed tale. He knew the history of events from the past. His father had told him about bad blood between these people going back generations. There were resentments there, smouldering discontent. Some wanted to burn the Manor House down, preferably with the Major inside it. There were only a few people not beholden to him. Drover was one of those 'free people'. His influence came from that. And they couldn't but accept, if he chose to invite someone to his house. 'Even Betty Flanagan drank tea with him,' they whispered. 'It finished her in the end, God rest her soul.'

But there was always someone listening, just to spread trouble. And they were all at it. It didn't matter if it was true or not if it sounded right for making trouble.

Bill was looking at the 'mobile bank' parked in front of his pub. Flash the politician just had a whiskey before going in to chat with the bank manageress. He wondered if she had given him the money for the car. That's why he was drinking so much with her lately. She was fond of a drop after work too. Wasn't she lucky to have a driver collecting her?

He only agreed to that mobile location for the business it brought the pub. The bank manageress's name was Miss Blackstock, from Belfast. She was reputed to favour loans for protestant people, so Flash told her he was one, even though he had no religion. He kept his best intentions honest for funerals only. If they figured out you were faking everything, they'd never vote for you again. Politics made no excuse for having genuine belief in anything that could soften you. Flash was doing his best to please her for all those reasons. If she loaned him some money for a car she might reach further if there was a property boom in the town. It was good business for her to have a direct link to government; Miss Blackstock knew the real story there.

CHAPTER 11

They headed out early in Glasgow, walking through side streets all the way to the hospital. There was a tense urgency of purpose driving them. Timer chose this high awareness time to rehearse their proper story, discussing new bits to make it fit better.

Joe listened intently. There was nowhere else to go.

A stern-faced security guard at the main entrance directed them to the 'Victorian building'. It was standing slightly apart from the main hospital, with a small well-maintained car park in front of it. The sign sticking up in a grassy verge read 'STAFF ONLY'.

Timer was confident in his approach. While he explained the purpose of their visit in some detail, the lady at reception listened intently. Then she smiled, nodding her head knowingly at the shy friend who'd made such a desperate journey from Ireland for a student nurse's position in Scotland. 'He must be a good lad so,' she said to Timer.

During her discussion on the telephone, she became visibly irritated and didn't try to conceal this frustration. Letting her feelings on the matter be heard and raising her voice, she spoke sharply. 'There has been zero response Sam, for a month now. So there's not many left to choose from, is there?' She put down the phone abruptly, "The recruitment officer is down the corridor, first left, pointing in that direction. She ignored them.

'Mr Samuel Kerr' was the name on the door. This middle-aged man's curiosity had already been primed with the story of a boy coming all the way over from Ireland to work in his hospital. He wanted to hear more about that. With his pen poised expectantly over a blank sheet of paper, he waited and listened to Timer relating his rehearsed introduction.

And he gave the relevant information very precisely. His line about them being in college together aroused immediate interest. Mr Kerr smiled faintly for the first time. There was education on offer here, as well as clean-cut strength. And apparently, some amount of intelligence also. There were not many young boys rushing to take up the offer of working in this intimidating place. Timer went on to explain how his friend had travelled immediately on receipt of his letter, with hopes of employment. The recruitment officer took his time reading the letter he was handed. He even checked the envelope for a postage date. This man was intent on providing a solution.

'You didn't waste much time getting to Glasgow, did you Joe?'

'No sir, my father gave me the money to travel over with enough funds to return immediately, if my application was unsuccessful. He didn't want me wandering around a strange city with no job. '

'Why does a career in nursing appeal to you so much?'

'Both my uncles were male nurses; it was always discussed in our home, when I was growing up. You might say, part of our family's proud history.'

'I see. Do you know the hospital names your uncles worked in?'

'They worked in the same hospital in England. I can write to my father. We don't have the telephone in our home yet.'

'There's a form for you to fill in. It deals with your previous work experience, but if you've just left college that shouldn't take long. You say that playing football is one of your interests. We have a team here that could do with some fresh talent.'

Joe had been coached by Timer to handle questioning. He must always hold eye contact with whoever was talking to him and speak slowly. His Irish accent was just as confusing to strangers, as the Glaswegian accent was for him.

Mr Kerr spoke directly to Timer then.

'You can wait at reception while we continue with our wee discussion here. It will not take long to get the details processed. On account of these unusual set of circumstances we can make preliminary conclusions today. There will be a requirement for character references, from local police that know Joe in Ireland. That can't wait for too long.

'We must ensure there are people of good character in our employment, at all times.'

Timer had heard enough to convince him that the job application had been successful. He sat on one of the hard wooden chairs opposite the reception desk. It was never intended as a place of comfort.

The desk was the only other piece of furniture in this vast

expanse of emptiness. The floor was marked out like a draughtboard with black and white square tiles. The cold concrete walls were all painted with a black border all around the bottom half, and then white to the ceiling. There was one powerful light in the centre of it all that lit the entire room. It wasn't intended to be a hotel. The only comfort here was getting away from it.

The desk had a small reading lamp, so the reception lady could see what she was doing. He thought it strange, having no natural light in a working area during the day. There were two doors either side of the desk. The one on the left was down to Mr Kerr's office. The door on the opposite side was bigger, more robust. It had two large keyholes on the side. Timer wondered about that. He knew this place was where Glasgow's hardest inmates finished up if they were taken ill in prison. One of the lads had told him this hospital was a very tough place to end up in. How Flanagan would get on was anybody's guess. He dismissed that caring notion as irrelevant. He liked his school friend, but he must keep away from him now. The boys sharing the flat didn't want him. He couldn't go against their wishes, there would be no one crashing out on the couch permanently.

When he saw his friend coming out the door with a broad smile on his face, he assumed the best. He took the piece of paper from his pocket in case he forgot. Even at this early stage he was covering himself for perceived misfortune in the future; staying ahead of the posse, was always his way. Timer knew how to gallop in a chase.

'I'm staying on here now Timer, thank you for everything. I told Mr Kerr about my luggage disappearing on the ferry like you suggested. It was a good thing to say. They're fitting me with a new outfit, trousers, shirts and black shoes, all I need.'

'That's great Joe, here's the address in Luton I was told to give you. You never know when you'd need it. We might meet up again for coffee in the town centre, sometime in the future. I'm always in there, have to rush back to the flat now though and get ready for a difficult class tomorrow morning.'

He'd have him out of his head before he got home.

There was a letter due to this Sergeant Nelson in Ireland. It would be no harm letting him know where the runaway was holed up. He couldn't have police calling around to his flat with his friends listening to the story. They wouldn't be impressed.

Joe was more inclined towards making an excuse for his school friend than finding fault with him. As far as he was concerned Timer had put himself out to help him in his hour of need. He got the message; his flat was not a place to visit. These friends of his were not cut from the same cloth as the Irish. They didn't understand the 'hundred thousand welcomes' like them.

He headed back into Mr Kerr's office. The recruitment officer wanted to introduce him to his new workmates. The door at the end of the corridor led into the staff canteen. A few people were sitting around tables having coffee. Mr Kerr encouraged him to engage with them. Joe was embarrassed being the centre of so much attention.

There were six small square tables in a row along the wall, covered with red oilcloth in floral designs and two chairs at each one. The small kitchen outlet was tucked neatly into the corner; at the very end, it looked like everyone helped themselves. Someone put coffee on the table in front of him. That he had never asked for. Mr Kerr explained that a woman came in to cook meals every day, and he proudly called out some of the menus.

Joe had forgotten about food. The inherent shyness within him came to the fore, so he only heard an odd bit of what was said to him. He nodded, saying nothing. Listening was hard enough. Trying to understand the accent was too much.

'Here is your new boss Joe, his name is Robert. Under his good guidance you'll learn everything there is to know about nursing sick people, and find out all about taking care of their needs.'

A young man got up from his chair, dark haired, with a lightly bearded face that had a fixed permanent smile.

'Hello Joe, I'm very pleased to meet you.'

Robert shook his hand vigorously. Then he held on with the other hand, for more sincerity of purpose, to reassure him. Joe hadn't expected so much enthusiasm. But this was his boss, so friendliness was a welcome beginning.

The head nurse fetched him another cup of coffee before sitting down again. Then the questions began coming at him. Every one different; where are you from? What age are you? Do you play football?

He latched on to that last question. But he soon discovered that the football they were into was not the same game he played. He didn't know anything about Glasgow Celtic. That soccer game wouldn't be allowed in Ireland. It had been banned by the GAA for many years as an undesirable foreign sport. But he couldn't say that.

The young lad appeared to take exception at his disinterest. He raised his voice to quiz him on this lack of knowledge. 'What kind of footballer are ye, don't know Celtic football club? Yer nay a Rangers supporter are ye?'

Joe sat there looking at him. He didn't know about Rangers either. Quietness settled in the room for a minute. Mr Kerr had been listening carefully to this interaction. He was taking stock of how the new boy handled the environment. And he came to his rescue, explaining a few facts to them.

'The football Joe plays in Ireland is not the one we know. The rules are completely different. I'm sure in his own time he'll tell you all about it. But Robert can show him to his room. He will want to settle in before any more discussions take place. He's most probably tired after his long journey. That ferry crossing can be exhausting when the sea is rough. Tomorrow morning he'll be working on your shift. Angus, you can become better acquainted then.'

At the end of the canteen, beside the kitchen, there was another door. It opened into a long hall with eight doors on the left side. A door across the bottom had TV room written on it. 'This is your new quarters Joe,' Robert told him, opening the last door to a spacious room. It had a wardrobe, wash basin, a toilet and a single bed. The place was spotless, like everywhere else. Robert continued explaining the layout of things.

'The bathroom is next to the TV room, you won't have far to go for a good soak. Mr Kerr told me your suitcase was stolen on the ferry. Bad luck that, but we have a rule, no jeans working the wards. You'll get a pair of trousers and two white shirts, black shoes are always required.

'The white coat like the one I'm wearing is compulsory. Some of the cost of this outfitting will be stopped from your salary every week, until it's paid off. You must have clean clothes for the ward tomorrow. We'll go to the supply room early, before starting work in the morning. So you had better get a good night's sleep.'

'Will do, thanks Robert.'

'Good, Joe. I might check in later on to make sure everything is all right for you. If you're asleep, I won't bother waking you up.'

Next morning the supply room in the main building was as busy as a high street clothes shop. Under Roberts's instruction the energetic young man behind the counter located everything in a short time. He praised the convenience of having a standard fit for the new student, Nurse Flanagan.

Being referred to as Nurse would grate on Joe's nerves. It wasn't like any aliases he'd ever imagined in former times. These experiences weren't coming from any past dream times. Nurse didn't feel the same as boxer, footballer or horseman.

Robert gave him two keys, one for the robust door at reception that opened both locks. The other was for the door after that, going into the ward. He told him 'never forget to lock all these doors'. The outside door was the last line of defence, he emphasised, if anyone got out of the ward. They could get into the hall area and escape from their place of confinement if that big door was left unlocked.

That information registered with Joe. It started him off security minded. He was a jailer so, with a ring of big keys hanging from his belt. It sounded tougher than nurse.

There was a door marked 'security'. Robert introduced him to two burly men in uniform inside before entering the ward. There were sixteen patients here, he explained, eight beds on either side. Joe got an instant flashback to the dormitory in boarding school. He'd much rather be here. That was the good part.

The nurse gave him privacy to change into work clothes before showing him around. Most patients were in bed continuously, he told him, and weren't much trouble. Then he made a flippant observation, which registered as a warning, in the ears of the new nurse; there were 'a few exceptions to every rule'. He'd remember those words.

'All eight patients on the right hand side are easy going and usually non-aggressive,' said the nurse. 'They have varying degrees of mental issues, but once they get their medication every day, they are no trouble. That's important to remember Joe, medication works. But if not dispensed properly, there will be problems. Those security guards are primarily for patients of the prison system. They are in the blue beds. And they can be difficult sometimes. Those beds on the right side, as you can see, are all white. The first four beds on the left hand side are blue; those patients require experienced nursing staff attention.

'Remember this; the last four beds in yellow colour are not suitable for student nurse care. They require the attention of two nurses. Do not go near any one of those, even if they demand your attention, unless I'm with you. Make sure you understand what I'm saying. This last bed here, Mr Mc Donald, is a very troubled man. Keep away from him until you get to know his ways. He'd spot your lack of experience, and use it against you.'

This man was in a crouched position, the pillows stacked up behind him. His bushy eyebrows almost concealed the bewildered eyes. His narrow mouth twisted in a permanent snarl, he stared hatefully at the two nurses discussing his problems.

Robert addressed him cheerfully. 'Good morning Mc Donald, how are you today?'

'Fuck ye dina kin,' he growled.

'That's what he's like; even a few caring words don't bring out any human kindness in him. He is a very difficult man. No matter what you do for him he doesn't appreciate it. In fact he sees everything as an attack on his person, a bitter old boy.'

They headed into a big bathroom at the end of the ward; washbasins, toilets, and an extra-large shower. A big freestanding bath with legs took up a prominent space in the centre of the grey tiled floor. It looked enormous.

'We like to have the bath in the open; it's easier access for patients and safer too. Watch everything I do, see where things are, and build up your confidence doing it. They would sense it if you were unsure and exploit it if they got a chance. They might be referred to as 'mentally deficient' but they have another gear, to exploit lack of confidence. They sense it very quickly.

'So Joe, first lesson today is: don't ever demonstrate reluctance in any situation. Be in control always. That's the only way they will respect you. If you're confident, you're in charge, got that? Now we are going to get one of our patients out of bed for a wash. He enjoys his bath, on a good day. But can be trouble, and if he lies down on the floor it's difficult getting him up again.'

He took a basin from a cupboard and half filled it with warm water. Then he put some disinfectant into it and a big sponge. He draped a small towel over his arm.

'It's always proper procedure to have a basin of warm water on the ready when you visit them first thing in the morning. You must allow for what the night time brings. A good wipe would clean them up. We will give them all their medication, after we scrub Chester first.' He took a pair of rubber gloves from his pocket and headed out into the ward again. The first bed on the white row, opposite Mr McDonald, was his destination.

'We start at the bottom; the other nurses begin at the opposite side of the ward, that's a security measure. When we are spread out, we have more presence. It's the system we use.

'Now, we must get Chester washed. He would never get out of bed if he wasn't encouraged. He's big and strong but harmless, always looking for money, don't ever give him any, he'd put it in his mouth and choke. "Come on Chester, we're going to bath you."

The man in the bed laughed hysterically at that shit, shaking his head furiously like a toddler with a hissy fit saying NO.

"Gimme a penny fucker!" he roared.

The head nurse whipped the bed clothes back to reveal deposits of solid excrement flattened on the bottom sheet.

'Chester, you're very bold.'

'Hungry.'

If Joe had any doubt that this nurse idea might turn out bad, it was magnified now. He wanted to throw up. Human excrement had disgusted him since the boy had fallen into the school toilet. He had never got over the smell of him. Now this was the worst possible start.

'Come on Chester into the bathroom.'

Joe saw he could barely fit into the bed. He would never

have expected him to tower over him, six foot tall himself. He wondered how he might go about handling this fellow if he got difficult, with a violent streak coming over him.

'What height is he Robert?'

'He's six foot six inches, twenty-five stone, eighteen years old,' he added proudly, like he was his own boy. 'He'd be some handful if he was a violent man. At least we have some things to be thankful for.'

The bath could fit his huge frame. Chester sat in it with a certain amount of glee in spite of his apparent reluctance in the beginning. This was a very changeable person. When Robert began to wash him, he never stopped until Chester was covered in a soapy lather. He handed the sponge to the student nurse inviting him to 'get into the hang of it.'

'Wash the soap off him Joe, you must start somewhere.'

Joe rubbed the sponge frantically over the back of his patient, to get it over with quick.

'Do the fronts, not as heavy handed he's very sensitive, you might hurt him down below. We'd never get him into the bath again if that ever happened; he protects his privates very much.'

Joe was rubbing his chest and he didn't like the eyeballing Chester was giving him. Not a comforting feeling at all.

'Move down lower, don't be scared of touching the genital area, he needs a good scrub down there, with the mess he made on himself, in bed last night.'

'Shouldn't I be wearing rubber gloves too?' He hoped to get out of doing it.

'Yes hold on, I'll get you a pair from the office.'

Chester didn't want his genitalia tampered with. He lashed out at the new nurse with a slap on his jaw; that was hard enough. The nurse glared at the laughing imbecile he was trying to care for. 'Chester, you hit me, I'm only helping you.' He was raising his voice for an apology, but nothing like that happened. The man in the bath tub was too busy masturbating.

This stand-off met the head nurse, when he came back.

'He gave me a hard slap on the jaw Robert; now look at what he's doing, interfering with himself.'

'Aha, that's no harm at all, it's a natural thing. Someone must have showed him how to do it. It doesn't mean anything to him. But it keeps him quiet, and nothing happens. Chester, you cannot hit Nurse, because he forgot his gloves. Say you're sorry.'

Chester ignored him. He never wore gloves.

The head nurse was picking at him. Chester didn't care if he was wearing gloves or not, just as long as he got his penis stroked.

It would take time working through this white line of eight beds. A few of the non-compliant occupants were carefully assisted to the bathroom. Chester's rapid response bang to his jaw was still ringing in Joe's ears. That kept him alert. He knew it was there waiting for him if he took his eyes off the patient.

Over the next few days he did his best on the job. There were a few things bothering him. Robert was too friendly, getting more inclined towards touching him, something he was never used to. In Ireland people were very friendly, but they didn't put their hands all over you, for a caress, for no reason. If someone died it might happen. He wondered if the head nurse was a touchy-feely person, but he hadn't seen him handling other nurses in such a way. He would be happier if it stopped. He couldn't get the nerve to broach the subject either, making him very uneasy.

Chester was making life more difficult. One day he waited until the new nurse went into the bathroom, and then lunged at him, gripping his shirt collar, demanding a penny. Joe would gladly give him one, to escape his desperate clutches, except he didn't have a penny to his name either. So they had something in common. When he told Robert about these attacks, his instruction was to remove his fingers one by one to release him, until he got the message. That soft approach wasn't having the desired effect. In fact, it seemed to give the monster more confidence. He still persisted in annoying the new nurse, more aggressively. It crossed Joe's mind to give him a slap, like the one he received. But that was not in the nursing manual. It was no harm thinking along self-preservation lines though, in case the worst happened. It was bothering him as much as the touchy feely way his boss was acting. He didn't know how to stop either one of them, just hoped it would end. The hassle was wearing him down, when he needed to be right to focus on the awful job he was stuck in.

He loved home cooking, that reminder of his mother's food. The kind middle-aged lady running the canteen was the recruitment officer's wife. She cooked meals at home to bring into the canteen. The Kerrs were a couple that didn't have children. She treated all the young nurses like sons. And she took special interest in the Irish lad who liked watching TV. He hadn't told anyone he'd never seen it before coming to Glasgow.

When the football mad Angus, a Celtic supporter, heard about the Irish football story, he forgave him and adopted him as a friend. The best one to protect a Paddy in Glasgow was a Celtic supporter, he informed him, making an honorary out of him.

'When you're using hands playing football you know nothing. That's why it's called football, only feet and head.' He was trying to prepare Joe for the soccer football experience he was planning. They were going to see a game together.

Thursday evening, Joe was watching the Lone Ranger and Tonto on TV. Robert came into the staff room with a big towel draped over his arm and a dressing gown over his shoulder. There seemed to be some urgency about him.

'Come on nurse, follow me.' He went into the bathroom.

'I don't know how long it's been since you've had a bath, but I have to tell you that there's a strong whiff of body odour from you. The other nurses all noticed it too. So I think it's time you had a good wash. I will fetch some disinfectant while you strip off; you can put this dressing gown on while you're waiting for the bath to fill up. Look at the positive side of this situation nurse, your bathing technique with the patients is less than heartfelt. I can see that you are struggling with the task. That's understandable when it's not something you've done before. Take this opportunity to learn the right way of doing it. I'm going to wash you now as if you are a patient, so you will know how to do it properly, next time. Maybe that's why Chester has taken such a pick on you. You're hurting him without knowing it. Relax now and enjoy the experience of being washed by a professional.'

Joe wasn't keen on this lesson at all. It started with his back getting scrubbed. Robert shampooed his hair something that hadn't been done for so long he couldn't remember. There could be 'graveyard mites' roaming around in it now.

His arms and chest were next for the diligent care of the nursing professional with eyes like a hawk, to feast on anything.

Joe washed his genital area, letting him see he was doing his part in the cleansing programme. The head nurse commanded him to remove his hands instantly. He said it with authority, so he complied with orders. But his knees were together for modesty.

The head nurse was having none of that shy cover up either. 'Open your knees wide, how on earth do you expect me to wash you properly? Relax, you're worse than Chester.'

Joe swore, spreading his legs wide in the bath. No person had ever touched him in such an intimate way in his life. The head nurse was down on his knees now, getting his hand in deep under him. The caring feeling was getting weirder. The new nurse freaked when he got an erection. That hard on did it. He sprang up so fast he sent him flying.

'Its fine Robert, I'm okay now.'

'I'm not finished scrubbing you yet.'

'Yes you are, don't ever suggest this again. I know how to wash myself. I know what you were trying to do just now. That's a no-go area for me. Do you hear me, keep away from me, you fucker!'

Joe gave him a threatening eyeballing, pulled on his dressing gown and picked his clothes up from the floor. When he left the bathroom, there was nobody in the TV room. He was in no doubt now about the true motives of the head nurse.

From now on familiarities would remain devoid of any physical contact whatsoever. It was getting to a dangerous level.

Friday was payday. Joe was looking forward to receiving his first ever pay packet, but it wasn't enough to dull the feeling of revulsion he felt towards the head nurse. Robert was behaving in his usual concerned way, enquiring about his mood, asking if there was anything he could help him with; the worst possible question.

An opportunity to broach the tricky subject arose when they were having lunch in the canteen. There was no one else there.

'You're very quiet Joe, is there something the matter with you? Do you have any personal problems you'd like to talk about?'

'Robert, the first thing I want to say is this. You're the one with the problem here. Where I come from there is no such thing as that kind of intimate touching you carry on with. It was never something that I experienced growing up. I'm telling you now I don't like it. I have never had contact like that with anyone, not even with a doctor. So I don't want it from you under any circumstances. Don't try it on me again, or I'll give you a thump.'

'Oh, you're over reacting. I was teaching you how to do your job. That's what I'm paid for. You're a trainee nurse with a lot to learn. Pity you're so full of Catholic hang-ups, get over it.'

The atmosphere remained frosty all day. Later that evening, when Joe had gone to bed early, there was a knock on the door. It was the head nurse seeking him out again.

'Nurse, I have your wage packet here with me, you forgot to collect it from Mr Kerr's office.'

Joe had been brooding in bed all evening about this tormentor. Now he was at the door, and Joe wasn't wearing any pyjamas. He wasn't getting out of bed without them. He'd heard the magic words 'wage packet'. That was enough information to gain admittance.

'The door's open,' he announced dryly.

Robert was flicking the pay packet like a fan in front of his face.

'Its okay put it there, on the locker.'

'I brought my butterfly collection to let you have a look. They are beautiful, I've been collecting for many years and some of them are very rare. Look at this white one with black spots.'

He held the book open like a photograph album, bending down towards the bed. Joe could see the lovely butterflies, their eyes still open, carefully spread out, mounted like a stamp collection. He was horrified thinking about these colourful, graceful insects, 'murdered', as old Miss Kelly would say. What cruelty was this? Hung trophy like, for want of someone's sick desire, someone who couldn't appreciate how wonderfully special they were alive. It was a truly pitiful sight. He remembered them flying low over the lake. He was so overcome by this that he didn't register the head nurse's subtle hand movements for a minute. He was kneeling on the floor groping at his penis under the bed clothes. Joe lashed out and sent him flying across the floor. The butterfly album went with him.

'Get out that door Robert. Never come back into my room again, for any reason. You're a real sicko.' As he was leaving, he had a more promising warning for him. He hoped he'd take heed of it. 'Next time you assault me I will give you a box in the mouth. Then I'll tell Mr Kerr what you're up to. Get out and stay out.'

Robert must have been in the pub after that episode, because when everything was quiet in the ward that night, the other nurses gone to the canteen, he pounced again. And there was a strong smell of alcohol from him. It kicked off harmlessly enough, with a song on Radio Luxembourg called Big John. Not a tune to make you spring up for a dance. It had nothing going for it in the line of rhythm, but that didn't bother the head nurse singing along with it, moving his body, to put some fancy dance steps together. But they didn't look right. And neither did he.

'Let's forget our differences, we'll have a little dance,' he slurred.

Joe was on alert again. This wasn't boarding school. In those days the boys waltzed with each other for training purposes. The nearby convent girls put on a play every year at Christmas, a full dress rehearsal, for the invited college boys. But they were only interested in dancing with girls when the show was over, the stuff of legends. Now this hospital ballroom was stuff of nightmares.

'No, I don't know how to dance,' he said, agitated.

'I will teach you everything.'

'Listen, you don't understand no when you hear it.'

The head nurse's face changed from a sneer into some other demented look. He grabbed Joe's shoulders, pinning him against the wall. Then he planted his boozy bearded lips on his mouth. The new nurse let fly with a punch into his stomach. Robert dropped to his knees gasping for breath and vomited. Joe had the last word. 'I told you to leave me alone, but you wouldn't, would you?'

At seven the head nurse instructed him to take a bedpan to Mr Mc Donnell. Joe approached his bed carefully to put it sitting on the locker; he then proceeded to turn back the bedclothes, warily.

That's when he saw it. A big pool of liquid diarrhoea and an overpowering smell of it. Then there was a sight of the biggest penis he ever saw, standing erect from this frail old man's body.

Like a wonder of the world. Bigger than any stallion horse he'd ever seen. He couldn't take his eyes off it; he was frozen to the spot. He stood staring gobsmacked.

Then the mad old boy eyeing him took his chance. Lunging for the breast pocket of his white coat, he pulled him down on top of him; drawing his long fingernails along the side of his face, with this tormented squeal of insane delight, the mad bloodshot eyes bulging from their sockets, he roared all he knew. 'I dina kin' I dina kin…I dina fuken kin…'

There wasn't a doubt he'd kill you, if he could.

The new nurse's hands were buried in excrement, and he was close enough to see the big penis was an amputated leg, curved into a point between knee and thigh. If you looked at it quick you'd still think it was a big cock.

Chester was sitting up in bed laughing, clapping hands joyfully like he was watching a circus. It was easy to see the clown.

When Joe washed his hands he vomited into the washbasin. Chester stalked him again, following him into the bathroom and grabbing him in the vice-like grip once again.

Joe had enough of them all now. He knew it was finished before it was over. He brought his knee up hard and Chester went down.

It took three of them to lift Chester up off the floor. He pointed to the new nurse accusingly, but he pointed out the soap on the floor, where he had slipped, showing them where it was. In the same place he'd left it.

Joe was leaving the nursing profession, but he wasn't telling anyone. The keys would be found on the locker in his room.

Doing the Irish goodbye was very silent; tell no one you're

going. He was a 'knee in the balls' type of nurse. They didn't mention having a preference for those in the advert, so he wasn't going to impose one on them.

When Joe walked out of the main gate of the hospital an hour later he knew his destination. He headed for it in no great hurry.

Later when he sat under the tree, peace consoled him. He felt the relief of taking in pure fresh air again. Wasn't it strange; the place he could breathe best, others couldn't breathe at all?

He had some clothes now, the hospital wouldn't miss them. There was money to buy a train ticket to Luton. He'd rest for a while after the long walk. The graveyard was that welcoming. There was peace here where no one else would go. With his first pay packet in his overcoat pocket, he was the richest man in the graveyard. And he laughed at the thought of that old saying.

CHAPTER 12

Back in Cody's Cross, the Gardai were still giving Bill grief about Ned Goat's death. There was hardly any crime around here, so the Dublin detective was getting a kick out of it. He was into making more serious allegations, just for the craic. The depth of the chair legs in the clay was suspicious. It would have taken the weight of two men, driving them that far down. The knot on the rope was professionally tied. Did Ned use tricky knots tying up goats? He didn't think so. Why was the knot damaged cutting it down? It was easier cut above it. But the location of that cut made things difficult to figure out. Detective Crotty made an issue of this.

'We know it was deliberately done,' He concluded.

They'd reduced the pub owner to nervous movements, like he'd lost confidence. If Bill was acting out a part, he was good at it.

Bill had the solicitor annoyed with nuisance visits, trying to allay his concerns. It was difficult for the legal gentleman to tolerate him anymore. Except Bill's family were his father's oldest clients, so he must remain respectful at all times.

Crotty and Nelson called into the pub to work the belligerent owner over. He was still doing a thriving after-hours trade. Nelson was always in uniform, so the whole town could see the shame of it. They started with the same accusations, 'allegedly interfering with a crime scene'. Bill regretted threatening Sergeant Nelson with the use of a gun. Some mistake in the heat of the moment. But now he was stuck with it.

The solicitor told Bill they were winding him up, but he had to acknowledge an illegal act, tampering with Ned Goat's body, 'interfering with a crime scene', as it was called. The Irish police didn't have much time for it, though. They hadn't the technical know-how to process DNA evidence, he said. 'That contamination stuff slowed things down too much for them.' He laughed.

'They could do me for something, couldn't they?' Bill shouted at him in his office, annoyed by his apparent lack of commitment, not discussing these so-called criminal proceedings.

'Yes they could, except they cannot prove a crime'. The solicitor was getting weary of him now.

'You don't know what they know, or less about what they can make up. They can summons me; I thought he was coming to arrest me when he arrived with the bad news about our son running away from college.'

The solicitor, a kindly young man, found a way out. He leaned over the desk to him. 'I heard about that Bill, I intended to mention it. It must be difficult for both of you.'

'Where did you hear it?'

'Oh, in court, they hear everything there. I wouldn't worry about it, worse things happen all the time.'

'Yeah, you want to hear how they talk to me as if I was a convicted murderer already? Out to get me I say.'

'Bill, they shouldn't be doing that, but it's their choice. Would they be after you for anything else?' he enquired, coyly.

'After hour drinking, PJ, the Gardai have me tormented.'

'If you get a letter, bring it to me, we will have something to go on then. Right now it's all hearsay, and hearsay's no say, OK? Otherwise we'd all be in jail. Now on a more personal level do you want anything done for your son I will be only too glad to help you, any way I can. I want you to know if you need me I'm available day or night. '

'Yes PJ, that's kind of you, never know what trouble is on the horizon. I appreciate your concern. I'm sorry for being so agitated and I can't tell my wife about it. That would worry her all the time. She has enough on her plate, I swear to you. And by the way, if you still want to open that office in Cody's Cross I can give you the room now. Miss Kelly passed on quickly in the end, God rest her soul. There's a lot of new development lined up for the town, as you probably know.'

'Thanks Bill, we'll get to work on that one,' the solicitor assured him, getting up from the big swivel chair in his office.

After all that, they shook hands warmly before parting company.

Susan Wilson heard all about her driver's life on that trip from the art auction in Dublin. She'd spent the night with her chatterbox hyperactive sister and her quietly subdued husband, so the opportunity to relax was welcome. She was fascinated by the serial history of Cody's Cross, this dark, unforgiving account of times past, when there was little else to worry them.

It was a painful recollection, the way he told it. And she was concerned for him, hearing all about it. The Yank's demeanour changed as he talked; his confidence took a dip. The raw emotion in his quiet tone was palpable. Now she understood some things that bothered her. Even after forty years you were still regarded as a 'blow in' to this town, a person that couldn't be trusted. Susan was taken in with the story. Just because he took two eggs, they had branded him a thief. She could see everything happening the way he described it.

These revelations and their damaging repercussions on a young boy's fretful mind made the journey home a learning experience. It was hard to imagine the cruelty inflicted upon him by so many ordinary people at the time. When they discovered who he really was, he'd be respected. Maybe that's why he wanted to 'change the look of the town'.

Susan thought it an admirable cause. She would remember this conversation, reaching a decision about selling the field. She agreed to the project, which gave him a feeling of belonging. And Susan had a new home for herself, with a big garden that would give her plenty to do. That was the best part. She looked after her own personal interests at the same time, and the Yank could live out his years in peace.

He confided in her that Blimey was the person he disliked most, this big bully that might attack you anytime he felt like it. He was always the tallest boy in the town, the strongest too. 'It was his total lack of compassion that made him such a monster,' he muttered, as if he'd been brooding about it for fifty years.

Susan took note of this reference to Blimey, a person she didn't care much about either. He was her nearest neighbour. He used the empty hay barn as a cinema, called it 'the moonlight', where patrons carelessly discarded cigarette ends, and other things. She never slept a wink when a movie featured in case the whole lot went up in flames. The town fire service was 'slow moving'.

Blimey's two-storey abode, once the best house in town, looked neglected now. It depressed Susan to look at it. He spent his time walking around in a blazer with a cigar bellowing smoke from the side of his mouth. Some imposter, he'd lived in London for a while, and he'd bought the blazer in a second-hand shop, they said.

It fooled nobody. He was the town idiot. His antics with the audience in the picture hall were funnier than anything you'd see on the big screen. It was the highlight of every show. His local crowd set him up for a bit of craic every time. He walked around before the movie started, smoking his cigar, and shouting at them to stay quiet. What did they think it was a pigsty?

He used the' Blimey' word very often in these rantings. That was how he got the nickname.

'Blimey, do you think this theatre's a pigsty?' he'd shout. And they'd all roar back at him from the darkness, 'You're the dirty pig in the pigsty.'

Susan had trouble sleeping after that Dublin journey. All her concerns were directed to Yank, her new dear friend. He insisted there wasn't another name to fit him properly in Cody's Cross.

He told her his poor head had given him problems in America. It was only with a good psychiatrist that he'd got to grips with his life. She thought he was a man on a mission. The town needed someone like that to get it together. She'd be watching.

She talked to WT about that Dublin trip, but some things

Yank had confided were for her ears only. WT was sympathetic towards the young fellow and more favourable towards him, but he'd get him to adopt a few real 'Irish customs'. Paying for whiskeys topped that list. He was caught once already, and once was enough. He often repeated that one; loudly.

Yank knew he was seen as a rich man about town now. And there was no doubt in his mind that Susan would tell WT about some of their chat. That would cut down on what he had to say. He needed both of them on side to make good on his plans.

So the great meeting of minds came about as a result. It led to discussions on the town's progress, how it should move with the times, now that the future was looking so good.

After a while they discussed doing a development for themselves, a project to keep them going. They would all learn from the Yank. The three-house project could work out cheaper with discount on building materials from Flanagan's hardware. There was lots of business to spread around, three houses constructed for the price of two. WT was impressed and a lot richer as a result.

Yank knew how it worked, down to the finest detail, and he wouldn't be deterred from getting his hands on the main objective. But he didn't want anyone to know about that yet.

Susan got a brand new bungalow to live in. She would never have been inclined to turn down such an offer. The new development was named after her departed husband, 'Dr Wilson's Close'. She knew well he would approve, and him looking down.

Susan admired Yank's positive character. He channelled his energy into working for the town's future benefit. They were all in it together. The nickname 'Three musketeers' suited them well, 'all for one, one for all'. There were bound to be interesting times ahead.

The newsagent's eldest daughter, Lucy, had arrived back home to live. Susan had long been an ardent admirer of the girl known as the lady of the town. Their combined force would smother the men at meetings to get their own way. Sure of it.

She smiled wistfully, living the moment, thinking about it. Her plan was already set in motion.

CHAPTER 13

When Joe walked into the Café in Glasgow, there was a great buzz about the place. She was on her own preparing orders, and serving tables. The seating space was all occupied. He was going to leave immediately, but she'd spotted him coming in the door and waved, smiling, pointing to her barstool at the counter. It was his first time in the place during lunch hour.

He wondered where her grumpy old dad was; she needed a hand.

'Can I do anything to help you out Connie?'

'Oh yes, take these orders down to the tables when I leave them on the counter. I'll tell you where to go. Dad's upstairs, in terrible pain with his back again, I wish they'd call him into hospital.'

Connie made coffee when it was quiet. 'The dish washing could wait for a while longer,' she said, 'just so the tables were cleared off and wiped down'. She wanted to hear where he'd disappeared to. He told her all about the hospital. She laughed about his wash in the bath tub by the head nurse, but she was furious about this so-called friend of his, dropping him in a bad situation. He should have cared for him better. It was the first she'd heard of him running away from boarding school in Ireland.

Joe told her about the builder his father knew in Luton who would give him a job. His friend Timer had given him the address. She frowned across the table, hearing that name again. He might be trying to get rid of him for good, this time.

She was furious about this so-called friend discarding him in a mental hospital. There was something innocent with this young Irish lad. Was it because he was carefree he seemed so gullible? And why wasn't he worried by the threat of misfortune that could lie ahead of him? She had a strange sisterly urge to mind him. She'd never felt anything like that come over her before, and it was quite enjoyable.

He went on to tell her all about sleeping in the old graveyard. She was horrified, saying how it was regarded with suspicion by everyone. She had to run past it every day for many years, going to school. He might be better off working in the café for a while where she could keep her eye on his progress.

'You must have more money before heading for Luton, Joe,' she said. 'Take a job here for a while' gather some cash together before you go, just to make sure you have enough. We have a spare bedroom upstairs on the second floor. I need a few jobs done that I haven't time for. That front you remarked upon hasn't had a proper clean-up or a good painting for years. Maybe you could do that. I'm embarrassed by it. I'll pay you the same money you were getting in the hospital. It's not much but it's all I can afford.'

'Right Connie, I'd like to do that for you. Thank you very much.'

In a big city far from home, he'd discovered a family business similar to the one he grew up in. The routine was almost the same, the challenges not very different. He began working for her full of confidence, without the apprehension that had smothered him in the hospital job. He wanted to do his best for Connie when she put her faith in him. He took into her list of jobs enthusiastically.

He remembered how good the bar front at home looked. The colours would be perfect together on this café, green, black and gold. 'The Cameron Café' in gold lettering would be similar to his family pub. It didn't take Connie long to realise her good fortune; without being told anything, he knew what to do.

He changed into his good shoes, grey trousers and white shirt to be a waiter for the lunchtime trade. Then he was back into his jeans again, doing jobs. The customers liked the quiet spoken Irish lad. Nothing was any trouble for him.

Connie finally got around to saying what was on her mind. She asked him to phone his mother in Ireland and let her know he was safe 'in a wee job' in Glasgow.

She got details of the police station back in Ireland. With his permission, she made arrangements through Sgt Nelson to talk with his mother. And that was a tearful occasion.

She reminded him he'd be sixteen on his next birthday, the 14th of May, and she wanted him to come back home where he belonged. He promised to write her a letter to explain everything better. Connie would ensure that task was carried out.

On his first night in the café, before he fell asleep, he heard a knocking over his head. Then a pause and the sound of more knocking, fainter than the first. He knew it wasn't mice. This banging continued about the same time every night. Connie told him it was her father's habit to knock the ceiling with his rubber ended walking stick to ensure she was safe in her own bed, alone, she added cynically. He thinks of everything.

If she went to the tavern, the curfew was ten o'clock. She'd knock back, letting him know she was there. If she didn't, he'd check on her, a prisoner in her own home.

She told Joe how much she loved her girlfriend. She had worked in the café for a few years. When her father found out about their intimate relationship, he banned the girl from the café, but they still corresponded in letters. They talked on the phone once a week. And every now and again they spent a night in Glasgow. 'Absence made the heart grows fonder;' Joe was very touched by that.

She invited him to the Tavern on a Friday night. She'd handed him his wages in cash, saying he deserved a few beers on account of all the work. It would never have occurred to her that this Irishman had never drunk beer in his life before, but he wasn't going to highlight his lack of experience now.

She gave him a sports jacket her father had worn when he was young, and one of his ties in the Cameron clan tartan, like her long skirt. He looked older in this outfit. There was a thing brandished about called 'baby snatching', and she didn't want to hear it directed towards her, not even in jest. And of course there was her respectability as a serious lesbian lady to uphold faithfully.

He'd watched men sipping beer, slowly, without getting drunk. That was how he wanted to be. He looked older with the jacket on him. The wide tie made him feel like one of the Cameron clan, with the mad Irish in him, heading to his first ever drinking session. He felt privileged by her confidence in him. He wasn't used to enjoying another person's company, and he liked it.

He had no problem with her choices in life. What you have to share in friendship shouldn't be anyone else's business. The bartenders knew Connie very well, so it didn't matter who she brought in for a drink. They lived off meals in her café, one big happy family. She liked them for being that way towards her.

Joe waited for her to sit down. The table she chose was just inside the door, her regular place of comfort. There was a noisy crowd in, exciting for the new Irish customer; laughter has the same ring to it, no matter where you go to enjoy yourself.

'What would you like to drink, Joe?'

'I don't know the beer names Connie; pick one for me. In Ireland I drink Guinness,' he lied.

'I enjoy a good local brew, I'll get you one.'

She was swallowed up in a crowd around the bar. He took out his bundle of cash to look at it and he sat up straight with his back to the wall, putting the cash back in his pocket. He noticed a lovely looking girl, smiling when their eyes met. To his surprise she came over to sit in Connie's chair. He couldn't believe his luck. This tavern was his favourite place already.

'I'm Vicky,' she said.

'I'm Joe from Ireland. I work in the Cameron Café every day.'

Her eager clutches stretched for a naïve sucker; on the lap of a seasoned call girl, this romantic type of dunderhead was rare. The smile broadened, looking him over. It wasn't important that he was good looking; she'd seen the wad in his pocket and didn't care what he looked like.

'Would you like to come with me for a good time? We'll leave now; I can take you to a nice place.' She spoke quickly. He looked at her. Was she talking about a party somewhere else? Flashing the mascara eyelids, pouting her scarlet red lips, lowering her shoulders, the cleavage so curvaceously exposed. His eyes devoured her charms. When he saw how warm they looked, huddled together, he nearly said how cold it was outside, but he thought she might cover them up if she heard that. Learning to become wise was getting easy. He never mentioned the weather.

'I'm here with my boss, she's up at the bar getting drinks. I don't think I can go anywhere without telling her first, in case she'd be worried where I went. Is there a dance near here tonight?' he enquired.

When she heard that, the girl looked at him like he was stupid. She wiggled her way to the door in her high heels, short skirt, long black hair and hooped earrings, waving and saying she'd see him again some time. When he was alone and more informed.

Connie arrived back with two pints, saying the bartenders thought she'd crossed over the other side for a 'wee toy boy' variety. Joe wanted that explained to him exactly.

'If she'd stopped being lesbian, turned on to young fellows.'

'No this was definitely a staff outing,' she assured them.

He told her the story about Vicky, how she'd invited him to a party, somewhere near there. She might be coming back for him soon, he hoped. Connie's eyes flashed to the ceiling. 'Come on Joe, let's get a few pints into us, we haven't much time left before ten.' She smiled, thinking of an idea playing around in her head.

Connie was well aware who he was talking about. She knew Vicky personally, and spoke with her regularly. She explained that this young girl was a prostitute; and how that arrangement worked out. She was explicit in her descriptions.

Connie suggested that she had seen him counting his money, and explained how the girl planned to rob him, when she got him excited enough to forget about it. Any thoughts about 'falling in love' were 'fantasy. Working girls were hard in their way, they had to be. Love didn't feature in their plans. Not all clients she met were as naive as he was. Some of these men might beat her up. They had a tough existence. There was a lot of risk dealing in this sex game. The girls deserved more respect than they got, and she had a lot of sympathy for them. It might be a good idea for her to hold half his wages every week and keep it all together for when he was leaving for Luton.

'Just to be sure you don't lose it,' she said sympathetically.

'I will have the café front painted before my birthday, Connie,' he said. 'I plan to move out the next day, Sunday. Just to put a time limit on everything now. Your father will still be in hospital. But if you could make arrangements for your girlfriend to arrive on the same afternoon I leave, that would be perfect. You could explain to him later how desperate you were and needed someone in a hurry. Make it sound like she was doing the Cameron Café a favour by providing cover in an emergency. You could tell him I left without giving you any notice. Blame me. How I left you stuck when I finished the painting'. You couldn't bear the thought of him finishing up in a nursing home, if you hadn't time to care for him. Just to sow the seed of doubt about nursing homes.

'I discovered growing up that the fear of this end quietens down the most belligerent of older people. None of them want to hear it. Use it as a gentle hint for getting your own way. You were left in a bad situation, with no help in the café. You turned towards the only person you could count on for help. Lay the guilt on him, Connie; it will stick when he's feeling unwell. You may think it a bit harsh but that's the way it must be if you're going to have any peace for the remainder of your days. Or else you will be his slave here until the day he dies. If he doesn't want to see it your way, threaten to leave with the girl. It shouldn't come to that, but you must fight for control of your life now. There's an old saying to remember: 'Sometimes you have to be cruel to be kind.'

'Maybe you're right Joe. One thing for sure, something has to change, I cannot go on like this anymore. It's wearing me down, ruining my life. The more I talk with you the stronger I get. I've lacked confidence to stand up to my father. I must do it now.'

They chatted on for a while longer until it was time to go.

Connie announced that two pints was her limit, just as he was starting to enjoy talking. He had no other option but to return to the café. She gave him an old copybook to write a long letter to his mother, and after all that, she laughed, heading for bed.

He felt carefree after his first taste of alcohol. He was an experienced pint drinker now, but he wouldn't be saying anything about that in the letter. And there was another anxious phone call home at the weekend. He was dreading that.

When Sunday came round, Connie busied herself in the kitchen. She couldn't help overhearing that telephone conversation. It was so poignant it made her cry. She wondered what to do with this stray young lad. He would have to grow up quickly. Heading down the London direction was tantamount to going into the flames of hell, from a Scottish point of view. There would be predators every step of the way; taking advantage of his naivety. She got a shudder thinking how he might finish up. She'd help him become more streetwise before he left.

That conversation he had with his mother reminded him again how the boarding school debacle negatively affected his whole family. His mother conveyed in particular how his father would never get over it. Dealing with this scandal had adversely affected him. There was a sickening shame attached to having a 'wild boy' son. She found the humiliation difficult to bear. And she was struggling to cope with everything.

Joe did a good job on the Café.

There wasn't much time for fun, if he had to obey a curfew, so he took to bed early, dreaming of what might have been if he had got to the tavern and Vicky. He'd listened to stories, heard descriptions of how it was done, and imagined situations without doing the deed. But he was getting ready for it. Connie would see the 'sticky sheets' on the bed when he was gone. And she'd forgive him. He was sure of that.

Nature's call was sudden and dealt with deliberately.

Connie organised a little party in the café for him; she'd baked a birthday cake. He tried hiding his lack of enthusiasm. It sounded like something you'd do when you were ten. But it was his last night, and they were best friends. Cake for two in the café, with the nicest lesbian in Scotland for company, he could hear the priesthood screaming out for him already. She said he was only beginning to find out things, winking at him when she said that. What her intentions were he didn't know. She gave him this handy suitcase, a leather one, for all he had.

The train was leaving Glasgow at midday. He'd be gone next morning; his time was over here, except for this party, which sounded like Mass. Alcohol couldn't be served in the café. He planned to leave the door off the latch when she went to bed. Then he'd make a final hopeful dash to the tavern. But now he was busy helping her with balloons, creating a party atmosphere, so he'd make the most of it.

At eight o'clock the table was covered in a white cloth. There was only one candle on the cake.

'I'm supposed to be one year old Connie, is that it?' He laughed.

'No, it's you're first time'.

He felt guilty about how much trouble she'd taken, singing happy birthday, blowing the candle out. Then she produced a big jug of orange juice and two glasses. The mood improved when she took a large bottle of vodka from the fridge. Things were looking up.

He danced around the café like a mad Highlander in her grandfather's old kilt. She said the look was a 'traditional memory' on his last night for a 'wee bit of craic'. And it would be his first time on vodka and orange.

Connie was thankful for the sound advice on her personal life. She praised his awareness for such a young lad. It must be attributed to his upbringing. She wished him good luck on the rest of his journey, before taking into serious drinking.

The music blared out from Radio Luxembourg. She was on the floor teaching him a dance routine she wasn't sure off. The laughing took the dance on a mind of its own. It might even be classed original. The legs pumped in all directions.

Suddenly there was a loud intrusive knock on the door. Joe was startled looking at Connie, thinking wrong things. She shouted 'answer it,' on her way to fetch ice.

All his dreams came true when he open the door, to Vicky, in a birthday greeting suit he could never have imagined. Her long overcoat hung open, revealing that it barely covered everything, reeking with the smell of perfume, leaving him gaping after her. He looked over at Connie. She was laughing at him. The evening was going to turn out better than it started.

This Connie girl would fit into the 'craic' anywhere. She might even be at her best, having it. A marvel the touch of difference can create.

Straight away, Vicky displayed notions of a more advanced dance routine. Stripping, it was called. Connie joined in the rude-nude mood too. He needed no more encouragement.

Vicky stole the show. That would turn out perfect for her new student's benefit. He willingly pursued, on the learning curve. In a small café in Glasgow at the age of sixteen he'd have his first ever sexual experience in some detailed practical lesson. His teacher was so mad into delivering it. It would have to be different, with adventurous detours taken for the pleasure of a keen learner. All night long, the 'young whore' got enough of it. And she gave it back plentifully. What more can we say?

Vicky was still in bed when first light made its appearance, but when he woke up again, she was gone. Next morning his boss was at the table, when he came downstairs. Connie was anxious to establish that he used a condom from the pack of three she had left next to his bed. Joe was confident answering.

'Yes, I used the three of them. I have them in the case to dump. I got good at it as the night went on. She didn't ask me for any money. I told you Connie, love matters, if you're good enough.'

She noted that he was annoyingly triumphant. That male thing had escaped from him. Connie smiled, turning her eyes up. They were all the same. She couldn't let him know she'd paid the girl to spoil it all for him. He would act like a typical man with the brazen feelings of sexual prowess they thought they possessed. The brain had clicked on in that department, so he was ready to travel.

Vicky had arranged a special agreement for her on this deflowering education. She'd be making some enquiries from her later, naturally. It proved to be money well spent. For Connie it was a special birthday present for a loyal colleague. He was such a pleasure to work with and a great friend in time of need.

She knew Vicky's lesson would help him on his travels. Now he was properly prepared, the rest was up to him. Sink or swim.

He sat down at the table for the last time. 'I'll fetch your coffee, I have all your money for you,' she said, looking at him. He felt heartfelt sadness creep over him. That look was her saying she'd miss him too.

If only for a short while, they had bonded. Sometimes on the journey, things happen between strangers when they connect. Connie and Joe were only friends for a short time, but it made a big difference. They knew they might never see each other again, but they hoped that connection would last forever.

'Goodbye Jonsie,' she said, 'it was real nice knowing you.'

'Yes Connie, I'll miss you. I promise I will always think about you, I'll never forget how much your friendship helped me along. But I thought you preferred Joe. First day I was here you said you liked the name Joe, you said Jonsie was childish, remember?'

'Yes I do, but Joe doesn't describe you properly, I think since I've got to know you. There's more rooms left in Jonsie's house for several characters to inhabit. All I've seen are wonderful. How I wish I had met them all, that's quite clear to me now. Step gingerly on your way Joe, stay true to yourself, until it gets too dark for our Jonsie. The whole place would be so dull without him, for sure.'

CHAPTER 14

Jonsie was the topic of conversation in stories told at the pub. Some past exploits in Cody's Cross came up for discussion. He was a strange young fellow; everyone had a tale to tell about him. He ran away from a college in the west, they said. Hopefully he'd get home in one piece. But you couldn't say anything out loud.

The boy was seen talking with Drover on fair days. Maybe that's why he finished up in a mental home in Scotland. Drover was able to drive people mad with tea he made from 'poteen' and he talked to the yew tree, to watch over the town. Jonsie must have learned the madness from him'.

Anyway he was coming home from Scotland soon, they said. They were pleased, for poor Hanna's sake. She had soldiered on bravely through bad times, with the lot of them. Everyone remembered when he almost blew up the house with a bag of explosives, before he was able to walk. Was he getting messages from the fairies even then, they wondered? This lad wouldn't benefit from what Drover had to say. He was too manipulative for a young boy. How did he persuade poor Betty Flanagan to worship the moon? And look what happened to her after. Something wasn't quite right with the two of them.

They nodded their heads; see what happens for another day. There could be more to it all than met the eye, they said.

Hanna knew how to talk through tricky situations with Bill. She'd defused a tense situation. The pressure was off. So she insisted on a few things before going back to normal.

Was this part of the Cody's Cross curse, she wondered? It would be great to discover something 'not quite right' going on. 'If you listened long enough, you'd believe in anything.' But the town was a different place now, with so many strangers coming and going. Things would never be the same again. And maybe that was a good thing. Freddy Brown's pub was a den of iniquity. The Yank's son and his overbearing wife had the place buzzing for themselves. Parties were talked about. Hanna was annoyed.

A new happening in town, would create scandal in no time. There was talk of wife swapping, but no one knew who was doing it yet. When you thought about it, the negative cronies exclaimed, there weren't many wives around suitable for swapping with if you had a woman to swap, in the first place. Anything could happen then. Sex was the new football.

Television was in several houses now and imaginations were greatly enhanced with modern happenings. Things were changing. Sex was mentioned more often and stories were drifting around. That pair in the pub were up for anything; frolicking with the liberal boat people. 'Anything goes if you knows', they said. But the good living locals wouldn't go near the place in case they were seen by someone. It was more about the thought of getting caught than anything else. Who would see you? And the guilty way they'd look at you, after saying it.

The big river was a favoured destination for 'boat people' who enjoyed leisure sailing. They mingled happily with the small local population, and seeped up the quaintness of the village where they wished they lived permanently. The Sergeant had become less diligent in his after-hours raiding patrol, as cordial greetings were readily shared. The boat people thought drinking all night was normal behaviour. Freddy Brown's pub never closed, except during the day. There must be time to rest, after all.

Hanna sat at the kitchen table holding her husband's hand. She'd been observing him, during a spell of quietness in their conversation. She remembered all the way back, and knew his rough honest way could never hide anything for very long. Not once in his life did he ever raise his hand to her or threaten her with physical harm, and that was not how it was in every home. She knew that sometimes appearances were deceptive.

'You're soft hearted at the back of that tough exterior Bill, that's what I love most about the way you are, such a caring man.'

'You're not short on caring yourself.'

Stroking her hand, he looked into her enquiring eyes. 'I love you very much, Hanna.'

'And I love you very much too, Bill.'

They would remember that little boy they raised, and talk more often about it. Try to stop worrying where he was now and how he was doing. They promised to help each other. When the bad thoughts arrived, they had to know it was the best thing to do.

Their son was out of harm's way for a while; Willie Magee was minding him. And he was the soundest man you could get.

When Hanna started thinking back on things past, she remembered that Ned Goat's death still bothered her. She knew her husband had driven Louie home that morning. Drover was saying 'they were parked 'discreetly' behind the yew tree near Ned's house for a long time. Hanna knew her husband never paid attention to parking. He pulled in anywhere he liked. But there could be something else to it. Not everyone liked the Flanagans. There were enemies hiding waiting to pounce. Old scores remained unsettled still.

Her husband said bad things about the goat man, when Jonsie's money was stolen. Surely he never meant them. But when the newsagent told him he'd changed three pounds in threepenny bits for him. He swore to her he'd 'kill that bastard goat man'.

Why didn't Bill tell her about the Louie incident when everyone else knew about it? Was it deliberate, for a reason she didn't know about? It felt like a cover up. One sure thing, she was going to find out.

Anyway, she was a member of the Development Committee now, helping the town to grow. And she liked working with the intelligent Mrs Wilson. She was getting close, like her mother. Hanna's mother heard everything that went on in the town; she'd tell her what they were saying when she arrived. But there was a kitchen table to set properly first, the day was moving too fast for her. And she was never late for a visit.

The Politician knew where his loyalties lay now. He was calling around more often, keeping up with things in Cody's Cross. It was all happening quickly. Yank was a respectful man; Flash had already experienced his generosity. So he'd provide any assistance he could. His man in the council was standing by. Information was slow coming, held up on some merry go round; this town needed something to speed it up. And the American was the right man for the job.

Flash knew he would benefit from any success coming Yanks way. The voters were watching everything going on; they had more awareness than politicians gave them credit for. It was all lining up nicely for him.

With this cunning grin on his face, the driver couldn't see. He didn't want him knowing how well things were going now. He might expect something out of it. The prestige of holding this driving position should be enough for him. None of the driver's cronies were driving a politician about. It was what made him important in the pub. They talked to him as if he was someone. And if he heard some things going on that ordinary people should know he'd put the word out there, where his efforts were well received. Sometimes he got a few bob when it happened right. Then again he might just be ignored. The latter was more common. But he'd heard there was a big one coming up in the pipeline. Maybe he could benefit from helping it along. Keeping his ear cocked would do no harm, playing his cards right.

CHAPTER 15

Joe had hours to mull over everything. His mood had changed to a more depressing state. The phone calls to his mother in Ireland forced him into enduring guilty heartbreak. That was why he couldn't contact her anymore. She wanted him to come home immediately. And he wasn't going back there yet. Not even for his mother.

As he sat alone in the eerily quiet train compartment, her words still advised him. And listening to them made him cry again. He regretted he hadn't taken the ferry home to Ireland instead. It finally dawned on him how much pain he'd caused his family. And he was sorry about that, but he wanted more adventure. What could he do at home? The world of 'free spirit' was a selfish one. So he'd have to keep on going.

London was a trouble-free changeover and they rolled on to Luton Town station in the dark of night. He remembered his fraught arrival in Glasgow not so long ago, except this time; he had a proper address and enough money in his pocket. When he got into the taxi he showed the address to the young driver. He banged on the door knocker of the big house, and it opened almost instantly. A square-set middle aged man with dark curly hair stood looking him up and down, a cheerful expression on his weather-beaten face. And what looked like a smile on his lips.

It could be he was expecting him.

Joe remembered this man from another life. He had seen him a few times in the bar at home; one of the noisy Christmas holiday crew.

'Hello sir, I'm Joe Flanagan from Cody's Cross, my father sent me to this address, looking for Mister Willie Magee.'

The man displayed a bigger grin hearing that. It relaxed Joe more when he put out his hand for a firm handshake.

'I know your father Bill, very well, a decent man.'

The strong grip tore at Joe's soft skin like rough sandpaper, an instant reminder, of the type of man he was dealing with.

'Come in, you're welcome, straight into the kitchen, follow me.'

Joe swaggered after him into a warm room, a big table in the centre with chairs around it, just like home. He got that Irish feeling 'we're all the same here boyo'. It was good.

His father would have told this man everything.

The unfortunate school departure, would, no doubt influence his opinion somewhat. He must be truthful. There would be several versions of the 'runaway kid' doing the rounds, hardly any of them forgiving. His reputation would be travelling ahead of him. He was wise enough to know all that.

'This is Bill Flanagan's son Brigid, you remember him running around the pub at home when he was small. That wasn't too long ago, was it; will you look at the size of him now?'

A pleasantly plump, cheerful woman with kind blue eyes got up from the table, running her fingers down her side for a warm greeting. He felt at home around the table with this small family.

Mrs Magee was busily making him a ham sandwich to have with a mug of tea. 'After such a long journey,' she said.

'The dinner will be ready soon.' Mr Magee did the talking.

'This is our son Michael, Joe, you will be sharing a room with him upstairs, he will be working with you every day too. So you will be seeing a lot of each other.'

Michael had that same gravelly grip in his hand too, genuine all over it. A quiet chap, but Joe got the impression he'd like to talk. He listened intently nodding his head sometimes with a smile. His father made up for all that shyness though; he had lots to say. The home gossip was satisfied early. No matter how far people wander; they remember their nests, and like to talk about them.

Willie Magee settled into a story about his working experiences over the many years 'in this country,' as he kept referring to England. He was very proud of his achievements, making sure, Joe knew, he didn't get anything handed to him. He knew all about it, because he lived it. 'I'm known as Digger Magee, Joe. If you asked someone about Willie Magee in the pub, they wouldn't know who you were talking about. It's how I made my way here in this country since I arrived from Ireland many years ago. I have to tell you about the digger man's work. These Irish navvies are some boys, I tell you. You could be proud of them for building this country when their own Englishmen wouldn't do it. Starting tomorrow morning, that's what you're going to be a pick and shovel driver.' He laughed. Digger revelled in his colourful account of the past; those days, when only the toughest of men made it to the latter years of their lives. 'God rest their souls.'

He made the sign of the cross over his broad chest, with humble reverence to their everlasting memory. The heroes of this folklore were giants of his time; their like would never be seen again.

'You had to have your own pick and shovel to get a day's work in those days. I carried mine around with me on my shoulder. If you weren't careful where you left them, they would be stolen. They were a passport to a job, you see. Some men took them to the pub with them. And that was often a big mistake, because they were stolen. It's no harm for you to know this history, Joe. It's your new job for a while, learn from it. You won't be stuck in it forever. Everyone else knows the stories. That's why I'm telling you, so you know. They talk about the old days a lot. They haven't much else to keep them going. They're set in a certain way of life; you'll be a novelty among them, for a while. 'You'll have to be tough, mind you. I'll be a different man on the job, you'll see. I'll be Digger Magee. I wonder what they'll call you, that'll be good.

'Now, your foreman, Leitrim is his name, will be tough on you until you prove yourself. He's a rough, arrogant man, but he gets the job done for me. The men work like hell for him. They're afraid of him, you see. His rule is obeyed: whatever you do in one day; you get paid for, and if you do enough, you're taken on again the next day.' He laughed over to his wife. He knew of her disdain for those men you couldn't clean the house after.

'You wouldn't be fond of looking after too many of them, Brigid. They lived to work for drink. And brawling was just part and parcel of their journey. They existed from one day to the next, you see.' Digger spoke proudly. 'I'm giving you this information so you know how it goes. Then you'll find out who y'are, won't ya?

"Come tomorrow you'll be hearing bad stories that I'm a slave driver. So I'm telling you how it is, Joe. There is nothing soft about me. Times have changed, you don't have to buy your own pick and shovel anymore. But by god you get to know how to work them. It's not all about hard work. Michael here will show you around at weekends, to the Irish dance halls. There will be lots of time for girls. It's full of them here. You never saw the like of them.' He winked at him. And Mrs Magee smiled, as that was 'all talk'.

But mention of girls sang the 'good times' to Joe; he was switched on there already. 'Oh Flower of Scotland,' he thought about Vicky quietly. He would never forget her knowledge, or her enduring energy. 'Just to meet her likes again' would be all he'd ever want. He had it bad all right. But she'd flattened the rising footballer in one night. Even highly charged youthfulness was no match for experience. The lessons were arriving fast since school. 'Thanks Jesus,' his grandmother would say, albeit with different intentions in place, of course.

'Tomorrow morning you will be heading off with Michael here to spread stones over a big ten acre site for electricity pylons,' Digger was saying. 'Sometimes you'll be taken off the job to do a bit of grave digging or a few foundations. I can assure you it will be a pleasant break from spreading stones. Look at me hands will you,' turning them up with pride for a look. A ploughed field would best describe the craggy crevices across his palms.

Joe knew some things defy a proper description. Mangled, twisted, lumpy and cracked doesn't sound good for describing hands. Joe was getting sharper already. Jonsie was never that careful. Now he was going to hear all about money. Digger's voice got more serious broaching the territory of payment.

'You'll be paid five pounds a day,' he said with awe in his tone. 'You'll have to pay the missus for your keep out of that. She's the real boss around this place. She mightn't be too hard on you, on account of who you are and how much respect we have for all the Flanagan family back in Ireland. They fed us when we were young, kept the house full of groceries, money taken, if it was there. And there was credit available for mother when it wasn't. That's the long and the short of it now.

'Flanagan's Hardware store kept Cody's Cross alive, back in the day when money was scarce. I just want to point out to you something about wages, Joe. The going pay rate for a day's work on construction is two guineas, two pounds two shillings. I pay more than twice, a fiver. Now don't forget to tell your father that when you're writing home. I wouldn't want him to think we were making little of his son when we got him over here to England. But you're getting top money now, young lad. Brigid charges a pound a day for keep, but she will only take a fiver from you instead of seven. Then you'll have twenty pounds for your own pocket every week. Make sure to save ten if you're wise, that's the way to start off, save all your money. How's that then, all right with you then Joe?'

At that very moment four burly men walked through the kitchen, intent on making their way without stopping, but Digger called out to one by name. When he turned, you could feel his tension. He had a bad eye in his head, his father would say about him.

'This is your boss, Joe', said Digger. The middle aged man never moved to greet him. He stood there, a sly smile loosening his cruel mouth for a second, like a pike wondering if he'd bother with a sardine. There was that sinister foreboding look about him. 'This is Leitrim for you now,' Digger said with a bit of pride in him. Not everyone had a bad ass under control.

Digger Magee knew well that his foreman's reputation as chief tormentor preceded him, but the young Irish lad wouldn't know anything about that yet.

Then Leitrim spoke, with his bad attitude and raw ignorance warning what to expect.

'I see they're still starving them, back in the old country, he won't be a good worker so. I'll make sure he learns the hard way, believe you me.'

He continued on out of the kitchen as if Joe didn't exist. But the new man would remember him; the high alert button was on. A wrong one looks the same everywhere.

'Leitrim is his own worst enemy,' Digger explained. 'He never learned to communicate properly. He told me his father only spoke fifty words to him in his whole life. He suffered from bad depression, I think. He told me once why the men work so well for him. He explained it like this: 'I just show 'em once how it's done, and make 'em better at it.'

'He does a good job for me, all I care about. And while he might lash out in a fit of temper on occasions, he's put no one in hospital yet; a tough man though, is Leitrim. Watch him.'

When Joe heard that last remark casually dropped into the mix of all evils, he picked up on it instantly. He wouldn't be Leitrim's first casualty for hospital. He'd stay well away from him, or there would be trouble as a result. No doubt about it. Must be heads down so, doing what needed doing. And mouths kept shut. This fucker was dangerous.

Lights out in the bedroom; Michael had enough talking done.

'Okay, six o clock doesn't take long coming. We must save our energy for all the dancing at the weekend. At least we have that to look forward too.' Michael dreamed on. Laughing quietly, this placid character was opening up.

Joe would drift off to sleep thinking about chasing girls again.

Next morning, Michael walked him to one of the five green vans parked at the back. 'The Digger Magee' with pick and shovel was painted on both sides. You could see at a glance what this outfit was all about. But it wasn't comforting seeing Leitrim perched in the front seat with his elbow sticking out the window. The warning was clearly defined with this fellow. He saw the Nasser bastard in him already. And that was a sobering realization.

They pulled into a big site, with electric pylons over their heads. Truckloads of stones arrived periodically, four-inch limestone coated in white dust, dumped everywhere. The crew took into levelling these stones with shovels. A little at a time, there was lots to go around. Mechanical diggers weren't available here.

Joe had a new shovel with a long handle and pointed blade. Michael told him some shovels were blunt at the edge from wear, and much harder to dig with. But the shovel jarred, painfully. This condition didn't improve. The inmates on hard labour in the American penitentiary might have had it easier by comparison.

July was a scorching hot month for the digger men. This job

was tough enough without the weather conditions conspiring to make it worse. Scattering stones was cruel work in the midday sun, and there was no end to it. The stones were piled high in open construction lorries, dried out on the journey. When drivers arrived in convoy, clouds belched from trucks dumping their loads in scattered heaps. White dust covered the navvies from top to bottom, until they appeared like snowmen. And it was not a good place to inhale. Masks were not available. The giant electricity pylons reaching into the sky over their heads didn't provide comfort either. It was like some strange other world, a place none of them would ever forget, or want to be in again. The piles of stones reminded them of who they were.

These men were hard nails, battered blunt with no expectations, and left driven into the ground, they had escaped too. It must have been a very bad place where they had run from.

Joe struggled from the beginning with this demanding work.

He tried against the odds. It wrecked his head, before it numbed his arms and blistered his hands. The constant resistance of big stones against the shovel was soul destroying. One of the older men said it was 'the greatest hoore of all jobs he ever worked', the voice of experience, adding this common caveat remorsefully: 'But you'd expect it hard in England, wouldn't you?' They cursed their sanctuary, remembering historic events.

And that nasty piece of work Leitrim didn't help matters. He was a typical Irish foreman with that bad attitude, the worst kind of bullying bastard you'd ever meet. That same violent streak ran through them all. When you knew about them, you'd realise how drink twisted their thinking. Blank eyes listening to demons that kept them going, their noses flattened across their jaws in fights. Big wallops should have put manners on them, but it made no difference. Nothing changed their way of life. And they were settled into it.

Leitrim was Nasser the Dean, let loose on a building site to do his worst, whenever he felt like it. Moving around the job shouting abuse, he'd hit you a wallop with the shovel across the arse just as quick as he'd look at you. He'd got away with it for so long he felt entitled to it. Built like a tank to carry it out. Every day Joe felt how hard it was to be a 'Digger Magee man'. It was the first time in his young life he was stopped.

Leitrim never tried to communicate in the house, after working hours, where they lived as tenants. He called him 'college boy.' It wasn't intended as respectful nods to his academic pursuits, more of a 'put down', the sound of failure all over it, sneering. 'What are you doing here, college boy? Did they kick you out?' You must have been a stupid fucker so.

He'd been getting the negative treatment from him. It started off with the smack of a shovel across the ass. He only did it once. Joe faced up to him and shouted 'never hit me again, I'm not your slave.' He got away with it that time. His sudden reaction startled the foreman. He wasn't used to it. Nobody had ever stood up to him before.

Michael advised not confronting him. 'He will attack. Those few words you roared took him by surprise. Be expecting hard knocks.'

Joe would have preferred any other nickname, murderer even, might work as a deterrent; or Jonsie with its soft inclination. That 'college boy' name was a target on your back. Like a lamb chop in a butcher's shop, a short expectancy in life.

These Irish navvies saw him as a figure for ridicule, because he had never had to do any hard work in his life. A college boy, 'but his family must have money', they said. 'He'd be a spoilt brat so.' You'd know that just by looking at him, they said.

Michael was listening to all these taunts, watching closely how his new friend was coping with the pressure. It was a good lesson for his 'human behaviour' studies. Michael said he attended yoga class with this girl he liked, on Fridays. And he also told his new friend how he paid his own way through college.

There were no freeloaders welcome in Digger Magee's house. His father had told him, just once. Joe thought about his own father. He had squandered all his money on the boarding school disaster. He had a lot of making up to do. One day, everything would be sorted out properly. He'd made that same kind of promise at the lake as a young boy.

Michael told him about his sociology studies. Joe thought he was trying to impress him, but no, it was all true. He said he wasn't interested in discussing college topics. Too far over his head, didn't he run away from all the education, he protested? Michael didn't care anyway. And he assured him he'd never mention education again.

They were having great fun together after the girls. Michael introduced him to the gym three nights a week. That's when Joe discovered his friend was such a good boxer. He'd been selected by a boxing coach as a prospect because he was big, handy and tough. Michael spent time teaching the moves to Joe, who was enjoying every minute of it. What he wasn't pleased about was Michael being 'too good' anytime they sparred. Something he had to suck up, not able to take him. It was apparent that he might never get there. Two years older means more experience, you didn't have that knowledge early on in the fight game.

He spent the sessions learning how to stay safe, developing his moves. Good footwork was essential; his well-conditioned leg muscles playing football were flexible around the canvas. Under Michael's tuition he became slick, training to dodge punches, learning to spot a delivery gap. And gaining experience of perfect timing, to unload the right hand; his lethal weapon.

Sex wasn't happening; he told Michael he had only done it once before. Michael wasn't keen on this discussion, so they dropped it from conversations altogether. They both agreed that girls were much better fun to be with than drunken brawlers. At least you could have a good laugh with them. These two lads loved the ladies' company.

Joe was the first one to wear a handkerchief around his mouth at work, like the bandit Jesse James, he told them. Leitrim took exception to it, when he saw a few men copy this bad habit. They were good men that would never have entertained a wimpy call in their lives before. This college boy was a bad influence on them, so it must be sorted. He took it out on him first chance he got. Coming up behind him when he was stooped shovelling, giving him a kick up between the legs 'to teach the young fucker a lesson 'that he hadn't learned in the college'. It delighted the foreman to see him squirm on the ground in agony. He shouted out at him, triumphantly, pausing for a second, to lean over him.

'Get up ta fuck college boy, if you're able' he roared, before walking away laughing. Joe swore he'd get him for that. One day.

He saw the foreman in action a few weeks later in the wine bar. It was a frightening display of savagery. He'd hit you with the first thing that came into his hand. Now that he was barred from the bar, Joe was happier drinking in there. It was called a 'wine lodge', where you could drink up to a maximum five pints of draught cider, straight from a wooden barrel to get launched to the moon with this mad stuff driving you on. The kind of place heavy drinkers went to for a high before going to the pub to get drunk. This mix was bad medicine.

You were expected to exit the premises after five pints, that was the rule. It was written up on notices. A few pints of this stuff could make you someone else; a bad detour for a nastier specimen to use for motivation, a troublemaker like the foreman didn't need it.

They had a security man watching out for this sudden change in demeanour. That was when Leitrim carried out his vicious attack, on a good man doing his job. He took into him until he was overpowered by a few more doormen. Now he drank with his cronies in the Black Stallion, the foreman's only bar, a place where young navvies never strayed.

They saw enough of the bastards all week.

One night, when Joe and Michael were on the town, their confidence was on a high with cider. And with their bravery boosted, they knew no limits. They decided to check out this 'foreman's only' bar for the Craic. See what it was all about.

After tanking up in the wine lodge, they made a bee line for the Black Stallion Inn. They weren't standing up at the bar for long when they were approached by Leitrim. He brazenly ordered them out, saying they shouldn't be using the same bar as foremen. He was making shapes, indicating he'd enforce the issue. There were a few hard looking men at the counter with him, smirking over, waiting to see which way it was going to turn. They would be ready if required. Leitrim ordered them to get 'de fuck' out of their pub. And never come back anywhere near it again. There were people looking at them.

Michael headed for a side exit, with Joe close behind him. Through this door they went, down two steps to the ground; the toilets were out this way, located in the car park. When Joe looked closer at it, the big plan hit him. He could see a way to settle Leitrim once and for all, with a dose of his own medicine. To put manners on him. College boy had a plan.

He practised the perfect delivery a few times in the gym. He got Michael's support, no physical help required. He was too close to the renegade foreman for that. It might have bad repercussions for him later on.

Joe talked to his mother on the phone when he wanted to. Bill was less inclined. He didn't want to know. He started wondering why his father hadn't seen Ned hanging on the gate, that morning when he drove past Drover's house on his way back into town. But he could only say that to Boxer, because it didn't sound right. The old fighter told him what they were saying around the town. It was to do with his stolen money. But he didn't believe a word of it. If anyone murdered Ned it was Louie. Boxer said that bald bastard hated the goat man. And from what he knew about him, he was sure he could do it.

Joe often cried himself to sleep at night, thinking about his mother, how good she was to him when he was young. She had minded him when the old one called him 'murderer', with the little dog dead in his arms. He was seven when he had made that promise, sitting in the tree. 'They will never change me from the way I am.' Not for the first time, he knew it was right for him to honour this promise.

Even though he was far away in England, Hanna felt nearer now. She was glad to get the phone calls; that kept her going. Her son would make his own way eventually, she was sure.

The annual funfair that Michael never stopped talking about finally hit Warden Park. It was part of the festival celebrations in August. The boy's plans for enjoying this occasion were well made in advance. Five pints in the wine lodge before heading for the funfair. They were in high spirits walking along the street. This cider could creep up on you though, they knew about that. It was a balancing act. Insanity was around the corner with this crazy shit.

The carnival occasion brought girls out on the hunt too. The boys were readily available to be exploited, if that's what it took. So they got lost in funfair time, and the music did it for them, strolling around. They were called on to try out the dodgems by a thick Irish accent. Bob was his name, from Dublin.

The boys tore into each other in the cars, followed soon after by a few whirls around on the Chair-o-Planes. The cider fermented, and they puked their guts out on the grass.

When Michael looked at his watch, it was time. They knew what they had come to see. The boxing booth at the fair provided a setting for Michael's 'carnival tales'. Every year there was someone badly beaten in the ring, blood everywhere. A slugfest was the way he told it. They were very 'dangerous animals', these men working in boxing booths. They didn't use fair play, and could open your forehead with a head-butt. He'd seen it happen several times.

They arrived to this colourful structure, the centre of all the attraction. Painted with Stanley Thornton's Boxing Promotions, in big blue letters, blending in to the carnival setting perfectly. It wouldn't have been much of a funfair without a 'combat arena'. The top of a well weathered marquee was visible, directly behind. But the current action was taking place in front, on stage. High off the ground, six boxers stood gloved up, ready to fight all comers. The man in the bowler hat and gold waistcoat was addressing the gathering. He called on the 'best of ye' to take on any of his fighters, encouraging words for the boozed-up listeners. The sound of fighters primed them for action. Sure they were all great fighting men, in their own minds.

'I'm Stanley Thornton,' he roared, 'with the best fighters in Luton town today. Where are ye now, tough men thinking ye can fight? Maybe in the pub, look here then. See how to win a five-pound note in nine minutes. Ye could buy some beer with that.'

His wife moved through the crowd, her headscarf tightened in a knot on her forehead, with a book of tickets in the apron pocket. 'Buy fights tickets from the lady now!' he roared.

The Thornton team had been a well-oiled unit for a long time. The boxing ring was surrounded by a good crowd of people. Many of them had resentment against booth fighters and longed to see a real good bloke from the crowd do a job on one of them. It sometimes happened; one of their own stepped in to sort out one of these 'dangerous scrappers'. But it didn't happen very often.

They could warn other fighters about Luton, the toughest town in England. When six fighters were selected from the audience, the show could begin. Joe watched the first two volunteers disappear down steps into the marquee behind. They didn't look tough, just older and shorter. His height advantage gave him belief. And the next volunteer was an old man of forty, he thought. The booth fighters were all ages, a rough crew of 'tough guys'. This was only a step away from homelessness for them. It could happen if they began losing too often, time to go then. Their next battle might be their final bout.

'Michael, why don't you have a go? I'd say you'd beat any one of them, you're a real good boxer.'

'Naw mate, they're a hard crew Joe, I've seen it before, wait till we get in for a look. You'll see then.'

There was two left and Joe was sure he could beat either of them. It was probably the cider advising him. Although he couldn't beat Michael in the gym, he'd best him by going in with one of these hard men types that he was obviously scared of. That would be the same as winning over him, wouldn't it? He stuck his hand in the air, thinking like that, shouting 'Me'.

Stanley Thornton pointed to the side stairs, and poor Michael instantly realised his worst nightmare. 'Oh no Joe, my dad will kill me.' The new fighter just ignored him.

Michael could see him being badly beaten up here. The wild young Irish fellow's self-belief was good, but this recklessness was bad. This carnival trip could finish up worse. Then there would be a lot of explaining to do. Michael could imagine it. His father could be subject to sudden personality change, if things went badly wrong. Anyway one way or another all hell would break loose. He paid for the fight ticket with a sense of dread in his head.

Stanley Thornton had a mood change after his confident delivery on stage. He wanted a word with the bloke that looked like he had run away from his mother', at the fair. There would be trouble if a young boy got the shit beat out of him in his boxing booth.

He faced him down when he was changing, with wild, accusing looks spreading all over his rugged face. He didn't want to hear excuses. He just wanted to make sure.

'Look 'ere son what fawking age are you?'

The young contender had the answer straight away. 'I'm twenty-two, Irish schoolboy boxing champion at ten. Why?'

'How come you're not shaving then?'

'Because I don't want to.' The fighter glared at him.

When Jonsie discovered he was the only one that knew his age, there was never going to be any doubt about it thereafter. He looked over at the man going to fight him, looking ahead in another world, dismissive towards his challenger. Stanley handed him a bundle of well-worn boxing gear and boots. There was no going back. Nor would he want to.

He relaxed; his days at the lake had given him self-awareness. Calmness would come from controlling his mind. Whatever came up, he'd deal with it. 'Look for the gap; hit as hard as you can.' Boxer had drilled that into him in Cody's Cross. He remembered now.

He sat on the stool looking across at his opponent, overweight and uninterested. He looked out at the audience. And the most unbelievable thing happened. You couldn't make it up. Sitting out there was a girl he recognised called Eileen, in the front row. He'd been at school with her only a few years earlier. He knew her very well. One of the many 'real life coincidences' he'd experience. He might have shouted out to her, but he was supposed to be in an expensive boarding school for the better off, not slugging it out for a fiver, at the end of 'no hope'. He was badly caught; the whole town of Cody's Cross would erupt with 'this story'. She'd hear his name and recognise his face, then tell them all at home about it. He was in a circus now, the clever college student, laughing at him for being such a clown. His mother would be mortified.

Suddenly the boss was standing over him, gesturing impatiently.

'What's your name, kid?' He roared.

"Digger Magee', the fighter roared back at him.

When Stanley Thornton announced the fighters in the centre of the ring, the loudest cheer came when Digger Magee's name was called. It seemed that everyone in Luton had heard about him.

The boss took note of the young lad's instant popularity. This was something he'd never witnessed; this sudden interest in youth. Maybe his older boys were not worth looking at. Rough and tough wasn't cutting it like it used to. Youth was good looking, very vulnerable; they cared more about that.

Young Digger Magee didn't rush the wise old veteran. He circled him, moving and dodging, weaving the way Boxer and Michael taught him, for space to land the right fist, watching for a 'gap' to appear. When he was caught with a left uppercut, he'd be more careful next time.

They exchanged a few blows. When the old fighter moved out of the corner he exposed a gap under his elbow, with a soft rim of fat on it. Digger landed a right punch there.

The fighter shook himself after; a better one would stop him. That's what he wanted to do, knock him. The one who fell first and remained there was usually the loser.

When Joe sat down between rounds, he was barely out of breath. The man on the other side was gasping for his. Joe felt he had this fellow's measure, and if he could block him from landing the uppercut, he could take him. There was nothing more dangerous in him than that, except a whole lot of experience, so he'd watch him very closely.

The middle round was slow and cautious, the pace reduced by the older man. The audience were getting bored by it, slow clapping. They had been cheering everything in the first round. Now they were expecting some blood spilled what they had paid their hard-earned money for. But when the fighters came into the centre for the last round the referee told them angrily, 'speed up the action, boys'.

Digger attacked, putting him back in the corner again. He made the same mistake coming out, so the young fellow buried his right hand in the fatty ring under his ribs again, and the bandaged knee folded. Ben Russell, seasoned fighter in Thornton's, was on the floor, dropped on the wobbly knee. He'd been carrying it a long time. Stanley depended on him to keep the rest of them under control, a fifty-year-old father figure. But his fight days were coming to an end.

Young Digger Magee had been caught in the eye with a good one, but he pocketed the five pounds prize money gleefully. It made him think, if he could make that in nine minutes, why would he shovel rocks all day, every day, for the same money? He wasn't college boy for nothing, he could count too.

So he chatted with the boss for a while afterwards. Stanley Thornton took note of the young fresh-faced fighter's appeal to this new audience. He admired his confidence. But he was no schoolboy champion. The crowd was getting younger all the time, with teenage girls turning up for fights now. The Irish boy was a green fighter, but he was different. And he was a survivor. It was hard to hit him. One of his boys was packing it in, after Luton. This lad could join until Southampton, end of season. He would have found out all about him by then. 'Digger Magee' would become part of his show.

Joe didn't need a college education to figure the maths out here. That digging job was a no-brainer. He had brains when it suited him. Would they be beaten out of him a few times? He had never even imagined that.

The boss gave him instructions, what time to turn up Monday morning, if he was serious about becoming a fairground fighter. If he was late he'd miss the chance, for sure.

When Joe walked into the dining room next morning, his eye was swollen and turning blue. He received a hostile reception at the breakfast table. Leitrim couldn't let it go; he enjoyed looking at it so much. He talked about blackening the college boy's other eye, when he lost the run of himself; a rare outburst in the confines of the house. He wasn't pleased when Michael told them all about Joe's winning fight in the boxing booth at the fair. It annoyed him to hear about any 'pugilistic encounter' he didn't have a starring role in. He glared, with jealous rage building up in him.

'Stupid college bastard, if you were smart you wouldn't be here,' he hissed low, in case Mrs Magee heard it. But he made it sound real bad. The bullying maniac was running stone-mad in this fellow's mind. And for some reason it was targeting Jonsie.

Willie Magee picked up on it quick though. He laughed; he'd never seen Leitrim so wound up before. Was there something amiss, he wondered? The foreman could be observed bristling.

'That kid from Ireland was made of tough stuff,' Willie thought. And he was sure Leitrim could see it too.

He smiled across the table like he was a son of his own. 'Boxing at the fair is not a job for the faint hearted, Joe,' he said. There was no bigger compliment to get from the top Digger man himself. He'd tell them all about it at home too.

Bill Flanagan's was his local pub in Ireland. He wanted to do everything right for them at home. It would pay off next time he went over there. He'd like to feel important an odd time. They would be showering him with free drink for years after this.

The following Sunday night, Joe and Michael were on the town for the last time together. A farewell trip, an Irish way of doing goodbye; tell nobody, just disappear. The old tradition for leaving people they really liked stuck in gloom.

The boys were set on a return visit to the Black Stallion Inn. The plan was discussed all week. Michael was a bit in awe of his young friend now, so he was easily led. The display in the boxing booth was impressive, just for having the balls to do it alone. But he had a great right hand, to deliver such a punch. Well he knew it must be accurate for this final tense mission. If Joe missed he was in big trouble. And so was he.

When Michael looked over at him, he appeared relaxed. That was another thing; he never got flustered. Why was that, he wondered? And while he was doing all the yoga, this other guy was getting all the calm.

Michael was so tuned into the plan that he couldn't hear anything in this crowded bar at ten o clock. The whole focus was on one thing only. The place was buzzing. Standing near the counter with a few pints in their hands, they chatted idly, waiting for the 'inevitable', their inner feelings made them fit for calmness. They occasionally smirked at each other, to keep confidence highly pitched.

Suddenly, the ignorant idiot sneaked up from behind like a thief. In typical arrogant style he wasn't doing any listening. It was the boss's way or the highway. His attitude head on.

'I thought I told you two fuckers, 'keep out of the foreman's bar'. We don't want any kids puking up milk in here.'

'Don't worry Leitrim, we won't be staying for long. You insulted me this morning so I challenge you, a fist fight in the carpark, if you have the balls for it. We'll see who the tough man is then.'

Leitrim heard it as one of the best propositions ever put to him. He said it simple, so there was no mistake about it.

'Do ya want to fight now college girlie?'

'Yah, you're no fucking good Leitrim, you're a cowardly bastard.'

Calmness threw the foreman off. He liked excitement when he was 'going to town'. That's what he called it. And it should be angrier. It could be college boy was afraid of him and he was trying to hide it. He wouldn't want people to know he was slaughtering a teenager either. Car park would do. He'd do a job on him out there. No witnesses. The Boss's son would say nothing. He'd know better. His father would have something to say about that.

Joe finished the pint in one go in front of his face. The message was clear; he'd be dumped that fast too.

'Come out after me now, you're a coward without a shovel in your hand. You assaulted me, now it's your turn.'

When Leitrim heard that he shrugged a few times, blinking rapidly, stretching his neck. He was hearing the voices in his head again. College was gonna be broke up.

'You won't be pretty when I'm done ripping ya apart, girlie.'

Joe turned, heading for the side exit. Michael moved discreetly after Leitrim, in case someone came between them.

Then, at the very minute the aggressive foreman was about to step outside, Michael shouted 'Jonsie', the agreed code word between them. The foreman was sent flying backwards, left sprawled out cold on the floor unconscious. Not a move in him. He never saw the punch from around the corner. Or felt it. He wasn't there after it happened either.

They ran out the back gate laughing. Someone would find Leitrim soon enough. Must have slipped on wet ground and banged his head. The foreman would be too proud to admit a 'college boy' had downed him with one punch, albeit a very false one.

That's if he even remembered it.

CHAPTER 16

Joe was travelling in the boxing lorry when it pulled into a transport café. Michael would be expecting his call. It was all arranged from the day before. He'd phone him from a café.

Michael gave him a good account of everything in the Magee house since his departure, with emphasis on their good 'friend' Leitrim. He'd been left with a sore-looking jaw from that perfectly loaded punch. Michael relived the action on the phone; he enjoyed the memory so much. 'The jaw was x-rayed, slight fracture, he said. There wasn't a word out of him now. His father said he should be in hospital. The story got out, Willie Magee made sure of that. Of course it was embellished. That would make it last longer, another bit of folklore in the making. The line explained it perfectly: 'College boy was a good boxer'. He decked Leitrim with one punch, that's all.

Leitrim was a silent heap at the table, where he was left to sit eating nothing. Drinking tea with a shut mouth was his lot. Digger asked him 'who beat the shit out of you?' without getting any reply. So he added without lowering his voice, 'about time too.' Respect wobbled when the boss was ignored. Even admirers turn on you, when you lose.

When Michael mentioned that their absent friend the College Boy was on his way to Cambridge University to renew his studies, Leitrim listened sullenly. Michael knew the foreman hadn't a clue what he was on about, so he shouted it out at him, 'College boy was good at sussing out people.'

Looking straight into Leitrim's face saying it, Michael was brave to stare him down. But he was the boss's son after all. And a fellow with a broken jaw finds it hard to look back.

Joe knew all was well, back in Digger Magee's house so. The chickens had come home to roost.

Michael was going to miss the mad 'college boy', he was sure. There were tears flowing during their chat. They would keep in touch, and remain friends for life, a promise made in stone.

Jonsie 'Joe' Flanagan, alias 'Digger Magee' was in Cambridge now. The Boxing Booth extravaganza arrived on the carnival site. After a quick cup of tea, boiled up like tar on the stove, the crew went into a well-worn routine, assembling their place of work. Joe was told by everyone what to do. And because they were such a savage looking crew, he did it. He knew he was outnumbered.

The big lorry had the tent, ring and other equipment packed into it. The seating was folded carefully and every inch was specifically taken up. One piece out of position threw everything else off.

The colourful wooden wagon they towed was the fighters' living quarters. Six men lived here all day, every day. They had stopped communicating on any meaningful level. Small talk was the order of the day and a variety of hand signals were understood by them. Like strangers with a common purpose, they proceeded on their own way of doing things. Nobody spoke, only in desperation. Stepping outside this way of doing things wasn't appreciated.

Everything was geared towards putting on the show, but for some reason it was never given the proper title that suited it best, 'the Slaughter', the purpose of this scary existence was least apparent. It was only a job for men that knew about nothing else.

The most attractive part of the living quarters wagon was the gaudy outside. Inside was dull; the place reflected the mentality of its occupants, angry silent loners with a chip on their shoulder. Now he was one of them. Nasser had fixed the chip in place for him a long time ago. He might be forced to regret this handiwork, should the priest ever be unfortunate enough to meet up with him again.

There was not a picture of a child, or a house, or a granny, or a song displayed, or any likeness of another boxer. The walls were bare of any pandering to longings of nostalgia. This was death row on wheels. A stove, six bunk beds stacked in twos. Waiting to fight another day, it could be the last one, for any of them. One 'bad trick' was enough for Stanley to get rid of you.

Joe was sleeping over his old adversary, Ben Russell, the man he'd fought in Luton. He'd been part of the furniture for a long time. He'd become his only acquaintance on the job, giving him some tips, how to deal with the rest of them. They weren't interested.

There was Brighton, then a few more before finishing in Southampton. He wasn't enjoying this particular experience. This kid fighter 'Digger Magee' would be blooded in Cambridge.

They weren't all 'college boys' either in this university town on the river. It was as rough as any other place after dark, with lots of construction going on in the area. The navvies were there as well. They wouldn't mind a scrap when it came their way. If they were going to get paid a fiver for it, bring it on.

Stanley Thornton had him sparring, a training session, out on the front stage with Ben Russell each day, to gauge the reception for his 'kid fighter', as he now billed him. Joe thought of the show his father had brought him to see when he was young. There was a two-headed calf, a dog with five legs, two cats joined at the hip. 'Freaks show' it was called. He was a freak in the same kind of show now. 'The kid you'd find easy to beat, if you were any good at all.'

The carnival crowd could see he was very young. He didn't look dangerous like the others, he looked lost, and they wanted to save him. The girls said he was better looking too. So they talked about him with their friends, and came to see him every night. He had a following.

The sparring sessions, well planned by Ben Russell beforehand, were attracting lots of onlookers. Stanley's wife sold tickets for the night time fight, a rare happening. Everything was changing for the better. The boss selected suitable opponents from the stage, careful not to include any of those battered ex-heavyweight types. They were often challengers and when one slipped through, he usually inflicted serious damage on the booth fighter. The crowd liked that as blood gave them a high. That's why they were there.

Joe pocketed a few fivers by staying away from trouble. Not a popular fight plan. Then he was knocked out cold in Cambridge town. He went down and there was nothing more to talk about. He couldn't remember anything. Stanley would need to be more careful selecting, or the boxing booth attraction might become the stretcher's best friend. Some of the girls were saying he shouldn't be there now; he should be at home with his mum.

He was lined up on stage one night, when two lads underneath started discussing him. He heard it all. 'Look he's not hard, no fucking tattoos, ya can do a job on him.'

'Come on man, we need money for booze.'

The bigger one came up to fight him then, a tough-looking character covered in tattoos. He was a muscular, square-shouldered twenty-five-year-old, with a broken nose and 'bad intent'. This was an experienced fighter and he left Joe knocked out on the canvas floor in the shortest possible time. Welcome to the real world, 'champ'. Things were going okay for a while till Stanley screwed up with the selection process.

Carried into the dressing room, smelling salts did it. All Joe could think about afterwards was 'get a tattoo'; they said he was soft with no tattoos, and they were proved right. It could happen again. Get the tattoo quick. He had to look hard, getting one on his arm, like the rest of them. He'd be knocked out more often if he didn't.

He spent next day in bed dumping the blues; not one of them came near him. Ben Russell hadn't anything consoling to say. Maybe it was because he slept over him he bothered speaking at all. They didn't care about getting beat up; it happened to them, sometimes. It was all part of the same job. When you're down that low, it doesn't matter anymore.

Joe was up first thing next morning for the tattoo parlour. It was time to get the identity right. So when the man asked him what tattoo he wanted on his left forearm, he said 'anything will do. It's just a tattoo for the boxing ring.'

'Ok mate, you're Irish, I'll do a harp, put your name on it.' That's how it happened.

On Friday night he went to the pub. There wasn't much time for pints after the show. He was lucky to bump into the cheerful Irish lad in charge of the dodgem cars. Bob was tall, with a set of white teeth permanently smiling, like a rock star. Joe could see an advantage hanging out with this character. There were girls everywhere when he was around. And so it turned out to be. Anytime they met up, they took into chasing the women, with great expectations and success.

One night, Bob told him his story. It started off sad, with his father running away from home. They'd been great friends, but the time came when his parents didn't agree anymore. His father became very unsettled. He told his son that he was going to join the French Foreign Legion. He would see him again when he returned to Ireland. That was two years ago. Now Bob wanted to reconnect with his old man. He was on his way to France and he'd be joining this famous regiment of Legionnaires noted for their toughness. Men enlisted from every country in the world, criminals, murderers evading capture, and a mix of people seeking adventure, like them.

From bank managers to doctors, there was no difference for Legionnaires. They just didn't fit into the world they inhabited. So they chose to hide away for a while. It helped them to find their true selves. Or they might get killed in the process. He made the motion of slicing his neck with his finger, laughing doing it. He'd fit in, knew where he was heading and was determined to get there, a man on a mission. Joe could hang out with this fellow.

His knowledge and his confidence impressed him. Bob said that when he returned to Ireland, all the qualities the ladies loved would be moulded into this French Foreign Legion soldier. Joe would like to feel that way going home. This lad from Dublin was on his way to France. If his father was still in the Foreign Legion, he'd find him.

When Bob talked about these men, it sounded like a great adventure. He was in no doubt about that. 'Can I come with you Bob? I'll join up too.'

Bob was delighted to have company, so they left the carnival behind them in Southampton. He was glad to escape from the old wooden wagon with nothing in it but five 'punch-drunk dummies' for company. He'd won and lost, learned a lot; how to give it and how to take it. And he was glad to escape from it. He had to sleep with his money in a sock all the time, he never took it off. That tells you. Wasn't he lucky he met Dublin Bob? He would never have thought of becoming a soldier. It sounded much better than being a nurse.

That's what adventures were for, being something you never thought of before. There was bound to be horses there; he could see himself galloping over the sand on a white Arab stallion, with the white turban on his head flying behind him, like your man in the pictures.

They walked around the docks, where ships and boats of all descriptions were tied up. It took Bob a while to gather any useful information, there weren't many people about. He'd made several enquiries about 'departure for France boats'. They visited a few before finding one that would take them to Le Havre, in France. That discovery was very well timed. It was getting dark.

It was a Red Star French-flagged vessel, and the captain agreed to take them if they worked their passage, shovelling coal into a furnace. They must show up next morning at six o clock, before the ship sailed out on the morning tide.

'If you're late you'll miss us' was made clear in broken English.

They located the nearest inn. 'The Gentle Inn' was inscribed in old scroll writing over the battered front door. The whole building was just a little wider than a barber shop. The boys found this quaint relic of the past very appealing. And felt lucky for discovering it. There was a dull ball light over the door that barely lit up the entrance. They stepped down into a dim lit, smoke filled room; this place was a laid back reminder of times long gone by. The conversations sounded good humoured, familiar old friends; telling each other things they already knew about.

It looked like intruding on a family gathering; such was the cosiness of the place and comfort in each other's company. Pork pies swilled down with pints of beer would lead to a comfortable night's sleep. They relished the thought. 'You could meet Dick Turpin in here,' Bob said.

An elderly couple sitting behind the bar beckoned them over. They were chatting with the old sea salts sitting up at the bar. This was where all the scented smoke was coming from. The landlord joined them with a pipe full of his own making.

'I'm Dot, my husband Arthur's beside me here, we're the landlord's boys, and you're welcome. Now what can I get yer to sip?'

When she served up two pints, Bob enquired about the availability of accommodation for one night.

'Yes laddie, we'll fix yer up right 'ere.' She took their bags in behind the counter. 'Don't be in any hurry now, everything is ready. You've had a long journey I know your accents. I always like to take the money in advance, in the event of an early departure,' she said, smiling warmly at them.

Joe picked up that she'd been stung by Irish men already, doing an early morning flit. He didn't blame her. And he'd encountered a lot of anti-Irish sentiment on his travels. Paddies could be very rough customers, and they weren't everyone's cup of tea.

They sat down near a log fire, where two well dressed women sat opposite each other, warming themselves. One of them got up suddenly, removing her long red coat to hang from a rack on the wall. When she sat down again, the centre of her attraction was much more revealing. She bulged out of her low top and Bob wasn't impressed with the view at all, sounding very cynical when he whispered to Joe. Laughing like an idiot.

'Looks like they're smothering, doesn't it, poor bastards.'

'Who?'

'The tits look squashed together like a baby's arse.'

'Stop it, they're too old for us Bob.'

'They don't think so Joe, prostitutes; we won't be going down that road. They're nearly forty for Christ's sake.'

This prostitute revelation switched Joe off; his 'Flower of Scotland' had more than adequately filled that position. There would be lots of nice girls in France, when they got there. He was sure of that.

The quaintness of the tavern appealed to him. It seemed like it hadn't changed for hundreds of years.

'Those rafters look as if they spent years washed up in the sea, they have that 'salty dog' look about them,' Bob said, with a knowledgeable expression on his face.

'Is the wall made up with blood and horse hair?' Joe asked. 'There's a pub in my home town, like that. Supposed to be hundreds of years old, and looks it.'

'Like the old dolls looking us over from the fire there,' Bob said, laughing. 'I'm going up to bed, we have an early start, and whatever you want to do is your business. You're hardly going to be a mamma's boy, are you? Any one of those ladies would gobble down your little Irish cock and blow you out again in bubbles.' In his Dublin dialect it sounded more hilarious than harmful. He laughed at his own brash humour, at least someone enjoyed it.

Joe leaned back in his chair to imagine what might lie ahead of him in France. He would have enough money to spend, not like when he had arrived in Glasgow. When he thought about it he put his hand in his pocket to feel it. Digger had saved ten pounds a week for him; one hundred and twenty pounds was a lot of money. He looked at it, turning it around in his hand absent-mindedly; as much as he had ever had.

The ladies winked at each other. They knew where it was stashed now. He had a zipper on the money pocket. There was enough cash to compensate for a bad weekend in Southampton before heading back to London next day.

When he finished his pint Joe headed for the toilet. The fireside woman in red was waiting when he came out. She'd been doing a little removing and they were in her handbag now. In the dim lit corridor she pressed her perfumed body against him, dropping her hand between his legs. She probed her hot tongue around his mouth, for a passionate promise. When she took his hand up to the hair he could feel the damp softness like Vaseline between her legs. She knew he was hers then. None of them could ever turn away from that moist offering. And only a chemist would know the difference. Vaseline was a must.

'I live near here; we can do anything you want there,' she whispered. There was no way of resisting her, even if he wanted to. He was well up for action now.

Her friend was buying a bottle of Jamaica rum. Dot took note of this purchase, shaking her head. It looked like Irish was planning on a late night. She'd give them a call in the morning. He would be much lighter then, for sure.

'I'll be awake all night, boys will be boys,' she sighed to the assembled crew.

They'd been surveying the transaction as well. One of them started talking about fishing to keep it nice. But another one ranted about sex, as a necessity.

'Aye,' he concluded, 'it might even be man's natural entitlement.'

Dot eyeballed him and he dropped his head, under her gaze. These crowd played games for sport every time they could. When she headed to bed at closing time, the front door was left off the latch for her guests, usual procedure in the inn.

At five o'clock in the morning she returned to give the boys a call. The youngster that had gone off with the ladies of the night hadn't returned. Nobody knew where they were staying. That was that.

She felt bad his friend was left alone. He wasn't happy about being let down. But he understood the mating call for a night owl. To her credit, she knew how it worked too. Pity though, about his young friend's lust for life. It was bad luck in meeting that one.

When Dublin Bob explained that their final destination was the French Foreign Legion, she was more consoled. It was good the youngster had missed out on that appointment so. Her own son had disappeared in the adventure direction; this Irish boy brought back that ache to her heart again. Perhaps a similar carefree attitude made him vulnerable as well.

When Joe woke up, alone in the room, the empty bottle on the window sill was all that remained of the party. The first time he had tasted rum, and it had knocked him out. He hadn't a clue what time it was, and remembering the ladies, he was glad they were gone.

Then he thought about them cavorting naked on the bed. Instructing him what to do, and the best way to do it, he had hated every minute of it. He had never seen girls kissing each other in that way before, downing the rum looking at them, he got sick. This wasn't the kind of night he'd visualized in his dream world. They had laughed at him for their own amusement, a novel way for them to spend a night. But they had never asked him for money. That was the good thing about it.

Then he got a panic attack. He remembered the boat journey to France. He dressed hurriedly, and made a desperate run for the docks. Sea gulls screeched at each other, diving on the seaweed rocks. The tide was gone out long ago and the boat to France with it.

Bob would be shovelling coal like hell, to reach his destination. And he was left in despair.

He made his way to the Gentle Inn in a very depressed state. The landlady didn't help his troubles when he came in the door. 'Where you going laddie, let your friend down have you?'

'Yes I'm sorry. Could I have coffee please?'

She stared at him, a faint smile on her wise face, weighing him up. She could see it more clearly now, for what it was worth. This was little more than a bold child.

'Rightly so laddie, hope you have your entire money safe in your pocket, after your night out with those ladies.' She sounded a cautious tone, heading for the bar.

Joe's hand darted down to feel his pocket. The gut wrenching thought hit him – gone, nothing to pay for his coffee.

The money was all gone. It was over. All he could do was cry, tears of hopelessness. What was he going to do now? Where was the nearest graveyard?

Dot Gentle watched him from the bar. She was a sucker for young lads' tears. Her husband had never got over the loss of their son either. It brought her back a few years, and the kind mother surfaced. Putting the coffee in front of him, she sat quietly to coax the whole story, listening patiently to his rambled tale. Her soft face never altered once.

There were Irish lorry drivers, going home from the continent, calling into the pub regularly. It wouldn't be difficult to send him home. But she was filled with compassion for his predicament. They must discuss options, after he had slept for a while. Her husband would hear the whole story first. There were rooms that needed a makeover. Maybe this was a chance to get it done. None had been touched up for years. If he'd painted a café in Glasgow he could tackle a pub in Southampton. It wasn't easy to get someone for small jobs. This fellow would give her a spruced-up pub. That expectation alone was worth all the fuss.

'I'll show you your room,' she said. 'Later, you can eat, meet my husband Arthur. There's some work here, painting for a while. A little bartending perhaps, like you did in Ireland. You'll need some money in your pocket going back home.'

'Thanks very much that would be most helpful, Mrs Gentle.'

Joe could take change of purpose in his stride. But being foolhardy, when survivor instinct takes over, can finish up bad. Thrills and spills along the way provide intrigue for the chase. And, they say lessons are learned better the hard way.

But this carefree attitude provides free spirits scope to pursue what's in them. It moulds the kind of character you need for taking chances; that's why survivors retain so much knowledge. Answers must come quicker in times of strife. They have to.

Practical experience should be about finding out how it's done right. Wild abandonment is forever the risk taker's route. And even if Jonsie sometimes overruled Joe, wisdom was in the same breath, especially when survival was the proper option.

Free spirits, through the progression of natural instinct, are very adaptable to change. And this factors in that prerequisite for survival.

The following quote is attributed to the biologist Charles Darwin: 'It is not the most intelligent, or the strongest of the species that survives; it's the one that's most adaptable to change.'

CHAPTER 17

Things went badly wrong for Blimey when he lost his home. The Gardai physically removed him on a court order and dumped him out on the street with nowhere to go. He was stuck in the worst house in town now. 'Lucky to have it,' they said.

And then he was forced into contacting Louie again, to give the place a good fumigating, though their past history was fraught with difficulty. However necessity proved to be a great leveller. Louie needed the work; his old boss still owed him some money. That might come along another way. Blimey was stuck in misery. Once the grandest man in town, he was sleeping in the gallows now. That's what they called the gates outside his door, where the previous tenant had hanged himself. This so-called Yank was a highly praised builder, living in his new home with big shots either side of him. But Blimey could see he didn't know how to dress properly. And the swagger of him on the street in tattered jeans. An enemy from the past was an enemy forever.

Blimey was able to boss him about when they were young. Those days were long gone. He must be calculating and careful now. This Yank was proving to be a thorn in his side.

He was one of the town 'committee people' who had seized Blimey's property. The bungalows he built blocked a beautiful view of the river. Then they'd got planning permission for a hotel, and he couldn't even hold on to his own picture hall. They took that away from him too. So he had a lot of animosity now. He was wondering for a while if this Yank was settling old scores. Blimey would have to watch him closer on account of that, even if that bastard tried to ignore him. He'd still watch as he pretended to sketch the hotel.

The Major was part of this phoney committee too. He couldn't intimidate him anymore either. They were all in it together. This old house of Ned Goat's was owned by the same crowd that had taken his home. They had all benefited from his misfortune in some way or another. Revenge would come his way; he thought about it every day. Blimey was deep.

At a meeting in Flanagan's bar, everyone agreed 'Cody's Arms' was the best name for the new hotel. It had a welcome 'arms wide open' feel. Like that comforting line in the gospel song; a blessing from heaven only pious people could feel.

They listened in case they'd miss what the politician was saying. It was in all their interests, he drooled. This top class hotel would fill the town with customers. Everyone would benefit from that. 'I have made Cody's Cross a destination now,' he roared, 'with this new hotel creating jobs. Not a small town for passing through anymore.' It was all due to hard work by the town development committee. This dedicated group gave their time to improving the town. They should be complimented for that. Tourists were coming to the river. And he told them he spoke to the planning authority, on 'all your behalf'. Then he went on to ramble what he'd heard as if it was his own. The hotel had twelve bedrooms, where the neglected old house and dilapidated picture hall once stood. The whole place was tastefully landscaped with different trees; pink and blue hydrangeas. They applauded and laughed at the flowers knowing he couldn't differentiate between dandelion and dahlia. 'A new beginning for a long established community,' he shouted. 'It was you the people with all you put into it. It's a credit to the whole community.'

Flash encouraged them to feel proud of their achievements. The town belonged to them all. 'A transformation of the old steward's residence, he bragged, an eyesore on Main Street for years. Blimey wouldn't like to hear his home bad-mouthed.

WT Flanagan was running the hotel his own way. Yank was keeping a watchful eye, and the bemused Mrs Wilson was 'overseeing' everything going on. The comedy of the situation wasn't lost on her. Of course she wasn't part of the hotel ownership, so she could be non-judgemental when consulted about 'business enterprise moves', or any other simple events.

Major Cody had no financial stake either; his interest was simply opportunistic. Hanna was keeping well away from it; the small hotel bar was more opposition for her husband's pub. It would present a clear conflict of interest for her, so she couldn't commit to anything like that.

Since the County Council had started tarring the street, for the first time ever, none of the kids in the town wore shoes. At the beginning of summer, all footwear was removed until September, when school started again. It suited the mood; tourists loved this old world place that never changed. They spoke of their forefathers arriving in America barefoot. How the stories growing up affected them, but they still prospered. It wasn't easy for them either. Prejudice everywhere. No dogs or Irish, they said. And 'they were still barefoot in Ireland'.

The limestone gravelled street was gone for good now. Motorized vehicles were making a regular appearance. And all this progress had brought about more changes. The horse transport service was coming to the end of its long, dependable journey. Petrol pumps that looked like spacemen were making their presence felt.

There were two of these pumps on the footpath outside Danny's house. No one knew how they got there, or cared. You could only get petrol when he was around. In a real emergency, he might be located in Flanagan's yard, and he'd oblige anyone, if they waited in the pub till he was ready. It might take some time to register the lack of speed in this petrol delivery system. Danny wasn't even trying to learn if it was fast enough.

Guided by personal interests, the development committee was talking up more projects, and everyone was behind them in their endeavours. It was a requirement that there were no objectors to slow down planning applications. The committee moved things along smoothly. Everyone was excited that the tourists were coming.

Molly put six window boxes on the front of the pub and the old walls were whitewashed, for the first time in years. It looked alive again. And now it was known as the 'best pub' in Cody's

Cross. Only old people drank in Flanagan's Bar.

The committee wanted to create a cultural image for the town. There were grants available. Some of that old fashioned decency lay in WT still; he was proud of Cody's Cross. That little weakness must not be mistaken for good character though. All building materials were supplied by his hardware store at a reduced rate. He didn't take much profit. And he knew well that he would be credited with the brains behind all the progress. This was turning out better than he'd ever dreamed off. The Yank was 'engineering' it with personal objectives in mind. Their coming together was a partnership's dream.

They kept an eye on the movements of one Major Cody. He was a man that shifted along a narrow track; his own plans were always paramount. The condescending attitude he regularly displayed was for intimidation purposes. When he knew he'd get away with it, enough whiskey gave him false courage to say anything.

Hanna made progress with a new committee recruit, Lucy Whyte. She'd returned home to care for her elderly parents, and they hijacked her for the town development cause. The newsagent's daughter would be perfect for the committee, with her Dublin experience, that pleasant way and cultured voice, to cope with the 'flowery accent' of the English Major that gave everyone the creeps. She'd cut him down to size in her own time. They were all sure of that.

Dr Wilson's Close was fully completed in time. And that paved the way for more expansive ideas. The people involved in this new beginning were in daily communication. This town development committee was proving to be a worthwhile venture for some of them. The hotel was a low key affair in the beginning. But it was promising.

WT was trying to learn the trade as he went along. It would have to be done right. There would be more than a few critics looking it over. And there were grants available. He was always brooding, thinking about all the money he could make.

Yank poured himself another cup of tea in the kitchen. They were admiring their job. Ongoing construction made things inconvenient for a time, but you'd never know it now. Everything looked pristine from the comfort of the home. Something they were both very proud off. And they congratulated themselves on account of that. 'Winning against all odds,' they laughed. For a moment or so they were close, like thieves in the night.

WT laughed, talking about Blimey employing Louie to paint the hall just before it was demolished, but Louie never got paid. Something had happened between them in England, and they had fallen out about money again yesterday. He'd never heard Blimey shouting such abuse at anyone on the street in all the years he'd known him, so it must be serious stuff. Blimey thought, if he 'painted his hall we couldn't touch it'. The Major was trying to get rid of him for a long time. And he was plagued by a shortage of money. His account in the hardware store was still unpaid.

WT mentioned this in passing, but he never forgot it when talking with him. He'd called him to order about paying it off several times. There was no comeback.

Yank said he was glad Blimey was gone from around the place. WT listened; he had respect for this Yankee man now. There was more in him, and the old dealer was attentive. He wouldn't miss any opportunity. He remembered Danny talking about Yank with him one day. They both knew him in childhood days when the judiciary victimised him. A young son's mistake, when he tried to provide food for his ailing mother.

'They set out to get him because he was poor.' The wagon master always maintained that. 'It happened that way then, still happening now, so we needn't wonder about it, divorce proceeding of our time.' His father went out to get an armful of turf for the fire, and he never came back into the house again in his life.

They were evicted out of their little house on the river by the Major's people, so they squatted in an old cart shed out on the road. It was still there, covered in briars, 'bad memories every time Yank passes by, I'm sure,' Danny said, and that scoundrel Blimey made his miserable existence even worse. They were always fighting coming home from school. Yank's mother was almost blind. It was a sorry state to live in, with no financial assistance available from state benefits either.

'They didn't even have a chimney; their fire was on the floor. I was out there once, never gone back again. I'll never forget it. Do you know, before he turned up, I often thought about him. She cut his hair with sheep shears, I remember that. It was chomped in patches. He was full of lice. Everyone ran away from him, in case they brought them home. When his mother gave him money for eggs, he bought two cigarettes instead. Ryan sold eggs stacked on a small table, outside his shop door then. The young fellow stole two eggs and the Gardai were called. He got six months in a reformatory school, pointed out on the street as a thief and he ran from the town in shame. Abandoning her to her fate ate away at him. He told me that. He got on a ship sailing from Liverpool, working his passage to America. He's a great man WT, living here in the community with us again. Blimey insulted him one day crossing the street. The Yank told me he spat the words out at him: "Do you still make the omelettes?" It wasn't intended to be light hearted.

He doesn't want him to forget the past. He wants him to remember where he came from and above all who was in charge back then, because nothing had changed. The Yank will remember that remark, I can tell you.

'Some of them never want you to forget where you came from, in case you'd feel good about yourself, when you're trying to do your best, WT. The Yank has an aura of wellbeing about him that Blimey hasn't. How could it be that someone from a hovel along the side of the road had risen so far above him?'

He'd never give Yank the satisfaction of feeling that good.

'A man with knowledge of American ways could do a lot of good; maybe get a struggling town on its feet. Let's leave him alone to see what turns up. But he will remember past torments, you can be sure.'

'He'd be well entitled to Danny, I'd be the same way', said WT. And he added more intently, 'I'd make it my business to get him for it no matter how long it went on.'

When Joe returned from England, he began working for his Uncle Tom in the hardware store. His first duty of care was the horses. Like his father Bill, it was a task he relished. But they were being gradually phased out; a red van with Flanagan's on the sides took care of deliveries now. Danny was still the driver. And Flanagan's funeral undertakers had acquired a motorized hearse. The team of black horses was still kept on for traditional funerals.

Joe was trying to drop the Jonsie name, but that's what everyone still called him. It sounded childish, he thought, having got used to people saying Joe in England. He preferred it that way now.

That long adventure had taken the 'wanderlust' out of him. Boxer told him that was how it worked and he might never leave Ireland again. Contented with his lot, the worst over him, he was settled back at home. After an absence of four years from the game, he was playing regularly with the town junior football team. They wore black and white shirts and were called the 'Magpies'. The new Garda in Muldoon's old job was a good footballer.

'The whole competition must be taken more seriously,' he was saying out loud, and the new football committee were listening. This Garda was seen as a godsend for the ambitions of the club, the only one to straighten them all out. 'The drinking must stop.' Training must begin in earnest. They had to win something. He lectured them. And they listened.

Rasp had nothing to do with the team anymore. At last, they were free of him. Not before he had ruined some of them, unfortunately.

Joe still had his coloured pony Ruby. Danny had taken care of her when he was away; she had her daughter with her for company. He was excited about doing the breeding job again. Although he had grown up fast into Joe, he was still Jonsie with the horses.

Bill viewed his hardware store appointment with mild contempt. His father had got his hands on him after all.

WT had full view of his hotel standing just outside the door. He could open it up every day, if he wished. But running a hotel was different from a shop. And he was still learning about it. He'd made some progress, and the small bar inside was ticking over nicely. There were bedrooms available on request.

Mrs Wilson recommended a woman who would keep the hotel aired and clean for a few pound a week. She'd make up beds for guests staying overnight for a little extra. WT knew there was money to be spent setting this place up, and he was calculating how he was going to get it back. He was determined that his partner would pay his fair share. It was not going to turn out that he'd be stuck, like a round of whiskey in the pub. Once was enough to get caught. The two of them would have a long talk about business commitments again, soon.

Joe was beginning to see something wrong with the new hotel arrangement. There wasn't anyone coming and going, like a normal run hotel. Quietness, like the graveyard he'd lived in. He knew a hotel should be a lively place, full of people all the time. This was just a drab sleepover where the odd commercial traveller spent nights drinking alone in his room. It should be a fun place, like the pub Molly and Mack ran next door. He'd been in there a few times for a pint. He took care his mother never got the smell from him. He was varying his times coming home. But he knew she was on to it already. There were tensions.

WT racked his brains about how he could make the Cody Arms more profitable. He wasn't paying out wages for nothing.

And if he didn't hire some people, he couldn't stay open. 'As a going concern,' he moaned, 'A going concern.'

Tom's new business idea was an electrical installation company. Houses were getting wired up throughout Ireland. There were two gangs of electricians working full time and electric light was being installed everywhere. The hardware store was stocked with all kinds, makes and descriptions of modern electrical appliances.

Joe started up a travelling shop, going around in the old red van. He went through the countryside selling toasters, kettles and radios, with every other electrical appliance available, on order. Washing machines were the new sought after commodity.

The young lad's popularity as a footballer helped. His knowledge of Uncle Tom's newly wired homes locations gave him access to eager customers. They were waiting to buy, and business was good.

Missing out on the hardware store broke Bill's heart. His bar business declined with Freddy Brown's singing lounge taking all the business. He complained about people all the time and falling out with people was what occupied him now. Even the after-hour trade he depended on had dwindled to zero. Nobody wanted to spend time with a grumpy person.

Complaining about Freddie Brown's all the time, there was a bad name associated with the place. They sniggered among themselves about calling into that 'den of iniquity' some quiet night, when nobody would see them. And they were all 'hard' enough for a visit, there would be no point going in there otherwise. 'Did you see the size of her?' They all saw them.

Dr Wilson's Close had a new name, 'Millionaire's Row'. There could be jealousy taking root after a few years, when novelty wore off. Nevertheless, the townspeople were a wily bunch of survivors who appreciated the value of good intentions. But wrongdoing was attached to some of these town development decisions, and they whispered that there were shady deeds being done. It wasn't hard to figure out whose pockets were being filled.

The instigator of these bad tidings was Drover. He instructed Mad Phil to shout his doctrine in both pubs now. Drover's solitary way made him strange. He worked on a lorry bringing cattle on the ferry across to England, and he didn't care what anyone thought about him. Some of his deeds were full of bad intent, like making poteen for putting in cups of tea, taking advantage of intoxicated people. Homemade whiskey was powerful stuff. It could take you away on hallucinogenic trips.

The old yew tree had witnessed everything going on in Cody's Cross for almost three hundred years, but there had been injustice bestowed upon it in the past. Drover was always saying that, even though his great grandfather was one of its victims. A vindictive man, he could put a 'curse on you', they whispered, with silver crosses dangling like bad luck from his hairy ears and a red bandanna round his head, like a pirate. Drover respected no one. Mad Phil was warning everyone there was worse going to happen. Spouting things nobody wanted to hear, he pointed his finger up at the old tree, shouting damning words as if they were gospel truth. People with badness would be found out. He laughed aloud as if that was funny; it was known who they were, another mad laugh. There would be a last day, and the mad words would freak them all out in turn, even for merely suggesting a doomsday.

CHAPTER 18

Freddie Brown's name was still over the pub, but the mood was different inside. There were no quaint loners whispering about the delight of the place anymore. It was all modern now; you could get carried away having the craic. Wasn't that what it was all about? The best of them knew it. And the rest of them ridiculed it like they always did. The town had moved on a long way. The new American landlords Mack and Molly were smooth operators, more LA types than small town folks.

The boat people were enthralled by the 'far out shenanigans', as they called it. There wasn't anything like it in Dublin. And they spread good stories along the river so everyone would hear about Molly's place. The townspeople talked about the antics with shock, awe and pure delight. There were 'big shots, politicians amongst them too'. What went on in there was better than the cinema, they said. Drover spread this news about moral decline. He primed Mad Phil with 'sex sins' he'd heard about, for the confessional. The people waiting in line outside heard everything the priest said too. Everyone listened when he went inside the box. The priest was very cautious. Money was at stake here. This thrill-seeking couple in the pub were generous in their offerings to the Catholic Church. Although never attending mass, they made kind donations. There was always a pardon for repentant souls. He'd been in to wish them well, in the name of God. The priest knew they'd find their true way one day, when healing time came around. It could even wait until the last day if they choose. They were still Protestants, after all.

WT had been watching Blimey's antics for a while. Same routine every time, he'd arrive at where Mrs Wilson's house had once stood and stare at the white hotel building, sitting on the spot where he was born. It was hard to explain, with such a refined accent. Could he describe his dire circumstances now, living in the goat man's old home? A place everybody called 'the gallows.'

But in spite of all that, he was still impeccably dressed.

'It tells you a lot about the man' WT mused, watching him. He probably wouldn't know he was a bollox.'

WT observed him take out a jotter, looking intently ahead of him. The old man figured he was sketching the hotel. He opened the door to call him over, and he could see his embarrassment. He was a customer in his shop, and his family before him, paying for everything they got. Always clean shaven with a nice shirt and blazer; WT admired a bit of style. Even though this character lived in the squalor of his present abode, he still looked the part. And some parts were hard to fill in this town.

When Blimey realised he had the ear of the richest man in the county, he felt important again. This store owner was the only one he'd bother having a conversation with. So he bad-mouthed the

Yank, reminding WT of those humble beginnings he had crawled out from under, and the old man sat still, as if he was listening. But he was doing business in his head. If this picture hall 'genius' could show films in the hotel, good news would spread. Not many people knew it was open. This man dressed like he was a manager, or something. And he wouldn't have to pay him a penny. In fact he might get a rent, like it said in the book about getting a hotel up and running that he was reading.

Wouldn't Blimey look good parading around his hotel like he was part of the furniture, giving the impression to strangers that there was a classy manager observing everything going on? With that awful 'West Brit 'speaking voice he'd cultivated listening to the Major. That he detested. But it could come in useful now.

The tourists wouldn't know he was a bollox either just by looking at him. But that didn't matter anyway; they wouldn't be hanging around long enough to let it bother them.

Image, WT knew, had everything to do with it. It was all about image.

'If you were showing your pictures in the hotel, wouldn't that get you back on your feet again?' WT said to him.

It stopped the picture hall man dead in his rant about Yank. 'Are you offering me the hall for my film productions, Mr Flanagan?'

With that hopeful sound in his voice, WT knew he must wait for a while. There was something he remembered of Yank's personal opinion about Blimey to consider first. The Yank detested this man; Susan mightn't like the idea much either. There were a few hurdles left to cross yet. But WT considered it done, and he gave him some good news to keep him going. The film shows should be back in action again.

'Yes Blimey, Saturday nights, to hell with the priest, how's that.' That was the first time Mr Flanagan had ever called him by his nickname. It let him know from the start who was boss. Blimey couldn't contain his enthusiasm. He was ready for more discussion on the matter, and made an attempt to sit down. But the boss got up quickly when the chat was over. Yank might walk into the present gathering.

'Think it over and we'll talk again. Oh by the way, I noticed you using a pad looking up at the hotel, are you drawing it, can I have a look? I might buy it from you if it's good enough.'

'Ah no Mr Flanagan, not yet, when it's finished you'll see.' He went out the door in a hurry.

'We'll work something out,' the old boy shouted after him.

Joe could see how much things changed since he'd been away. Attitudes had hardened. But the houses were all softened, newly painted, colour coordinated by the development committee's cultural advisor, Lucy Whyte. And all the residents came together for this effort to clean up the town. There was a tidy town competition to enter that would make the Cody's Cross name. The footballers had a dance in the hotel for funds towards the town painting job. Every evening when he finished work, Joe headed for the football field. He was one of the best players on the town team now, and with perseverance he'd become a good electrical goods salesman in the area. There was something settling about being back at home after all his adventures. He'd seen a lot and the wanderlust was gone.

If it did that to him, wasn't it worth all the hard times travelling?

This new street development would provide more opportunities in the town for business outlets; it was all they ever talked about now. And Joe knew the motivation was all down to the Yank. He seemed to have the town's interests at heart. It was good that everybody rallied round him, except for the renegade loner Drover. And that Blimey person nobody wanted to know about. Louie was working as the Yank's chief foreman now. Anything Yank wanted, Louie took care of it.

But the County Council was breaking Yank's heart. He was too progressive for their nonchalant way. 'There was extra work with this American nuisance,' they complained among themselves. And these comfortable veterans, used to sitting around with cups of tea, weren't on for shifting. Where did this fellow get the idea he was an engineer? Maybe he had too much money in America.

The university graduates all agreed that there would be less work to bother their heads with in future, if he was closed down early. He was a tin can to kick down the road. And 'blow in' made the sound sweeter.

Drover was getting Mad Phil to annoy these council men, for sport. 'Get a statue of Yank erected on the green,' Phil shouted, to everyone's amusement. No one would listen to him, but everyone heard what he had to say. The council generals did nothing, as usual.

The Yank wanted Flash Politician to promote his cause, to fulfil this solemn promise he had made when he was young. He'd get even with those 'tyrant landlord people' that had burned his mother's home before he was old enough to understand.

On this quiet stretch along the river bank, where his family cottage had once stood, he would build a new home for her. One she richly deserved.

When he tried to buy this land he was told politely that it was not for sale. Mr Whyte was honest, saying he had given the land to his daughter Lucy. She would be looking after them, he told him, and she might want to get married one day. That would be a perfect place for her house. And that was the end of that.

The Yank got more interested in Lucy, from a business perspective, of course. He'd made enquiries about the shy young lady who had once been a librarian in Dublin, and every story he heard about her was a good one. She was the quiet darling of the whole town. So he'd started calling into the newsagents more often, to 'feel her consideration'. She was only half his age. 'Not interested in romance,' he heard. There were anxious whispers of a disastrous relationship in Dublin. No one wanted to discuss this private matter, in order to protect her.

This young lady didn't use careless words or share any disposable phrases. Yank had been talking with her. Anyway it was all about business now, but once upon a time his reputation in Boston was as a ladies' man.' She wasn't at ease talking with him for some reason. He could see that. Maybe her father had said Yank was after the land.

But he was very pleased when she joined the town development committee. And when she spoke with such sincerity, he respected her more. That was all very different from his Boston experiences. However, his interest wasn't reciprocated in the newsagent's shop.

She registered his presence with casual customer exchanges, and he could see she wasn't like that with everyone else. This situation would remain for the time being. But the town development meetings were getting more interesting. Lucy Whyte came into prominence when she had something worthwhile to say. Maybe a man of the world would know how to wait; for a time when it was proper to proceed. And heed the needs of a special lady.

One day when Joe was visiting his grandfather, he began telling him all about his friend Timer from school. He was now a college-trained hotel manager living at home in the west.

WT picked up his ears instantly, hearing that. His grandson's friend, the hotel manager, college trained in Scotland, trying to get away from home... it all sounded good to WT.

'A gambling casino, bejesus!' he roared. 'Now you're talking, son.' He had this slobbery grin on his face, like a fox thinking about hens.

Joe told him good things about Timer and added a few bits he had made up, just to fit the success profile of a real winner. He sounded a confident note, telling the positive story. Timer living in the town would be fun company. There was no social life to be had here for a young wild man who was convinced he had seen it all before. His school pal would surely bring out the best of it.

'Timer is a wizard at getting things done,' he told his grandfather. He had promised to open a gambling casino one day, with a new approach that nobody had come up with before. Cody's Arms could benefit from some of those ambitions, if they had a holiday resort for gambling. Like Las Vegas. The 'Green

Oasis Casino' with all the trees and water around here, like an oasis. It's the perfect place for saying goodbye to your money.

WT kept saying 'Green Oasis Casino'. He liked the sound of it, giggling like he was young again. 'Bejesus!' he shouted jumping up from his chair, 'This is all between the two of us, Jonsie. Not another person to know son, promise me that. We must keep the gambling quiet for a while; the church would come down on us hard for that. But we'll get a story going to best them in the end.'

'I swear to it grandad,' the boy said, eyeballing him. He only used 'grandad' to soften him; for the 'firm horsey handshake' the grasp was tight. It was safe going so in proud family tradition 'amongst us is the best way forward'.

The old man was dealing with another true blue like himself who would 'never let you down'. He emphasised that loudly when he was saying it.

Joe was looking forward to renewing acquaintance with Timer, burying that Scotland experience for good. It was just a bad time for everyone at the same time, was his logic.

WT was getting a powerful smell of money from it. He must act quickly, in case the scent went awry, before Bill got big ideas. 'Now son, tell me something, this hotel manager, where is he now?' He spoke in a slow, deadly way, emphasising some secret urgency in the matter.

'Less than an hour's drive grandad. Less than an hour's drive.'

'Right son, we're going to visit him me and you. Tell no one, do you hear me?'

A few days later they headed off driving west. They were going round looking at horses all day was the story. That particular excuse never came in for ridicule. Respect for the horse.

Timer wasn't enthusiastic on seeing Joe arrive at his family's run-down hotel. This job was not portraying a success story. His weird father was hovering around keeping an eye on everything, and they were fighting morning, noon and night. Timer explained that small detail nervously, to cover himself.

Joe told their story confidently. His grandfather was interested in a gambling casino for his new hotel. There was a job for a manager to run the place and make some money. Was he in?

It was the best news Timer had heard for years. His father had threatened to kick him out several times for drinking and carousing, and he had had enough of it. If it was possible to start immediately, he was ready to leave with them.

The Flanagan's were delighted to have him along. 'Sure, you could move into a room in the hotel,' WT said. The Yank couldn't complain about not being informed when the new manager arrived. He'd firmly knocked WT's idea for Blimey's cinema show in the hotel, insisting he wouldn't want him near the place, so he felt obliged to give way on this one. In any case, a manager might be the best way to get it up and running properly. Sometimes it made him ill, just looking at it. It looked like the best kept ruin in the whole country.

He wasn't told about any gambling casino plans either. It was sprung on him. Yank was starting to count down the hours on this hotel shift.

But there wasn't time for discussing that problem yet; he was preoccupied trying to get his hands on Lucy Whyte's bit of land.

He was making no headway even with broaching the subject with her. The newsagent's daughter was in her early forties, tall with a fresh complexion, attractive to the eye, challenging for the mind; she dressed plain, reserved. You'd know when you were talking with her for a short period of time that she had style. Yank knew it put 'careful' in front of your face without saying anything.

Lucy had been over visiting Mrs Wilson several times; they liked each other's company, with subtle similarities in their makeup.

Susan was delighted when she got involved in the development committee, with such a keen interest in the town she had grown up in. And of similar opinion that 'those men shouldn't have it all their own way' that statement she made, put her firmly on the girls' side.

Hanna was around the same age as her, so they had a lot in common. They all spent time talking over personal matters that drew them closer as friends, finding camaraderie in each other's company. Some words of wisdom between them were well heeded, and they learned different things from each other. As this sisterly relationship grew stronger by the day, they agreed to influence the new town expansion by giving it some feminine feel.

Susan discussed 'this new street' with Lucy. She said her father had told her all about it, and he would give his blessing to any arrangement she came up with. It was her place now. She confided in Susan that she planned to build a house at the river one day, when she got her hands on enough money. Her parents could live out their days happy in their new home on the water. She'd never let them finish up in a nursing home.

Her mother lived upstairs, unable to walk, and her father was a wonderful man who waited on her hand and foot. He was riddled with arthritis, which he hardly ever complained about, but when she saw the pain registering on his face sometimes it caused her great anguish.

Susan listened, feeling sad for this young woman, giving up everything to care for her parents. Life had given her a few bad turns she had never expected or deserved. But Mrs Wilson wanted to part with some motherly advice. It might help to point her in the proper direction. She told Lucy the whole story about selling her own field. How much it had changed her life, still living in the town she loved, just a slight shift in location.

There were many advantages to living in Dr Wilson's Close, and she said how happy she was with her next door neighbours. She gave the newsagent's daughter a rundown on things, with particular emphasis on members of the town development committee. A young lady must always be on her guard against controlling men. The older they were, the worst they were, Susan counselled.

She showed her around her spacious home, all wheelchairs friendly, she emphasised. No nursing home requirement here.

'When we get to old age, we will be able to manage ourselves.

Susan knew Yank couldn't talk about land with Miss Whyte. She remembered him telling her they had several chats about books, art, even the horse fair. But it seemed she wasn't on for discussing her land. No heavy business mood. He couldn't get past that barrier; and things were still distant between them. This thought was foremost in her mind.

Susan was in a perfect position to mediate if required.

WT was dozing in the chair when the door got an urgent bang. He had a visit from an irate Blimey, demanding a specific date for his opening. He had new movies to show. The eyes were bulging out of his head; Drover had given him a cup of tea earlier, persuading the picture hall owner to talk with old Flanagan in person. 'Businessman to businessman' he said, to instil more confidence into him, since he was behaving so badly.

WT started explaining how the cinema idea wasn't happening now. The new hotel manager had blocked the idea. This fellow out of the catering college knew what he was doing. No one could go against the man in charge of everything now, he told him. It was his job to do the right thing.

Blimey started roaring abuse at him when he heard that, telling him about all the preparations he'd made to get back in the cinema business. The disappointment was unbearable. 'I'll burn the hotel to the ground!' he swore, tearing a page from his sketch pad to hurl at WT before storming out the door.

WT picked up the crumbled page. It wasn't very consoling to see his new hotel in flames like that. This angry man had been drawing for some time. He looked out the window at Louie doing the gardening. He wondered if he'd heard any of the loud exchanges, the threats, and he called him in for a word. The cinema man was unstable. This time around he might cost Louie his well-paid job. And he'd never had a job like it before.

'Blimey is going to burn the hotel,' WT said, showing him the drawing of the hotel in flames.

Louie the gardener gave a vicious sneer, looking at the sketch. 'He did it before Mr Flanagan, in England when he set fire to the projection room for insurance money. He told lies; I got jail. He swore he'd give me money for taking the blame, but he didn't.'

WT gave him a strict order: 'watch Blimey at all times. If he burns this hotel down you're out of a job'.

Louie complained he wasn't paid for painting the picture hall either, and now it was gone. He cursed the day he ever set eyes on the picture hall owner who'd told him he was a millionaire when he wasn't.

Not for the first time, he would put an end to him. He said that a few times.

CHAPTER 19

Joe played a club football game one Sunday afternoon. The referee was a selector for the county team, a famous ex-footballer. When the game was over, he had a word for the promising young centre field player. 'Be ready this evening for a county trial game Joe, the car will collect you outside your father's pub at six o clock'. This county football approach was very direct. And they wouldn't expect any rejections.

Joe's playing experience in junior club competition was far below county footballer standard. This was a monumental move up. But apparently he'd impressed a man that knew the game well. It was unusual to see a nineteen-year-old playing inter-county senior football, especially at centre field, the most demanding position on the pitch, where two of the tallest team members usually took charge.

When he lined up for the throw-in to start the trial game, there was a marked difference in their appearance. His opposite number was an imposing 6ft 4in 27-year-old in his prime, with years of tough county football experience to his credit. Joe wasn't too fretful; some calmness inside him was always there in time of need. He'd had to rely on it several times already. Big occasions weren't that intimidating for him anymore. He'd seen a lot, and could take things in his stride now, with all the calmness of a more experienced young man.

His centre field partner was one of the top four players in Ireland in that position and he gave him a piece of advice. 'Back into him Joe, run for the high catch.' It was good advice for the new recruit. The ball handling he'd practised in the boarding school handball alley would come in useful.

Catching a ball above everyone else's head was a great skill. On this trial day his performance fielding the high ball got him noticed as a future prospect. That's how it all began. With a total of two years' experience at the lowest junior level, he was selected to play against the all-Ireland champions, at the highest competitive senior level. This game was a highlighted challenge match for the opening of a famous football park. Against the best players in Ireland, he started the game off at full forward. The fullback, his marker, was a seasoned warrior, like teak, and tolerance wasn't part of his nature. However in the battling tousle for possession the new recruit held firm. At half time the selectors moved him out to centrefield – this was a more demanding position – to get a closer look at him.

Joe was pitched up against another top player with a few all-Ireland medals. There were no mediocre players at this level except him. The match reports following the game were favourable enough though. The critics formed similar opinions, a promising debut; it was all ahead of him. He was only a very young lad yet.

There were a few county matches that stood out, for different reasons. Some were memorable, others better forgotten. But there was a bit of fun going around too. His sisters were young teenagers who had never been to a football match in their entire lives. They wouldn't know about rules; they were just developing notions of boys. And their interest grew when their brother started playing for the county team. They knew one sure thing: 'It's full of good lookin' fellas'. They saw their friends looking at photographs from the papers, and formed a better plan. They insisted on personal introductions to his new friends the county footballers; girl power over older brother.

Joe had no intention of doing anything as embarrassing as that. You'd want to be missing a few brain cells to fall for that one. And in the way a mistake can happen, when you're trying to get rid of someone, mind alteration takes over the situation. He would live to regret this sudden departure of all reason, for sure.

'The next match I'm playing, I'll introduce you to them all,' he said. It was intended to end that conversation, with no serious intent implied; just something nice, to get away from them in a hurry.

Joe developed a painful boil on his wrist, before an upcoming county match, and his father said he wouldn't be selected again if he didn't turn up to play. He had a dog remedy to fix it, and he produced a bottle of iodine, for greyhounds' legs. Perfect for boils, he assured, 'it'll kill it immediately'. The footballer had no option but go along with the doctor.

Bill covered the boil with this so-called iodine healing liquid, and then wrapped a white bandage around the wrist. A stain coming through this bandage indicated a visible sign of injury, and when the game kicked off, his opposite number saw it first thing. Every time Joe reached over him to catch the ball, he gave the bandage a box with his fist. That pain sent the ball flying. When half time came along, he hadn't held on to one of them. The mood was stuck in a grave downward spiral. It was the first time he'd ever got a roasting.

His two mischievous sisters were bored waiting for the end game, but they would be meeting boys. They were thinking this football nuisance thing was a good excuse for a great day's outing with 'all the fellas on view'. They should have thought of it years ago. So they saw nothing happening on the pitch. What was going on didn't matter.

The teams didn't head for the dressing rooms at half time. They huddled in circles, at opposite ends of the pitch, sucking on oranges, listening to words of wisdom, tactics for the second half. Spectators were not allowed on the pitch during this interval.

But the star-struck girls sitting along the sideline saw a different picture. They thought this boring game they hadn't bothered watching was over. They picked their way across the pitch, laughing about what was in front of them. It was a perfect chance to say hello, their high heels sticking in the mud, helping each other along.

That was how it looked when Joe spotted them, linking arms in the usual hysterics. A feeling of dread came over him then. They were heading straight in his direction.

He stepped out from the circle so they could see him in his blue jersey and white shorts, their county football colours, hoping they wouldn't make a show of him. The oldest one spotted him first. 'There he is Ann, look,' her screechy voice turned up full volume. 'Joe, what colours are Cavan playing in?' She roared, as if it was a good question, having watched the game for half an hour. These girls had a way of blowing the situation up in your face. They were at it forever. And it always finished up bad for him. They were so good at it.

Speaking with the deadly tone his father resorted to in times of desperate need, Joe gave final instructions: 'Go back and sit down till the fuken games over. Don't make things worse for me here today, please.'

'Oh we thought it was over,' Marie cut in.

'Get back to the side line NOW, it's only half time!' he shouted.

Away from the football field, Joe had other things keeping him busy. There were days spent on the road selling electrical goods. He enjoyed talking to the country people. They liked this fellow who always did his best, taking a few bob off a kettle or a toaster to suit their strict budget. He was a decent young man in spite of his wild ways. They all agreed on that.

He was pleased his pony produced well-marked filly foals, fit for any future plans. There were long cold nights spent alone in the field, watching for her to foal. The dealer said mares should be called nightmares, for the worry they caused. It took a long time to get anything out of foals, so he didn't bother with them.

Joe bottled beer and Guinness for the pub. There were big wooden barrels to shift around. He sucked beer from the pipes when the air locked, and swallowed it. That was what he told his mother when she accused him of drinking. It all happened in the line of duty. Her animosity towards alcohol was intense, but he had developed a taste for it. There was a more wary form of interaction between them now. The drinking binges with his so-called friend who had dumped him out on the street in Scotland, everyone in the whole town knew about now. She had become a more anxious person than ever before.

Her son was staying in a hotel room, next door to his friend. Hanna had objected to this move but was overruled. She knew what it was all about. Getting closer to the action was the primary reason for the shift. There were girls arriving to holiday on the river, and the boys would be there like wolves waiting for them. And the drink would be flying.

Timer was doing a good job in the Cody Arms. There were laws prohibiting gambling on licensed premises. The boss filed for a day in court, and they were biding their time.

He'd introduced a few inspired décor touches that made the place more attractive for visitors. Good reports spread and the hotel got a positive review; a homely place for commercial travellers on their rounds. It attracted the local elite, as they saw themselves; the hotel was the place to be seen. You could even have a drink and a cigarette sitting down at a table. Like at home.

Molly from the pub was covered up well for her night off. You'd think she wasn't the barmaid at all. Her brassière was tastefully cupped with modesty in mind. A silver Celtic brooch fastened the cloak around her shoulders.

She crossed the street as it started to rain, making a mad dash for the hotel door. She was watching him from the pub window, going inside earlier. He'd caught her eye a long time ago. Her mission was searching a quiet town looking for fun. Midtown Manhattan it was not; she'd been looking there already. That's why she was here, hijacked into coming on pilgrimage. And she was still desperately trying to make the most of it.

Molly was in Ireland to keep in touch with her 'green side'. Growing up in America her Irish parents had told stories about the old country. She listened to the music and dreamed about going there one day, when she got lucky. All her life she had worked as a barmaid. It was a good job for a sudden change of location. Now she was part owner in a pub, and it couldn't get any better than that. Still into fun ways of the past, she was forty and couldn't behave respectfully even if she wanted to. Her husband didn't love her, and she didn't care. They had got married in Mexico, on a hangover. That loving feeling had never entered the equation. Yet in some strange way, they depended on each other to survive. It seemed to work. She didn't know how, or care why. Something must be paying for everything.

The object of her interest right now was sitting up at the counter. She had caught him peering down her front when she worked. He must have a huge desire for forbidden fruit. That notion could be well satisfied if he looked around. Molly was feeling fruity too.

A fertile imagination roamed the barmaid's head, when young men were involved. Bad boys trying to break out was her speciality, she'd teach them how it was done stateside. A trip 'around the world' in her bed was whispered favourably already. It was real easy to get in there too. You just stayed hard at it.

She smiled, sipping her gin, shaking her knee, feeling the

tremor of action already. Then a young couple arrived in to sit beside him. He seemed pleased to enjoy their excitable company. Molly would give this special treat a miss until next time. Nobody was going to get lost. That rude smile had never left her face since she started looking at him. How good would it come off after all that tension build-up?

Joe was delighted when they walked in. They were off to a motor club party and she was bringing her new camera with her, for taking pictures. He was travelling with them.

Timer was missing from the hotel, having fallen for the charms of a nice foreign girl. Danny was working behind the bar and he was busy enough. It was very early on in the night for this place. Joe had spotted the pub barmaid, sitting alone behind him at a table. He made sure not to make eye contact with her. She reminded him of the women who had robbed him in Southampton.

Timer told him about sex exploits with commercial travellers. Some of the more promiscuous types detoured to the Cody Arms Hotel with her renowned experience especially in mind, he said. They laughed at the hotel being 'a noted place of ill repute'.

The young couple at the bar were saying the 'motor party' was open air, and hoped it didn't rain. Taking pictures was the newest craze. When they described photographing 'the tranquil lake' with the woods all around, he got more interested. They were pleased to have the county footballer along for company. It would take some time to arrive. And there were lots of things to talk about along the way.

The journey's end covered a two-mile dirt track through a dense pine forest. They came to a halt near a wooden footbridge over a shallow river. In this spot, the quiet presence of an old cottage seemed mystical, like a picture painted on canvas; only an artist could describe such alluring grace. This place would never again leave his head. In years to come, he would reflect on its haunting beauty, with the same love of his life. Never to take any of these treasured memories for granted. He'd dream them, always to call them his own.

There was a group of people enjoying themselves around a blazing bonfire. A sing-song could be heard starting up. It was all very friendly and inviting. The young couple excused themselves, till later, and walked over the grassy knoll to join the revellers, camera on the ready. Joe turned back for a quieter stroll in the opposite direction. He looked to that tranquil cottage that drew him in again. The door was wide open now and a warm, yellow glow spread out into the darkness; it seemed so inviting he kept going on towards it.

There was a tall girl standing at the door, indicating a food table behind her. Despite her kind, welcoming gesture and pretty appearance, the hunger got to him first. But he didn't know how to attack the spread with manners. So he sought a bit of help.

'Do you work here?' he said, looking at the food.

'Why do you ask?' she enquired, her chin stuck out with a humorous grin.

The answer to that simple question wouldn't come to him quick enough. He took stock of her good looks when she spoke again.

'I'll help you.' She picked up a plate, pointing her finger at the food. 'Would you like some chicken?' It made him more careful, when he heard her polished accent. 'Yes please.'

On a sudden impulse, he said, "I'm Joe O'Flaherty, the County Cavan footballer".

It felt essential to be honest. And it might impress her. He'd used it successfully in the past. 'Oh I am sorry, I've never heard of you.' She apologized, moving around again.

He felt like an idiot; it had worked so many times before. She had an English accent. Maybe she was on holiday and knew nothing about Gaelic football.

Her hair bounced as she walked serving food. The pleasant, well-meaning smile never left her youthful face. Everything seemed so effortless for her. He watched and wondered.

No matter what demands were made, she reacted with genuine caring interest. There was no phony performance to create any false impression here. And it was obvious she wasn't aware of her laid-back manner. It was just the way she set about doing her thing.

'Why do you ask' was still ringing in his head. He couldn't come up with an answer to that simple question. All he could do was stand there, wondering, while she attended to the needs of some very civilized party people. They took their food with great manners, and all of them chatted casually with her. It looked as if they knew her by their friendliness.

'My name is Norma,' she said when it had settled down and they were alone again.

'When I said do you work here, I meant are you from here,' he said, trying to make a paltry excuse for the perceived blunder. He even knew it was a stupid thing to say. But he wasn't gifted for choice.

'Oh, sorry, never heard you, I was listening to music.'

'Where's the music?'

'My little radio.' She took it out of her bag. 'I've used it all through boarding school, my constant companion.'

'When were you at boarding school?'

I've just finished, I'm starting college in Edinburgh next term.'

That bit of information convinced him she was from Scotland.

'You must enjoy school; did you never have any bad experiences there? I ran away from it, horrible place for bullying.'

'Yes, I'm like a beanpole, I got a good bashing around the ankles on the hockey pitch. I was singled out as house leader, you see. I could give it back though,' she told him quickly, nodding her head slowly. Her jaw was set in this fierce hockey face look. It made him smile. He could see how the determination changed her face, and found that very attractive about her. It looked like a warning that she could handle anything that came her way. He admired that single mindedness, and knew she wouldn't tolerate any messing. Trying a hurried kiss here, he felt, wouldn't be well received. But she was so easy to be with. It would be real nice to get to know her better.

He remembered how Connie had appreciated his help in Glasgow. So he volunteered for work, because she was on her own. She gave him a bemused look when he said that. Without saying anything, she stepped back, to allow him pass. He took plates from her. Sometimes their eyes met when passing each other, and they smiled. This simple sharing made the experience truly felt. Like-minded souls feel the same way in each other's company. It's a compelling human attraction, a wonderful natural feeling, for sure.

Love at first sight – is there such a thing? But something very real, 'sincerity of purpose' gave this unusual urge to tell the whole truth, no matter what was said. He had never had such a feeling in his life before. This was against all his secretive ways. There were lessons learned for 'the hunt'. A constant rule was telling lies in all forms of contact with girls. Only the foolhardy spilled everything at the start, like it said in the instruction manual 'How to woo women.' They're lovely, but be careful of them till you get to know more about them.

But those meaningless advice stories for winning a girl's attention would fall by the wayside this time. Now was very different. He wanted Norma to hear it all from him. See him as he really was. Honesty of purpose was his first urge on this occasion.

A strange feeling came over him; it stopped him in his tracks. It was very warm in the close confines of the small house, and he couldn't take his coat off, with the tattoo on his arm. They were taboo in Ireland. It was embarrassing and not for the first time, he wished it wasn't there. She might see some form of 'dubious character'. That realisation could drive her away. His mother had kept telling him this scenario would occur.

Yet he rolled up his sleeve to reveal everything. Norma wasn't the least bit put off by the tattoo; instead she talked about learning from mistakes. 'Everybody makes them.'

How could he tell this well-educated girl about his rough ways, if he was going to say everything? He would have to tell all at the start.

She turned over her arm, describing her own bad circumstances. 'See here Joe, this is my diseased arm, that's what the girls called it at school. They would run away from me shouting horrible things about my diseased arm. Of course it hurt, but I never let it shame me, and I couldn't hide it all the time either. If you let other people's opinions affect you negatively, it's you that's wrong. When you're influenced by the way you feel.

'When I was just fifteen months old, I pulled a pan of boiling water off the kitchen stove. I spent a long time in hospital with third degree burns, very bad. Everyone has their own story to tell. Try to do good things, and stay away from bad people. That's what I think, most times it works.'

She looked at him and giggled, and he could see her relaxing. She must have been feeling some of that pressure too.

'You're not a bad man, are you, Joe?'

She smiled into his eyes, saying that, and he felt captivated. It was so powerful. He heard what she was saying in slow motion. How could you be bad to this one, he wondered?

'We must learn to make our way through life. We're all like little birds learning to leave the nest.' She was saying that laughing. But there was no doubt she believed it too.

'You know a lot of good things, Norma.'

'My aunt is a librarian; she reads books and I listen to what she has to say. There's no TV in her home. I lived with her off and on over the years; she educated me about many things. A wise lady, she found answers that explained the world we live in, I listened.'

He discovered that Lucy in the newsagents was her aunt.

When she left to speak with some other people he stayed there on the spot. This strange meeting of minds took on a life of its own then. And how they connected set a relaxed mood. They talked about things as if they had known each other for years.

It could be perceived as a strange coming together, but it never felt like that to them, not once. He didn't have to care what he said to her. Norma spoke her mind, while he responded in kind.

She blamed her Scottish grandmother for upholding such a strict code of moral values. They were passed down in her family for everyone to judge for themselves.

'I refrain from intimate contact, in true Victorian style,' she said, laughing. A strict deterrent, or maybe she didn't think that way. Life's intimate secrets are closely guarded by the pure at heart. Norma was one of those. The idea of a goodnight kiss never registered. There was no way she'd be entertaining a proposed stroll in the wood.

They parted company with a firm handshake, like concluding a horse deal. Whatever took place between them during their long conversation, it would last for much longer in their minds.

Going into the night with a carefree feeling, he looked at her phone number, neatly written. He took great care putting the note in his inside pocket. Something kept running around in his head all the time. And it wouldn't stop for a minute. This was the girl he was going to marry. He felt it in his bones.

It was an original thought, the first time marriage had ever come into his mind. It just came over him, and it got stuck in the pure spirit of sincere belief.

Earlier he'd told the young couple to go on home without him, but they wanted to take a photograph for posterity first, they said. He was in no hurry to leave. Norma's long hair, pushed back tidily from her temples, looked elegant. His mood was more pensive when they took the picture. And that's how they left him, with big smiles on their faces.

They seemed to 'fit' perfectly, albeit from different cultures. This togetherness would stand the test of time, their difference made loads of room for exciting stories to grow in.

Her parents were waiting for her when it was all over. They discreetly avoided meeting their daughter's new friend. This old cottage was part of their family history.

He had a fifteen-mile walk ahead of him and he didn't care. The first two miles were along the forest trail. Then he'd take to the quiet country road all the way home. The birds would be singing the dawn chorus, those sweet sounds would keep him company, and he had many hours to think.

He felt like the happiest man in Ireland, so wrapped up in her he could think about nothing else. How can you explain a wonder? There weren't words he knew to describe the feeling. 'Love at first sight' should be easy to explain now with such compelling proof.

The Yank had fallen for the quiet, lady-like manner of Lucy Whyte. That feeling occupied his mind these days. He knew how futile it was. They had been in close contact during the land deal, but it had never become romantic. It hadn't even reached very friendly.

With the book shop extension, something should have clicked when they worked so closely to get it right. In Boston, you learned body language very early on in the game; how you were doing. You found out quickly if your expectations were well received. And there was definitely nothing happening for him here. When all the work was done he was getting bored. The house was complete;

the interest in things was gone. And there was no female company. Yank could be starting to feel old.

An old flame had just moved into Cody's Cross, but she was married now. The religious wouldn't tolerate adultery. 'Sins were sins'. And he might finish up being shunned in the town.

He had never experienced loving feelings for any woman. He'd been abandoned, with the mixed-up motherly affection he then endured as a young man. His marriage was destined for failure. What good was money when you were alone? Bar hopping around Boston looking for romance never stood a chance. It only kept romantic notions at arm's length. It had hit him properly recently, when he had time to think more about it. He only now realised what he had missed.

He was sitting at home now having coffee, doing his favourite thing, looking out at the river. So far, he'd done what he said he'd do. His mother was taken care of, finally.

He had to make adjustments to get the exact location right. It was important to have it where the family home stood before it had been burned to the ground. Over the road lived Major Cody. In his big house of self-importance, thoughts of it going up in flames were satisfying. This Major's father had drunk brandy from a hip flask, watching his mother's house burn. He was sitting on his horse at the time, so the story went. It had never cost him a thought.

The County Council blocked Yank's plans in the beginning. If there was going to be a new street, they'd like to own the idea. However there was a young engineer who saw merit in the plan, and he applied pressure on his elderly colleagues for serious consideration. He proved relentless in his pursuit. River Street came about as a result of his endeavour. There were nuns taking casual strolls there, and it became the most respectable place in town.

Everyone had a positive opinion of 'Riverside Walk'. For religious locals, the nun's preferences for gathering in groups confirmed its status as a place of sanctity. And there were those that despised the presence of the ladies' underwear window when it arrived, presented on the corner of the street, in the midst of all the devotion, like a beacon for pleasure.

It was Susan who persuaded Lucy to part with the field she'd inherited. Then she'd have enough money to do everything she wanted. First move was into the house beside her in Dr Wilson's Close. It was Yank's house, properly done, and ready to step into.

She was excited about having Lucy as her next door neighbour. The young woman had agreed to the sale after discussing with her parents. They were very happy now in their new home by the river. Lucy's niece Norma was helping out in the shop for the summer months. She had just finished boarding school. Now it was the time for her to gain some work experience.

Lucy could spend all her time sorting the bookshelves, a never-ending pleasure for her. There was a reading space where you could sit and browse through any number of titles, or she could help you read, if you wished. There was nothing too much trouble when it came to books. She would like a town of avid readers.

This was an alcove in the shop, shelved and stocked like a library. She was there for anyone to talk with that required assistance.

A young man with special reading requirements spread the kindest words about her: 'She was like a really kind teacher'.

Molly's bar was notorious for scandalous behaviour. She was the chief instigator of all things lewd. With enough gin in her, the pearl necklace would get pushed down her cleavage deliberately, and she'd pick someone to fumble between her breasts to retrieve it for her, if she got frustrated enough.

'I worked topless joints in the US. I'm not shy,' she bragged. 'It's feel-free time. Well fit to be seen, as my mother used to say about them.' Her husband Mack schemed a lot. He'd discovered that pulling strokes on the Irish was tough going. They didn't like parting with money, because they didn't have any to part with.

It was known Mack would do anything for cash and didn't care if it was legal or not. He was convinced that his way of going on would make him respected. He could never imagine their contempt for him. This man was programmed to take control of every situation. Acting out different characters to fit his plan concealed his scheming ways, most of the time. He bossed Molly, giving her little money. And he whispered about CIA operations like he was still part of it all. They were on to him, a 'pure bollox'.

But he was Yank's son. That made a difference. The blacksmith said people only tolerated him on account of that. Otherwise he would've been drowned in the river long ago. His whorish wife wouldn't be far behind him.

She had men of all ages driven mad. And to a blacksmith who had never had sex with a woman in his life, the wonder was great. She was a perfect 'devil woman'. The town was getting a notorious reputation far and wide. Smithy heard everything going on in the forge. He warned of 'trouble coming down the line'. You'll see, he told everyone that listened.

WT was fully occupied with fixing up the hotel, while his eldest son took care of the hardware shop. Tom had been snared into a hasty marriage by an ambitious woman who besotted him. The old man made it his business to find out all about her.

The name was Pearl. Whatever story she told him to speed up the wedding, it wasn't a pregnancy. There was no sign of that tell-tale bump. 'Peril', as Bill called her, was only interested in fashion; 'not particular about what she wore and not all that caring about where she took it off.' Fit to be seen from the inside out, she imagined. Wide open, she was known as too. A big shot, the kind they all wanted to be. When you were a big shot, you looked down on people. She had learned that in her hotel receptionist job. But when she married into the biggest hardware store around, she'd arrived. Now it was her time to do a little 'looking down' of her own.

When 'Peril' started working in the shop, she got very inquisitive about the financial end of the business. The boss noted that from the word go. WT knew trouble when he saw it. He'd keep an eye on her. She had met his son when he was doing a show in her hotel, but the old man figured it wasn't his singing that had captivated her. More likely she'd heard about the big shop. And she would know how to hold on to a good thing when she found one. He found out her pedigree was noted for that trait. Tom would tell her 'good news' about the property he owned. It made up for being bald. And there were other shortcomings we can't talk about, yet.

Hanna was always very well aware of everything going on.

Tom's wife was making a bad name for herself without working too hard at it. And everyone knew about it except him.

WT advised him to set her up in a fashion shop to get rid of her. 'Negotiate for one of Yank's rental properties on River Street. You could hide her in there until she gets some manners.' Then he told Tom the whole story, out straight. 'Keep an eye on that woman of yours; she has a roving eye in her wandering head, dangerous. I'll tell you that, me boyo.'

WT knew she had tried joining the town development committee but was side-tracked by a tactful Mrs Wilson. Susan knew what an unpopular choice looked like, and she'd make no mistake. 'Oh no my dear, you are far too sophisticated for a drab old Town Committee, you would be more in keeping with the extravagant tastes of an exclusive fashion shop.' And Pearl believed her.

Yank gave her a shop on the corner with a big window. They were saying he was backing her financially, that's why they were on such friendly terms. He was in and out and fussing over her as if there was something wrong with him. That old story from years ago about modern clothes from America was doing the rounds again. They sneered about Tom away singing, what he was missing. And felt sorry for Yank, who had stooped so low to get what he wanted. But every success story must have similar motivations driving it on. 'When you can't do what you want, do what you can.'

It could be Yank was doing all the crooning in his absence. 'Singing for all he was worth,' the gossip lady said, nodding her head. She claimed the American was 'backing her' in more ways than one. This gossip woman said too much, that's why her husband was happier living with her own cousin in London.

This fashion shop brought something different to a quiet town. Two mannequins in suggestive poses in the window were realistic. Men gazed at them longingly, and some were seen 'gratifying themselves in a self-indulgent way,' they said. That story came to the notice of the priest. This God-fearing shop was a distraction for Catholics, he roared from the pulpit, but they weren't listening anymore. Everyone knew about his gambling addiction now. Donations to the church fell. He lost respect. The priest never made any reference to illegal gambling in the local hotel. He must be getting church donations from there so.

A hotel was a blessing in the town, he preached. 'He'll soon be going with the women, wait and see,' they whispered about him all the time now.

Then the nuns suddenly stopped walking past the boutique window. It was rumoured one of them had turned Protestant and bought something unholy in there. This knickers shop was suddenly getting to be a turn off for good Catholics. If these skimpy knickers didn't cover up everything, what was the point of wearing them? Everyone knew if you wore no knickers there was something bothering you. And it wasn't good.

After a town committee meeting, it was agreed that 'River Street' was a perfect name with that running water sound everyone liked. They might erect a 'tourist waterfall' there, sometime. They could use the rocks from a local quarry; no other place in Ireland had them.

Timer was doing good business in the hotel; couples staying

overnight didn't have to be married anymore. That was a new thing. He'd made changes with gambling opportunities especially in mind. The residents' lounge was converted into a games room. There were a few toys tastefully placed around for authenticity and distraction purposes. The full-size roulette table was spinning all night and sleeping with a colourful rug over it all day.

There was a sign stating 'The Green Casino' on the wall, at WTs insistence. The games were more serious after dark. Timer's passion for gambling had taken off in style. This was a great attraction for 'fancy free' visitors. The river travellers were magnetically drawn to it.

The Yank's house was on the same spot where his mother's had once stood. She would be proud looking down on it. He didn't think about her with as much guilt now. But there were current matters bothering his mind, causing him embarrassment in the town. Everyone was talking badly about his family. His daughter-in-law's antics were discussed openly in his company, a deliberate attempt to keep him informed. And his son was a pure laughing stock. He didn't ever learn from past mistakes, taking after his mother that way. There was nothing between the ears except scheming. Both of them were no good. He'd finally admitted what he always knew, the pity of it. There was no point in pursuing such a lost cause anymore.

At last, he'd decided to do something about it. He took his son to Ireland to get the stupidity out of him. His hope was some of the 'clever survivor Irish' would rub off on him, that didn't happen. The wise guy New Yorker didn't fit many places. It was a big mistake. Now it was over.

The Major had lived alone since his wife died. There were no children. Nobody knew the full extent of his entitled behaviour in the past; he had taken what he wanted when he felt like it. Rumours about his exploits were intriguing. If you listened to them for long enough, you might think the whole countryside was full of Major Cody's children.

They even said Louie was one of them. When they rambled on about his mother, you would never hear her proper name mentioned. She had abandoned him as a baby in England, where she went to have him. Her family refused to acknowledge it ever happened.

Louie had a small house on a few acres and called himself a farmer. This man was a bad distraction to the peace of the town. He constantly displayed evil intent. If he had anything in for you, it would surface. This caused problems with him fighting on fair days.

And many people in the area were afraid of him. Some said it was better to ignore him, but that didn't always work. He wasn't easily distracted if he wanted something.

When he was going looking for it, he knew that fear was his ally.

CHAPTER 20

Blimey was found hanging from the 'gallows'. The people going to mass saw him first.

Stiff as a board, a rope round his neck, and a chair stuck fast in the ground beside him, the scene could have been set, it looked so perfect. 'No one will miss him,' the religious said. And the whole town came out for a look. They blessed themselves to pray like hypocrites for a Protestant they didn't like.

'He should have done it sooner,' some of them said. Others saw a doomsday warning. 'He's the second one left hanging, one of each religion. There will be more, mark my words'. It was good there were terrible things to talk about. Bad things lasted longer.

Drover's grandfather finished up hanging from that same gate. He wasn't able to herd cattle on one leg. How he hanged himself with one leg missing, nobody knew.

The Cody curse was whispered about. It had taken a new lease of life with Ned Goat's departure, and now it was off again with Blimey's sudden demise. No one had seen it coming. What made him do such a desperate final act?

Having spent such a long time putting up with it, there was more to it than met the eye. But you couldn't be heard saying that. There were strange happenings under the surface that nobody knows', they said. Different people said different things to each other.

He never paid anyone, they said. The Major was out to get him. But there was no proof about that; Louie knew something about money from England. And it was never that simple with him. Maybe Blimey got tired living in a small house. Drover was saying, 'The curse came down hard on someone else like that before.' Hinting at the goat man tying it all in. 'Who'd be next?' He asked them. Nobody answered. He grinned, staring wide-eyed at them.

Drover knew they were all afraid of his 'supernatural power'. He knew that advantage. Total control of the situation was his game.

Mad Phil said Yank had paid Louie to do Blimey in, for past grievances against him. Some things he said could be true. And in this small place where nothing ever came out in the open, paranoia reigned. There was nobody alive who had nothing to hide.

One bad spin off misfortune was all it took; everyone shut up then. The Major said there was madness in them all. Maybe he had helped to put it there. And religious hang-ups made sure it stayed that way. As long as a few 'our fathers' would fix it, everyone toed the line.

Drover's travels had prepared him well. He had advantages when playing the guru, with this gift of supernatural power. They responded with less enthusiasm, like it was only a game. But the magic mushroom tea helped convince them that he was possessed by his grandfather's spirit, and that power came from the tree's curse. It was in him.

'The evil sign was passed on down,' Mad Phil shouted. 'The yew tree's ghost hanged Blimey.' Phil's voice sounded like he knew something more. The picture hall man had cursed at the tree two nights before he died. 'They're after me!' he roared. That's how Drover heard him when his house window was open all night.

Blimey's body wasn't moved until detective Crotty had collected the evidence. He carried the hangman's rope in a big bag, calling into Flanagan's pub, the uneasy Sgt Nelson by his side. To be fair about it Nelson didn't approve of Crotty's procedures for solving crime. The Sergeant was old school; everything must be done by the book, not 'Crotty's everyday convenient diary', as this case would reveal. There was a serious side to this play-acting that wasn't considered well enough. The detective made all necessary self-interested adjustments.

Bill got a fright when they walked in. There was never comfort when these two were hunting you down. Anyway, he was past caring, nothing much had changed. Crotty threw the rope on the counter in front of him. He talked like a gangster when he shouted out loudly at him 'Billy boy, ever seen this rope before?'

They watched the pub owner say 'no' and shut up.

'You know you cut the last one from Ned Goat's neck. Isn't that knot tied the same? We might be looking at a serial killer.'

Crotty decided to move it up a gear. 'Was the picture hall man hung up there by somebody he knew, same as the goat man? Was he strangled inside the house as well?' he asked the perplexed bar owner. That didn't matter either way. Crotty could see possibilities everywhere, but he knew the best route to take. These two corpses had no living family relatives to care about. Undoubtedly the case could be enlarged with more investigation, but that would entail visiting this creepy village more often. Not a good prospect. It was easier to wrap this double suicide up and forget it. No one showed up to sympathise. They had that much in common; nobody cared that they were dead. Same as when they were alive.

There should be nothing more to say about that.

Bill had seen that same 'tying knot' around Ned Goat's neck too, like the one on Louie's pony. He remembered it well.

'I swear I never saw it before,' he roared with a big grin on his face. But Crotty wanted the fun over. The fact that the ropes looked the same was not a coincidence. There could be more to it, he knew that. But no one else gave a shit one way or the other. Why should he?

'Blimey ended it all his way; he couldn't live life anymore, simple as that,' Bill said. He wasn't under suspicion like before, so they could fuck off with themselves now.

And that's what they did.

Crotty explained exactly how it was to Sgt Nelson. 'We mustn't bother probing around these suicides too much looking for alternatives, just in case we find any. The story here is straightforward. They did themselves in.'

'But Sam, how does the hangman's rope look the same on both?' Sgt Nelson asked him seriously. He knew this ready-made, suit yourself police procedure wouldn't be condoned in Depot headquarters. But anyway, he was no detective. That's who was making the calls.

Crotty gave a dismissive gesture of his hand before replying.

'The thing is Nelson, that's the only kind of rope available around here, obviously no demand for rope at all. You see? By and large they all seem a happy bunch of people'.

Nelson heard it better. That initial urgency of doing everything well was gone. He'd felt more a part of the 'town gathering' for some time. The runaway boy had brought everyone closer together. He couldn't be bothered chasing 'after hours drinkers' anymore. 'A much easier life with so little to do was better for him,' his wife said. And he'd convinced himself. A quiet life in such a small community was easy to maintain, just so long as there were no troublemakers to contend with.

CHAPTER 21

In 1964 the Cavan senior football team played in an all-Ireland semi-final, at Croke Park. I was a team substitute on the day, watching events unfold from the bench, in the beginning.

The opposition were Kerry, the county with the highest All Ireland success rate. It was thrilling to be part of such an occasion, but a little daunting too, for a young fellow out of his depth, with seventy thousand people roaring their heads off. It was a far cry from Malone's' small field where I had learned to play the game not so very long ago. I had featured in the previous Ulster semi-final. But a bad mistake I made that day would haunt me forever. So I was apprehensive about being called on to play in this crucial encounter. All part of the pressure build-up for this big occasion. The green well-manicured grass surface of Croke Park was slippery underfoot, and the day never let up, with showers of drizzling rain.

The full team squad had been in collective training for one month to help prepare us for the massive task ahead. We lived in a monastery that felt like boarding school all over again.

A Cavan centre field player took two heavy falls in quick succession during the first ten minutes of the game. It left him limping because he agitated an old injury. But Gaelic footballers don't depart the field of play easily. After twenty minutes I was called off the bench to partner him. I'd taken to the playing pitch in this role a few times in the past, but expectations weren't as high then. This was going to be my first experience at all Ireland finals level. The lack of playing experience never entered my mind. So, when called on to deliver, I'd give it my best. 'Get stuck into them', I was told. The ball wasn't mentioned.

Kerry didn't drop many high balls on my centre field position; something they had discussed during match tactics made them careful maybe. A feature of my game was catching the kick out and distributing good possession to benefit the whole team.

The mistake I had made in the Ulster semi-final resulted from carelessly kicking a wet ball from the side of my boot. The shot was too far out for a realistic goal effort. I'd only just come into the game when I caught a high ball, to the roar of the supporters, only to blast it wide, which brought jeers from the opposition crowd. It was a really bad attempt, to be honest. I'm still ashamed of it.

That's why I gave my Ulster medal to someone I didn't know and might never see again. Of course it was a stupid thing to do, but that's what usually happened when alcohol was leading the way. Rational thinking was missing. When you're young, things seem different when bad ideas take hold. Everything seems like fun.

Talking to this nice girl at an after match party in a Dublin hotel, I made some complimentary remark about her amazing charm bracelet. Without any thought I took the football medal off my keyring for her. I'm not sure what she thought, but she took it. The Ulster Medal was a beautifully crafted piece of artwork, striking to look at, a gold Celtic cross with tiny engravings, featuring a white ivory centre piece for the 'red hand of Ulster' emblem'. I wish I had it now. You only appreciate some things when you've lost them. I liked the medal, but I honestly felt that I didn't deserve it.

Anyway, I still remember that girl's full name. I only saw her once again after that though, at a house party in Dublin. I think the Ulster medal story was one of her party pieces. She might have acquired a Gaelic football players following as a result.

On this particular occasion she was with a very good college player who I remembered from my time in boarding school. He was also renowned for his sense of humour, and although we had exchanged hostile words during tense past exchanges on the pitch, he was okay with me, and so was I with him. It turned into a fun meeting. He'd know of my footballing ability, and that would ruffle him for confrontation. These 'county footballer' bigheads must be taken down a peg. He was absolutely sure he'd stolen my girlfriend. That was 'one up' for him. She would surely have shown him the medal.

He could see I was alone and probably assumed I was still interested in her. If you gave them your important football medal, you'd expect to be seeing them around you more often; that would be a logical way of thinking. But logical was another word I was never sure off.

This fellow had an attitude, winking at me slyly behind her back. His smirk said I was no longer in contention. There was a better player in charge now. At 6ft 2in, he wouldn't be parting with his new girlfriend. It didn't matter how many all-Ireland semi-finals I'd played. 'The only one you were in, you lost,' he roared. 'You gave my girlfriend an Ulster Medal to win her over. But she has a better man here.' He was pumping his big chest with a fist like an ape in the jungle to emphasise his dominance over me. It made me laugh a lot, it looked and sounded so comical. And to be fair about it, he was only half serious.

I was up for the craic as well, and I let him have some rough football banter, in keeping with the rivalry tradition. The low grade level he was playing in was a start. 'You'll never win a medal for her. You wouldn't get picked for the minors,' I shouted back at him. He saw the funny side. He'd played for the minor team already; I didn't know anything about that.

It was all good craic, remembering where we came from, with some praise exchanged for getting there. We were long-lost pals, but he'd won the ball in this game. He was still holding her tight under his arm, and maybe my Ulster Medal was in her bag.

'Gimme the ball!' That war cry spurred you on in the heat of battle on the pitch. After that bad shot at goal, I was dropped to the bench for the Ulster final, but now in the very next game I was going out in Croke Park.

I saw an incident from the bench develop on the field of play. There were small things going wrong from the start. Settling down was problematic for this Cavan side. Wily Kerry sensed disarray. On this all-Ireland semi-final day I was in familiar territory; in the deep end without a paddle.

The young red-haired priest who had helped me out with a six-pound cash donation when I was running away from boarding school turned up at the dressing room door at half time. I was so embarrassed that I didn't have the money to give him. It was all I could think of. He quickly stopped me trying to explain all that, and told me I was doing okay on Micko, the greatest footballer to ever grace the game. This man was in his prime. While I was only starting out on mine, the young priest advised me not to be disappointed; 'that man you're playing on was never equalled'. There wasn't much consolation when you knew that. The final result would confirm Cavan had a very bad day on that occasion unfortunately.

During my time playing Gaelic football I came up against the best centre field players in Ireland. Croke Park against Dublin was a memorable occasion. It was my second appearance on the hallowed turf and I settled in better with the benefit of that semi-final experience.

In a write-up years after, it was said that HB came on to play at centre field in that all Ireland semi-final game against Kerry in 1964. To keep the record straight, HB wasn't there on that occasion. It was me. They made a few mistakes in that write-up. A picture taken in Croke Park on the day is still in my possession, and it proves the truth without any doubt.

The following year I fractured my ankle in two places playing against champions Down. That finished my Gaelic football career.

There were a few rugby games in me as a cumbersome prop forward. In those days speed wasn't a requirement for the front row position like it is now. Strength was a must, though.

I didn't know the proper rules in the beginning. The authority of the Gaelic Games Association banned foreign games to protect our national sports. Rugby and soccer were classed as unwelcomed foreign games in Ireland during that time.

One night I was boozing after hours with a rugby coach. I complained how I never got coached properly. I could have been a star, I told him, if I had had individual attention. Just to get him going. His big brown eyes surveyed me cynically and there was venom in the reply. 'How could anyone coach you?' Maybe we should leave it like that so.

Some things don't sound any better when explained. You find home truths sharp edged when you drink late at night with tolerance for egos turned down low. You'd hear them in a whisper. But by all accounts they should be heard.

When I got a Leinster junior rugby trial at tight head prop, it was too late for me. I was in America by then. I played half a dozen games for New York Rugby under the accomplished Canadian coach Ed Lebow. Then the cursed booze lined me up for a vicious turn of fate. I was ready-made for the call. The drink won the battle, and it left me in a very bad place for far too long. I was lucky to get away from it. The fact of the matter is this; I would never have made it on my own, never.

Norma was there to pick up the pieces. Not an easy task, but she stuck with it until there was no other option available to her, and she had to take care of family first.

The heart-breaking event that smothered our lives took us to America. We would never get over this harrowing journey and not in our wildest dreams could we have envisaged what would happen to us. It would turn out to be one of life's harsh lessons. It's a long story for some other day. Everything comes out in the washing, when it's caringly done.

But we must wait to find out how we got there first.

It's all just another turn in the tale of a lifetime.

CHAPTER 22

When we had our picture taken in the cottage at Killykeen Lake, I was smitten. Every time I look at that picture I can see the joy in our faces.

She had this calm presence about her. Not once in the entire conversation did I think about ravishing her in the wood outside, a remarkable achievement in itself.

To make it positive, if the room was full of talent you'd want to enjoy her company. With no one else there to confuse the issue, I found out why. And it was such a revelation, this refined, natural manner. That blew me away. I wasn't used to anything like it. I had this feeling I had known her forever; I'm trying so hard to explain that without making you sick. We talked about everything. There was reluctance parting with her at the end of the night, but we would be meeting up again, for sure. And that thought alone stayed with me for the long fifteen-mile walk home.

Knowing the story as I do now, I'm so glad I did my share down the years. I wouldn't want to have any regrets now. Those initial troubling times never dented the bond; we got closer on account of it as time passed. We had to be strong in adversity. The changes forced on us were drastic. A mad time in America took its toll. 'Fill my life with flowers,' she said, when I asked her how I could make things better. What could I possibly do to improve?

That's the way it must be. I'm telling the tale for what it's worth; I'm getting it all off my chest. Some things aren't easy to go back over, that's all I'll say.

I was just lucky when we first met up. So was she, as it turned out. The love story was always very real. But it wasn't always easy going; the hasty decisions, those narrow misses when things might have gone wrong, and sometimes did, could have finished me. You don't feel danger when you're young. Never think if it's wrong or right. With no responsibilities, things have less value. The way of going on is all choices. And they're dangerous things.

I tried doing it right for Norma. She deserved the best effort; her passions were simple things, baking, flowers and plants. I was there at her right hand, to dig holes, and I learned to love flowers too.

Good intentions make simple pleasures bloom. When, one day, you listen to yourself truthfully, it's worth hearing. There are always good intentions. As for taking it all in, adapting to change is sometimes a daunting task. But whatever has to be done.

I thought she was English, that first night, Scottish later, when she mentioned going to college in Edinburgh. I was trying to figure her out, as you do, on another night out in the chase. The company of an attractive girl and a wood all round to explore; if the opportunity arose. Time would tell, but now it was all about talking. And the conversation; I'd never had a sensible chat like it before. Many of her views were different from mine.

I mentioned sex like it was normal conversation, just to try it out, but she didn't like that. Didn't shy away either, making her opinions clear. 'Strictly not my cup of tea,' she emphasised. Promiscuity wasn't on her chosen path. It never would be. She wasn't like that. Her interest was baking; home industry, it should have sounded boring but it didn't, and she liked the Beatles. I wasn't a fan of the Liverpool group. Mick Jagger was my man.

Such a meeting of different minds could start off slow. But we were saying things that made each other laugh. And there was ease there when urgency never arrived.

For the next few years when she came home on holidays, I was delighted to spend time in her company. I looked forward to it. We were unusual in our naturally shy way. A bit withdrawn; we didn't take messages from the outside world easily. Wrapped up in each other, with sincere intentions, it's hard to explain love. It sounds so made up when I try.

We shared a dry sense of humour too; fun took malice out of the hard times. Harmless things we got up to kept us going. Every time we met was an adventure in itself. Something might happen. One time we were around the lake, and she was wearing a light, flowery summer dress. I thought of a gentlemanly plan to feel her body through it, so I took her up in my arms to step across deep water, but put my foot down on floating moss close to the edge. That embarrassing soaking for the two of us took the belief off me for a while. But the dress was very light and clingy when it got wet, so I suppose everything worthwhile has a price.

We wrote long letters every week when we were apart. Ten pages was nothing. And through all this heartfelt contact we grew closer. I will always remember how much those letters meant to me as I waited, on the seat outside the door, for a postman's visit.

She was always precise with her replies. I hid them carefully in a private place, to read over again, but my mother found out where they were, and she was reading them out to my father. They were highly impressed by Norma's well-written letters, and the interesting subjects she wrote about. Soon my parents knew everything there was to know about her.

I was pleased about them finding out how nice she was. My family never stayed quiet with a good story. They always had so much to say and never kept anything to themselves.

Then my father's heart condition deteriorated. There was a blockage in his heart, and he needed a bypass operation, but he refused to have one. Too dangerous, he said. You might get a heart attack, he'd explain, warning everyone off it, but the heart attack would get him, eventually.

We didn't know why so many people seemed to be against us. That was before we started getting nasty correspondence; why anyone should bother, we never truly understood. We didn't care. It was a great interest to some very peculiar people. Religious fanatics from both sides lined up to cause trouble for us. A Protestant electrician told my father about bad things he heard said. Small town talk is for begrudgers. It's always without meaningful substance, idle ramblings for drunks to amuse themselves with. We knew it wasn't going to rattle us, and it didn't. We thought it was funny, but it wasn't.

Ignorant connivers tried making trouble. Nasty stuff, sometimes delivered as fun to me, was uncalled for. That's to put it very mildly. 'This mixed marriage isn't acceptable,' they ranted. 'Such a nice quiet girl too, what was she thinking off, having anything to do with him'. The Catholic bigots can do bigger bastards, when they want to get their claws stuck into you. 'Too much of that posh education' turned her head. The nicest people were more understanding. They may have had businesses to worry about. Customers kept closer.

'It must be blocked somehow,' the bitter bastards railed. 'How did he get in with her in the first place? He's not even a good catholic, if there is such a thing in those bastards.'

They wailed about Catholic leaving such a bad taste in the mouth. Has no Protestant man, over the border, got a son fit for her, they wondered? And this active group of naysayers grew bigger when they heard each other talking the same.

Why is kindness so elusive? And yet there is always some on hand in times of strife. Maybe it's not shared often enough. But good people seek kindness in likeminded souls.

Leo Tolstoy, the Russian writer, wrote meaningful words on that exact topic. It should be compared with what we know. Norma's fervour rarely varied. And there were some tough times on the way to test her resolve. But I learned from her, and we held fast like a well-fashioned wedge. You know bad times can bring people together very tight.

Closeness has been our bedrock for sixty years. It doesn't move easily when it's rattled, or tolerates any excuse to stop talking overnight. It's a better strategy to practise, never sleeping on a fight. That stops it waking up feeling like a war.

She was used to coming on electrical sales trips. When she was at home, it was all good, more time together. Picnics and kissing at lunchtime comes to mind. I never complained once. But she enjoyed meeting people, especially the country women who cooked and baked bread in cast iron pots on a hearth fire. She had so much to say to them; one short visit was never enough. Norma liked discussing recipes, telling them all about the buns she baked for our picnics at the river. She never mentioned how fast I ate them, to get into the kissing.

Electricity was the new acquisition, and there was always some requirement missing, whether it is a toaster or a washing machine. Electric kettles were so handy everyone wanted one. And electric cookers were so expensive they were only for the well off.

But if you needed a fire in a hurry you could buy an electric one to carry around with you. There were some deals made available to people where money was scarce. They'd pay something off next time. But not once was there a request for money owed, in all the years. These were very honourable people. It would be shameful to know of their circumstances.

Everyone wanted to talk about football, and that gave Norma a great idea. This footballing game could be advantageous in sales promotional contexts, she reasoned one day at the river. I wanted to listen as she outlined a plan to get me a good job. One I deserved, she said, and she meant it, looking up vacant job applications every day in the *Irish Times*, with this wink to keep me tied into the project. I wasn't happy working at home anymore.

We talked a lot about it. We had often discussed spending the rest of our lives together, and projected many things we'd like to do in the future, talked about them as if they were destined to be. This belief we had in ourselves came naturally, and it made us a great team.

A secure job was a must for any married man's future ambitions. Norma believed I could do it. Her encouragement made me try harder; that's how it was. Our dates were a lot like going back to school, and you know how much I liked that. But there was something about teachers too that made a difference. We kicked into project mode job finder automatically.

She talked to me about interviews and methods for dealing with different kinds of people, stuff she'd learned in her own education. And she'd been a prefect in a very posh private school for young ladies. I know its tiresome having to listen to all this praising her, except there is no other way to say it. Suck it up. There was some letter writing to carry out and she polished my communication skills with a few well considered lessons. It was a very pleasant task. In such attractive learning conditions, I found my own way into becoming a salesman.

Anyway, after a while, and some rather terse interviews in a big hotel in Dublin, I got the job. I could never have imagined this kind of luck. But I must say the football connection mattered a lot; it was a major interest for this top American Refrigeration Company in Ireland. They could identify with the sporting appeal. And I could tell them about my 'Ulster medal' as if it was still in a glass case at home. Not dangling of a charm bracelet somewhere else. I was now in the world of make-believe for real. But it still felt the same way. Maybe I couldn't make out the difference anymore. Wasn't that some form of progress for me?

College education wasn't as important to this company when you had stature, presence and intelligence. There was a good salary. And a new saloon car supplied free every year, with all expenses and commission. There was a few weeks' training with full pay as well.

With electricity almost everywhere now, grocery shops were installing refrigeration counters. This new job would help me make enough money to build a house. So I bought a one-acre site on the edge of town for this purpose. Commission money paid for it. I was on my way. We could start building when we saved more. These progressive sixties heralded the beginning of supermarket food providers in Ireland.

One day we went around the lake for a walk. We climbed the white tree, and I produced the ring with three stones in a straight line, like my mother's. Norma often admired it on her finger. Even though we'd planned the time forever and knew all about doing it, it was still very emotional. We were in tears when we embraced each other, looking at the ring on her finger. That was a very special day.

Things were looking up, and I was drinking very little now.

When the word got out about our engagement it was met with frosty arrogance. There was nobody with any opinion in favour of the marriage. It was easy to get a sour comment. And when we heard some of the worst stories, we couldn't believe them. Small town talk, Norma said. 'You'd never think an ordinary young couple could cause such waves when all they wanted was to live happily together'. 'Why on earth is it anyone's business to comment on our private affairs?' She was perplexed by the whole thing.

The first sense of things not being perfect came across in a cynical way. I didn't really understand its implication until years after. But on the day it was said to me, I got the sense of impending doom. Try and visualize hearing this sort of stuff in the light of day.

We came upon the blacksmith sitting outside the pub. This old boy heard it all shoeing horses. A grumpy bachelor couldn't say a good word about anyone. He sneered, shaking hands with Norma as if he knew something we didn't. She'd never take notice, or care what way he looked, while the extreme state of his mind never reached her either.

This occasional Catholic had some deep rooted prejudices, but he managed to keep them to himself until she went inside. Beckoning me closer, he let me have it then, in the hateful way he spoke from the corner of his mouth.

'I feel sorry for you son, they'll hate you for this.' He stared hard at me like he knew more. His voice took into some sound of sheer delight, when he went on talking. 'If you marry this protestant one they'll never leave you alone.'

I remember how shocked I was hearing that for the first time. But a local carpenter gave similar warning words to me a long time after that. So, it was always there, without a shadow of doubt. Whatever it was, only they knew the mixture.

We were three years dating together when the word got out about us getting married. We never covered up anything. It wasn't how we thought. This negativity wasn't such a funny distraction anymore. It made us stop socializing. There were nasty comments at horse fairs, you wouldn't believe it, and from people I didn't even know at all.

Let's be clear, this resentment was intended to create hassle. The bad news was enough to make people sick. We heard what was said, and we knew where and who said it. I hope they are still vomiting. I want to say to that crowd, we've had a great time, and it's not over yet. But everything we got we worked hard for. And we enjoyed the journey, not like you.

They made up their minds that Norma was too good for me, and it was their business to disapprove; that was what it was all about. They didn't want to discover the 'amazing room for improvement' in me. Like her, I duly delivered in spades. 'What Norma wants Norma gets', a woman said to me in a shop many years ago; I liked hearing that. Someone knew the truth about the way we were. I was on the right track from the start of the action. They will forever be prisoners of ignorance. It's all they're good for. I'm so far ahead of them I could sit down and they still couldn't catch me.

On both sides of the fence, there is no fundamental difference in the type. Bigotry's sickness is like vomit on humanity. Prisoners of ignorance are all the same.

Nothing was ever going to stop us, though they tried their best. Decades on, it's still there; I hear it coming back to me.

Norma had a last meeting with my father before our wedding. He was forty-eight years old and on his deathbed. Unknown to me, he'd made an effort to ensure our wedding never took place.

Let me say first, this gesture was well intended on his behalf, for Norma's benefit. Like my mother, he knew her well from the letters. And with such great respect, he made a plea for her ears only: 'Please Norma, don't marry my son. Leave him be on his own, and find a nice young man in your own religion. He broke my heart, and he'll surely break yours too. It's in him, you see. He can't help it.'

He was full of admiration, you'd know by the sound of him. It was so emotional, very tearful saying it, she said.

I often wonder if I would have done the same thing myself in similar circumstances, to protect a lovely girl. I know I would. And she told me what her reply sounded like.

'I'm going to marry Joe, no matter what happens, I love him very much. You see sir, the only thing I can ever do is follow my heart, I don't know how to do it any other way.'

She mentioned how he looked at her before putting his hand under the pillow for a bulky envelope. Inside was £500 in various notes, saved from the cash box, quite a bit at the time. 'Take this cash Norma, a few pounds for you, don't let him see it. He'll spend it on drink, you won't get a penny.' That was that.

No mention of my broken heart. I wonder why that was. It's not hard for me to see the gun pointed at me all my life, is it?

So it appeared there was discontent about our marriage from all directions. Believe it or not, sixty years later it's still going on. What's wrong with them? I had such a bad effect on them, whatever I did. We were always aware of it and it never ceased to amuse us. But I can attack its stupidity. To regret it had to come in our direction. Like a tornado.

It always came to me that mistakes were easy things to make. And I was good at finding them, to be positive about it. But over the many years there were personal attacks that crossed the line. I was great at dealing with them, when I found out. But Norma was never singled out for personal attention. They thought she was okay for insults, it seems.

Miss Blackstock, the bank manager, made a spectacle of herself at a gathering in the town one night. Norma and I were just back from our honeymoon and we were sitting opposite her when she was totally overcome by everybody congratulating us. There would be a lot of acting going down at this drink-sodden moment in time. She glared across the table for a while, getting the 'phoney voice' right, no shrill East Belfast accent here; it was doctored for proper sound, by the convincing power of gin.

'Tell me Norma,' she spewed out of her red crossed lips. Looking over at us, she slurred her nonsensical palaver. 'What did you see in this fellow? What did you see in him?' she persisted. 'What did you see in him?' for the third time. It was unbelievable to witness.

Norma dropped her head in shock embarrassment for her and her stupidity. She would never answer such a stupid schoolyard question. It wouldn't be ladylike. When Miss Blackstock got no reply from her, she turned her wrath on the next available victim for her frustration. That would be me. I was waiting to destroy her, I swear it to you.

'Joe, how did you get her? She screeched, 'How did you get her? I want to know how you got her to marry you.' Eyeballing me, daring me not to reply. The boss wanted answers.

I was up for it now all right, three times was enough. I knew exactly what I wanted this bitch to hear. Perhaps next time she would remember not to prod the bear.

'If you put your hand under the table, you can feel it between my legs. It might help with your frustration.'

That gesture of 'friendly understanding' stunned her, I think, drunk as she was. You'd think by the look on her face I was the mad person. It never even occurred to her that her questions were bad mannered, and none of it was any of her business.

But maybe rudeness is necessary for the job, especially dealing with people whose confidence is shattered, struggling to make ends meet. Rudeness would intimidate them.

If you're in charge, you can say anything you want as long as it puts them down on the spot where you'd want to keep them. When you're behaving like a Major over them.

CHAPTER 23

When she was coming to the end of her college studies, Norma invited me over to Edinburgh for a weekend. 'It would be a nice break for you,' she suggested, too see how she lived.

Was it expected to be a revelation? That's what it turned out to be. Clear the air to straighten up the act.

Women are versatile decision makers, when they select. Men just plop in, hoping its right; women starts making it right from the word go, like thoughtful nest builders. She was inclined towards openness, to take good stock of events. Maybe she'd discover if jealousy was one of my hidden demons. It certainly wasn't one of hers, in any shape, colour or form. She was comfortable that way.

That first night I arrived in Edinburgh we went off to a college bar. Norma wasn't much of a drinker, one or two was enough. I made up for that, so she had a long night watching me downing pints of beer. She drank Babycham, in a tonic bottle size with little alcohol content. However, that was enough to make her giggly. She wasn't pretending.

We loved to dance, and I liked it that she knew all the moves. I could learn with her. We never left the floor until we got tired, and we were quick to get back out into it again.

But on this Edinburgh visit, my excessive drinking got to her. She'd never been in my company in such circumstances before. We had a deadly serious talk about it, and I made promises to her I really meant. This together ethic was part of our mentality from the beginning. The fact that I was listening earnestly to her was a consoling factor.

She spoke calmly in her cultured way of speaking English, making great sense.

'Joe, alcohol doesn't agree with you. It will ruin your life.' She said that last bit in a lower tone, a sad afterthought. And continued on to state her beliefs, calm, and level-headed.

I remember the scene vividly. It was another coming of age moment. Every time I look at this Edinburgh picture, I feel it was timely delivered and I remember it.

She made me sit to hear her words, in the three-piece suit that my mother bought me for the trip, to impress the lovely girl she so openly admired. Mutual respect would bond these two women, with similar love interests, and a share of heartbreak that could last forever.

Norma's words sounded foreboding, so I listened.

'Joe, drink changes your personality.'

She continued expressing her views in a detailed way. So early on in the relationship, she could see that problems lay ahead. In the way she saw things she was trying to sort it first.

She was sharing an apartment with three other girls, so I had her room all to myself.

Whatever her wild abandonment when it came to boyfriends, there was a strict limit to her commitment in relationships. Kissing was as far as it ever went. And if subjected to any undue pressure her reply was always the same: 'Cut out pressuring me if you want sex, you should go and find it somewhere else'. She gave that advice very clearly. It was definitely not her scene, and she wasn't going to make changes to her current situation: lots of boyfriends, but no sex. That's the one that seemed to work best for her.

She introduced me to her friends James and Pip so casually. 'They are my boyfriends,' she said, while I was getting that thing older people call seizures. Later she explained how the two fellows shared the 'boyfriend detail' so adequately, as she casually referred to it. That one took me by surprise. She'd never mentioned them before, anytime.

'I have two boyfriends here Joe, that I like being with. Pip has a motorbike, I sit up behind him and off we go on our merry way. He takes me into town shopping and waits patiently outside boutiques, a real godsend. But you couldn't get him dressed for a formal party if you paid him. Where suits are a requirement he won't co-operate. That's why I have my other friend, James. He's more distinguished looking with his black beard, and fits more easily into the dinner events,' she explained. The best of both worlds, she enthused.

I should have asked if I was still required, I suppose, to be on the safe side, but I always knew I was her number one. Maybe I was delusional, but from the very start I trusted her, and we were convinced that we'd been planted in the same soil with the same spade. There would be a better chance to grow from there. And we did. Something honest always made me respect her way. She wouldn't know how to hide anything or make a reason to do so.

'I must sound like a harlot,' she said, laughing at herself. When she spoke she saw a funny side to everything.

I was struggling with the funny side of the situation though. I listened with my heart beating. How could she kiss a man with a beard and all the food on it? The girl on the pedestal got a sudden rocking. Why was she telling me all this, was it supposed to feel normal? Or was she going to dump me for my drinking?

Amazingly, Norma wouldn't mention either conversation ever again.

Now, sixty years later, I surely understand her thinking more clearly. It fits her perfectly, to be honest. Typical Norma, I'd say. Back then she was telling me something I didn't want to hear, so it was up to me. If I didn't like it, that was too bad, and if I didn't want to see her again, that was ok too. She never made demands. It was always just a matter of how you want to take it. Or leave it. 'Such is life,' she could ramble sometimes unconsciously. She was picking up some of my mother's lingo. The thing was, she did what she wanted. This free spirited woman must have set her expectations high very early on in life. There was no compromise.

She knew to put it across with no bad feelings taking hold. There was never any problem with her way of doing it.

'The best way Joe is honest and open,' she said, and I thought she was right. Wasn't I a free spirit too? It sounded okay when it was properly explained; you could make yourself accept anything.

'Look Joe, I'm alone here, I would prefer a boyfriend to accompany me where I want to go. I will get no hassle then. I don't like being bothered when I'm out trying to enjoy myself. That's why I have two boyfriends.' The way she said it could sound like it was what everyone did. It made good sense to her. I got it too, after a while, when I finally figured out how to stomach it.

What else could I do bark and growl? Wagging the tail is better. You might get a bone for doing that.

'And,' she added, when she had me on the run, 'as you so famously remarked to me in Ireland, after my first year here, the improvements I made on the kissing front, You even said so, I'm in training here, putting in a lot of work.'

She pouted in such an embracing way, enjoying every bit of it. It seemed very French kissy to me. If it sounds like a loser's excuse I don't care, but I admired her.

I told her, with an edge in my tone, she wouldn't be to every man's taste. The hint of jealousy poked its nose in with that one. How could you conform one like that? Why would you want to? It just wouldn't be right. Where could you put her?

You'd think I might react jealously and clock one of the boyfriends, or maybe the two of them; that would have been no trouble for me. It wouldn't have been right though, I'd be letting her down doing that. But I felt no anger or resentment at all. It was part of the setup she had for a trouble-free existence, her way of doing things. Trusting her judgement came naturally to me now.

One time many years later I was looking through the religious scripture she reads, the Book of Revelations. I was writing something and looking for a suitable quote. A photograph fell from this book on to the floor. I picked it up and it was Pip, alone on his motorcycle; she had probably taken the picture. I brought it away with me, and got a nice frame. I never said a word. When she was asleep I put it on her locker, beside our bed. When I woke up next morning it was gone, and I never saw it again. I didn't bring it up for discussion until after Christmas. It was a laugh for us, but it was never funny enough to reappear again. I wouldn't mind that. I was more established after twenty-five years. I'm not sure what happened to it, it wasn't dumped anyway, she'd never do that. It's very safe somewhere, wherever she put it.

When my mother first met her I could only see mutual respect, and I was so pleased. My mother asked me once, intrigued by this refined girl's interest in her wild son, if we had ever had fallout. She hadn't heard of any rows going on between us.

'Joe, do you and Norma ever have a row?'

I had the truthful answer. 'No, how could you fight with her?'

By this time Norma was more like a daughter.

My drinking habit got more exercise. It seemed like the order of the day, young fellows going mad on the town and some of the hardened drinkers going on pub crawls for days after matches. It just happened off its own bat, when it was wind-up time, drinking for your life. The fun boys went at it together.

There was still opposition to us as a couple. The bad people thought we didn't belong together. You know, the ones that didn't have any love for themselves so couldn't identify it in anyone else. And there were more sinister reasons; religion was a nasty thorn in the side. These charlatans were located on both sides of the religious divide. Sometimes you could tell what they were just by looking at them. Their conniving pain made hatred grow on their faces.

That boarding school torture still bothered me; I used to get flashbacks in England, drinking the rough cider. There must have been something in it to bring up past hardships.

After I returned to Ireland I borrowed my father's van and drove the long road to the college that had once held me prisoner. I went back there intending to confront Nasser. Luckily for both of us, he wasn't there on that occasion. It wasn't many years since I'd left the place. I was impetuous, under the influence of alcohol, and there was no reasoning. When wrong messages arrived, I didn't know anything about turning the deaf ear. I listened, intently.

Mad fellows hear a special noise of their own. They can bring it upon themselves like a war chant.

I met a fellow called Noel from boarding school, at a horse fair. We were having a chat about old times in 'jail', and we started talking about this priest that still haunted us. Noel had got done by him a few times as well. Amazingly though, he befriended this scumbag Nasser later on in life. He used to visit him in his parochial house, where he was still carrying on his newly modified priestly calling. I heard that one loud and clear.

'Where did the fucker go?' I shouted. I could scarcely believe what he was telling me. I honestly felt a bit light-headed, losing control in some strange way. If I ever met him like that he was done for. Thank God I had missed him.

Nasser was a priest in a neighbouring parish just five miles from where I lived, and I never knew it. Wasn't I lucky? I knew straight away. All the fights in the boxing booth, I had seen his face. Can you imagine if I saw him in reality, drunk or sober? Nasser would have been in real danger. So would I.

I told Noel about going back to get him, telling him how it was, the way I walked boldly into the refectory when they were all sitting around having lunch in one of the places where I had got some of the beatings, during lunch time too.

I arrived in looking around me for the fucker. I had drunk a few whiskeys in the pub, waiting for a proper time. My whiskey head was telling me to beat the shit out of him, as he had done to me. But it wasn't baldy Nasser at all. This priest was young, with lots of hair on his head. I made a hasty retreat.

'So they transferred him to your neighbouring parish, Joe? That's exactly where he finished up?' Noel laughed.

I wanted him to stay quiet so I could think more about it.

Nasser the dean was lucky we never met up. I wouldn't have been able to control myself. I wouldn't have wanted to. I still haven't got him out of my head for getting away with it, a pure bastard in every way.

'That's the story so, right there beside you, for ten years Joe, until he died of a heart attack. Soon as he'd see you at his door he'd have another one. You'd be arrested for murder.'

'I couldn't have resisted if I'd known that he was only five miles away from me. I'd still be in jail,' I said. Now I want to forget it for good.

Isn't it a good thing that I never attended any church ceremonies for all those years? If I ever saw him spreading his hands out like a holy man I'd make a run for him. Noel was still saying, 'we all got abused' I was pleased someone else knew the story; the holy man wasn't winning this one. No way.

When I finally got my hands on the teacher Rasp, I was minding my business hitchhiking home from the big match in Dublin.

Imagine for a minute the feeling I had in my head when he pulled up in the car on the road. I knew he was goosed. There was a job to be done here of some description. God sent him.

He was delighted to come across me, as if we had no history. So he invited me into a pub along the way, for a whiskey treat. He started praising my football ability, like he'd been responsible for creating it at school. It was as if he knew everything good about me now, and I couldn't listen to it.

Rasp had told me I was no good as a footballer. How much he had tormented me in front of his daughters would never leave my head.

I downed the drink of whiskey in one gulp and headed for a piss. I decided what to do there. He'd remember a good smack on the side of the head, when he got one. Not a person in the place; the barman had just stepped out. I walked back, cupping my hand, and gave him a good hard smack over his ear. He was on the floor squealing like a pig. And it was great to hear it. This was him getting a little taste of what it was like, how he had treated me. He had often left me helpless on the floor after fighting him off me to keep my trousers on.

So I left him there, as I had sworn I would that day.

He had tied me into the seat at school, for asking that simple question, 'who are the Jews?' when I only wanted to learn. I'll get you for this one day Rasp, I promised. And I made good on my word. It was the teacher's turn to get sorted.

What goes around in a bad way comes back to get you in a worse one, when you're an evil person. You'll get what's coming to you, eventually. It's the way of the world.

After working as refrigeration salesman for less than a year I found out you could make good money. We'd bought an expensive site to build our own house. When I sold three refrigeration counters to a big supermarket chain, it was good luck for me. And I loved everything about my job. I had my foot in the door of a very good customer who would continue to purchase. And there was the commission cheque. It paid for the site with enough money left to fence it in, and a nice gate in natural wood hung invitingly on the entrance.

Then the drink beckoned. I went missing in action for a while.

I called to tell my mother I was coming around a few days later, to hear if there was any trouble brewing for me. When I showed up at my mother's house, Norma was waiting, sitting stiffly on a chair in the kitchen when I walked in, the last person I wanted to see until the next day.

The atmosphere was very tense. There was another woman there. I knew her. Anyway, Norma started off with very serious stuff that made me laugh in her face, so she just jumped up off the chair to deliver a straight hard punch into my laughing mouth. It put me back, and cut my lip against my teeth. There was blood all down the front of my white shirt.

When my mother saw the blood she looked at Norma with a kind of worship in her eyes.

Norma finished up as my mother's hero after that. The first time and the last time she ever raised her fist in anger, the memory of that display would serve for a whole lifetime. No one suspected that this power play was in her. Least of all me, remember the rallying cry again: 'Why would you want to fight with her?

CHAPTER 24

We never talked about our wedding day again when it was over. That's how bad it was. To try and explain it as a drab, lonely affair would be doing it justice. There were twenty people in attendance. All my family were dressed in black because my father had died a few days earlier. We had paid for the wedding in advance and couldn't afford to lose the money. Norma's family were doing their best to mingle in uncertain circumstances. It might have felt like a shotgun wedding, but of course it wasn't. There was no music with respect to the recently departed. And all that gloom felt like another death in the family.

It was a good excuse for not inviting people. Maybe we didn't get married at all, they could say. Then everyone would be happy. When would those old wives' stories about being in love go away?

We often laughed at how things were for us. It felt normal most times, but it wasn't. She was a lady and I was a boyo. That comparison brought with it a certain animosity, directed towards me. It hid in the most deceptive places. And it's called jealousy. That was something we would learn to expect. You couldn't make it up, and sometimes, on rare occasions, it was even funny.

We couldn't wait to get to Connemara on our honeymoon. That was a great week, but very private, as you might expect, for such an intimate occasion. We sat with the powerful sound of the sea for company and those mysterious mountain ranges protecting us from all harm, in the west of Ireland, this wonderful place where it seems life stands still, and we were alone at last. No matter where we went from now on, we promised we would always remember this place. 'Too renew our strength with the memory of it'. We promised together.

One fellow my age said something to me once that I couldn't believe. He was supposed to be a friend and very serious when he said this. 'You know Joe, you'd be nobody if you weren't married to Norma,' he said, with a three-piece suit on him, gold watch and chain, never worked a day in his life, lazy bastard, using his father's money and social standing to create this impression of who he was.

I saw him many years later, touching people for money. I saw it. When we locked eyes, we knew each other. He knew I'd been there once, but he was the one alone now, nobody, where he could have had it all. There wasn't any value left in him. He'd spent his time pretending to be who he thought he was. A plastic version of who he'd like to be.

We were really looking forward to raising a family of our own, and we had made plans for the upcoming arrival. Boy or girl was fine, we discussed both options gleefully, and we had no special preference, hoping everything would turn out all right. Norma's nine months pregnancy passed normally, without any worrying ailments or side effects. The doctor was watching her closely with regular check-ups. And we couldn't wait for the birth of our first child. I was continuously watching her for falling; something I had in my head. Delivering foals had given me some knowledge I shouldn't have. But nevertheless I worried more than normal. I knew it wasn't all clear cut.

We couldn't wait for it to become a reality. Yet when the time arrived suddenly, it took everyone by surprise. Norma was rushed to hospital, in labour. That was the first indication of anxiousness; not everything works out according to plan. We weren't properly prepared.

I was doing business for a big refrigerated cold room in a butcher's premises at that precise time, one hundred miles away from home. There was no telephone service operating. And I arrived back at our flat to discover she was in hospital. I drove to Dublin anxiously and booked to stay in a small place near there. They wouldn't allow me visit her immediately and I sat outside intensive care for three days, until she was well enough.

She'd had a twelve-hour labour and the resulting complications proved detrimental. The cord was around the little girl's neck, which resulted in a lack of oxygen. And the bad consequences of that unfortunate occurrence were profound brain injury. She was kept in an incubator for a number of weeks.

The doctors and nurses were very evasive when questioned about our child. They were very friendly to us before the birth and with the dismissive attitude shown to us afterwards, we were anxious.

When we tried quizzing one doctor he told us there was a slight problem, but nothing to worry about. Slowly it filtered through to us that all wasn't well with our little girl. We even tried telling ourselves that we were imagining everything, because we had been told there was nothing to worry about.

Eventually, someone bluntly informed us that the child was 'a cabbage'. She would only have a lifespan of seven years. Our feelings after receiving that information were gut wrenching and we were unable to process the horrendous future for our special daughter, Marise.

But after she came home it really sunk in what we must do. She had epilepsy, which resulted in seizures very often. She was unable to swallow and after slow feeds for an hour or more she could vomit the whole lot back up again, and we had to start all over again. It was a desperate situation; truly awful to see our little baby like this. She had no recognition of anything or indulged the normal things babies do, just lay there motionless and soundless. It was heart wrenching to watch from one day to the next. And there was no help or special consideration at all.

I'm sad to reveal that bigotry was in hot pursuit of our trouble. And if the card I received when the baby was about three months old was anything to go by, the 'prisoners of ignorance' were taking to the pen when swords weren't lethal enough.

I receive this card in the post when Norma was staying with her mother for a few weeks. One morning it came in my door. The devil's postcard; I think the anonymous person that sent the card knew that my wife was staying with her mother. I don't know for sure, I just think that.

Anyway, it was one of those big black writing 'Sympathy' cards when someone dies.

The word NO in pen prefixed SYMPATHY.

No Sympathy. You Catholic bastard, the best you could do for a lovely Protestant girl was give her a DAFT child...

That was the heartfelt message of a religious person.

I read it twice and burned it. I don't ever remember it causing me pain. I only thought about it fleetingly, never told another person about it. And thinking about it recently, it wasn't the worst thing ever said to me in my life, by a long shot.

I don't know why anyone would bother themselves with such evil intentions to make broken-hearted people worse. But as we know, bigotry is source for the devil's work. It's the kind of people with nothing to give, no kindness, no love, no tolerance and above all no understanding.

Keep a wary eye for them, they are dangerous and they are everywhere. Like humanity's curse.

Norma didn't hear anything about that sympathy card for over fifty years.

I thought it was necessary to tell her after our daughter Marise passed away when she was fifty years old. I told her all about it then. Just to complete the sequence of events for her. She always likes being kept up to date about everything.

We were overcome with great sadness at Marise's condition. It took a while for everything to sink in. How could it be so? Nothing we had heard had ever forewarned us to expect that. And we would have to live with the pain of it forever.

We accepted it was our burden to bear. We'd battle on together like always. The disappointment was great, promises were made.

There would be no more children, when we talked about it. We were both instantly in agreement about that. Never could we endure such a feeling of loss again.

How could it all go so wrong on us?

But acceptance was ready made, and we got through it. It's all in a lifetime, we told each other when we hugged. That's just the way it was for us.

We were lucky with each other and we can't expect everything to be rosy.

A few months later we were making preparations to take Marise to hospital in Philadelphia. The doctor in Dublin had arranged it. It was the only place that catered exclusively for her condition. We struggled to get the money together and eventually succeeded.

So it was America up next.

We wondered what that would be like.

I would like to thanks my old friend Gus Hanley,
playwright and theatre director, for all his thoughtful
advice over many years

www.ingramcontent.com/pod-product-compliance
Lightning Source LLC
Chambersburg PA
CBHW010554200726
48283CB00018B/3032